PRAISE FOR THE NOVELS OF LISA VERGE HIGGINS

Friendship Makes the Heart Grow Fonder

"This novel reveals the excitement of European travel while honestly reflecting on the pain and confusion that accompany the grieving process... [This] story of self-discovery is both heartwarming and thought-provoking."

—*RT Book Reviews*

"Compelling...Readers who lose themselves in this wonderful book will be rewarded with the discovery of the value of true friendship.

—*Kirkus Reviews*

"Higgins does a nice job of balancing the characters' voices, and with each woman at a different stage in her life, diverse readers will find something to connect to. A natural for group discussions."

—*Booklist*

"Do not miss this rich celebration of friendship—its power to heal, to fulfill, and to put life's adventures into perspective. This book is as comforting as a cup of tea with your best friend."

—Susan Wiggs, *New York Times* bestselling author of *Return to Willow Lake*

One Good Friend Deserves Another

The Proper Care and Maintenance of Friendship

"Quirky, original, and startlingly refreshing, this is a novel about friends. It's a novel about risks. And it's a novel about dreams, what we thought they were and what we discover them to be...Great novel. Great reading."

—TheReviewBroads.com

"A lovely novel with moments of deeply moving insight into what it means to be a mother, a wife, and a friend. Read it and share it with your own friends—you'll be glad you did!"

—Nancy Thayer, *New York Times* bestselling author of *The Hot Flash Club* and *Beachcombers*

"An amazing novel of love, friendship, and community. A truly joyous read that marks an impressive debut."

—Jane Porter, author of *Flirting with Forty* and *She's Gone Country*

"Poignant, romantic, and funny...about the need for our closest friends to occasionally give us a shove in the right direction when we've lost our way. You'll recognize yourself in these women. I loved it."

—Claire LaZebnik, author of *Knitting Under the Influence* and *If You Lived Here, You'd Be Home Now*

"Expertly woven together by Lisa Verge Higgins...simply but beautifully written...the common thread is Rachel, who has given the best gift a friend can give—a second chance."

—RomanceJunkies.com

RANDOM ACTS
of KINDNESS

Lisa Verge Higgins

GRAND CENTRAL
PUBLISHING

NEW YORK   BOSTON

Grand Central Publishing
Hachette Book Group
237 Park Avenue
New York, NY 10017

www.HachetteBookGroup.com

Printed in the United States of America

RRD-C

First Edition: March 2014
10 9 8 7 6 5 4 3 2 1

Grand Central Publishing is a division of Hachette Book Group, Inc.
The Grand Central Publishing name and logo is a trademark of Hachette Book Group, Inc.

The Hachette Speakers Bureau provides a wide range of authors for speaking events. To find out more, go to www.hachettespeakersbureau.com or call (866) 376-6591.

The publisher is not responsible for websites (or their content) that are not owned by the publisher.

Library of Congress Cataloging-in-Publication Data

Higgins, Lisa Verge
  Random acts of kindness / Lisa Verge Higgins.—First Edition.
    pages cm
  ISBN 978-1-4555-7285-4 (pbk.)—ISBN 978-1-4555-7286-1 (ebook) 1. Female friendship—Fiction. 2. Kindness—Fiction. 3. Self-realization in women—Fiction. I. Title.
  PS3558.I3576R36 2014
  813'.54—dc23
                                        2013034419

To my mother, Ann Verge
A survivor and an inspiration

Chapter One

T hrowing her past away was easier than Jenna expected.
She turned off Interstate 5 halfway through Oregon and took the exit to the Umpqua Highway. It had been more than seven hours since she'd glanced in the rearview mirror and watched the skyline of Seattle recede. A rattling came from the backseat as her suitcase slid up against a plastic crate. That crate overflowed with the only things worth keeping. Black-and-white photos she'd pulled right off the walls, a Parisian coffee press that Nate had bought her in better times, and the tattered remains of Pinky Bear, a stuffed animal loved to baldness that she'd discovered swallowed in dust under her thirteen-year-old daughter's bed.

She flexed her fingers over the steering wheel. A soft jangle of metal brought her attention to the passenger seat. Her Chihuahua mix lifted his head from his puppy bed, rattling his license tags as he pleaded with her with bulging brown eyes.

"Don't worry, Lucky. We'll be stopping soon." She slid

her fingers along his nicked ears. "Claire's house isn't far from here."

The GPS urged her on, guiding her through the twists and turns of the rural road. Her foot lay heavy on the gas. In her mind, she was fleeing an apocalypse. In her mind, the glowing trail of a meteor still streaked the sky behind her, ending in a mushroom cloud that billowed as it belched smoke from the crack it had made in the street in front of her home. Any sensible woman would run from that scenario. It didn't matter that her particular meteor had been a sheaf of papers sliding across a kitchen table, the sound of the impact the click of a door closing.

Her sight went so blurry that she nearly missed the rusted sign that tilted off its pole. She jerked the steering wheel to make the turn onto Single Tree Lane. Her old Chevy Lumina kicked up a spray of rocks as the sedan swayed onto the road. Jenna drove under a canopy of pines until there was no more gravel to drive upon. She pulled the car to a stop in front of the lone house buried in ivy. The leaning mailbox sported a number. It matched the scribbled address she'd spent an hour digging out of her e-mail archives.

She sat with her hand frozen on the door handle, disturbed by the sudden loss of forward momentum. An impulse had propelled her here. But now, parked in front of Claire Petrenko's house with its front yard tangled with grass and wildflowers, her impulsiveness ebbed. *Normal* people called ahead to say they were dropping by. Normal people sent e-mails or texts to reestablish a relationship with someone they hadn't seen in a decade. Normal people didn't just follow plans hatched in desperation while sobbing over the contacts list on their cell phone.

I must do this.

The small muscles at the nape of her neck tightened. She blinked at the house with its moss-streaked roof and sagging porch. A bike leaned against the corner of the porch, a metal basket hooked on the handlebars. Jenna could just imagine her old friend pedaling on the rural roads, skirts flying, bringing home organic groceries.

Then Jenna tumbled right back to her high school self, where she spent all her time clutching her binder against her chest, keeping her gaze on the laminated floor, recognizing people by their footwear, hoping and dreading in equal measure that someone would stop and engage her in the kind of superficial conversations that girls were expected to enjoy—*Did you see that new boy in English class? Did you hear what happened at last Saturday's hockey game?*—the kind of small talk that would finally seal her place as part of a group if she didn't freeze, stutter, or shrink back into her whorled shell like a startled whelk.

Lucky dug his paws into her thighs. She tucked him close. She made herself envision her daughter, Zoe. Zoe, with her water-blue eyes and Nate's dimples. Zoe, who was three thousand miles away sleeping in an Adirondack camp that banned all cell phones and any communication with parents that didn't arrive through the U.S. Postal Service. Zoe, who was too far away to scream at her mother that she hated her and thus didn't care about what had just happened.

Jenna shoved the door open and stumbled out of the

car. She lurched on her bad leg as she tightened her grip on Lucky. If she moved fast enough, she could outrun the fear. So she crossed toward the porch, ignoring the goat tethered in the yard and the flash of sunlight off wind chimes swaying from the porch eaves. The second stair bowed under her weight. A big black bird on a perch by the door rustled his wings. The creature cocked its head, skewering her with one shiny black eye.

Lucky whimpered. She dropped him to the floorboards just as he loosed a stream of urine.

Yes, throwing her old life away was easier than she expected.

Starting a new one was not.

❧

Please, Claire thought as she heard the knock on the door. *Don't let it be another rotisserie chicken.*

Claire stood in the kitchen with the heels of her hands braced on the counter, hoping beyond desperate hope that if she just kept still, the visitor would leave on the porch whatever she was offering—another pan of lasagna, perhaps, or a head of kale to add to the ones wilting in her refrigerator—and then drive away. She knew it wasn't one of her sisters. Her sisters didn't bother to knock. And they'd just left a half hour ago, a flock of starlings that descended twice a day to see that she'd eaten, peck-peck-pecking at her about keeping her arms elevated, taking her meds, working less in the garden.

Her broken-winged raven cried *caw-caw-caw*.

A stranger, then.

"The eggs are out back," she called over her shoulder. "Just leave the money in the tin box."

She paused, listening for footsteps. Every morning she gathered warm, freshly laid eggs and then put them in a labeled box in front of the house. Buyers took how many they wanted and deposited the cost in cash. It was a lot like a drug drop.

"Claire?"

The voice was faint, unfamiliar, and female. Claire pushed away from the counter in surrender. She weighed the cow-spotted teapot, found it full of water, and lit the burner underneath. Such "quick" visits to check how she was doing usually stretched to at least two cups of green tea. She wished her sisters had never set up that blog after her diagnosis. Now every person she'd ever met in thirty-eight years knew where she lived.

And that she no longer had boobs.

Claire crossed the den and swung open the front door. The woman made an awkward little jump that loosed a lock of blonde hair from whatever kept it off her neck. Pale, thin, and somewhat rumpled, the woman had the tense look of a dancer afraid she'd just missed her cue. Her fingers dug into the sleeves of her lightweight sweater. A ragged-looking dog quivered by her feet.

Then the woman glanced at the dog and shifted her weight, a subtle tripping rhythm of knee and shoulder that triggered a memory of a girl Claire once knew in high school, a shy little creature with a bad leg.

Oh my God.

"I'm sorry about that," the woman said, eyeing the wet trail weaving toward the stairs. "If I could get a bucket of water—"

"I'm hallucinating," Claire interrupted. "This is what happens when they change my meds."

"No, no, Lucky does this whenever he's nervous—"

"I can't be seeing Jenna Hogan standing on my porch right now." Claire pressed a hand against the doorjamb as the woman drew in a sharp, little breath and nodded. On the bureau of Claire's bedroom stood a dusty picture of her high school graduation day. It was a photo of twelve grinning girls with hot pink hair proudly fluffing the evidence of their last high school prank.

Jenna was the one peeking just over Claire's shoulder.

Speechless, Claire drew Jenna into a hug and held her until her skinny friend loosened up enough to hug her back. Claire's mind raced, seeking a reason for this woman's unexpected presence, until she realized there was really only one reason why an old high school friend would suddenly turn up at the house of a buddy with cancer.

Claire pulled back so she could look into those nervous blue eyes. "How long has it been?"

"Sixteen years." Jenna slipped her hands into the pockets of her khaki shorts. "I haven't seen you since the five-year high school reunion. Everyone was there for that. You were there. I was there." Jenna did that bi-level shift again. "Everyone was there."

"You're a little early for the funeral."

Jenna started. "What funeral?"

"Mine, of course." Claire gave her a wink. "On that silly blog, my sisters make sure my woes sound worse than they really are. They would have you all think I was on my last breath. I assume that's why you're here."

Jenna's gaze dropped to Claire's shirt, as Claire knew it would. Claire hadn't bothered with reconstructive surgery. She hadn't even bothered with a padded bra. She was what she was, and that was that.

Jenna said, "You look good for a woman on your last breath."

"I've disappointed my sisters thoroughly." Claire grinned and took a step out of the doorway. "Why don't you come on in? Then you can tell me what prompted you to make the long trip. Preferably over a glass of wine."

"Can you have wine?"

"I've had cancer. I can have anything I damn well want. And frankly, you look like you could use the courage."

Claire led her into the cool interior of the house. A window was open in the kitchen, but even the breeze couldn't completely eradicate the medicine smell of the place or the sight of a well-pillowed chair pulled up in front of a television, a pile of amber-colored plastic medicine bottles collected on the side table.

Claire fled straight for the kitchen, where there were fewer reminders. She shut off the flame under the teapot and instead reached into the refrigerator for a half-filled bottle of what was left of the Oregon vintage she'd traded for some heirloom peppers from the garden. She turned to find Jenna slipping into a kitchen chair, the dog tucked on her lap. Back in high school, Jenna was the quiet mouse who hid in corners and chewed on the end of her ponytail. She'd gotten more artful about her blonde hair—caught up in tousled imperfection in a claw clip at the back of her head—but she still looked as if one sudden move would make her diminish to the point of invisibility.

Jenna Hogan…Claire's mind filled with memories. Jenna had been one of the group that Claire could always count on to help at a fund-raising drive for the Key Club, or a coat drive for the Baptist Church, or to join her on a weekend cleaning up the wilderness trails near Pine Lake, the little Adirondack town they'd all grown up in. That was a long time ago, when Claire believed that she could change the world.

"I've come for two reasons." Jenna reached for one of the two jelly jars Claire clattered onto the table. "The first is to apologize. I should have gone to your sister's funeral all those years ago."

Claire used the excuse of struggling to pull the cork out of the bottle in order to avoid responding.

"There's this thing about weddings and funerals," Jenna continued. "I was never very good at them."

Claire didn't like to think about that day. Most of Claire's high school friends had sent something—an e-mail, texted condolences, flowers, a wreath. Her good buddy Nicole had even flown in from California, abandoning her young family for an extra three days so she could stay with Claire during the painful task of sorting through Melana's clothes. But Jenna, who lived closer than all of them, didn't even text.

Claire could have used a few friends around her then. In the weeks after she'd buried her sister, she'd been gripped by a strange euphoria, an almost trippy intensity of existence that made the world seem brighter, full of odd possibilities. She'd wanted to shake the dust off her boots and flee the world. Without friends to temper her impulses, it had made perfect sense to run away to Thailand, shave her head, and become a Buddhist nun.

The cork came out with a hollow *thunk*. Claire reached over to fill Jenna's glass. The look her friend gave her was tremulous.

Claire sighed. It really wasn't kind to kick kittens.

"That was ten years ago," Claire said. "Water under the bridge. So, what's the second reason why you're here?"

"To help."

Ah, there we are. "You know, there is this amazing invention that can pass messages over long distances. It's called a phone."

"Yes, I know I should have called—"

"If you had, I'd have told you that it's been six weeks since the operation. I'm recovered."

"But I read on a blog somewhere that it's harder for someone to say no if you make an offer in person."

Claire tried to keep her smile, her spirits sinking as she sank into her chair. Jenna reading was a dangerous thing. For a stretch in high school, Jenna had become obsessed with personal self-help books, which tasked her to do things like say "hello" to one new person every day, or strike up conversations with strangers, which only enhanced Jenna's reputation as a quirky little oddball and also led to the young girl's great familiarity with the shopkeepers of Pine Lake's main drag.

Now Claire noticed the twitchy way her friend ran her hands over the dog's head, saw Jenna's good knee vibrating. The universe sent creatures like this to Claire all the time. A three-legged goat, saved from the side of the road, now mowing the lawn in front of the house. A blind possum snoozing in the shade under her porch. A crow, saved after flying into the front window.

Jenna was another broken-winged bird.

Claire gripped her wine. For the past six years, she'd cobbled out a living by caring for her uncle's land, growing her own food, bartering eggs, and working during the school year as a teacher's aide at the elementary school two miles away. Since the diagnosis, she was barely capable of keeping her own skin together. She wasn't sure she could handle another wounded creature right now. She needed to take the advice given on airplanes and put on her own oxygen mask first.

Jenna stuttered, "I didn't mean 'help' in the medical way. I know you have three sisters helping you—"

"Smothering, you mean. Hovering around me day and night, telling me what to do and how to do it. And frankly, Jen, I can't envision you changing my diaper if I ended up in hospice."

"I wouldn't be much good at that anyway." Pink blotches

began to bud on Jenna's fair skin. "Nate did most of that in our house. Diaper changing, I mean."

Claire had changed Melana's diapers in hospice. Claire had squirted the morphine under Melana's tongue. She'd bathed the bruises in the crook of her elbow, reminders of the young resident's faulty attempts to find a vein before Melana finally got a chemo port.

"I'm here," Jenna explained, "because Nate's under deadline doing a sculpture installation in the waterfront district of Seattle." She picked at the rim of the glass with her fingernail. "He'll be at it for weeks in the garage. He's only half human when he's working, so it's best that I'm not there. Since Zoe's at sleepaway camp for the next three weeks, and I've got some time off from work, I'm free to do anything. Anything I want."

Waves of hurt and desperation and maybe a little bit of crazy emanated across the table, but Claire couldn't help herself. "Spit it out, Jenna. What, exactly, are you offering?"

The little blotches on Jenna's chest bloomed into the size of cabbage roses. "Do you remember in eighth grade when we watched the middle-school musical *Cinderella?*"

Claire held tight to her patience. "Of course. Riley and Sydney played the wicked stepsisters. Riley sweated right through the polyester costume, and we spent the whole night teasing her about it—"

"And after, over pizza, you and I joked about how if we had a wish, we wouldn't waste it on a pretty dress and a date?"

Claire nodded. It had been one of many long conversations she and Jenna had shared in the attic of her house, or while lolling on the green in front of the Pine Lake library, or basking on the sun-warmed boards of the dock at Bay Roberts. Jenna confessed that her wish would have been to lose all her painful shyness. Claire couldn't quite remember what she'd wished for. Probably something foolishly idealistic, like an end to poverty in the world.

"Well?" Jenna rolled the wineglass between her hands. "What are you wishing for now, Claire?"

Claire went very, very still, half-expecting to hear the rumbling of the floorboards under her feet along with the tinkling of glasses in the drain and the rattling of silverware in the drawer as the earth shifted beneath her feet. She'd experienced an earthquake once before. She'd rushed outside only to witness a flock of birds rustling out of the trees in noisy confusion, much like the possibilities that now swirled in her mind.

One of those possibilities gripped her with a strange euphoria, an almost trippy intensity. She felt her pulse race, a sheen of sweat break out on her forehead. How wonderful it would feel to get away from all this, to shuck off the shackles of the label *cancer patient* and just be Claire Petrenko in the great wide world.

Then she took a good, long look at her old friend, sweet, trusting, shy Jenna, and realized they would need a very special kind of help to make this work.

She knew exactly where to find it.

∼

Please. Nicole squeezed her eyes shut at the sound of the doorbell. *Please don't be the police*.

Nicole knelt on the floor of her kitchen with her head deep in the gutted dishwasher, holding on to the vain hope that she'd hear the sound of a bedroom door bang open or the clatter of footsteps on the stairs. She was deluding herself, of course. Lars was at work and the kids were out of the house at preseason lacrosse practice. Not that they would have rushed to answer the door, anyway. Over the past eighteen months, they'd all learned that unexpected visitors only brought bad news.

Her spine knotted one vertebra at a time. Nicole tipped back on her heels and braced herself as she stretched to her full height. She edged her way around the flotsam of plastic and metal dishwasher parts on the floor then walked on soft footsteps through the hallway. She bent to peer through the peephole.

No blue uniforms.

She drew away and let out the breath she hadn't been aware she was holding. Of course it wasn't the San Mateo police. For the past two calm, quiet weeks, she hadn't had to worry about frantic neighbors or impromptu visits from California state social workers or squad cars pulling up to the house at unexpected hours. Yet she was still reacting like a lab rat conditioned to expect an electric shock at the sound of a bell.

She put her eye to the fish-eye lens and took a better look at the women waiting on the porch. They looked vaguely familiar, but not like any of the social workers Nicole

13

had come to know. The woman in the back was chewing on the inside of her own cheek. Her face was hidden behind a pair of oversize glasses, and she clutched a small, fat dog under her arm. The other had a bohemian look—a loose auburn braid, drugstore sunglasses, and a T-shirt that screamed *EARTH FIRST! We'll strip-mine the other planets later.*

Nicole settled her face into a mask of calm and then mustered the courage to pull the door open. "May I help you?"

The bohemian gasped. "You've cut your hair."

Nicole swept her fingers up her neck to where her hair curled at the nape. Any social worker she knew wouldn't have commented on that. She'd cut her long, long hair before she'd had the need to know anything about social services.

"You're all cheekbones now," the woman said. "It looks wonderful! But I imagine that when it happened, legions of your ex-boyfriends spontaneously woke up wailing and gnashing their teeth."

Then the bohemian laughed, and the sound of that deep-throated amusement burrowed into Nicole's brain, unearthing a memory of a hot June day under pine trees, washing the sap off cars to raise money for something, something, something. The softball team? Or was it the hiking trail restoration project that Claire Petrenko ran—

Claire.

Nicole blinked. The woman's features wavered and morphed as if she'd been looking at her through rainwater glass, but now those features grew as sharp as the photos Claire's sisters frequently posted on her cancer blog.

Claire winked. "Go Pine Lake Beavers."

"You've got to be kidding me."

"How long has it been?"

Nicole's mind raced. The last time she'd seen Claire in the flesh was nine or ten years ago on vacation in their Adirondack hometown of Pine Lake, clear across the country, when Claire had made a quick stop there before flying to Thailand. The last she'd *heard* of Claire was on the cancer blog Claire's sisters kept for her. Lately Nicole had been skimming that, wincing at Claire's sisters' relentlessly upbeat posts. The only thing she remembered amid the myriad medical details was that Claire had come out of the mastectomy with flying colors.

When was that? Six, eight weeks ago?

Then Nicole realized she was standing openmouthed while a high school friend stood on the porch bouncing on the ball of her toes. So Nicole opened her arms. Claire threw herself at her, squealing, and Nicole rocked in her embrace while Claire's laughter bubbled over.

"You're so skinny." Claire pulled out of the embrace and held her at arm's length. "Both you and Jenna. Don't you guys eat Cheez Doodles?"

Nicole glanced at the other woman. Seeing Claire was a shock, but having Jenna standing in her shadow was just bizarre. The two of them could have time-traveled as a set from twenty years ago. Jenna had always been Claire's particular pet, an odd little bird limping along in her wake.

"Hey, Jenna." Nicole leaned over for a quick hug, but it was like wrapping her arms around a plastic mannequin. Or her eldest son. "What an adorable dog."

"He's a rescue mutt. He's ugly as sin." Jenna tightened her grip as the dog shuddered. "Do you always open your door with a weapon?"

Nicole glanced at the screwdriver still gripped in her hand. "You caught me in the middle of a home repair."

"Just tell me it's not the toilet." Claire threw a thumb toward Jenna. "Kiddo here has a bladder of iron, but not me. I haven't peed since we left Sacramento."

"There's a powder room right down the hall."

Nicole felt her smile tighten as she stepped back to let them in. She hadn't welcomed visitors for a long time, and unexpected ones put her on guard. She reminded herself that Jenna and Claire weren't the kind of unexpected guests she had to worry about. At least, she didn't think so, as her mind stumbled to come up with even *one* plausible reason why they'd suddenly show up at her door.

The thought crossed her mind that Claire and Jenna's visit couldn't *possibly* be unexpected. Jenna lived in Seattle, Claire somewhere in rural Oregon; now they were both here in the San Francisco Bay Area. And Nicole had been losing track of schedules these past few weeks, dropping balls in ways she'd never done before. Her sudden freedom of movement after living in a high-intensity-monitoring mode had left her feeling slack and disorganized. She'd checked her e-mail just this morning but hadn't seen anything from either one of them. She hadn't received a text, either—and she would have known, because her cell phone never left her pocket.

The uncertainty embarrassed her. She hesitated to ask in case this visit had been prearranged and in the hell that had become her life, she'd just forgotten.

"I like the pictures." Jenna stood in the hallway with her sunglasses perched on her head, eyeballing the framed, whimsical charcoal sketches of oak trees upon the walls. "Who's the artist?"

"My eldest son."

"You're lucky he draws. My husband sculpts. You can't walk five feet in my house without tripping over one of Nate's installations."

Nicole mentally scrambled for what little she knew about Jenna. Pine Lake High had been small, but she and Jenna hadn't really been friends. And though the cancer blog had put everyone in touch again, it gave only hints of everyone's life through their brief, sympathetic, cheering posts.

"Could Lucky have a bowl of water?" Jenna gave the dog a nuzzle. "I didn't dare give him a drop in the car. Sometimes he pees when he's nervous."

Numbly, Nicole led the way toward the kitchen. Eighteen months ago, she'd have been deliriously happy to welcome guests, joyfully enfolding them into her happy, unruffled suburban life. She'd be handing Jenna a stiff drink and asking about her family, trying to coax the woman out of her shell, find out what she'd done with herself, maybe joke a little about that one time they went whitewater rafting and

Jenna had surprised everyone by being the first to hurl herself into the water off Elephant Rock.

Neutral questions only, Nicole thought. If she asked probing questions, then they would ask probing questions, too.

"So," Nicole said, choosing her words carefully, "did you call to tell me when you were arriving, Jenna? I've been elbow deep in replacing chopper blades, but—"

"I told Claire to try, but she wanted to surprise you. She also said you're not so good at answering phone calls."

Her breath rushed out of her. So she hadn't missed a call or an e-mail or a text. She wasn't completely losing it. "With three kids, the phone's always ringing. Do you want something to drink? Water? Lemonade?"

"Lemonade."

"I'll have some of that, too," said Claire as she joined them a minute later, blinking at the metallic guts of the dishwasher on the floor. "What, are there no cars to reassemble around here?"

"It's been a long time since I took apart an engine. This is a lot easier." Yesterday it was replacing the inner tubes in her bike, and the day before she'd spackled a hole that her daughter Julia had punched into the hallway wall with her lacrosse stick. "It's less greasy than under the hood of my old Lynx."

Claire grinned. "It's good to see some things never change."

Nicole set out a cereal bowl of water for the dog and poured a second glass of lemonade for Claire. "Listen, I promised Lars I'd have this all cleared up before he got back from work and the kids from practice and that'll be"—she glanced at the antique clock on the wall above the sink, calculating how soon she could gracefully shoo these two out—"about an hour from now. You don't mind if I finish this while you guys tell me what brought you so unexpectedly to my door?"

"Of course, Nic," Claire said, her eyes dancing. "I know we took you by surprise."

Nicole laughed as if she hadn't panicked at all. Then she leaned into the dishwasher and removed a torx screw in the chopper cover.

Claire added, "Jenna did the same exact thing to me the day before yesterday."

Jenna? "Really?"

"Yup, she just drove down from Seattle and showed up at my cabin and offered to take me and the dog on a road trip for the next three weeks."

Nicole paused, more at the number than the news. It'd be three weeks, six days, and ten hours before Noah would be home again.

"Wow." Nicole's voice sounded flat even to her own ears. "I don't remember what it's like to be that spontaneous."

Claire leaned affectionately into Jenna. "Isn't it the most selfless, generous, random act of kindness?"

From the shadows of the dishwasher, Nicole's curiosity tingled. She glanced at Jenna pulling dry kibbles out of a plastic snack bag and feeding them, one by one, to the dog on her lap. She tried to remember Jenna's story as she pulled a paper towel off a roll and started wiping gunk from the filter. Jenna had at least one daughter who must be a teenager by now, probably her own son Christian's age. Jenna worked in the money business, at a bank or with a broker. That didn't sound like the kind of situation that would lead easily to three weeks off without family.

Not that this was any of her business. "A vacation sounds like just what the doctor ordered, Claire, especially after all you've been through. Although isn't it awfully soon after your surgery to be taking a long trip?"

Claire said, "How did you do that?"

"Do what?"

"For a minute, I thought I heard my sister Paulina's voice coming right out of your mouth."

Nicole slipped two screws on the counter above and raised a brow. "Does your sister have a reason to be concerned?"

"The operation was six weeks ago. I'm right as rain and ready to see the sights. So tell me, how's the life coach business going?"

Nicole plunged her head back into the dishwasher, wiping clean some deeper part of the inside so neither Claire nor Jenna would see her face when she stated the next bold-faced lie. "I'm on sabbatical now. In August my clients are basking on beaches and too busy to worry about things like how to potty-train their three-year-old or motivate their teenagers to clean their rooms. So, do you have a route planned?"

"Jenna's driving," Claire said. "I've never been much for maps. And I've always believed that plans and travel frequently work best when they aren't made together."

Nicole tried to hit the mental brakes, but she couldn't stop her mind from vaulting ahead of her better sense. In her kitchen sat a woman who'd just emerged from a brush with death and another who'd somehow untangled herself from a knot of domestic and professional obligations. If Nicole were a real therapist—which she *wasn't*—she'd say this was a classic avoidance scenario, spurned by some stressful life change. If she were to give them advice—which she *wouldn't*—she'd suggest they make plans, set an agenda, make reservations, decide on a final destination.

Two lost sheep.

"Ah, Nic," Claire said, "I can tell from your silence that you're sitting there thinking the two of us must have gone totally crazy."

"I don't have enough letters after my name to make that kind of diagnosis." She squinted up at Claire. "But I do remember that the last time you took off on a long trip, you ended up doing a stint as a Buddhist nun."

"This time I'm not subject to the lure of holy temples. My only job is to keep costs down as Jenna and I discover the lower forty-eight."

Nicole remembered that Claire had once bragged she'd lived on three dollars a day while backpacking in Thailand, mostly by charming herself into the homes of many a native family for the sake of a free bed.

A free bed.

Ahhh. The quest for a free bed would certainly explain this surprise visit.

"The truth is," Claire said, "I really do have a goal. Back

in high school I left something unfinished, something I always wanted to check off but never did. So Jenna and I are planning to head back to Pine Lake."

"Pine Lake?" Nicole knocked her head on the top of the dishwasher as she fell back on her hip. "*Our* Pine Lake? Three thousand miles away in upper New York State?"

Claire drawled, "Is there any other Pine Lake?"

Suddenly, Nicole was no longer sitting on the hard kitchen tiles. She was transported to a beach chair lakeside. The wind riffled the grass. Katydids chirped in the trees. She envisioned the sun turning the surface of the water late-afternoon gold. Her toes curled as she remembered the feel of sand sliding underneath her sandals. Her shoulders suddenly ached, a sunburn ache, crying out for an evening breeze under star-blasted skies.

Claire's voice was tinged with concern. "Hey, are you all right?"

"I haven't been home—there—in so long." Nicole rubbed her head where she'd knocked it. "You took me by surprise."

"I see that. What do you think, Jenna?" Claire nudged a startled Jenna with an elbow. "Is there enough room in the car for a life coach who appears to be in desperate need of a vacation?"

Nicole stood up and placed the screwdriver on the counter. Rather, she tried to place it down. Instead it clattered out of her fingers, the noise jarring.

"If only I had three weeks to spare." Nicole stepped around the dishwasher parts and headed toward the hallway.

"Why don't I just make up the guest room for you two? I would love if you both stayed the night."

Claire called out her name, but Nicole took the stairs pretending she didn't hear. Nicole flung open the hall closet and hid behind the door to stare blindly at the folded linens. She was a fool to even consider the possibility. She had too much to do here at home, plus two other children and a husband who needed her.

And she didn't deserve to be jaunting off on a three-week road trip as free as a bird.

Not while her son wasn't.

Chapter Two

Reno, Nevada

S tanding on the second-floor walkway of the Silver Dollar Motel, Jenna drank horrendous motel coffee while watching trucks kick up dust on the busy road. Last night, the Reno skyline had been a blaze of neon bling, bright and enticing from a distance. Now those buildings were dull and wreathed with a blue haze, ugly in the harsh light of morning.

She turned to return to her room to pack the last of her stuff and noticed someone waving at her from the motel parking lot. She stilled as a dark-haired woman shaded her eyes to squint in Jenna's direction.

No. Can't be.

Jenna blinked to loosen the grit from her vision. She blinked again, hoping this was just a mirage born of heat and air pollution. That couldn't be Nicole standing in the blazing Nevada sun. Yesterday, Jenna and Claire had driven away from Nicole's home, leaving the former star athlete back in

California. But no, there Nicole was, crossing the cracked asphalt toward the motel stairs.

Jenna lifted her arm in greeting and tried to hide her dismay. She didn't really like Nicole. Her aversion to this woman was stupid, and she knew it. It was a musty remnant of high school. Nicole's only crime was being born well-mannered, efficient, confident, and gregarious. While Jenna had plotted for a week how best to approach her English teacher for the embarrassing necessity of asking for a college recommendation—then spent four days hovering at the end of class trying to balance the risk of being late for Calculus with the opportunity for a private moment—Nicole had just popped her head around the door and chirped, *Hey, Mrs. Peters, you think you could write me a rec?*

Now Jenna watched the former star softball player bounce up the stairs to the second floor of the motel and then stride past the row of chipped maroon doors as if she were loping across the outfield to the pitcher's mound with a hundred people cheering.

Jenna's daughter, Zoe, walked like that, too, her sails billowed by easy confidence as she navigated through the mean-girl storms of middle school.

"Hey, you." Nicole approached, digging into her wicker purse. "I bet you've been missing this."

Jenna felt a sinking darkness as Nicole pulled a familiar smartphone out of her purse.

Nicole gave it a little tilt. "I misplaced mine once, and I felt like an amputee for days. I found this buzzing under the guest room bed."

Deep under the bed, Jenna knew, because she'd kicked it there herself and then went down on her hands and knees to make sure it slid far. Now she glanced at the screen and saw a single bar of power and a bunch of missed calls. It must have been vibrating madly on the hardwood floor for Nicole to have found it so quickly.

"Jenna?" Nicole dipped down to catch her eye. "Didn't Claire tell you I was coming?"

"No. No, she didn't." She slipped the phone in her back pocket and wondered why Claire had kept mum. "Please tell me you didn't drive all the way up here just to deliver this to me."

"I did." Nicole shrugged. "Reno is not so far away."

Delirious relief seeped through her. Yesterday, Jenna had assured Claire that she would have been *thrilled* to bring Nicole along on the cross-country trip. It had been an easy enough thing to say after Nicole had turned the offer down flat. But the last thing Jenna wanted to do was share a car for three thousand miles with the Girl Most Likely to Succeed.

"I couldn't help but notice that your husband called a few times." Nicole's smile was curious. "How sweet that he's checking up on you."

"I'll call him later."

She looked away from Nicole. Jenna was convinced that therapists received special ocular implants along with their licenses, mini-MRIs that beamed through flesh and bone, right to the gray matter where patients hid all their thoughts and secrets, motivations and lies.

"So." Nicole leaned back to glance into the open motel room. "Where's Claire?"

Jenna gestured to the far corner of the front parking lot where her Chevy was wedged between the concrete base of the motel sign and a muddy Ford pickup truck. From her vantage point on the second floor, Jenna could just glimpse Claire sitting on the hood of the Chevy, her legs crossed, her face lifted to the sky, completely oblivious to the flickering neon sign of the Silver Dollar Motel just above her or the sketchy group of men just by the road, watching trucks rumble down the drag while sucking on cigarettes.

Jenna said, "She does this every once in a while. Sits for hours. Sometimes in the car while I'm driving."

"Meditating?"

"Lucky will even crawl onto her lap."

"I'll say hello when she's done, then." Nicole sank into one of the two slatted chairs and dropped her purse beside her. "This will give us a chance to chat."

Jenna slipped a hip onto the metal railing, hoping Nicole didn't see her knuckles go white. She wondered if Nicole wanted to "chat" as in fill the air between them with empty discussions about the weather or "chat" as in open up a vein and bleed her feelings over the second-floor railing.

"This trip you're making with Claire is really wonderful," Nicole said, tugging on the creases of her tan capris. "It was your idea, yes?"

Pass the razor, then. "She's leading the charge. I just showed up on her porch and offered whatever help I could."

"Help?"

"You've read the blog, right? I thought Claire would

still be housebound. I thought I'd be fetching her meds and taking care of the chickens. But she had other things in mind. Did you know she has a blind possum living under her porch?"

"Honestly, I'm not a bit surprised. Who's taking care of that blind possum now?"

"She left a note for her sisters. She said they're up her ass 24/7."

Nicole choked on a laugh. Jenna felt her face go hot. She didn't swear by nature, but she rarely had the good sense to filter other people's comments, either.

"I remember her sisters from Pine Lake." Nicole stretched out her legs and squinted into the middle distance. "They showed up for every one of Claire's fund-raisers. All four of them wearing batik blouses and long auburn braids, looking like the sister wives of some polygamous cult."

Jenna remembered them, too, running out of one another's rooms in Claire's crowded house, borrowing one another's clothes as they chatted about hair care and bra sizes and menstrual cycles, the atmosphere so much livelier than her own quiet house with its bubbles of personal space and deep silences.

Nicole said, "I remember Claire calling them the chick brigade. Though since Melana died, there are only three of them now." Nicole fingered the cross at her throat. "I'm curious, Jenna. How did an offer to help a sick friend turn into a road trip?"

Jenna glanced away to scan the trucks zooming by the diner across the street. "She told me what she really wanted

to do is get the hell out of Roseburg, Oregon. I said okay."
Jenna shrugged. "I had this crazy idea that maybe that's what
friends do."

Nicole's silence stretched out between them, a yawning
gap in the conversation and a shimmering moment of tension. Unnerved, Jenna shifted her weight on the railing. On
the trip to Reno, Claire had reminded Jenna that Nicole had
a degree in psychology from the University of Chicago. With
a pedigree like that, Jenna figured there was no reason to
go through the agony of spelling everything out. It wasn't
like Jenna had changed so much since she'd been a gangly,
socially awkward mouse in high school. All her life she'd
struggled with relationships. She was finally trying to do
something about it.

Zoe's angry words rang in her mind.

You're so stupid, Mom. You're so blind.

"So," Nicole said, "I assume your daughter must be out of
the house for the rest of the summer?"

"Zoe's at Camp Paskagamak until the end of the month."

"Camp Paskagamak." Nicole made a two-fingered salute
and recited the camp's motto: "'Self-Reliance, Self-Esteem,
Self-Respect.' Do they still expressly forbid communication
with the parents?"

"Except by snail mail."

"Wow. I haven't thought about those musty cabins in
years. That place gave me a permanent phobia of spiders.
I guess being home with Nate in an empty nest must have
been a little unnerving, huh?"

Jenna regurgitated the easy lie. "He's working on an installation. Usually he's mild-mannered Dr. Jekyll, but when he's in this phase of the process, he morphs into Mr. Hyde. He doesn't want me around."

At least that last part wasn't a lie.

Nicole mumbled, "Artistic temperament."

"Uh-huh."

"It can be a nightmare to live with, I know. So your daughter is away, your husband in the heat of artistic creation, but how did you manage to get three weeks off from work? Your boss must be very generous."

"My boss is a jerk." Jenna winced at her own reaction. She took a moment to debate what to say and then decided there was no harm in the truth. "He's the type who'll scream at me red-faced over the numbers I just crunched 'incorrectly,' only to realize an hour later that it wasn't my report in his hand."

Nicole made an empathic grunt. "And then he won't apologize."

"Absolutely."

"And yet, he let you take off for three weeks."

Oh, Nicole was good, Jenna thought, she was really slick, slipping little needles of questions between easy banter. Jenna breathed against the ache in her chest, wishing she and Claire could just get back on Interstate 80 and head east. She breathed in and wondered how much longer Claire was going to meditate amid the rumble of trucks and the burned-roast smell of coffee rising from the diner across the street. Jenna breathed in and wondered why she was bothering to keep so many secrets.

"Jenna?" Nicole's voice was hesitant. "I don't mean to pry...but is there something going on with your job?"

Jenna turned her face away from Nicole's X-ray eyes. All during the ride to Reno, Claire kept harping on the fact that Nicole looked stressed and unlike herself. But back in San Mateo, Jenna hadn't gotten that impression at all. She'd seen a slim, fit woman stretched across a kitchen floor wielding a magnetic screwdriver like a conductor's baton. She'd seen a woman as calm as a hurricane's eye while her children swarmed around her setting the table and her strikingly handsome husband made dinner and brought them each a glass of wine with a charming wink.

The last thing Jenna wanted from a woman with such a perfect life was pity at the imperfection of her own.

"My boss sold the hedge fund." Jenna leaned back against the railing and crossed her arms. "He cashed out so he can go build houses in Peru with his fifth wife. Teenagers like to do those things, I'm told."

"Oh, Jenna—"

"I've got fifteen solid years of employment. I specialize in the semiconductor industry. I'll get another job." Although the thought of writing a new résumé and making cold calls to colleagues made her blood congeal. She searched for another subject, any subject. "Did Claire tell you we're heading toward Salt Lake City this afternoon?"

Nicole hesitated just long enough for Jenna to know that Nicole had noticed the swift change in topic. "On the phone Claire mentioned something about visiting Jin Ng."

"*Dr.* Jin Ng. She works at a cancer center. Claire said she helped her out early in the diagnosis."

"And any free bed," Nicole said, waving a hand at the cracked asphalt parking lot and the haze of highway dust, "has to be better than the Silver Dollar Motel."

"Oh, honey, if you're wrinkling your nose at this you'd never last three days in Wat Ram Poeng."

Claire sauntered down the hallway, hauling Lucky under her arm. At her approach, Jenna felt a physical rush of relief that she would no longer be the center of Nicole's undivided attention.

Nicole grinned as Claire approached. "That's not on my bucket list, babe."

"As a life coach it should be. A little time spent in a Buddhist temple would be spiritually transforming."

"My clients aren't looking for spiritual transformation. They're looking to keep their teenagers away from Internet porn."

Claire, her eyes crinkling gently at the corners, handed Lucky to Jenna. "You have your phone back?"

Jenna patted her pocket in response and let Lucky down to sniff around.

"That's good," Claire said. "We need your phone if we're going all the way across the country. Mine's so old I swear it's powered by mice running on treadmills."

Claire settled into the other chair, her T-shirt billowing out and then ballooning back in. Under three pink ribbons it said, *Yes, they're fake! My real ones tried to kill me.*

"So," Claire asked, her gaze settling on Nicole, "couldn't resist trying your luck in the lovely casinos of Reno?"

"You know why I'm here, you manipulative witch. You put the bug in Lars's ear."

"Good man, your Lars. He got any brothers?"

"He told me I'm banging off the walls in my house. I told him I was *fixing* them. He told me that if I kept spackling plaster and soaping up double-hung window sliders, I'd completely unman him."

Claire raised her brows. "I met the man. I don't think that's possible."

Jenna bent over to give Lucky a scratch, for no other reason than to hide the fact that she hadn't a clue what was going on. She was as lost in this conversation as she had been the other day in Nicole's kitchen. It crossed her mind that maybe this was what it was like to really *know* someone—to be able to talk past each other and yet still understand, instead of swimming in incomprehension.

"Lars actually packed my bags," Nicole confessed. "But he's not the only reason why I'm here."

Claire's eyes danced. "I put the hook in good, didn't I?"

"You told me that you left something unfinished in Pine Lake, something that you had to do."

"Now, Nic, it's not like Jen and I are going to knock off any convenience stores or anything."

"Jenna?"

Jenna started and glanced up to find Nicole tilting her head back, looking at her with those clear brown eyes.

Nicole prodded, "Do you know what this mysterious goal of Claire's is?"

Jenna hesitated. Claire had mentioned going to Pine Lake only yesterday. Jenna had gone along with it, because she didn't really care what she did for the next three weeks, as long as it took her farther and farther away from Seattle.

Jenna said, "I'm sure the details are forthcoming."

"Oh, it's hardly anything." Claire waved her hand in the air. "It's a whim. You're both going to think I'm making mountains out of anthills."

Nicole lifted her fingers to her cheek in a contemplative way that made Jenna nervous, even though the intensity of Nicole's stare wasn't directed at her.

"This must be really good," Nicole said, "if it makes you so uncomfortable."

"I forgot that you actually get paid for this." Claire spread her hands in surrender. "Do you remember the senior year trip?"

"Of course. The whole class rafted the rapids of the Hudson River Gorge."

Claire said, "Well, you did, and Jenna did, and the rest of our class did. But I bailed out completely at Elephant Rock."

Nicole splayed her fingers. "That's it? You're going back to Pine Lake just to ride the rapids?"

Claire's grin grew slow and sly, and seeing it, Jenna felt a sinking sensation like the concrete of the walkway softening under her feet.

"Is it good enough," Claire said, "to convince Nicole Renard Eriksen to drop everything to join us on a road trip?"

Chapter Three

Salt Lake City, Utah

When Claire had been ordained at Wat Ram Poeng eight years ago, she'd worn a pure white robe consisting of three parts. Under the three-tiered roof of the Siamese temple, she'd lit three sticks of incense and offered three fresh-cut flowers to the abbot. Her host mother had knelt to her right and her sponsor to her left as she'd publicly stated her wish to become a *maechi*, a Buddhist nun. Then, in old Pali, she'd recited three times the precepts of the triple gem.

In Buddhism, the number three was sacred.

Maybe that was why, while being mindful of Nicole at the wheel and Jenna in the backseat, Claire meditated in the passenger seat and experienced for the first time in too many years a rising euphoria, a sense of exhilaration and giddiness, a light-headed rapture, as if she were flying above the white moonscape of the Utah salt flats. What had begun as an impulsive act, hatched in a moment of desperation around

35

her kitchen table, had led her to be part of an unexpected trinity.

It was about time she got some Karmic payback.

A nudge on her shoulder jerked her out of deep meditation. She blinked her eyes open to the sensory assault of the bustle and buildings and traffic of Salt Lake City. She glanced at the dashboard clock. She'd been meditating for a full ninety minutes.

"Sorry to wake you," Nicole said, "but we're only a couple of minutes away from Jin's office."

In a plummy British voice, the GPS announced a right turn in eight hundred feet. The GPS was one of Nicole's many contributions to the road trip. Before Lars had kissed Nicole good-bye in the parking lot in Reno, she had transferred jumper cables, a pup tent, a medical kit, and an emergency radio to Jenna's car. The radio was so cutting-edge that Claire wouldn't be surprised if it could register cosmic microwave radiation.

Claire unfolded her legs and rolled her shoulders, willing herself to stay loose and relaxed, to not get nervous about entering the office of yet another oncologist.

"I'm glad we're stopping," Jenna said from the backseat. "Lucky just started giving me the yellow eye."

Nicole turned into a parking lot. "Tell Lucky I see a tree with his name on it."

Once they parked, Claire stepped out into searing ninety-plus-degree heat, realizing how far she'd traveled from the mossy shade of her little house in her uncle's thirty-acre wood. The modern, glass-faced office building was set in the kind of fanatically clean place that made her wonder where all the green things were hidden. Inside, no amount of air-conditioning could mask the nauseating doctor's-office scent of magazine ink and antiseptic.

Claire announced her arrival to the receptionist only to see Jin bound around the central desk, shouting her name.

The oncologist wrapped her in a hug and nearly poked one of Claire's eyes out with the pencil tucked behind her ear. Jin was four foot nine tops, her hair so short it stuck up in straight, stiff pieces. Little Jin—everyone had called her that—had been the topper of the cheerleading squad at Pine Lake High, climbing up bodies to perch at the height of a human pyramid and then launching herself off to perform a split in midair. Now, as Jin greeted the three of them, she vibrated like a human hummingbird.

"Claire, so glad to see you looking so flush! And, Jenna, is that you? I remember you from last-semester Calculus. Without you, Mr. Walton and his vector functions would have crushed me. And look at you, Nicole." She poked Nicole in the abdomen with the pencil. "Still fit as always. Are you still playing softball?"

They chatted for a few minutes while Claire tried not to notice the two patients lingering in the waiting room. One was an exhausted teenager sitting with his mouth open, a sure sign of chemo lesions. Across from him sat a young girl in pink jeans playing a video game, absently tugging on the Hello Kitty scarf wrapped around her head.

Claire was relieved when Jin finally cut the chatter short. The doctor directed Jenna and Nicole down the street to a

French brasserie, where she'd promised to join them all for dinner after she had a chance to meet with Claire "in a more official capacity."

Frying pan, Claire thought. *Fire*.

Jin's office desk was swallowed by files, Styrofoam cups, framed photos of her twins, and an array of samples in brown tincture bottles. No sooner had Claire sat down before Jin strapped a blood-pressure cuff over her arm. Then Jin moved her face very close, the way she used to in high school. Claire used to think Jin was really nearsighted, until she realized Jin just had a completely different sense of personal space.

"It's a good thing," Jin said, blinking, "that you are doing this."

Claire glanced at the cuff, confused. "Last time I was checked I was a healthy one-twenty-three over eight-two—"

"No, it's good that you're out of your house, away from the sickness and on an adventure." Jin watched the gauge as she flicked the screw with practiced fingers. "It's good that you're with friends."

Claire nodded, her feelings of Karmic alignment confirmed. "My six-year-old nephew spins like a top whenever he eats too many Pop Rocks. These past days, I'm starting to feel the same energy."

"That's the power of the mind." Jin dropped the bulb and tapped her temple. "It's almost as good as chemo against the cancer. Have you been doing your arm exercises?"

"In the mornings, yes."

"I'm sure your oncologist warned you about lymphedema—"

"I elevate, I check every day."

"Good. Now you know my specialty is in pediatric oncology," Jin said as she unstrapped the cuff, "so this visit is no substitute for continuing your regular care. You be sure to check in with your regular oncologist when you get home."

"For the sake of Buddha, my sisters have mouthpieces everywhere."

"What?"

"Don't worry. Paulina has already scheduled my next appointment."

"Good." Jin tossed the blood pressure monitor on the desk. "Did you ever get that shot of alpha lipoic acid like I suggested?"

Claire grimaced.

"Let me guess. Your Doctor I-do-things-by-the-book didn't approve. And you let him talk you out of it."

"That man never colored outside the lines in his life."

"In med school, I tripped over guys like that every day." Jin slipped the cold disk of the stethoscope under the stretched collar of Claire's T-shirt, blithely riding over one of the scars as if it was the most natural thing in the world that Claire no longer had breasts. "Your doctor, he's like a stubborn dog. You just have to pet him a little, and he'll calm down."

"Even if he were about thirty years younger—"

"I'm speaking metaphorically."

"Well, that's a relief. I'm not sure I could get past the ear hair."

"Your Dr. Straitharn, he's like a big general. He has big

39

weapons, lots of military toys. He likes to make frontal assaults on the disease."

Claire's mind drifted to the space where her breasts once were. "Lots of collateral damage."

"Mind, he's *very* good in lots of ways. He's working in a public hospital. A man like that could set up a cancer clinic and make a lot more money. He could take private clients who demand more than ten minutes at appointments." Jin circled a finger in the air to her own clinic then leaned over Claire's shoulder to slip the stethoscope down her back. "Still, his way—the usual way, strafing the enemy with the medical equivalent of napalm—is a great shock to the body. But just because you're spraying napalm doesn't mean you can't sneak in a small special team. Now breathe in."

Claire took a deep breath and noticed the crystal necklace swinging at the doctor's throat. In high school, Jin was the cool science nerd who dressed like a manga heroine when only a small geek community indulged in Japanese comics. Jin volunteered in the hospital, pushing patients around in wheelchairs while wearing pigtails, microskirts, and stockings to her thighs. Now Claire's gaze traveled over the diplomas on the wall, and she noticed the Yale undergraduate degree, the diploma from Johns Hopkins medical school, as well as several certifications. Claire smiled. Her Oregon oncologist had impressive diplomas, too, but no certifications for Reiki.

Then Claire's attention was snagged by a different frame, of Jin leaning over the bed of a young patient. "Wow. Is that really you?"

Jin glanced over her shoulder. "That's me and Jamahl. Don't I look like one hot rocking mama?"

"You make a better-looking bald woman than I ever did."

"Jamahl was one of my first real patients, a baseball fanatic suffering from acute lymphoblastic leukemia. When that picture was taken, he was between phases of treatment, just like you. He still had chemo ahead of him."

"At least you got to keep your eyebrows. Shaving your head didn't scare the hell out of him?"

"It made him laugh." Jin pulled the stethoscope out of her ears, slipped it around her shoulders, and then ruffled her own hair. "I did it a couple of times as a resident until my superiors asked me to stop. They said I was getting too emotionally involved with my patients."

Claire looked more closely at the photo. The boy's chin jutted out as he smiled. He was horsing around, grinning by pulling his lips back as if he were showing off his teeth.

"After the treatment," Jin said, "when he was feeling better, Jamahl went on a road trip, like you. His family spent two weeks in Florida. He did Disney World, Universal Studios, Sea World, the whole place." Jin's smile softened. "For weeks, I got minute-by-minute updates, texts, photos."

Claire didn't need to hear the rest of the story. It shimmered in the room, a sad, hungry ghost.

Jin said, "Let's get you some meds, huh?"

She turned her attention to the brown bottles on her desk, twisting them to read the labels, until she found what she wanted. Then Jin tore the paper covering a fresh syringe.

Cancer had long turned Claire into a human pincushion, so she just held out her arm and let Jin swipe it with an alcohol wipe.

"So," Claire said, "what's this stuff again?"

"Alpha lipoic acid. It's an antioxidant. I'd give you mistletoe extract, but some people are allergic."

The familiar sharp pinch, the cold wash under the skin.

"You still have to keep up the usual vigilance over the next few weeks." Jin pressed a cotton swab over the pinprick and leaned back to toss the needle in a sharps container. "You know the drill. Take antioxidants, drink carrot juice, maintain a macrobiotic diet, drink lots of green tea."

Claire thought of the Cheez Doodle wrapper she'd left in the car and the Snickers bar melting in her purse. "You know, they don't sell a lot of macrobiotic foods at gas station convenience stores."

"Do your best. You're not going to keel over in the next two weeks. Not unless Jenna and Nicole ply you with too many banana daiquiris."

"I like banana daiquiris."

"I'm officially prescribing you some then. Are you taking Interstate 80 straight through?"

"Not if I have my way." She'd have to confront Nicole about their route plans soon enough. "I'm hoping to visit Sydney in Denver. Then maybe Maya, if she's still at that archaeological dig in South Dakota. And rumor has it that Lu is back in Pine Lake."

"Consider me envious." Jin's gaze drifted to the closest photo, of two boys about six or seven, so identical they even had the same gap in their front teeth. "In another situation, I'd be climbing right into that car with you."

"The twins are keeping you busy."

"Little monsters. You'll meet them later."

"You know we're going to Pine Lake."

"You mentioned that." Jin pulled a paper bag out from a pile and stood up to poke through the samples on a nearby shelf. "My parents moved away years ago. New York City has a bigger Vietnamese community. I haven't been back to Pine Lake in years and years and years."

"Well, my plan is to ride the white water on the Hudson Valley Gorge."

Jin paused and raised her brows. "Like senior year?"

"Exactly."

"After that trip, it took about six years for my ass to thaw." Jen slipped a couple of bottles into a paper bag. "It's a funny thing, though. I remember that day. Clear as a bell."

"The icy rain or the spandex wetsuits?"

"Neither." Jin held out the brown bag of homeopathic remedies. "It was at Elephant Rock when I first saw Claire Petrenko quit something."

Chapter Four

Cheyenne, Wyoming

Nicole stood in the Union Pacific Depot staring out the arched window at a square in Cheyenne, waiting for a tumbleweed to bounce through. On one side of the plaza stood a vintage steam engine, on the other stood a ten-foot, sandstone-pink cowboy boot painted with peacock feathers. She pressed her forehead against the warm glass, looking from the nineteenth-century train to the funky boot, struggling to draw some thematic line between the two displays. Cheyenne's mix of old and new, classic and kitschy, was only adding to her sense of fractured dislocation.

Three days driving east on Interstate 80 and the images of this trip fluttered through her mind like stills on the hand-cranked Kinematoscope standing by the gumball machine, the one you could turn for twenty-five cents.

They'd been driving since seven thirty that morning, Jenna's Chevy wheezing up and over the Rockies. Now in

Wyoming, they'd crossed the Continental Divide once before driving through the high desert of the Great Basin Divide to cross the Continental Divide again. Claire and Jenna had taken plenty of photos of those white jagged peaks, sweeping red vistas, and soaring eagles. Nicole had just leaned against the Chevy until the heat of the hood sizzled through her jeans, watching Lucky do his best to water both the west and east sides of the country.

A squeak of rubber soles against the depot's black-and-white tiles announced Claire's approach.

"Do you see our waterlogged Seattle rat out there?" Claire adjusted her newly purchased pink-straw cowboy hat and gestured toward Jenna, who stood outside in the plaza with her arms outstretched, worshipping the High Plains sun. "How long should we let her dry out?"

"As long as she needs, I guess."

"There's a railroad museum on the other side of this building." Claire dipped her hand into a wrinkled paper bag, pulled out a little blue pill, and popped it in her mouth. "But it's only open for another hour."

"Let's give her a few more minutes." Nicole watched as Claire rooted through the bag. Nicole knew those questionable meds had come from Jin's office—Jin, who spent dinner that evening exhorting the therapeutic benefits of legal marijuana. "Shouldn't you be more discreet about that?"

"These? They're just herbal supplements."

"I'm sure police officers have never heard that excuse."

"Honey, I'd be disappointed if we didn't have at least one run-in with the police before this vacation is over."

"Well, just assure me that none of those pills are contraindicated with your meds."

"They're harmless, Paulina."

Above the lip of the water bottle, Claire's brown eyes danced, but Nicole sensed the rising of high, thick walls. "It's not like you just recovered from a tonsillectomy. All these miles we've traveled and you haven't once talked about your surgery or your treatment."

"Believe me, I'm taking pity on my captive audience." Claire dropped the bag and the water bottle back into the canvas tote that served as her purse. "Once you get me started, I'll be spilling things you don't want to know. Like how my extended simple mastectomy started with a cut just above the nipples and how they removed my lymph nodes like a trail of stringed grapes all the way up both arms—"

"Wow. What were you saying about a museum?"

Claire laughed as she pulled out her phone and checked for a signal. She waved in elaborate figure eights in the sunlight pouring through the glass, stopping periodically to check the face.

Nicole swayed back so she wouldn't get hit. "You know that's a myth, right? Waving your phone like that is not going to help you get a cell phone signal."

Claire tsked. "Oh ye of little faith."

"Did you check your map for reception before you left?"

"No, but clearly we're in a dead spot or something."

"So, what are you going to try next? Incantations? Killing a squirrel?"

"All right, I give up." Claire dropped her phone in her

purse and held out her palm to Nicole. "Hand me your interstellar communicator, Captain. It's the only way I can call our good friend Sydney again."

Nicole made no move toward her smartphone, which was tucked neatly in her back pocket. She had hoped Claire had given up on this idea. Visiting Jin had been a smart move because the good doctor had been on the direct route of their travel. But Sydney was a two-hundred-mile detour and thus one more way to delay their arrival at Pine Lake.

"Claire," she said, "we've already left Sydney a voice message. And two texts."

"So let's call again."

"There's this unwritten rule: if she got the messages and was able to host us, she would have called right back."

Maybe it was because Claire was unmarried and childless, but she just didn't seem to understand that people had complicated lives, things they needed to do, responsibilities they can't rearrange on a dime when a friend called from out of the blue asking for a bed—or three. Yes, Nicole knew Claire's financial situation wasn't so great. The new pink cowboy hat was a moment of minor extravagance, but Nicole had watched Claire refill her water bottle at public taps, perk up at the sight of a roadside cantina, and joke about sleeping roadside in Nicole's pup tent. But driving two or three hundred miles round-trip for a free bed didn't even make financial sense.

The sudden scream of a ringtone made Nicole jump. Jenna wandered toward them clutching a handful of pamphlets. Lucky trailed on a leash in her wake. The shower music from the movie *Psycho* screeched from Jenna's purse.

Nicole's chest tightened. It was none of her business why Jenna had chosen such a ringtone—or for whom.

"Hey, there's a bison ranch nearby," Jenna said, ignoring the ring as she perused a pamphlet. "They'll actually drive you out into the pasture and let you feed them from the flatbed."

"A bison ranch." Nicole heard Jenna's call beep mercifully to voice mail. "That sounds like a lot more fun than driving to Denver, doesn't it, Claire?"

"We can feed bison all over these plains, but if we leave soon, we could be knocking on Sydney's door by six."

"I'm sure our Sydney would *love* that," Nicole said. "Six in the evening is always such a tranquil time in a working woman's house."

Claire waved away the objection. "It's a hundred-mile detour, Nicole. Embrace it. Unleash your inner gypsy."

"My inner gypsy is exhausted from hauling the caravan."

Claire gave Nicole a squinty-eyed look. "You've got it all mapped out in your head, don't you? You've made up some one-shot route, arrow straight all the way to Pine Lake."

Nicole tried not to look sheepish. Yeah, so she'd planned an efficient route already. Next stop Lincoln, Nebraska, then Iowa City, Chicago, Cleveland, Buffalo, Pine Lake. She liked knowing where she was going. Mapping out her little pins on her phone app was like cleaning the dishwasher trap or oiling the closet hinges. It made her feel like she had some kind of control.

And, honestly, she couldn't get to Pine Lake soon enough.

"Wow, look at this." Jenna held up another pamphlet. "There's a bar here called the Outlaw Saloon. It has sawdust floors and a mechanical bull."

Nicole raised her brows. "Did you hear that, Claire? We can't possibly leave Cheyenne without riding a mechanical bull."

Claire swiveled one arm with a dramatic wince. "I suspect mechanical bulls go against doctor's orders."

"But two-stepping in sawdust doesn't," Nicole countered. "Personally, I think we should stay here tonight and enjoy everything Cheyenne has to offer. We can hole up in the Plains Hotel there, that lovely building right across the square. I've already made a reservation on my phone. It's historic, reasonably priced, and it'll even allow us to bring in Lucky for a small fee."

A strange emotion rippled across Claire's face, an expression that passed so quickly Nicole couldn't get a bead on it. Once, she would have read the flicker of an eye or the jump of a muscle in a jaw with the skill and confidence of a major-league pitcher reading the body language of the hitter before hurling a slider. It was a terrible thing to lose faith in one's own judgment.

She turned her face back to the window. How had she let Lars talk her into this, anyway? When she'd shown him Jenna's abandoned phone, he'd actually packed her suitcase *for* her. He'd even mimicked her life coach philosophy, talking about the importance of getting perspective, of retreating from everyday existence for a while so when she returned she could see it more objectively.

Well, she knew Lars right down to his fallen arches, but only after all these hours in a car with these women was she getting an inkling of what he'd been trying to do. He wanted to kick-start her back into the former, energetic, happy Nicole. Not the new Nicole who slept late every morning and avoided phone calls and visitors and spent hours painting the chips on the moldings so she wouldn't have to think about the unthinkable.

As if sending her off with the owner of an incontinent dog and a Buddhist with a junk-food habit could bring about any real change.

"Well," Claire said, "I suppose I can't really say no to two-stepping if there's beer involved. But"—she raised the face of the phone toward Nicole—"I still have a call in to Maya Wheeler. Rumor has it that she's at an archaeological dig somewhere in South Dakota. So don't you get it into your head, darling, that we're going to get in the car and make it to Omaha by tomorrow, you got that?"

"First round is on me." Nicole swiveled on one heel, taking some grudging pleasure in the small victory. "Now, how about we check out that museum?"

In the museum, she stared at some paintings of boxcar graffiti art while Claire wandered about, chattering over the display cases. Jenna disappeared into the gift shop long enough to purchase another postcard. Now Jenna sat at one of the benches, her pen poised, pulling faces as she tried to choose her words. This would be the second postcard Jenna had written to her daughter today; she had purchased the last one at a gas station some miles over the Continental Divide.

Not that Nicole was paying any attention to the difficulty Jenna was having communicating with her daughter. Nope, she wasn't paying any attention to the fact that Jenna was refusing to answer her phone. And she certainly wasn't dwelling on the fact that this morning while Jenna had been in the shower, Nicole had glimpsed on the face of Jenna's smartphone an all-too-familiar application entitled myinstantCOACH.

Who needs a real life coach when there's an app for that?

Then an image popped in her mind of Norman Bates knifing a blonde in a shower as Nicole heard that ringtone again.

"Oh, look, there's a second floor," Nicole said, gliding away. "I'm going to see what's up there."

She climbed the creaking stairs. She reminded herself that Pine Lake was at the end of this road trip. She imagined herself diving from the end of the pier into the soft waters of Bay Roberts, plunging deep into the dark green silence, burrowing as far as she could until she touched the powdery silt at the bottom of the lake. She imagined lingering there weightless, where the sounds of the outside world were muffled to nothing, lingering until her lungs screamed from the pressure.

"Wow," Claire said, coming up the stairs behind her, "my nephews would never leave this room."

Nicole rose up from her reverie. She found herself in

a room with an elaborate elevated model railroad. Claire poked at a switch, and a train idling by a dusty shingled depot lurched into action. The train swept through papier-mâché hills and a copse of furry pines, past sheds that read *Feed and Seed* and side rails full of wooden boxcars.

A mournful electric whistle filled the room. In that moment, Nicole was transported back to a Christmas when Noah was four years old. Lars, in a moment of fatherly exuberance, had bought a railroad set that he couldn't wait until Christmas morning to set up. Noah had squealed and raced around the house in his excitement, knocking over the boxes of ornaments, bouncing off the walls in his exuberance, pausing only to hover by Lars to "help" assemble the pieces. On subsequent Christmases, Noah had taken over the task, learning the names of each piece, jealously guarding the sections from the curiosity of his brother, Christian, and, later, his sister, Julia, assembling the ever-growing set in precise order and with frightening efficiency. She'd been so proud of his skills, so happy he'd found a passion. She imagined him as a future engineer.

Now she remembered that volcanic enthusiasm and wondered if that was just another sign that she'd missed.

"This is unbelievable." Jenna emerged at the top of the stairs, her face buried in a Cheyenne penny saver. "I could afford to buy thirty acres of land outside of Cheyenne for half my current mortgage."

"Jenna." Nicole pressed her teeth together but not quick enough to stop the question. "Are you ever going to answer that phone?"

Jenna lifted her head, dazed, then she fumbled in her purse to flick the phone onto vibrate. "Sorry about that. I was keeping tally of the rings."

"Three times," Nicole said. "In about fifteen minutes."

"Actually," Jenna said, glancing at the face of her phone, "it's been about seven times in the last hour."

Don't ask. Don't ask. "Are you sure there isn't some kind of emergency?"

"No emergency."

Not your business. "You mentioned that Zoe is at Camp Paskagamak."

"Fifth year."

"So if nothing has changed since we went there, then Zoe's under lock and key. No Internet, no cell phone, no off-camp calls allowed, no parental interference at all. Except," Nicole added, "in an *emergency*."

"I know it's not Zoe."

"How?"

"Because of the ringtone. If there was an emergency with Zoe, my mother would call," Jenna said, "and her theme is the Wicked Witch."

Nicole waited for more of an explanation, but Jenna just bent down and swept Lucky into her arms, running her hand over his back as she pressed her lips to his head. The sight gave Nicole a sharp, unexpected pang. Jenna shielded herself by hiding behind the clipped, ragged, chewed-up ears of her rescue dog. Noah's shield was his oversize hoodies and pants that sagged halfway to his knees, and the hair he'd grown long over his eyes. His shield was to turn his face away at the

53

simplest of questions, slam the door on her curiosity, drown out the world in deafening music, pretend that nothing was really wrong even as she stood outside his door willing him to communicate, willing him to crack himself open so she could dig into his mind and fix what was wrong.

The warm weight of a hand landed on her shoulder as Claire came up beside her. "Hey, I think we've seen everything in this museum. Why don't we check into that hotel you mentioned?"

Nicole took a deep breath. Claire was offering her a socially acceptable reason to just shake off Jenna's comments and continue to travel in swift, straight lines to Pine Lake without getting entangled in complications, but inside her crept fingers of worry, alarms of trouble, and dysfunction.

Nicole curled her hands until her nails bit into her skin. She told herself these women didn't need a life coach. They didn't need someone to tell them to outsource tasks they didn't like to do, or to teach them how to be efficient by breaking their day up into fifteen-minute intervals. What these women needed was a real *licensed* therapist, someone with training in dealing with deep psychological issues arising from a bout with a serious disease, or a sudden loss of employment, or whatever other dysfunctions they were both doing their best to bury. Most certainly they didn't need the advice of a woman with a psych degree who'd dropped out of grad school, who never even managed to gather enough credits to become a licensed family counselor, who'd earned her certification for life coaching after a six-week course at a retreat in Sausalito.

Words tumbled from her lips. "No one can really help you, Jenna, if you don't tell us what's wrong."

Jenna shot her a look, and the anger in her eyes was so lightning quick and unexpected that Nicole leaned back as her stomach dipped in a looping drop as she relived the feel of a young muscular arm swinging back to connect.

"It's my husband calling." Jenna's expression hardened. "It's just my husband."

Nicole managed a breathy "Okay."

"Right now Nate is sitting with a lawyer in Seattle waiting for me to show up for a meeting." Jenna hefted Lucky into her other arm. "Nate's trying to take my daughter away from me."

Chapter Five

J enna didn't remember exiting the museum, crossing the cavernous lobby, or pushing open the doors to the depot square. She didn't really come back into her own body until the hot breath of the Chinook wind struck her. Only then did she realize she was half-walking, half-stumbling across the open square toward the building called the Plains Hotel, pausing only to wait for the traffic light to change.

She'd never meant to keep her situation a secret. Back in Oregon, she hadn't told Claire the details because it just didn't seem right. Claire didn't need to know about the domestic explosion that had destroyed every relationship that Jenna held dear. Claire had problems of her own. Had Claire *asked* for the truth, Jenna would have relented long before they'd crossed the Sierra Nevada. But by then, Nicole had joined them, popping the fragile bubble of her new closeness with Claire, making confession impossible.

Jenna believed there were three kinds of people in the world. You could sort them according to how they reacted at the sight of a big, hairy spider. The first sort would bolt screaming to the far corner of the room. The second sort would labor to coax the creature onto a paper towel so that they could release the living thing into the wild. The third sort, casting a withering glance at all the trouble, would cross the room, raise a foot, and crush it beneath a heel.

She'd always been afraid of the third sort.

As the traffic light changed, she continued her awkward bolt toward the far corner. She plunged into the cool interior of the Plains Hotel. She made a beeline across the faded tile floor, through the halo of light falling from the skylight, past a player piano that had seen better days, to the reception desk. She asked one of the concierges about the reservation.

"I got it, Jenna." Nicole came up beside her and slapped a card on the counter. "This one is on me."

Jenna turned away before Nicole could use her ocular therapist implant to perceive the true mess she'd made out of her life. The lobby was blessedly noisy, full of tourists, full of chatter. She glimpsed Claire lumbering in through the doors with their overnight bags, and Jenna hurried to relieve her burden. Moments later, the three of them were sandwiched into the smallest elevator in the universe, crushed so close together that she could smell the acid-tainted scent of Lucky's nervousness mixed with the intensity of Claire's and Nicole's curiosity. They found their room down a hallway and opened the door to a mixture of red-patterned bedspreads and a couch covered in buffalo-themed upholstery.

Claire remarked, "Holy nineteen fifty-three."

But Jenna didn't pause to take in the ambiance. She trotted quickly into the bathroom. She slipped Lucky in the tub just in time. He did his business while gazing up at her with sorry eyes.

When she emerged a few minutes later, murmuring comfort into the back of his head, she found Claire standing with her hands on the small of her back, and Nicole collapsed in a chair hugging a throw pillow.

Jenna hated silences like these most of all, silences that weren't really silences, because of the full force of attention of two pairs of eyes. This was a *screaming* silence. In it all her failures lay exposed, as if both of them knew, just by looking at her, what a screwup she'd always been.

Nicole spoke first. "Jenna, does this situation with Nate have anything to do with your job?"

The small muscles of her neck tightened. Lucky whined plaintively. Jenna let him down. He sniffed around the legs of the couch while she imagined plates of armor clicking together to cover her brain, her ego, her heart.

"Listen, I know it's not my business, but I'm just trying to connect the dots." Nicole pushed the pillow aside and planted her elbows on her knees. "All the cell phone calls you ignore, the evasions when we ask you about home, the utter lack of conversation during a nine-hour drive—"

"Driving makes me zone out," Jenna said. "I drift off while watching the scenery change."

"—and now when I ask questions, you become defensive."

"I'm not defensive."

Nicole sucked her lower lip between her teeth, worrying it for a moment. "So...should I be keeping an eye out for federal agents? Should we be ducking into alleys at the sight of police cars?"

Jenna blinked. "That's a joke, right?"

"You lost your job, ran away from home, and your husband is trying to take your daughter away." Nicole splayed her hands. "I'm thinking embezzlement, insider trading, the Irish mafia. Please prove me wrong."

Jenna's bark of surprise got mangled by a stricture in her throat. "I suppose I should be flattered that you think me capable of that."

"I don't know you very well."

"You don't."

The moment the words left her lips a volcanic heat flooded her skin. She didn't say rude things like that. Not *ever*. Even when her boss, Samuel, came striding into her office with his colors flying looking for the projection reports she'd e-mailed him two days earlier, she suppressed the urge to bark back. Instead she listened to his rantings from behind a shield of mental armor, while waiting for him to run out of steam. Then she'd speak in a monotone, giving him detailed instructions as to where he could find whatever he was looking for.

She tried to stay calm behind that armor now, but the plating felt brittle, the joints slipping.

She dropped a hip on the arm of the sofa. "I thought it was obvious. Nate asked for a divorce."

Claire and Nicole exchanged a glance, one of those sad,

knowing glances that pass between people who understand each other on a cellular level. That shared moment made her feel smaller, odder, more alone than even when she was in high school, like a little brown sparrow lost amid a chattering flock of purple finches and screaming blue jays and swooping cardinals.

"Jen, hon," Claire said, all soft brown eyes, "I'm so very sorry."

I'm so sorry was something that you said when nothing else could be said. You need therapy? *I'm so sorry.* You're having trouble with your teenage daughter? *I'm so sorry.* Your husband is leaving you? *I'm so very sorry.*

"Well," Claire said as she turned and crouched by the hotel refrigerator, "I think we all could use a drink."

Jenna watched Nicole drop her head between her shoulders. Jenna could see the way Nicole's dark hair whorled out from a spot on the back of her scalp. Nicole didn't lift her head until Claire tapped her on the shoulder with the butt of a whiskey nip. Then Nicole seized the small bottle as if it were a branch held out to a drowning woman.

The cap cracked as Nicole twisted it. "You know, from the moment you two showed up at my door, I just knew something was up. Women don't just take off from the world, their families, and their lives."

"That's a myth." Claire leaned across and shook a little bottle of whiskey at Jenna until she reluctantly took it. "I've run away at least twice before."

Nicole said, "You've never followed the rules, Claire."

"Well, you just think too much." Claire winked at Jenna

before she sank into the other upholstered chair. "Jenna and I could argue that you yourself are doing the exact same thing."

Nicole shot down the drink. "I'm not running away from anything." She choked her words against the back of her arm as she wiped away a drop of whiskey. "But our friend here just lost her job. And if my memory serves, Jenna, you're the main breadwinner in your family, yes?"

Jenna crossed her arms. Nicole would remember that. Everyone seemed to remember *that*. Jenna supposed it was quite the subject of shocked curiosity among the Pine Lake girls, how little Jenna Hogan managed to snag a Pacific Northwest artist whom she now kept as a househusband.

"All I'm saying," Nicole continued as she opened her mouth for the last drops of the whiskey, "is that most people in that position are in a panic. They polish their résumés the next day, make cold calls to potential new employers, and buy new interview suits. They don't go off to ride mechanical bulls or feed bison on a Wyoming ranch."

"I'm looking forward to that ranch." Jenna, sensing opportunity, stood up from the couch and clanked her untouched nip on the table next to the statue of a bucking bronco. "I'm looking forward to the saloon, too. What do you say we all go get some real drinks?"

Preferably in a dark room full of music too loud to talk over.

Nicole tilted her head in that trademark empathic-therapist way. "Running away solves nothing."

"Technically, you can only run away if you have a home to run away *from*." Jenna found herself gripping her own

61

shoulders. "And if Nate has his way today, he'll get to keep that, too."

Every time she came close to thinking about what was written in the petition of divorce, the walls closed in on her. No room was big enough. It was like she was called in Mr. Chella's class, sent up to the front to read her essay aloud, twenty-six pairs of eyes staring at her, and a pulse pounding in her ears and someone snickering in the back. She opened her mouth, and the words froze. Suddenly there was no air in the room, nothing for her to suck in and breathe.

She had to get *out*.

There was a coffee shop downstairs. She'd smelled the aroma of roasted beans in the lobby. If she had a shot of espresso, maybe she could stop her ribs from squeezing. Maybe she'd stop choking on the attention and the concern and the pity.

"Hon, why don't you sit down for a piece?"

Claire loomed up in front of her so fast that Jenna swayed back a step. Zoe used to perform this trick back when her daughter was in the Harry Potter stage. The girl would leap out from behind a doorframe with her cape flying, stopping Jenna on a stutter when she cried out, *Look, Mom, I Apparated!*

Jenna tried to step around Claire, but Claire only shifted her stance, so Jen said, "What, are we twelve years old now?"

Claire's smile went soft. "You did a lot a running back then, too."

"I just need some air."

"Then I'll open the window." Claire put her hand on her

62

shoulder, warm and weighty, urging her down into the sofa without actually using any force. "It's stuffy in this room, that much is true."

Jenna felt the cushion give beneath her. Claire moved away in a rustle. Jenna thought if it were just her and Claire in this room she wouldn't have any problem speaking freely. Claire would listen. Claire always listened. When the old newspaper clipping of Jenna coming in second runner-up in the Little Miss Pine Lake pageant had somehow been passed around school, making her the butt of excruciating teasing for the pink tulle dress and the clown-cheek makeup, it was Claire to whom she confessed that her mother had forced her to enter. It was Claire to whom she confessed that she'd frozen in the floodlights and tripped over the heels her mother insisted she wear. It was to Claire that she'd confessed how disappointed her mother had been when she didn't win the sad consolation prize of Miss Congeniality.

Claire fiddled with the window, rattling the latch until Jenna felt a breeze blast against the back of her head. "We'd better keep these sheer curtains closed against flies," Claire murmured. "The screen is stuck wide open. Lucky can't jump this high, can he?"

"No," Jenna said, distracted. "No, he wouldn't try."

"Well, I'll tell the front desk about it later."

"Jenna."

Now it was Jenna's turn to grope for a throw pillow to press against her chest, as she glanced up to find Nicole perched on the edge of her chair.

"This is way above my pay grade," Nicole began, in that

soft therapist's voice that made Jenna's skin crawl, "but I know this much: There are certain life events that are the most stressful things that anyone can experience. They're the things that knock you flat. Loss of a job is in the top five. So is divorce."

Jenna snorted. "No kidding."

She couldn't be sure, but she thought she saw Nicole flinch. Or maybe it was just the slightest of muscle spasms in Nicole's throat.

In any case, Nicole plowed on: "Did the divorce papers follow the job loss? Or has this divorce been in process for a while?"

"I got the pink slip at my job last Friday afternoon."

She'd driven home that day in a haze with the contents of her desk rattling in the trunk of her car. The house was in upheaval. Zoe was going off to camp the next day. No one really noticed that Jenna had come home early. It was easy to sneak that box into the attic. Nate was wrapped up in the packing and Zoe...Zoe was angrier than usual. Every time Jenna approached Zoe's room to ask if she was excited about becoming a Master Ranger, Zoe just yelled at her.

I'm busy! Get out of my room!

"And on Saturday," Jenna continued, "after we dropped Zoe off at the airport, Nate handed me a nine-page Petition for Dissolution of Marriage."

Nicole leaned forward so far she practically pitched herself onto the coffee table. "Did you sense something was wrong before that?"

"Not a clue." Jenna looked longingly at a whiskey nip on

the table. "Maybe I should have paid more attention. Maybe I should have noticed the looks the neighbors were giving me. Her name is Sissy Leclaire," she said, the name sour in her mouth. "That's who my husband was—*is*—fucking. She lives three doors down."

Claire's little indrawn breath was a sharp sound in the room.

"I guess he got thirsty while I was bringing home the bacon," Jenna said. "So he reached for the nearest beer."

When he'd slipped the divorce papers across the table and quietly explained how they'd been *drifting apart* and how he'd *made such an effort* but he couldn't continue like this, it wasn't fair to him and it wasn't fair to her and it wasn't fair to *Sissy*. All the while, Jenna had stared at his sculptor's hands, striped with old scars, one a long, thin scab over a newer one, rough from his latest project. Sitting across the kitchen from her while his coffee went cold, he'd tried to act calm and rational, but she knew him. His skin was ruddy high on his cheekbones. He'd scraped his fingers through his hair so much it stuck straight up. He looked like he'd been caught watching porn on his laptop.

He couldn't meet her eyes.

When they'd first met, fifteen years ago, it had taken her nearly two weeks before she could muster the courage to look directly at his face. It had been beyond her comprehension why any man so attractively disheveled and so very *normal* would take an interest in shy, crippled little Jenna Hogan. But those days he was hanging artwork in her building lobby, he specifically looked for her. He greeted her by name, once he had teased it out of her. He complimented her on her hair. He grinned when she blushed. He'd asked her for coffee, and when she'd stuttered excuses, he just asked again the next day, promising he'd keep asking so she may as well just say yes and get it over with.

Later, after she'd tumbled in love with the man, they scraped together enough money to take a trip to Massachusetts to visit the artist colony in Cape Ann. They wandered among the galleries. They spent hours sitting on the rocks listening to the cold surf sucking and swirling in the caverns beneath, all while picnicking on whole-grain bread and artisanal cheese and cheap wine. He was a quiet man, fathoms deep, who liked to run his hands over the surface of things: rocks, weathered driftwood, her naked back.

You're an oasis, Jenna. When I'm with you, I can think.

Her purse suddenly rattled.

Nicole stared at Jenna's handbag vibrating on the table. "That's him again, isn't it?"

"At four thirty p.m. Pacific Time today, I was supposed to meet Nate in his lawyer's office to discuss custody issues."

Nicole raised one eyebrow. "One week after he served the petition?"

"I have thirty days to respond. Nate's hoping to move things along."

Let's not drag this out.

After he'd left the house that terrible Saturday morning, she'd sat at the kitchen table with the papers in front of her. She might have sat for an hour, maybe more. She didn't count the ticks of the clock over the kitchen sink—the clock he'd installed in a crosscut of white pine not long after they'd bought the place. She'd sat trying to process what had just happened. She remembered that she didn't feel quite *right*. The walls of the room bowed and shifted as if she were in a Salvador Dalí painting. Her head was a helium balloon, and the string was slipping. At one point, she'd shuddered in the seat and glanced down, only to realize that she'd lost control of her own bladder.

Nicole's voice, unexpectedly reedy. "Oh, no, no, Jenna. Don't tell me he's asking for full legal custody of Zoe?"

Jenna pressed her thighs together and felt the same dropping queasiness as when Nate had spoken those same words aloud.

"He's the primary caregiver, isn't he?" Nicole spoke to herself, as if she were just beginning to grasp the rapid tumbling of the consequences. "It's the same as if a full-time mother requested legal custody of the children in a divorce. Only here, the genders have been reversed."

Jenna's purse rattled on the table again. She waited for Nicole to insist that she answer it. Like every other therapist she'd ever spoken to, Nicole would certainly implore Jenna to face what she feared instead of collapsing back into her shell. That was what all the therapists always told her, and always in a tone of voice that suggested this should be the easiest task in the whole wide world.

Instead, she raced ahead of her fear.

She stood up so fast she felt the blood rush from her head. She reached in her purse and pulled out the phone. She rounded the sofa and strode toward the window. She pushed aside the billowing sheers and glanced at the photo lighting up her screen. It was a picture of Nate in the garage workroom. Black grease streaked his forehead just above the strap of his face shield. The pulled cotton collar of his work T-shirt revealed the sawdust-flecked hollow of his clavicle.

After Nate had left her alone last Saturday, she had scrolled desperately through the contact list of this phone, pausing once on her mother's name, considered the conversation that would arise when she told her mother about the divorce, and then continued swiping. The names flew by—the clients she called for algorithm updates, the work colleagues she could occasionally be dragged to lunch with, the carpool moms she exchanged brief, to-the-point changes-in-plans with, the cable company, the newspaper subscription number, the electric company, Zoe's soccer coach, and yes, even Sissy Leclaire—all the while searching for someone she could talk to. Someone to take her and shake her and tell her it would be all right. A three a.m. friend, an I'll-bring-the-wine friend, a *true* friend.

"Turn it off, Jenna."

Jenna started. Nicole stood so close that Jenna could see the little starbursts of gold edging Nicole's pupils.

"You've been hit by a sledgehammer," Nicole said. "You're still seeing stars."

The phone vibrated in her hand.

"You'll have to face him eventually." The breeze from the window blew up the fringe of Nicole's hair. "But he has absolutely no right to choose the schedule. That's something *you* get to do."

Claire moved behind Nicole, closing in, nodding in agreement.

Then, in one quick motion, Nicole pushed a lock of Jenna's hair behind her ear. Nicole did it so fast that Jenna wasn't sure if it had really happened or if she were only imagining the fading pressure of her touch.

"So go ahead and shut off that phone." Nicole nodded in encouragement. "You were right to run away."

Lucky made a high whining noise and leaned his weight against her ankle. Jenna glanced at Lucky, then glanced at the phone one more time, taking a deep breath of the Chinook wind as she absorbed the sight of Nate's face.

She shifted her grip. "You're right. I'm going to need a lot more than thirty days."

Then she leaned back and hurled the phone out the open window, watching it spin in an arc that cleared the near sidewalk and reached the yellow midline of the street, where it bounced once, twice, the pieces scattering just as a pickup truck zoomed by and crushed it under its wheels.

Nicole gave her a nod. "Nice curve."

Chapter Six

Rapid City, South Dakota

Claire flexed her bare toes on the glove compartment while the fan flirted with the hem of her skirt. Outside the car window, the grasslands of the high plains waved like the glossy fur of some wild animal. She cracked the window and let the hot wind tug her hair, experiencing the same light-headed elation that she'd once felt motoring through the Thai landscape, past dry paddies of golden rice, into towns with stucco houses dripping with bougainvillea.

Claire scooped up another handful of cheddar cheese popcorn and closed her eyes in mindful gratitude. After their dispute in Cheyenne about visiting Sydney, Claire had doubted her ability to convince Nicole to take a detour all the way to South Dakota. But this morning, after feeding bison at a ranch ten miles outside Cheyenne, Nicole had agreed— abruptly and with no explanation—to veer 250 miles off her mapped route.

In Claire's mind, her friend's Karmic change of heart proved the old wisdom that every good journey was a creature of its own making, a bronco that would buck against all efforts to rein it in.

"Hey, navigator." Nicole nudged Claire with her knee. "There's a turn coming up, and I suspect my GPS isn't programmed to find archaeological digs. Do you have Maya's directions?"

Claire leaned over and dug under an empty bag of jalapeño chips and two discarded water bottles. She pulled up a few slips of hotel stationery and feathered through them. "Here they are. You need to find the sign for the—"

"—the Fort Pierre National Grassland. We just passed it." Nicole turned the fan down to lessen the white noise in the car. "Read ahead to the part about the turnoff to River Runt Dam."

Claire guided Nicole over ever-narrowing roads while the tires kicked up gypsum to ping against the undercarriage. Around a bend in an area of shrubby and stunted hillsides, she caught sight of a collection of canvas tents. Among the tents stood a large canopy with the side walls tied back, open to the elements.

"Unless that's some sort of revival meeting," Claire said, "I think we've found Maya's dig."

Nicole pulled the car to a stop by a cluster of mud-splattered pickup trucks, a dented Volvo, and a food truck belching blue-gray smoke. Claire glanced out through the haze of the upper windshield and caught sight of a shadow wheeling in the sky. "Jenna, you might want to be careful with Lucky out here. From on high, he'll look like a really tasty groundhog."

Claire stretched out of the car. She switched out the cheesy pink cowboy hat she'd bought in Cheyenne for another she'd purchased at a rest stop just over the South Dakota border. This one was a wide-brimmed Stetson made out of felted bison fur that cost her about a month's worth of egg money. For a good twenty minutes, she'd debated whether she should buy it, petting the soft brim, mentally calculating. Cancer patients whose stats ran low for five-year-survival rates didn't have much use for 401(k)s, but still, the old penny-pinching habits died hard.

Jenna clutched Lucky close as she fell into step beside Claire. "Okay, can I admit that Maya always made me nervous?"

Claire gave her a look. "Hon, everyone makes—"

"Yeah, I know, I know, but Maya's different. Once, in biology class, she brought in the boiled bones of a raccoon."

"I got one better. In Global Studies, she used to tell stories about her mom in Peru digging up mummified children."

Jenna gave a shudder that Lucky echoed. "I never knew if Maya was going to grow up to be a Nobel laureate or a serial killer."

Claire scanned the half-dozen people kneeling in the dirt under the canopy. One khaki hat popped up as the three of them stepped into the shade. Maya Wheeler, who'd appeared twice in the glossy pages of *National Geographic* for her ongoing work on the Zapotec cultures of ancient Mesoamerica. Fluent in a half-dozen languages, she bore a bullet scar on her leg from a tussle with drug dealers in the jungles of Guatemala. The archaeologist unfolded herself from the ground and made her way around the roped-off area. She walked in the easy, loping gait of a woman who knew people were watching. Her slim, black tank top slipped up to show a wink of navel.

"Damn," Maya said as she approached. "Look what the prairie breeze blew in."

Claire stepped into Maya's open arms, knocking her friend's hat off her head with the brim of her own. Maya smelled of musk and earth and rain and sweat and something spicy, like cardamom or star anise. Tracking this friend's world-skipping adventures had become something of an embarrassing hobby of hers. Back in Pine Lake, Maya had been a college brat, the daughter of an anthropology professor at Saint Regis College, a few miles outside of town. Maya had missed whole months of high school following in her own mother's footsteps. Jenna may have questioned Maya's path, but in Claire's opinion, this particular Pine Lake friend was the only person she knew who never doubted her life's purpose.

Claire pulled back to get a better look at her, from the scar cutting across Maya's chin to the silver studs winking along the arc of her right ear. "Do you have a portrait aging in an attic somewhere?"

"What's an attic? I'm still renting an apartment." Maya hugged Jenna then turned to Nicole and paused. "Did somebody die?"

Nicole gave her a quizzical look.

"I'd never imagined you'd cut off that long, gorgeous hair." Maya shrugged. "And chopping off hair is a universal sign of mourning."

"It's not universal in San Mateo."

"C'mon, Nic, you remember CCD. Jeremiah 7:29: 'Cut off your hair and cast it away; raise a lamentation on the bare heights...' No?" Maya's brows rose high. "And I always thought you were the good Catholic of the crowd."

Nicole ran her fingers up her nape. "I did it about eighteen months ago. On a whim."

"Well, it suits you, anyway." The suntanned creases by Maya's eyes deepened. "Gawd, it's so good to see you guys. You have no idea how exciting it is to get nonacademic visitors when you're living in the back of the beyond. Did you ladies come ready to camp?"

Nicole grimaced as she hefted the tent pack. "My pup tent was meant for my three kids, so we three are going to be cozy. We'd better pray for no rain."

"I've already danced to my Mohawk ancestors for good weather." Maya linked her arm through Claire's and tugged her deeper into the shade. "Come on, let me show you the glamorous life of an archaeologist."

Maya led them to the edge of a grid. Spikes jutted from the ground in geometric precision. Strings stretched between them, demarcating the large area that was being unearthed. Within, a dozen people knelt, gently scraping away at the damp soil with small tools. Maya launched into her explanation, pointing to some depressions in the ground as evidence of a dry moat fortification—suggesting that, a thousand years ago, this had been a Mandan or an Arikara Indian village of some sort.

"So," Jenna piped in, "have you found any bodies yet?"

"No." Maya pulled a face. "We're hoping when we dig deeper we'll find a jawbone or at least some teeth." She tilted her head at the food truck. "Are you guys hungry? I wouldn't trust the burgers but the chicken fingers rock. If we're going to eat, we have to get food now because Pedro leaves at six sharp."

Claire murmured assent for all of them. Maya turned to one of the college kids and directed him to set up Nicole's tent near her own. By the time they all purchased food, that minion had assembled the pup tent and started a small campfire carefully banked by stones. Half of the volunteers piled into a pickup truck and waved their farewells, while the other half—mostly college students from what Claire could discern—tucked into dinner around their own tents a bit farther away.

As they ate and chatted, the enormous western sky put on a show of colors, fading from blue to mauve and indigo, the sunset lighting up the scudding clouds in shades of rose. Claire chewed on a juicy chicken finger and dropped her head back against the bar of the lawn chair. She drank in the wide-open sky, so overwhelming for a woman used to only a sliver of blue glimpsed through trees in Oregon. She felt the same giddiness she'd known the first time she glimpsed a *wat* and heard birds singing in bamboo cages and geckos clicking across the roof, while clusters of the saffron-clad monks engaged in peaceful walking meditation.

She decided she would wake early tomorrow morning and sit atop the shrubby little knoll just beyond the tents. She'd listen to the rustle of wind through the grass and try to meditate. Maybe in this vast place, the space behind her eyes would go dark and her breathing would grow shallow. Maybe here the whole world would fall away into the stillness that still evaded her, the place of stopped time that, before she'd quit the Thai temple, she'd been assured would leave her feeling sated, loose, happy.

"Some Buddhist you are," Maya gestured to Claire's chicken fingers with a chicken finger of her own. "Aren't you supposed to live on rice and flower petals?"

Nicole snorted. "You should see her dig into the Slim Jims."

Claire raised a chicken finger to the sky like a sacrifice. "Now you know why I abandoned the temple life."

"Well, I wish I could have fed you better." Maya swung one leg over the arm of her director's chair. "But honestly, Pedro's food truck is Nirvana compared to last summer in Belize. We were fishing for our dinner until a boy in the nearest village started walking three miles each way just to sell us tortillas and beans." She leaned back to rifle through a bag by her chair. "Fortunately, I did bring libations."

Claire grinned as Maya pulled out a bottle. For one shimmering moment of heightened consciousness, she was transported *back there*. Back on the fallen log by the fire pit on Coley's Point, listening to the pine logs snap and hurl sparks toward the darkness of the sheltering boughs. Sitting with warm mittens on her hands and warm bodies on either side, excitement thrummed through her body as someone thrust a bottle in her hand while Jenna leaned over and whispered a secret into her ear. She could almost taste the minty flavor of schnapps on the back of her tongue.

"Holy junior year," Claire laughed. "Just tell me it isn't cheap applejack."

"Only the purest Slovakian vodka, my friend. I've been hiding it for weeks from the undergraduates. I'm doubly glad you're here, because it would have been really pathetic if I had to drink it alone."

"No repeat of prom night." Claire had hoped for oblivion that night, and she had gotten it in spades.

Maya said, "I'm sure you've all learned to drink in moderation since our misspent youth."

"Not me." Jenna fed crumbled little bits of hamburger to Lucky on her lap. "I never drink."

"You of all people should take a nip now and then," Maya exhorted. "Vodka makes extroverts of all of us. Now"—Maya cracked open the cap—"there's a game I play whenever I come to a new dig with a brand-new crew. It's an icebreaker. The four of us haven't really spoken for too many years, so I propose we give this a go."

Claire said, "The last time you proposed a game, Maya, Theresa Hendrick nearly set the school on fire."

"That was Truth or Dare." Maya shrugged. "And Tess was just starting to go off the rails. This game is more cerebral. More spiritual. So I'll take the first swig and ask a question, and then the person of my choice will have to answer it."

Claire noted that Maya didn't wait for debate. She raised the bottle and took an impressive gulp.

"Okay." Maya coughed, her voice rough. "My first question to all of you is: why are you here?"

Maya thrust the bottle at Nicole. Nicole, looking baffled, seized it. "Why am I here?"

"There's nothing wrong with your hearing," said Maya.

"Clearly," Nicole said, starting to stand, "you meant to start with the Buddhist."

"She's on the other side of the fire." Maya touched Nicole's arm to keep her in her chair. "I'm asking *you*."

Claire's heart skipped a little as Maya's grin went sly. That look reminded Claire of an evening on Coley's Point when Maya, limned by fire, looked Claire straight in the eye and asked her what she planned to do with the rest of her life. Maya had been fixed, intense, questioning. The next day Claire found herself starting projects she'd never before considered. Both Maya and Nicole had that effect on people. So Claire settled herself more comfortably in the rickety chair in order to watch the clash of the titans.

"Do you want something existential," Nicole asked, "or another Bible quote?"

"No need to please me." Maya curled into her chair. "Just answer it honestly, any way you'd like."

"I'm here to make sure these two sheep"—a careless flip of her hand toward her and Jenna—"don't get eaten by wolves before they reach Pine Lake."

Maya cocked her head to the other side. "That's kind of a literal response. You're not doing this at all for yourself?"

"Well, it's a vacation." Nicole took a sip of the vodka and wiped her mouth on her sleeve. "I haven't had a vacation in nearly two years."

"So you're not on some soul search." Maya rolled her hand toward the grasslands beyond the circle of firelight. "You're not seeking some essential truth in American life?"

"Wow," Nicole sputtered. "How long have you been living in academia?"

"Only a couple of months a year. Aren't you a therapist, Nic?"

Nicole paused a beat. "I started a business as a life coach."

"How is that different?"

"Therapists have about as many letters after their name as you do. They're licensed. They can deal with clinical situations. For example, my fifteen-year-old son won't talk to me no matter how hard I try to coach him, so he is seeing a therapist."

Claire felt that little bit of news hang in the air for a moment, like a spark amid a cloud of smoke.

"My daughter won't talk to me, either," Jenna said abruptly. "Maybe I should have her see a therapist."

Claire glanced at Jenna in surprise. Her friend usually stayed quiet in groups, preferring to whisper personal details rather than state them in an open forum, notwithstanding yesterday's extended confession in Cheyenne.

Nicole must have sensed the change, too, because she shifted her attention to Jenna. "With teenagers," Nicole said, "it's hard to know what's normal and what's not. Exactly how old is your daughter?"

"Thirteen." Jenna slipped Lucky onto the ground and then placed the napkin full of hamburger meat in front of him. "Do you guys remember what it was like to be a teenager?"

Claire certainly did. At thirteen, she was the new girl in Pine Lake, seasoned enough to hang back until she got a bead on these folks with the flat northern accents who kept calling her a come-away. She was used to having to work to fit in. Her father had shipped his family of eight across the country several times as he moved his way up into better-paying park ranger positions. He'd made a conscious decision to stay in the Adirondacks after Claire's mother's terrible diagnosis.

She remembered *that* day. She'd been only seventeen years old.

"What I remember," Nicole said, "is that the softball coach finally gave me a chance to pitch. That's the year we won the regionals. Jenna, didn't you run for class treasurer or something?"

"My mother thought it'd help me be more popular. She made those stupid posters with the glitter glue."

Maya barked a laugh. "I've heard that being an American teenager sucks. I spent so much time overseas I hardly remember those years."

"Being a teenager didn't suck for all of us." Jenna hugged her own knees. "Nicole didn't suffer."

"God, no," Nicole said. "Those were some of the best years of my life. The hot lights during a spring softball game, the maple pecan pie after school on Fridays, swimming out to the island at Bay Roberts. Long after I moved away and my parents retired to Boca Raton, Lars and I used to visit every August. It hasn't changed, you know: the lake shore, the uptown drag, Coley's Point, the tiny aisles in Ray's general store—"

"—the drunks down by the cannery, the seasonal unemployment," Claire added, "the occasional alerts about the mercury levels in the fish."

Nicole gave her a raised brow from across the fire.

"I'm just trying to point out that your idealized town of our mutual past had its problems, too."

"You never let us forget it," Jenna said in a rush, "even when Nicole pulled you over in the hall and asked you to help at her fund-raiser car wash, and you agreed only if *she* would join *us* in your winter coat drive."

"That sounds like just the kind of idealistically futile thing I'd do." Claire's gaze drifted to the hollow of the open sky beyond the flames. "You've got quite a memory, Jenna."

"I remember it," Jenna continued, "because I was standing there right next to you, and Nicole didn't think to invite me."

The firewood popped and collapsed in the subsequent silence. Maya snagged Claire's eye in curiosity. Nicole looked like she'd been hit upside the head.

"That wasn't fair." Jenna stiffened in her seat. "You were a popular softball star who dated Drake Weldon. I was just a gimp who dragged a thousand middle-school gaffes behind me like Marley's clanking chains."

"And apparently, I was an oblivious jerk." Nicole tossed the last of her boneless chicken fingers in Lucky's direction and then thrust the bottle at Jenna. "Now it's your turn. Tell us why you're here."

Jenna reached for the bottle. "I'm here because of Zoe."

Claire had expected Jenna to say she was here to get away from the situation in Seattle. Jenna hadn't said much about Zoe, other than the fact that Nate was trying to get full custody of their daughter. The surprises just kept coming.

Claire asked, "Is Zoe having trouble in school or something?"

"No. Trouble in school I could handle." Jenna, raising the lip of the bottle to her mouth, winced as she took a sip. "I mean, really, what awkward situation *haven't* I experienced as a teenager? The problem is that Zoe hates me."

Claire raised a hand in protest. "She doesn't hate you, Jenna. She's thirteen, right? Helloooo, hormones."

"No, she really *hates* me. She slouches downstairs to family dinner wearing attitude and then only picks at Nate's parmesan chicken."

Maya murmured, "My God, you have a husband who makes parmesan chicken."

"His sirloin roast is better," Jenna said. "But all I ever see is Zoe just moving it around on the plate."

"Classic teenage behavior." Nicole took great interest in a thread that had come loose in the side seam of her shorts. "She probably thinks you're probing. She's misinterpreting your efforts at conversation as an invasion of privacy."

"Is that why Zoe's calling me dumb, blind, and stupid?"

Nicole glanced up, raising her brows. "Jenna, when a teenager says something like that, it sounds to me like…well, like she's dragging a thousand troubles behind her like Marley's clanking chains."

"If she is, Zoe's certainly not telling me." Jenna leaned forward, watching Lucky struggle to choke down the last of the chicken. "And that's why a week ago, I set off to find Claire."

Claire was starting to wonder if Maya hadn't spiked the fire with something more than dried old brush. Jenna was rarely this voluble—and she certainly had never *really* explained why she'd decided to show up at Claire's door a week ago. At the time, Claire had been too excited about the prospect of getting away from her sisters to probe too deeply. In fact, she hadn't wanted to probe—the gift Jenna offered was a juicy ripe plum, and Claire had lived in the fear that her friend would have second thoughts and snatch it away.

Jenna leaned down to scratch behind Lucky's ears as he sniffed around the grass for more food. She scratched and scratched, making no indication she was going to elaborate, even as Lucky stretched out from under her hand to wander farther afield. So both Maya and Nicole then looked straight at *her*, as if Claire might have an explanation. All Claire could do was shrug to mutely confess her own ignorance. Jenna's mind had always run in strange, concentric circles. Sometimes it took a little while to hit the bull's-eye.

"I've screwed up every relationship I've ever had in my life," Jenna finally said, with Lucky out of reach. "My father's dead. I've never gotten along with my mother. My husband is leaving me, and my daughter hates me. In the middle of all that, the thought came to me that I needed to go back to the *beginning* of things." Jenna pulled her knees to her chest and then hugged them so close that she could rest her chin on them. "The beginning of things is Pine Lake, where I once had a really good friend. Someone who seemed to like me, even if I was a freak." A flicker of a gaze, swift and nervous, across the flames. "I thought, maybe if I connected with Claire again, I could finally learn how to stop screwing up all my relationships."

Claire's face started to burn with a hot shyness as her friends' gazes shifted back and forth from Jenna to herself. She didn't quite know what to say. She didn't dare admit how uncomfortable it made her feel to be so needed, to be the central object of so much hope. There were reasons why she'd retreated to the isolation of a Buddhist temple after her sister's death. There were reasons why she'd come back to America only to hide in a cabin in the Oregon woods. Too many times she'd grappled with failed expectations, not the least of which were her own.

"Damn, Jenna," Maya murmured. "It's always the quiet ones, you know?"

Claire heard rustling, and a shadow passed between her and the fire. A bottle appeared in her lap. Before Claire could lift her head and raise her arms for a hug, Jenna pulled away and hustled back to her chair.

Then she noticed six eyes fixed upon her.

"No, no," Claire said, hiking the bottle. "It's end of game. No way am I going to be able to top that."

Maya said, "It's not a competition."

So Claire looked at Maya, still wearing her battered khaki hat with its wooden bead though the sun had gone down. The archaeologist sat at ease with her fingers laced on her belly, looking like the modern female version of Indiana Jones.

Maya, who never doubted.

Claire stretched her legs out toward the flames, flexing her bare arches as she felt the heat on the soles of her feet. "Did I ever tell you all what I did after I graduated from Saint Regis?"

Nicole leaned sideways in her chair toward Maya, forming a wall of inquisitive solidarity. "Tell me it has to do with why you're here."

"I'll get to that. After college, I ended up in a roach-infested studio apartment in Hell's Kitchen along with three other idealistic young pips. We were so eager to move to one of the most expensive cities in the world for the joy of working at a nonprofit."

Maya snorted. "That's so Claire."

"It took me almost two years at a land preservation company to realize that only about eight percent of the funds we raised actually went toward conservation. What was left was sucked up by the mortgage on my boss's penthouse on Central Park West."

Jenna piped up, "That doesn't sound legal."

"It wasn't. He was indicted and spent a few years in jail. But long before then, all my pretty illusions about the good work done by nonprofits had been shattered. So I quit."

Maya said, "Good for you."

"So I flew back to the nest, which, by then, was in Oregon. After a few years slinging hash at a diner, I decided to go back to school and get my master's in education."

Nicole's brow furrowed. "I remember. Second grade?"

"Special ed."

"There goes Claire again." Maya clasped her hands around one knee. "Running into burning buildings when most people run away."

"I intended to mold malleable minds." Claire swirled the bottle until she could feel the weight of the liquid shifting inside. "I was going to reach the most unreachable children. I was going to lift the disadvantaged out of poverty. You know, I was going to turn water into wine."

Then Claire's mind turned to Jason. A five-year-old covered in freckles with a mop of tangled red hair. He had quick eyes, agile in avoiding her gaze.

"There was this one boy there," Claire said, "the sweetest five-year-old you could ever know. Until you broke his routines. And then he'd completely *lose it*. He'd throw a full-body, screaming-at-the-top-of-his-lungs, all-out, flailing tantrum."

From across the fire, Nicole murmured, "Autistic."

"He hadn't been diagnosed because he was new to the school system. The teacher I was working with was at her wit's end. She had twenty-seven other kids in her class. I was a student teacher and the only one available to take him on." She had spent most of her time talking to the top of his head. He spoke in short sentences, in a flat voice, and he'd rock himself whenever the world became too much for him to handle. She'd labored to find the rhythms that kept him calm. Every once in a while, he'd rise up and say something almost poetic, like, *This morning I woke up inside a flower.* "It took about three months before it all came crashing down on me. Jason ended up in the hospital with a concussion. The mother accused me of being the one who gave him the bruises all over his body."

Around the silent fire, Claire could see the luminosity of their eyes. She didn't want to talk about the hellish details of those following weeks. The quick suspension, the small-town rumors, the suspicions of the weary social workers, the legal wrangling, the multiple interrogations.

"The truth is I probably did give Jason some bruises. You had to hold tight when he lost control. If you didn't, he might wriggle free and throw himself through the glass door. He'd tried once before."

Nicole sank her head into her hands. Claire supposed Nic had seen such things before, maybe in grad school.

"I was told that the investigation was mercifully quick, though it didn't feel that way at the time. Within a week, Jason was taken away from his mother and given over to social services. I was cleared not long after. But by that time, I'd seen enough. With three more classes to finish my master's, I quit."

Claire's throat went dry. That was the beginning of the hardest time, when her sister Melana got sick and everything went to hell.

Maya said, "Is that when you went to Thailand to become a nun?"

"No. That was a little later. But I quit that, too."

Crickets in the grass chirped. A breeze swept across and teased the fire. If she looked away from it, she could see the breeze rippling over the grass, silvery in the starlight. An expectant silence settled around the campfire.

"It looks like Jenna and I have something in common." Claire lifted the bottle to her lips and took a good, long swig. "I need to go back to the beginning of things, too. To the very first time I quit."

Chapter Seven

Sioux Falls, South Dakota

Stepping into one of the dusty batting cages at the Sioux Falls Empire Fair, Nicole eyed the selection of baseball bats. The aluminum bats gave a hollow clang that probably pleased the tween boys who were the main frequenters of these carnival cages. But aluminum bats always felt odd in her palms, slippery and cold. So she curled her hand around the neck of a battered wooden bat, hefting it up. *Ashwood*, she thought, as she rolled it to sense the balance. Then she lifted it to her nose to sniff the cinnamon grain, dusted with alfalfa pollen and sticky with pine tar.

In batting cage number three, she dug her front foot into the fairgrounds' dust. The bat felt heavy as she swung it over her right shoulder. She heard the drop of the metallic arm at the other end of the cage just before the ball shot out. Instinct kicked in, and she swung at the white blur.

Crack!

Nicole glared at the far opening and tried to concentrate on the next ball instead of the troubles that kept rattling in her head. Road trips were supposed to be about leaving those troubles behind. They were supposed to be about immersing yourself in the world you were in, like here in South Dakota with its crowds of brawny ranchers at every truck stop, its dusky, multihued horizon, its billboards advertising Wall Drug three hundred miles ahead. Yesterdays weren't supposed to exist when you were flying through fields of sunflowers listening to Jesus stations and soft country rock.

Yet when they'd first left Maya's dig this morning, Nicole had kept scanning radio frequencies for talk of a tornado watch. The skies had been low and ominous. She'd driven eighty miles an hour along the infinite ribbon of highway, and every shiver of wind sent silt pinging against the chassis. Every two minutes, she glanced in the rearview mirror so she could spot any change in the shape of the underbelly of the clouds, foresee the pea-green twist of a chasing funnel.

Crack!

The impact shuddered all the way up her arm. If only she could have connected as easily with the other fastballs, sliders, and curves that had whizzed by her on this road trip. Last night, Maya's potion of wood smoke and Eastern European vodka proved so much more potent a psyche opener than any of her halting, bumbling, straight-from-the-life-coach-handbook questioning techniques. Her failures just kept chasing her. Her friends' confessions in the South Dakota grasslands had made it official: how fortunate it had been for all of Nicole's potential psychotherapy patients that she'd been forced to leave graduate school when Lars knocked her up.

Crack!

"Oh, great." Claire's voice came from somewhere behind her. "You camped in the wild last night, and now you're working up a sweat. You're going to stink like a bear when we get back on the road."

Claire leaned against a post just outside the chain-link fence of the cages. Her T-shirt was splattered with colorful balloon creatures and said, *I Support Balloon-Animal Rights.*

Nicole turned her attention back to the ball launcher. "Are you going to answer your cell phone, Claire?"

"Is that darn thing ringing again?"

"I can hear it buzzing from here."

"I swear, my sisters have some kind of radar. Whenever we come rolling into any town big enough to have a cell tower, they decide it's time to call Claire to make sure I'm urinating clear and often."

The vibrating sound distracted Nicole, so much so that she didn't hear the drop of the mechanical arm. She swung but caught nothing but air.

She rolled the bat back over her shoulder as Claire made a clucking noise.

"It's just Paulina again. That girl can hold her horses. I spoke to her an hour ago, while you guys were listening to that banjo band. She wouldn't let me off the phone until I counted how many more pills I had left in my prescription and I swore to do my stretching exercises."

Crack!

Nicole cast a glance over her shoulder long enough to see Claire bite the head off a corn dog. "I see you're doing your best to keep to Jin's suggestion of a macrobiotic diet."

"No actual dogs were harmed in the making of this corn dog."

"Aren't cows sacred to Buddhists?"

"You're confusing Buddhism with Hinduism. And I am certainly *not* breaking one of the five Buddhist precepts that all good laypeople are bound to follow."

"I pass no judgment." She crouched and leaned heavily on her left foot as she heard the drop of the metallic arm. "During Lent, I'm not supposed to eat meat on Fridays, but somehow sausage appears on my pizza."

Crack!

The fence links clinked as Claire slipped her fingers through them. "Some Buddhists believe that even cracking an egg is killing a living thing. So the wife of the house orders a servant to crack the eggs. The wife is absolved because she didn't do the actual cracking; and the servant is absolved, too, because he was *forced* to do it for someone else. Of course, in most Thai markets, the eggs are sold precracked anyway."

"It's a strange, strange world you live in."

"This corn dog is delicious, by the way. You want me to get you one, once you're finished taking out your frustration on those baseballs?"

Crack!

Nicole didn't need to turn around to know that Claire

was twirling the half-eaten corn dog like a lollipop. Claire's head would be tilted, her long auburn braid falling over one shoulder, one leg crossed over the other with a toe of her battered boot dug into the dirt. For a woman who had no therapist training, Claire knew how to give a welcoming look while her body screamed *I know there's something on your mind.*

Nicole fixed her attention on the open box where the balls were hurled, setting her stance, shifting her weight, settling the bat at just the right angle over her shoulder. Yeah, there was something on her mind. It was the memory of last night, when Claire through smoke and sparks confessed a lifelong series of failures with easy cynicism—while Nicole sat still, guilty, hotly embarrassed at her vain urge to keep her catastrophes to herself.

Crack!

Claire said, "You still got some whopping power in those arms."

Nicole rolled her shoulders, feeling a pull in the tendons of her right shoulder. "Where's Jenna?"

"She's trying to win a stuffed animal for Zoe."

"For a thirteen-year-old?"

"Compensating, I guess. Or maybe Jenna is imagining Nate's face on the bull's-eye when she hefts that plastic rifle to her shoulder. Maybe target shooting is her version of pounding a dozen baseballs."

Nicole switched to the other side of the plate, pointedly not commenting, because this life-coach-fraud-of-a-therapist didn't know a damn thing about how to help a haunted, traumatized woman like Jenna. Nope. Nicole was just here with her friends. She was just taking a break from Interstate 90 to enjoy a state fair. She was just working on her left side swing, her weaker side as a switch-hitter.

Crack!

Nicole dropped the bat off her shoulder. The end hit the ground and puffed up a cloud of dust. "Claire," she blurted. "Are you going to quit on me?"

Claire stilled with the corn dog halfway to her mouth. "Quit on you? How do you mean?"

"I mean are you going to decide halfway to Pine Lake that this trip isn't what you expected? That you can't afford the gas anymore, or that Lucky has to pee too often, or that it's too much dealing with Jenna the bundle-of-nerves and that I'm too"—her mouth moved but the words didn't come out at first—"emotionally constipated?"

Claire twirled the stick of the corn dog in a perfect little circle. "You really think I'm going to bail."

"I really, really need to get to Pine Lake."

Nicole twisted away to hide her weakness and then dropped into her stance and waited for the next ball. How could she explain the feeling that if she just walked barefoot over the old pier and dove into the waters of Bay Roberts, she would somehow emerge psychically clean? If she just swam across to the little island, that spit of a thing with a half-dozen pines, she would somehow emerge as confident as the high school girl she once had been? One day was all that she needed. One day basking under the mountain sun, and her will would strengthen, her insecurities would melt, her spirits would rise to meet the challenges waiting for her when she returned home.

The ball hissed by her. She hadn't even heard the mechanical arm drop.

Claire said, "I did shoot my mouth off last night, didn't I? I never could hold my liquor."

"Forget it." She wiped the sweat off her brow with her forearm. "I shouldn't have mentioned it. I'm just jonesing for a nice cold Corona on Coley's Point—"

"You've got every right to wonder. I *do* have this thing about commitment. There's a reason why I didn't marry that Kiwi with the sheep farm outside of Wellington."

Nicole blinked. She'd never known Claire had had a fiancé.

"Hell," Claire continued, "I even chose Thai Buddhism because, unlike most other forms, it allows *temporary* ordination of monks and nuns."

"Shaving your head sounds like a commitment to me."

"Hair grows back quicker than you think. Don't stop hitting balls for me, Nic. You've only got a few more minutes in the cage."

Claire suddenly squinted in the direction of a carnival game clear across the fairway, watching a squealing group of kids as if she had money on their water pistol competition. Nicole recognized the body language. Apparently, the chainlink fence between her and Claire wasn't enough of a scrim, so Nicole turned away and dropped back into position to give Claire some emotional space.

"You may be surprised by this," Claire said, "but sometimes there were good reasons for me to quit. I didn't really leave Buddhism just because of a passion for mesquite-flavored beef jerky."

Nicole wiped the sweat off her brow with her forearm. "The six a.m. meditations would have put me off. And the celibacy."

"For me, I had serious problems with the Dharma itself. Buddhism is the study of suffering. Where it comes from, why it exists, and most importantly, the path one must follow to end it. When I took off for Thailand, I had this crazy idea that if I just followed the precepts, I'd make some sense out of the mess of my own life. And Melana's suffering."

The mention of Claire's sister's name split Nicole's attention. The mechanical arm dropped, and a ball zipped by, but she caught only a piece of it.

"Long before I got my own diagnosis," Claire continued, in the kind of airy voice Nic had heard her use to point out a wind farm amid an alfalfa field, "I had a front-row seat to the joys of stage IV breast cancer. With my mother, but more so with Melana. I saw the blisters from the radiation. I saw what lymphedema can do to a slim, graceful arm. I wiped her down when she was feverish, tried to get water into her when the sores in her mouth were the most severe." Claire's humorless laugh sounded more like a clearing of her throat. "Yes, those were good times."

Nicole undercut the ball, cracking it with the top of the bat so that it flew straight up, tenting the netting before dropping at her feet. She was breathing hard, realizing how far she'd already pushed the softness of her out-of-shape body. Her mind scrambled back, trying to remember what Claire had told her about discovering her own disease at an earlier stage than her sister—was it stage III?—and realizing in the process how very little Claire had actually shared with her.

Realizing how little she'd asked.

"Right up to a few days before Melana died," Claire continued, "she kept telling me that she was fine. That it really wasn't so bad. She'd caught the disease a tick earlier than our own mother, you know, so that meant she would be the Petrenko woman that would survive. I'd be researching treatment strategies and she would ask me in her reedy voice, 'What have you found, Claire? What new vitamins should I try?'"

Nicole stood with her bat on her shoulder with her head turned away, but she saw nothing in front of her, nothing at all.

"In the end, I realized that me holed up in a Siamese temple eating pea pods wasn't going to change anybody's suffering. Melana's suffering was long over, and walking the Middle Path sure didn't seem to be helping mine. I just couldn't accept the idea that happiness and suffering are nothing more than states of mind. I just didn't believe the idea that if I could control my mind, then I could be happy."

For Nicole, the world went a little mute, as if someone had tossed a thick blanket over the barks of the carnies, the sizzling grill of a hamburger stand, the clanging bells of an arcade win, and the tinny music of a nearby carousel.

If you can control your mind, then you could be happy.

Her mind drifted to Noah in his residential facility, sitting in circles with other sufferers, seeking patterns, mulling over the loops and twists of his broken thoughts, the swell and surge of his unruly emotions. Like Claire once had been, Noah was tucked away from the world. But unlike Claire, Noah had all the strength of Western medicine to teach him ways to control his mind. He had skilled doctors leading him through therapy; he had experienced professionals offering him new tools to deal with the stresses of life.

He wouldn't quit as Claire did. He couldn't quit.

She wouldn't let him quit.

"Anyway," Claire said, "what I'm standing here chewing off your ear to say is that you don't have to worry about me quitting. My diagnosis was like Karma holding a bullhorn to my ear. No more second chances."

༺

It was Nicole's turn to drive again, so she slipped into the driver's seat of Jenna's car and put on her sunglasses. Her stomach sloshed with blue slushy and the grease of a funnel cake, well mixed after a group ride on the Tilt-a-Whirl. She was sure to regret that later, but for now she was determined to get them back on Interstate 90 to Minnesota without glancing in the rearview mirror for imaginary tornados. In her mind, she'd already hopped and skipped forward to the sight of the spires of Chicago and the lights of Wrigley Field.

A day or two at the most, and she'd be back on her college stomping grounds.

"Hey," Claire said, tossing her Stetson at her feet, "do you guys ever wonder what happened to Theresa?"

Uh-oh. Nicole plunged the key into the ignition. "I assume you're talking about Three-Tat Tess, yes?"

Claire said, "She's probably Ten-Tat Tess by now."

"All I remember is that she tooled around at community college for a while." Nicole stretched her arm across the back of Claire's seat then was speared by the beady black stare of a three-foot purple bear. "Hey, Jenna, are you sure you want to ride beside that thing? There's still room in the trunk."

"I like it here." Jenna pressed up against it. Lucky, cowering on Jenna's other side, gave a little whine. "It's like a mascot, sharing the road with us."

"Okay then." Nicole eased out of the parking spot. "Anyway, after college as far as I know, Theresa pretty much fell off the face of the earth."

"I had Theresa's old e-mail." Claire reached across the dashboard to flick on the air-conditioning. "But it bounced when my sisters tried to add it to the blog."

Nicole ventured, "So what got you thinking about our rebel classmate?"

"Maya mentioned her the other night over the campfire, remember?"

Nicole straightened the car and headed for the fairground exit. "Let me guess. She lives just a few miles from here."

"I wasn't going to say that at all." Claire gave her an eye while replaiting the tail of her braid. "I was just going to mention that Maya told me she got a Christmas card from Theresa just last year. She's living on a farm."

"Theresa is feeding chickens?" Jenna rustled in the back-seat, kicking off her sneakers. "Our Tess, with the purple hair and the nose ring?"

"People change." Claire clutched the Jesus strap as Nicole poked the nose of the car onto the country road. "And you'd have acted out, too, Jenna, if you lived like she did in one of those houses by the old cannery."

"Saint Claire." Nicole shook her head. "What a soft touch you are. You called her, I suppose."

"You'd have killed me if I hadn't."

The car rumbled onto the gravel-scattered road. "One long detour just wasn't enough for you, was it?"

"Unfortunately, nobody answered the phone at Theresa's house. Maya did give me her address, though."

"Good. Then you can write to her. Maybe on the way back—"

"Nicole, you're a jet streaking across the sky, and I'm a bee seeking flowers."

"I'll get there faster."

"But twenty bucks says I'll have a much better time. Aren't you curious as to where she lives?"

Nicole accelerated as they approached the on-ramp for Interstate 90. "I suspect it isn't Chicago, which is where *I* want to go. And I know it's a long way from here, or you wouldn't be tiptoeing around the subject."

"You're so busy running here and there that you've forgotten that the goal of life is learning."

"Wow, for a moment there you actually sound like a Buddhist."

"And Buddhists teach that we only progress in life when we open up our attention to the universe. I didn't go looking for Theresa—Maya mentioned her. Now, all day, she's been prancing in my head."

"There's an image."

"It's Karmic. We have to take action."

Nicole glanced in the rearview mirror. "Jenna, you're awfully quiet. Do you want to visit Theresa?"

"Theresa scared the hell out of me."

Nicole gave Claire a nudge. "You're outvoted."

"But then again," Jenna added, "any side trip that takes me farther from my cheating husband is a positive thing."

Claire raised a slow eyebrow. "Well, Nic, aren't you the least bit curious as to what happened to that wild girl we all once knew?"

Nicole was curious, yes, but not about Theresa. Nicole hardly knew the girl except by reputation. Claire had hung out with Theresa in middle school before the girl started breaking into hardware stores and setting garbage bins on fire. Three-Tat Tess had been suspended from school too many times for Nicole to remember. But Claire tended to keep her hooks in people, especially the broken ones.

Nicole's curiosity ran on a completely different track. "You know," she said, "when most people take a cross-country trip, they tend to map out their journey depending on the landmarks or the tourist attractions."

"I've always had a deep suspicion of 'most people.'" Claire slipped her bare feet up against the glove compartment. "They tend to be a downright boring bunch."

"Just imagine everything we've passed by," Nicole said. "We could have made a detour to Yellowstone, or the Grand Teton National Park. We didn't see Devils Tower or the Crazy Horse Memorial. We hardly explored the Badlands, and back by Maya's dig, we couldn't have been more than a few dozen miles from Mount Rushmore—"

"Tourist trap."

"Instead, Claire, you've got us on some kind of Pine Lakes cross-country magical mystery tour."

"I haven't the faintest idea what you're talking about."

Nicole raised a hand to count them off. "Jin, Sydney, Maya, Theresa. Even me."

"Intelligent company."

"And free beds."

Claire gave her an all-knowing look. "Whatever you're looking for in Pine Lake, Nic, it'll still be there if we arrive just a few days later."

Nicole flexed her fingers over the steering wheel. Claire spoke the truth, a truth that was just beginning to bite. Nicole didn't want to be the rigid coach following some prewritten playbook. She certainly had never been like that in Pine Lake.

Moreover, she was weary of spending this whole journey like a fugitive hearing the distant baying of hounds.

She pressed the accelerator. The car surged forward. She felt an old, familiar, slipping sensation, as if the ground beneath the Chevy was slick with rain even though the South Dakota sky was crystal-blue and every car in the distance tossed up a haze of dust. She'd always been wary of abrupt changes in plans. A whole future could transform because of a single unfettered impulse. Like a moment of passion in a graduate-school dorm after a high-stakes billiards game with a sexy young man.

"So," Nicole said, strangely breathless, "where, exactly, does Theresa live?"

Chapter Eight

Kansas

Since Jenna had tossed her things in the back of her sedan and left Seattle behind her, she'd felt like a top—spinning, spinning, spinning—and as long as the world was a blur outside and events kept hurtling at her, then she could maintain her momentum with no fear of that first fateful wobble.

Now nearly three hundred miles south of Sioux Falls, just crossing the border into Kansas, Jenna stared out the bug-splattered window as she drove past the soaring poles of a wind farm. In the backseat, Claire napped with her mouth open, sinking into the purple stuffed bear, with Lucky curled up in the hollow of her lap. In the passenger's seat, Nicole bent over her phone, humming in her absent, repetitive way to some country song she'd heard about a hundred miles ago, during the long stretch where the radio could detect nothing but Dwight Yoakam and hair bands.

The wind farm's unholy whirr was audible above the high-pitched wheeze of the engine, and that was when Jenna's whole body started to shake.

It was a mistake to remember the last time Nate slipped his hand across her hip and burrowed his fingers beneath the waistband of her pajama bottoms—as she just had, moments ago, when she'd startled out of the memory only to notice that she'd drifted halfway to the other side of the road. Too long a stretch of driving was dangerous. Remembering the better times of two weeks ago was dangerous, too.

She watched the odometer tick over another mile, keenly conscious of Nicole in the passenger seat sweeping her fingertip across her phone. Jenna just knew Nicole would have seen the divorce coming long before the papers were drafted. Nicole would have picked up on all the subtle signals of a husband growing distant and not be left wondering afterward how he could have made love to her right up to the night before he'd handed her the petition.

"Nicole," she found herself saying, "what do you know about divorce?"

Nicole's humming stopped on a hitch. Her fingers stilled, poised over the face of her phone.

Jenna had never really understood why people reacted this way whenever she asked a simple question.

"I don't know much," Nicole stuttered. "I mean, Lars and I have had some hair-pulling screamers, but we never go to bed angry, and the makeup sex, well…"

Jenna made a sound that was meant to be a laugh, but she suspected that it came out more like a hiccup.

"I did have a client who went through a nasty split." Nicole slipped her cell phone in the purse by her feet. "I know, in the beginning, the timing is important. I hope you don't think I was out of line...but after what you told me in Cheyenne, I checked out Oregon's divorce laws. I was worried about that deadline you mentioned, the thirty days you have to file a response."

Jenna nodded. She wasn't in the least surprised Nicole had looked into the situation. She'd been quietly observing Nicole for so long that she'd memorized the pattern of sun freckles across the top of Nicole's shoulders. Nicole was the kind of woman who threw herself deep into things. Jenna had noted how many hours Nicole spent looking things up on her phone. Jenna had even seen Nicole sneak a look at Claire's phone when it buzzed only moments ago.

"I have to say," Nicole continued, "I'm having a hard time wrapping my mind around the fact that he scheduled a joint appointment with a lawyer only a week after he served you papers. That hardly gives you any time—"

"Nate must have spent hours with an attorney already," Jenna said, "working out child support payments and how to equitably divide my 401(k)s."

Nicole allowed a beat of silence. "It's odd that he's rushing."

The center yellow line wavered in her vision as she remembered the moment. She'd hardly taken her raincoat off after coming home from the airport. Nate stood in the kitchen and asked for a minute of her time. She'd thought he was going to hand her a contract to review for his next commission—instead she found herself named as a respondent in the Circuit Court of the State of Oregon.

"Zoe doesn't know yet." Jenna winced as a truck zoomed by on the left. "He waited until Zoe was on a plane to camp before he served me."

"He doesn't expect this to be over and done before you guys tell her, right?"

"I think he does." If the air bag explosively inflated and punched her in the solar plexus, Jenna didn't think her chest could feel sorer. "Zoe once had a stuffed toucan. She'd loved the fuzz right off the fabric to the point that it leaked stuffing. So one week, when we went off to Disneyland, he hung back at the house to hide it in the basement. He pretended ignorance when we returned and she couldn't find it. She searched for it among her stuffed animals for a little while. Then, soon enough, she found a pink bear to love. Pinky Bear, she called it. She forgot she'd ever had a toucan."

"You're not a stuffed toucan, Jen. Zoe isn't going to forget her mother."

"It might be better for everyone if I just went away—"

"*Don't say that.*"

Nicole's fingers dug into her shoulder.

"Listen." Nicole gave her a little shake. "On the fairgrounds in Sioux Falls, I watched you spend forty bucks trying to win that silly purple bear for your daughter. You've bought a postcard at every single gas station and truck stop from Reno to Omaha. I've watched you agonizing in the backseat as you tried to write. I've seen you drop those postcards in the mailbox only to run back and try to dig them out again."

Jenna blinked and kept her eyes forward, intensely aware of Nicole's ocular implant burning a hole in her profile.

"You love your daughter," Nicole said huskily, "and whatever is going on between the two of you, this much is true: it's never better for *anyone* if someone you love just 'goes away.'"

Nicole released her. Nicole turned her face away so Jenna could only see the familiar whorl of her hair as she pressed her knuckles against her lips.

In work, Jenna trusted Chinese translators to repeat her words to her foreign clients in a way that was culturally sensitive and idiomatically correct. Into that language gap fell a hundred thousand verbal gaffes. She only wished there existed emotional translators she could hire to follow her around and prevent her from saying the kind of things that evoked such strong reactions in her friends.

And in her daughter.

When Nicole spoke again, her voice was low and controlled. "Nobody likes conflict. But this is one of those times in your life when you're going to need to dig deep and find the courage to face Nate and speak your mind."

"I can manage conflict. There's conflict at the hedge fund all the time." She'd long learned to slip on her work persona like a suit of armor, and then shuck it off when she got home. "My boss only got things done when we worked under pressure—"

"That's professional, and that's admirable, and it explains

your career success. But, Jenna, be honest. Personal conflict is something you avoid."

Two thousand miles, Jenna thought. *Maybe she is finally getting to know me.*

Nicole reached over to fiddle with the knob for the fan. "Tell me, did Nate's papers have any kind of temporary status quo order of custody, or ex parte order or anything like that?"

Jenna didn't like to think about the papers, but those terms were unfamiliar. "I don't remember anything except where he checked the form saying he wanted full legal custody of Zoe."

"It's important that you know. I'm worried that since he filed first, he might have the first say in any custody battle."

Custody battle.

"Is there any way you can document the extent of your role in the parenting of Zoe?"

"Document?"

"I know that sounds cold-blooded. But because you're the primary breadwinner and Nate's the primary caretaker, you've got the burden of proof. If you want full legal custody, or even shared custody, you may have to show evidence of how much you're involved in Zoe's life."

Jenna hesitated. "How much I'm involved now? Or before?"

"Both." Nicole drew her brows together. "Always. You need to think up the names of witnesses who've seen you yelling on the sidelines at Zoe's sports events. Teachers who've sat down with you at the parent-child conferences.

Collect ticket stubs from weekends you've taken Zoe off to the zoo or to a movie while Nate finishes whatever he does. Did you work any fund-raisers at her elementary school? Did you run for office in the PTA? Did you take her to the last pediatric visit? Orthodontist? Dentist?"

Jenna felt the small muscles between her vertebrae tightening, the slow, cramping urge to bow her shoulders and arc inward, draw her knees to her chest and bury her head in the blue weave of her jeans, except she couldn't do it, because she was driving, because the road was racing past beneath her feet at—she checked the speedometer—eighty-five miles an hour.

Images flooded her mind. Zoe as an infant swaddled in cotton blankets, a warm bundle she'd lift out of the crib at two a.m. in the light of a single princess lamp. The slow ease into the rocking chair as she unbuttoned her pajama top. With a pinch, she remembered her daughter latching on, the weighty drop of her milk, the lullaby she hummed until Zoe stopped sucking and gifted her with a smile.

For three months, Zoe had been completely hers.

But the mortgage had to be paid. Nate's commissions were sporadic and unpredictable and didn't provide medical insurance for the specialists they needed to monitor Zoe's heart murmur because of a septal defect, a tiny hole between chambers that the doctor promised would close up as she grew. Nate took up the child care responsibilities with an efficiency that she'd admired, that calmed her worried mother's heart, so that when she kissed them both good-bye and returned to work, she didn't fear for Zoe's safety. She just left the house with a vague sense of hollowness that she'd attributed to her milk drying up.

When had it happened? She became the payer of the bills while Nate became the master of the neighborhood playdates. She washed the dishes while Nate placed his lips on Zoe's brow and gauged instantly whether the fever merited medicine or a swift trip to the pediatrician. When Zoe scraped a knee or tumbled off a swing, she would lift her arms to her father, though her mother stood right beside him on the playground.

Once again, the little brown bird ignored.

"Jenna?"

She'd told herself that when Zoe got older and less dependent on Nate, then Zoe would look to her more. When Zoe became a tween, they would talk about periods and bras and boys and how hard it was to make friends. As a teenager, Zoe would beg her mother to take her shopping, steal her high-heeled shoes from the closet, and vote for romantic comedies for Friday movie nights at home, both of them dipping their hands into the same bowl of popcorn.

Surely she could not be the only woman in the world who'd expected that the child who slipped from her own womb would mirror her not just in the color of her eyes but also in other ways, both good and bad. She'd ushered Zoe to her first day in preschool, cringing and terrified for her baby girl, only to arrive at pickup to watch Zoe tripping out of the schoolroom laughing, having conquered it with aplomb. It was a touch of the changeling. The little shock of those moments multiplied over the years, until one day that same child turned around with unexpected grace to look at the woman who birthed her with the eyes of a stranger.

"Jenna." Nicole shook her shoulder. "Mind the road."

She was straddling the lane as a car honked and tried to pass. She eased the car back between the white lines.

"Keep your eyes on the road and listen," Nicole said as she braced her hand against the dashboard. "I don't believe for *one minute* that you've been a complete outsider in the raising of your daughter."

"Not always."

There had been a golden period when Zoe first went to grammar school. Jenna's heart breaking as Zoe struggled with the heartless mean-girl machinations of fifth grade, running through best friends with alarming swiftness, Zoe's little Teflon heart rebounding while Jenna suffered every little prickle, every little scorn, holding grudges Zoe airily waved away. Until Zoe—sensing her pain, perhaps—stopped confiding in Jenna and started confiding in Nate instead. He made jokes of everything, teased and ribbed Zoe into laughter while, all at the same time, giving sage advice about friends over his special grilled cheese sandwiches and bowls of tomato soup.

"Zoe wrote an essay once, after Bring Your Daughter to Work Day." Jenna's throat felt dry, but Nicole's silence was like a vacuum begging to be filled. "She liked my office, the computer, and all the monitors. She was proud of me. We weren't always so estranged."

Overnight, it seemed, a sullen creature emerged from the cocoon of that happy tween. All the force of Zoe's hormonal swings focused on her *stupid* mother, her *clueless* parent, the adult she couldn't get away from fast enough.

"There's no way around it," Jenna whispered. "For a long time now, Zoe has belonged to Nate."

Jenna focused on keeping the car between the two white lines, her hands at ten and two o'clock on the steering wheel. She let go momentarily to pat the console beside her, searching for a water bottle, feeling the bite of a straw in her palm as she hit Nicole's diet soda, knocking fast-food napkins onto the floor. She heard a crack and then felt the smooth sides of a bottle as Nicole shoved it in her hand.

Nicole spoke with slow hesitation that made Jenna wary. "You do understand that full legal custody doesn't mean you won't ever see Zoe."

"The way Nate set it up, I have visitation rights every Wednesday." She fumbled her grip on the bottle. "Every Wednesday, and every other Saturday."

Jenna had suspected the schedule was sparse but had nothing to compare it to, until, out of the corner of her eye, she saw Nicole cover her face with her open hand.

"Okay." Nicole straightened up from under her hand. "There is something else you may want to consider. Oregon is a no-fault divorce state, but fault can be taken into account in the case of custody disputes."

She stuttered, "F-Fault?"

"The fact that he's cheating on you. With a woman who lives in your own neighborhood."

"The mother of Zoe's best friend."

"Oh, God."

Sissy Leclaire, who still sported the long, straight, part-in-the-middle hair of a girl of eighteen. She had a honking laugh and wore vintage clothes of patterns that didn't match, beads hanging from her neck, a compass tattoo on the back of her hand. Sissy Leclaire, an unmarried mother who'd bought the house with an inheritance from an aunt. She cobbled a living working as a doula, or bartending private events, or throwing parties selling candles. In the autumn, she made fantastical forest creatures out of acorns, sticks, and a bit of moss and glue. Miniature whimsical sculptures.

How long did Nate resist?

"As horrible as it is, Jen, that's your key to custody." Nicole had tumbled into a heap in the corner of the seat, rubbing her brow with one hand. "I have to believe that if you stand in front of a judge and state that Nate committed adultery with the mother of his daughter's best friend, the judge will raise questions about whether he's an appropriate role model to be the full legal custodian of a teenage girl."

"But Nate's an amazing father."

A vision of him bathed in multicolored lights from the Christmas tree, twirling Zoe in a dizzy dance, sweeping her in his arms before she could fall.

"Nate," Nicole pointed out, "is trying to keep Zoe away from you. Why do you think that is?"

"Zoe hates me. We've done nothing but fight for the past year."

"Is there a reason why?"

"Other than she's thirteen years old, rules her seventh-grade world, and thinks her socially awkward mother is an idiot?" Jenna's chest rose, defying the unspoken question. "Why else would she hate me?"

"Neglect." Nicole shifted. "Abuse."

Jenna glared at her. "I'm a breadwinner but not a beast. Just because I've given over the main child-rearing responsibilities doesn't mean I've neglected her any more than any other traditional household. Nate knows this, too."

"I'm not so sure you know what's going on in Nate's head. *This* is why you need a lawyer."

"I don't want a lawyer."

"If you don't get one, he'll steal everything you've worked for your whole life, including—"

"I don't want a divorce."

She gripped the steering wheel. Her blood swelled inside her ears, tightened her throat, rushed to her scalp and to the very tips of her toes. Nate's face flashed in her mind, the smile he gave her as he lifted his head from his work, the way his left canine was twisted a bit, the dimple deepening into shadow. The way he cradled her hand in his at the office parties she'd dragged him to, the way he ignored her dismissive bosses, pumped the flames of the other women's curiosity as he called himself a "ho" man and pulled her onto the dance floor, seducing her in front of the entire office. She still heard him, teasing her, tugging a piece of hair free of a clip right before he sauntered across the driveway to the garage to work. She let that piece hang all through the day as a promise.

The memories wobbling, wobbling.

"I should hate him, I know."

"Pull over, Jenna."

"I should hate that he betrayed me."

"You're veering onto the shoulder—slow *down*."

Then the world really was wobbling as the car vibrated over the shoulder strip.

"It's crazy," she breathed, lifting her foot from the gas. "But I'm still in love with him."

Chapter Nine

Kansas

"Well, this is not what I expected."

Claire stepped out of the car in front of the once-white house, standing solitary amid acres of flat Kansas farmland. The gravel of the driveway poked into her sandals. The house must once have been a proud, two-story testament to farming grit, but now weeds sprung through the slats of the front stairs. The door hung from a hinge. A few soaring rafters remained of the roof. Soot streaked up from the broken windows, making them look like eyes dressed with the thick mascara that her old friend Theresa used to favor.

Claire eyeballed the scorched furniture discarded by the porch. "To think my major worry visiting Theresa was that she would greet me with a loaded shotgun."

Nicole came up beside her. "Is that about your fourteenth birthday party? After all these years, she wouldn't load you up with buckshot for not inviting her."

"Maybe. Then again, maybe not. Are you sure that GPS of yours didn't steer us wrong?"

"It's the right address."

"Maybe Maya switched the digits or something—"

"Sorry to disappoint you, Claire, but the numbers are on the mailbox out front, stenciled right next to her name."

"But she would have told Maya if she'd moved away. She would have sent her a text, an e-mail, or left a forwarding address, something."

"People aren't always so eager to share bad news."

Claire kept blinking the Kansan dust out of her eyes, wishing she could clear her vision of what stood before her. Back in South Dakota, Maya had told her she'd received a Christmas card from Theresa just last year, a picture of a scarecrow sporting a Santa hat. The news had given Claire hope that maybe her troubled friend had finally fallen in love with some strapping farm boy and was now riding tractors and birthing litters of roly-poly little boys.

Jenna limped her way toward them holding Lucky, who raised his snout to the wind. "It still smells charred. The fire couldn't have happened all that long ago or the rain would have washed the smell away."

Claire eyed the parched brown fields. "Lord knows when it last rained around here."

Nicole pressed her forearm against her nose. "Ugh, that burned-plastic smell. I hate that smell."

"This farm is just begging for a mistress in a ruffled apron," Jenna said. "Can you see her dressed like that? Can you see her hanging wash out on those lines? Tending a garden? Sweeping the floorboards in the evening?"

Claire had to admit the task stretched her imagination. In high school, Theresa had always been on the edge of expulsion. She carved symbols into the wooden desks with the point of a Swiss army knife. She smoked brazenly on the front stairs of the school. On a dare, she tossed a lit match into a garbage bin and watched while the flames grew. The only reason Theresa had made it into the group graduation picture was because she happened to already sport hot-pink streaks in her hair. When they'd all lined up to fluff their dos for the camera, she'd leapt in to photo-bomb them.

Claire had always liked that particular shot the best.

"People change." Claire made her way toward the porch, stopping to gather a couple of daisies from the weeds. "Theresa once told me that after everything she went through with her parents' divorce, she would never get married. Yet clearly she married."

Jenna let Lucky down in the clearing to sniff around. "I didn't know her parents divorced."

"Her father screwed around with Theresa's middle-school English teacher." Claire eased onto the first step of the porch, testing the board with her weight. "You don't remember that?"

Jenna's brow puckered. "I guess. Vaguely."

"It was a huge scandal."

"I was out of the loop."

"Well, I could time-stamp the changes in that girl from the moment of the divorce proceedings."

Theresa the mischievous prankster that Claire had adored had suddenly turned brooding; her pranks, dangerous. She spurned Claire's efforts to clean the wooded trails in favor of beer, black clothing, and the stoners who hung out behind the old cannery.

"So those divorce proceedings," Jenna ventured, "they wouldn't have happened to have started when Theresa was say, twelve or thirteen years old?"

"No, no." Theresa had been fourteen when her parents divorced, but Claire figured Jenna didn't need to know that fact. Claire cast a glance at Nicole for help, but Nicole had swathed her mouth and nose with the sleeve of her T-shirt and seemed grimly fascinated by the bits of charred wood on the ground. "I was just speculating. In any case, the old Theresa we knew certainly isn't the same woman who ended up here."

Nicole added, "In a burned-out shell of a house."

"I'll take precautions anyway." Jenna crouched down by Lucky. "No matches. And black eyeliner is now banned from my house."

"Let's head back to town." Nicole's voice was muffled behind her hand. She swiveled toward the car. "We can ask some locals what happened, if they know where—"

"—not just yet." Claire raised the daisies to her nose as Nicole stuttered to a stop. "Just give me a minute to think this through."

Claire paced past a rocking chair to the end of the porch, seeking some evidence of her friend among the torn cushions and broken chairs. She peered through the cracked window to the cobwebbed interior, blackened and in shadow. She kept thinking there should be odd sneakers or lost jackets or scattered tools cast about. Fast-food wrappers or empty cigarette cartons or milk jugs. But no tire swing hung from the oak by the barn. No tricycle stood rusting underneath it.

Claire turned back to the porch. She ran her hand across the gritty back of a rocking chair. The wooden joints creaked as she settled into it. She nudged the floorboards to send herself rocking. Claire squeezed her eyes shut and remembered the young Theresa pretending not to shiver as she sat on the front porch of her old Cannery Row house. Claire remembered the sight of Theresa blowing out cigarette smoke, glaring, as Claire unloaded boxes of clothing donations from the trunk of her mother's car.

Then Claire opened her eyes and took in the new view—Theresa's view—of the long, empty ribbon of highway. She wondered how long Theresa had sat here staring down this road after her house burned down, trying to wrap her mind around the grim truth that there was no guarantee in life that everything and everyone would come out all right.

The rocking chair creaked as Claire stood up. She stared at the daisies in her hand, scentless with their petals spread wide. She thought about when she'd traveled through Thailand and had witnessed supplicants leaving betel nuts in a house where a woman had died in childbirth. She'd watched her Buddhist sponsor, Narupong, pull over to the side of a dangerous road in order to lay a painted figurine at the Tree of 100 Corpses. For a long time, Claire had assumed that these signs of respect were no different from the Western custom of laying flowers on a grave. But the Thai didn't pray for the repose of the souls of these hungry ghosts—no, they came for other reasons. Supplicants came to pray for a good harvest, a healthy baby, or the winning numbers of the next underground lottery. The Thai believed that great luck can arise from terrible tragedy.

Claire placed the daisies on the seat of the rocking chair and hoped that Theresa's tragedy—whatever it was—would someday gift her troubled friend with an equal measure of luck.

The porch steps creaked as Jenna took a seat, twirling a dandelion in her hand as she kept an eye on Lucky. "What do you think happened here?"

Claire eyed the drainpipe that hung off the porch eaves. "It could have been so many things."

"Maybe a grease fire?" Jenna bent down and plucked a sliver of glass out of Lucky's path. She tossed it behind her, into the hole in the upholstery of a broken love seat. "Or maybe lightning? The roof is caved in."

"I vote for arson." Nicole stepped into the conversation, her arms crossed tight, making trails in the gravel with her heels.

Jenna said, "Arson?"

"Absolutely." Nicole eyed the house as if she were spoiling for a fight. "Burning down a house is a physical manifestation of anger or frustration."

Jenna tossed the dandelion into the grass. "I know Theresa used to be crazy, but that sounds a little harsh—"

"You don't think our old friend was capable of dousing her issues in gasoline and then tossing a match?"

Claire hadn't smelled gasoline when they'd driven up, but now the scent seemed like a ghost in the air.

"People deal with difficult issues in different ways." Nicole eyeballed the wreckage. "Some people have difficulty dealing with the stresses of the world. Sometimes, nothing will make a teenage boy feel better but to strike a match and toss it into an iron barrel full of gasoline-soaked rags."

Claire froze, not sure she'd just heard right, rerunning that statement over in her head as Nicole's face blanched.

Nicole turned her back and headed for the car. "Can we just leave now?"

Chapter Ten

Mom, I think the garage is on fire."
Her daughter's high-pitched voice rang in Nicole's head. When Julia had phoned her that terrible day, the words hadn't made an immediate impact. Nicole had raised three kids. She'd learned that "Chris fell off his scooter doing tricks on the deck rail" didn't mean her son was paralyzed from the neck down. It meant a scrape on his shin or, at worst, a broken hand. So at the sound of Julia's news, Nicole's heart had skipped one beat, maybe two. She didn't click into full emergency mode until Julia mentioned the black smoke seeping around the garage door.

She'd made Julia call 911 on the landline while she abandoned her shopping cart in aisle six. She'd fast-walked to the car thinking about the gasoline in the lawn mower and the paint solvents lined up on the shelves. She told Julia to cross the street to a neighbor's house and not to hang up her cell phone until she got there.

Nicole arrived home before the firemen. Just as Julia had

described, smoke seeped from the seams, but she didn't see any flames. She did a mental accounting of her children and remembered that Noah wasn't in school today. He'd spent a restless night with a stomach virus, so she'd let him stay home. She swung through the front door and bounded up the stairs to rouse him—only to find the bed empty.

Listening to the rising wail of sirens, she noticed that the desk was clear of gum wrappers and pencil shavings and the gummy pink erasers he wore down to nubs. She stood in the hall and felt a tickle of mother's intuition as she noticed that no dirty jeans or cast-off socks littered the floor.

She didn't remember running outside as the fire engines pulled out front. She didn't remember fighting a fireman who bodily yanked her away from where she struggled to pull up the garage door. She remembered screaming that her son was in there. She remembered the sound of the ax digging into the wood. She remembered the men hauling him out, sooty, her son's arms dangling. She remembered the paramedic saying *smoke inhalation*.

Later, she remembered the doctor saying, *He'll live.*

Back home, the smell of charred wood in the air, in the grass, in the trees, in her skin, in her throat, grit in her hair no matter how many times she washed it, a clinging reminder of how much she'd failed him.

Now, curled up in the passenger's side of Jenna's car, Nicole blinked up at the scudding clouds trying to force the scent of charred wood out of her lungs. She breathed in the car's aroma of stale potato chips and damp dog and the reedy scent of old peppermint from the worn Christmas-tree air freshener dangling from the mirror. The engine whined, a high-pitched and vaguely alarming sound, and though she was grateful for the noise, she found herself worrying about the car's transmission fluid levels or wondering if there was a problem with the power steering. Those were worries she could check. Those were problems she knew how to fix.

Then Nicole caught sight of a low building up ahead, and she slapped a hand on Jenna's shoulder. "Take a right up there."

Jenna, driving, flicked on her directional. "At Fast Eddy's?"

"The pool hall, yes."

"But I thought we were looking for a restaurant—"

"It serves burgers." Nicole gestured to a sign that said *Burgers as big as Kansas*, as Jenna turned into the parking lot. "More importantly, it has a bar."

As Jenna pulled to a stop beside a dusty pickup truck, Nicole uncurled herself from the passenger seat and tumbled out. During the short trip from the car to the pool hall door, she tried to shrug the tension out of her shoulders. She wished that the skies would open just long enough to wash her face clean so she wouldn't look like such a panicked wreck.

Fortunately, the pool hall lived up to nationwide pool hall reputations. The sun could be going supernova outside these blacked-out windows, and not a sliver of light would penetrate. The place had a long bar and a recessed wooden dance floor with an area for a DJ. Some Top 40 country hit played on the speakers, twangy background noise for the two-dozen folks eating burgers and playing keno. Nicole passed a row of cowboys with their heels hooked on the bar's boot rail. She followed her instincts to the back, where she found three pool tables, two of them open. She breathed in the scent of cigarette smoke and stale beer, the perfume of another time, and it worked like Prozac to loosen her up.

She pulled her wallet out of her purse and slapped a dollar on the first table. "You guys know how to play eight ball?"

Jenna shrugged off her purse. "I worked for a hedge fund, remember?"

"Then let's lag."

Nicole seized two balls and lined them up behind the cue line. When Jenna was set, they struck their balls down the length of the table to bank off the short rail and return. Nicole's ball landed closest to the shooter's side rail.

Nicole said, "I'll break."

She racked the balls and then decided to pick a different pool stick from the selection on the wall. She rolled the new one in her hand with her back to the ladies. Nicole wondered how long Claire would hold her tongue. She figured she had one game, one drink, and maybe a half a game more.

When she turned around, Claire was seated by the pool table giving drink orders to a waitress in a gingham skirt and a denim snap-front shirt.

"A Coke for that one," Claire said, pointing to Jenna, who was dusting the tip of her cue, "and I say Nicole will want one of your specials. A Cody's Revenge."

Nicole lifted her stick. "I'll take two."

"Two's the house limit," Claire warned. "That means, Jenna, you're driving. In the meantime, I'll have a cold and frosty, whatever you've got on tap."

Nicole broke the balls to a satisfying crack. She watched two solids fall into the pockets, then waited for the balls to stop rolling before focusing on her next shot.

"You got yourself some competition," Claire said to Jenna, as Nicole pocketed another ball. "So, Nic, where did a mother of three learn how to play pool?"

"Chicago, graduate school days, at a hall called Get a Cue. They had ratty pool tables and watered-down beer by the pitcher." Nicole stepped back to eye the whole table. "They also had biannual tournaments for a fifty-buck prize."

Claire leaned back in the chair. "Fifty bucks will buy a lot of ramen noodles."

"That's where I met Lars." She squinted down the cue at an orange ball, sliding the stick over her bent fingers. "I played against him in the finals one semester."

"Lars won, I bet." Claire shrugged at Nicole's surprised look. "He'd have to impress you or you wouldn't have given him the time of day."

Nicole hadn't realized she was quite so transparent. She bent over the table, eyeing another ball, as the waitress slid an electric-pink drink on a nearby table. She hit the ball but with too much force, wondering how much of her troubles Claire and Jenna had already guessed despite the fact she'd let them grow like mushrooms in the dark.

"So," she said, raising her voice above the guitar twang of a Merle Haggard song on the speakers, "have you both heard the joke about the so-called family therapist who put her son in a lockdown facility?"

She hit the solid ball but it spun out and missed the pocket. She stepped away from the pool table, out of the spread of light cast from the overhead lamp, out of the direct scrutiny of Claire sprawled back in her chair. She wished she could take another step back.

She wished she could back up to, say, Idaho.

"I've been waiting about two thousand miles to hear this story," Claire said. "You finally up for sharing?"

"With about the same enthusiasm I'd have if I were facing a mammogram."

"Fortunately, I don't have to think about those anymore."

Jenna grunted as she lined up a shot.

"This isn't the kind of story you bring up over fast-food tacos. I blurted out the truth once before, and I paid a price for it." With half an eye, Nicole watched Jenna's technique as her friend knocked a ball into the side pocket. "Back when it happened, I unloaded my troubles on a woman I considered a friend. That friend had a son Noah's age. I figured she'd relate. I miscalculated." She tightened her grip on her pool cue. "That friend spent the next six months performing Cirque du Soleil acrobatics in order to sidle out of my sight in the hardware store."

"Oh, hon," Claire said, "I promise we won't leave you by the side of the road. Right, Jenna?"

"Right." Jenna frowned as she missed the shot. "Anyway, I'm starting to like your humming."

Nicole dropped her chin to her chest. A prickling started at the back of her eyes. Her friends' easy attitude was like a shot of vodka, straight up. The last thing Nicole wanted right now was to be drawn to some intimate corner table where the two of them would listen to her story with watery eyes filled with pity.

"The official version," she said, "is that Noah had seen some crazy web video about making colored flames. He'd imitated it by putting gasoline-soaked rags in a metal drum. He didn't mean to burn the garage down or anything. It was just a mindless teenage experiment. Ha ha. Ha ha. Oh, look at the time." The balls clattered as she took another shot, but nothing dropped into a pocket. "The truth was that my son was in the low-point swing of one of his moods. He wanted to see something burn. In the process, he nearly set the neighborhood on fire." Nicole tapped the edge of the pool table. "Call ten in the side pocket, Jenna."

Jenna startled and then made a quick, careless shot. The ball spun, badly hit, but torqued into the pocket nonetheless.

"The neighbors didn't exactly call out the casserole brigade even when they heard the official version," she continued. "There were no bagel deliveries or rotisserie chickens left at my door. That was my first hint that I would have to be very careful about whom I commiserated with." Nicole moved around the table, searching for a good angle. "Secrecy was a way to protect Noah, so at some point, when he learned a measure of control, he could come back home and pick up his normal life."

Normal life. Nicole flattened the cue against the side of

the pool table and then bent over to squint down the length. The stick quivered under her grip. Noah had once had a normal life. She thought of the preadolescent Noah, the intense boy bent over pads of paper almost as big as he was, kicking his feet up as he sketched vegetable gnomes and imagined dragons in cloud formations.

Nicole bobbled the shot then reached for her drink. It was sticky-sweet. The kind of drink loaded with liquor that tasted like cotton candy. She felt the attention of both women, even if Claire seemed intent on Jenna lining up her next shot. Nicole debated how much to tell them. Should she go all the way back to the forced forty-eight-hour lockdown? She'd been so furious, even knowing that it was standard procedure in situations the doctors deemed suspicious. She was more furious when the psychiatrists reassessed him after that time and decided to keep Noah for another two weeks. She had been adamant. She knew her son. He was an intense, curious, artistic young man struggling under the flux of hormones.

He was *not* mentally ill.

During a cocktail party at a college reunion, Nicole had once met an old graduate school friend who'd finished the clinical path Nicole had long abandoned. The colleague now worked in private practice. Her old friend had expressed frustration about her own struggling business, how no one really wanted to have years of weekly psychotherapy sessions with no guarantee of success, no guarantee of change. What people wanted, she'd said earnestly, was what Nicole was giving them—enthusiasm, practical advice, and quick-and-easy solutions to real-world problems. Nicole had left that conversation numb. Her friend had essentially called life coaching the therapy equivalent of McDonald's.

But even a drive-through therapist should be able to see signs of mental illness in her own son.

"You're up, Nic."

Nicole startled at Jenna's voice, then walked around the table and stared at the setup of the balls. Her brain made no sense of them. "Do you guys know that moment in a horror movie when the main character is creeping down into the dark basement?"

Jenna bobbed her chin against the felt tip of her cue. "You just know there's someone down there with a chain saw."

"Well, that's sort of how I felt when Noah got sucked into the system. I knew what they were going to do to him in that ward. He had ECGs to check his brain waves and MRIs to make sure he didn't have a tumor and a million other tests, physiological and psychological. They were looking for some reason for his 'aberration in behavior.'"

Jenna hissed, "Holy Clockwork Orange."

"I was so crazy with worry during those months that there came a point where I actually hoped they *would* find a tumor."

She shouldn't have said that. She'd never spoken those words before, too ashamed of the feeling. She hadn't even shared the sentiment with Lars. And here she was blurting it out in front of a woman who'd just had a double mastectomy.

Claire didn't seem the least fazed. "A tumor can be cut

right out," Claire said, patting her flat chest. "A tumor means the possibility of a cure."

Nicole sagged against a post. That was the heart of it, she supposed. Noah's issues were deeper, fully embedded, more complicated. She'd thrown herself into them. The months that followed had been a flurry of research. In order to keep fed and clothed, her vegetarian daughter learned to make baked macaroni and cheese, and her two-sport younger son, Christian, learned how to bleach the whites. Lars had been a rock, keeping the house running and keeping track of Noah's meds. Meanwhile, she'd lined up therapists—only the best of the best—and researched troubled adolescent behavior as if she were in graduate school again.

Why, why, *why*, after dropping out of her PhD program, hadn't she pushed to at least become a licensed professional counselor? It might have taken three years to finish the sixty credits required, maybe a few months more in supervised training, but then, at least, she might have been able to *help* Noah. She pointedly ignored the fact that she and Lars had started a family young and therefore had to build a life from scratch. If she'd only been more determined, she could have done it. Then she might have been able to pick up the subtleties between normal adolescent behavior—the occasional angry outbursts, a slammed door, increasing withdrawal—and the something-more-complicated that was the fascinating, frightening mind of Noah.

"So," Claire prompted, "did Noah ever give any kind of explanation for what he did?"

Nicole shook off the troubling thoughts then lined up

another ball for a side pocket. "Do you have any teenage nephews, Claire?"

"Paulina has two."

"Have you ever had a conversation with either one of them?"

"Briefly."

"Precisely. That was one of Noah's blessedly normal traits. When Noah spoke in sentences longer than three words, we served dinner on china."

Jenna piped into the conversation. "Honestly, Nic, after all that time in therapy, he was probably all talked out."

"I wouldn't be surprised," Nicole said. "I think teenage boys have a daily word quota. Once that's used up, pfft, that's it for the day."

"No, I mean, talk therapy itself is overrated." Jenna leaned down and aimed. "Maybe it's good for you, for some people. But for me, it's like a cow chewing cud over and over, only to be forced to vomit it back up before chewing it down into a different stomach. After a while, it all turns to some formless soup in your mouth."

Nicole let the odd image sink in. She thought about the weeks after Noah finally came home when she posed more and more direct queries. Why had he lit the rags in the garage? *It was stupid.* Why had he waited until she was out of the house? *I dunno.* Not only had Noah's attitude become more sullen and dismissive, but the more she probed, the more his responses became muddled.

She remembered sitting by his bed in the hospital the evening of the fire. She remembered how Noah had opened his bloodshot, sooty eyes in the ER, blinked at his surroundings, and then, when he realized where he was, his whole face crumpled.

She'd plunged her hand through his dark curly hair, gritty with soot.

Why? Why, my baby boy?

Nicole dropped into a chair. The shock joggled her spine. She gripped the cue so she wouldn't slip right down to the sticky floor, so she wouldn't let Claire and Jenna see how bad it all really was.

A shadow fell across her, and she glanced up to see Jenna standing between her and the pool table light. "Did they ever classify him?"

Nicole felt the grit of the blue chalk on the smooth wood of the cue. First they'd classified him with depression, which was what she'd expected, but then they suggested he suffered from a more serious mood disorder. One therapist proposed that he might have a borderline personality disorder. The next considered him mildly bipolar.

"Noah has always been an outlier." She shrugged, hoping it looked casual. "He never fit into a neat diagnostic box."

"In my teens, my mother dragged me to dozens of child psychologists." Jenna set the pool cue standing right in front of her. "I think the sixth doctor finally satisfied her by saying I had 'pervasive development disorder not otherwise specified.' It even has an acronym, PDD-NOS."

"Better known as 'physician didn't decide.'"

"Exactly."

"Noah got that one, too, early on."

"I tell you, my mother was so relieved. It explained everything. I had a *condition*. Inherited from my father, of course. He had the same strange affliction that I did, the one that made him prefer to stay indoors and read."

Claire scraped her chair so she sat beside her. "So how long have you been dealing with this, Nic?"

"Eighteen months." *Two weeks. One day.*

"How's he doing?"

Behind her eyes rushed the series of doctors she'd brought him to, the group therapy she'd insisted on, the litany of medicines they'd tried—sertraline, fluoxetine, lorazepam, risperidone, divalproex—measuring side effects against how they affected his moods, watching her once-active, happy little boy grow sluggish and sullen and plump. Some antidepressants, she'd been warned, can cause morbid thinking, and his room contained a light fixture and shoelaces.

That was the problem that kept her up at night, every night, when he was home. Listening for movement in the small hours of the morning. Watching him over breakfast for signs that he'd tucked his pills between his cheek and gum. Checking his room to see if he was obsessing over his sketch pad, or, more frighteningly, lying slack-jawed and catatonic on his bed, wearing earbuds that leaked the scream of heavy metal.

"He's spending six weeks in a treatment center." She reached for her drink and sucked the last of that cotton-candy sweetness off the clinking ice cubes. "We're trying something called dialectical behavior therapy. It's specialized for teenagers with a mixture of mood and behavior issues."

Claire raised her beer. "I was so sure you were running away from something. A malpractice suit, maybe. Or a midlife crisis. Maybe an angry ex-lover."

"If only. And I didn't run away," she reminded her. "I was pushed out by Lars."

"Like Bilbo the Hobbit," Jenna piped in, "nudged into an adventure by Gandalf."

"That explains things," Claire laughed, "because life was so much simpler back in the Shire—I mean Pine Lake."

Nicole caught Claire's wink, and the memories tumbled over one another. Noah, eight years old, laughing as he splashed into Bay Roberts. Noah painting his body scalp to foot and playing the mud monster to send his sister squealing. Noah, falling asleep wrapped in a towel by the bonfire, whispering how he wanted to live in Pine Lake forever.

"Personally," Claire remarked, "I think you should take up meditating."

"I'm not sure that'll help Noah much."

"I'm talking about *you* right now. Noah will be home before you know it, but right now, it sounds to me he's in good hands. But Buddhism could teach *you* a little about how to handle anxiety and suffering."

"I've got a religion, thank you."

"The untrained mind is so vulnerable. If something good happens, all is glitter and joy." Claire leaned toward her. "And when something bad happens, it's in pain."

"You read that in a fortune cookie."

Claire's laugh was honest. "I think you'd make a great *maechi*."

"I'm not moving to a place with cockroaches the size of llamas." Nicole rattled the ice in her empty drink. "And I'm *not* shaving my head."

"You look me in the eye and tell me you don't believe it was Karma that sent us to Theresa's burned-out house today?"

Nicole had to admit that the coincidence was odd. Then she tugged on the cross hanging from her neck. "The Roman Catholic Church might give me another reason for that coincidence."

"Fair enough. So how do you feel, Nicole, now that you've confessed your so-called sins?"

Nicole stopped jiggling ice cubes at the waitress. She froze with her glass in midair. She took a long, deep breath. When she exhaled, she felt a new looseness in her ribs as the air rushed out of her, right to the bottom of her lungs. She felt loose-jointed, elastic, like she did after a long, leisurely Pilates session. She glanced into the pink dregs amid the ice in her glass as her senses tingled. Some realization eluded her, hovering just outside her now well-lubricated mental grasp.

It was probably the liquor, she told herself, shaking the cubes again. Yes, it was the liquor giving her this unexpected lightness of being.

"Are we done playing pool?" Jenna clattered the stick on the table behind her. "I see a crowd on the dance floor, and I think they're line dancing."

Claire stood up. "We can't leave Kansas without line dancing."

Nicole laid her pool cue on the table. Jenna led the charge, and Nicole followed Claire. She floated in Claire's wake as they headed past the bar toward the dance floor where a crowd had already gathered.

Then Nicole slammed into Claire's back.

Nicole stumbled. "Hey, Claire—"

Claire flung out one arm to hold her back, and then Claire lunged forward to seize a fistful of Jenna's shirt. Claire dragged Jenna bodily back, pulling both of them around the curve of the bar.

Jenna said, "Claire, what—"

"*Shhh!*"

Claire shoved them behind her. Then she stretched up on her tiptoes, bobbing her head perilously close to the bald pate of the nearest bar patron, who stopped sipping whiskey long enough to give them all a baleful look.

Nicole ignored him and followed Claire's gaze. She saw a woman standing just inside the doorway to the pool hall. Nicole shook her head and looked again.

Maybe one Cody's Revenge was all she could handle. The woman at the door looked a lot like Claire's sister Paulina.

"Come on." Claire swiveled on a heel and darted back toward the pool tables. "Every pool hall must have a back door."

Chapter Eleven

Getting the heck out of Kansas

J enna shot out the back door of the pool hall and slammed into a white apron. The white apron stumbled back. She glanced up at the man wearing it as he flung his cigarette out of the way and shot blue smoke toward the moon. Above the shouts of cooks, the clatter of pots, and the plunging hiss of frying oil, she mumbled an excuse, only to have Nicole and Claire barrel out behind her. The young man gave her a shrug as if women escaped through the pool hall kitchen every day.

Jenna caught up with her friends as they raced to the corner of the building. The sky was gray in the gloaming just after sunset. Claire hesitated, peering around the corner, then minced down the narrow alley between the pool hall and what smelled like a dry-cleaning establishment, rounding the garbage cans as if hitting them would alert the hounds.

At the front corner of the building, Claire pressed her back against the wall. "Jenna, take out your keys."

Jenna plunged her hand into her purse and curled her fingers around the Hello Kitty key chain Zoe had gifted her on her thirty-second birthday.

"Nicole," Claire said, "you take the backseat. I'll ride shotgun."

"But you don't know how to use the GPS—"

"You don't need a GPS when you're fleeing an angry sister."

"So that really was—"

"We'll talk on the road. Jenna, are you ready?"

Jenna jingled the keys.

"Lightning-fast. Let's go."

Jenna shot out behind her friends and followed the tail of Claire's braid. Claire skidded to a stop as the front door of the pool hall opened. Jenna braced herself to dive between parked cars—she figured that was what Claire would want her to do, though Jenna didn't know why—until she saw a couple emerge, too wrapped up in each other to notice the three women frozen in the glow of an overhead fluorescent light.

She had a quick flashback to senior year. That freezing winter night when she sat with Claire and a bunch of fellow Key Club members sharing a bottle of peppermint schnapps around a fire at Coley's Point. They'd heard a shout beyond the firelight. They'd squealed and scattered willy-nilly into the winter woods, outracing the scanning beam.

As the door of the pool hall slammed shut, they zipped back into action. Jenna shuffled around the car to unlock the doors. She hauled her purse over her head and tossed it in the back. Lucky's tags rattled as he jerked awake. Jenna dove into the driver's seat. She plunged the key into the ignition, and the engine roared to life.

She put the car in reverse and slapped her arm on the passenger seat behind Claire to scan the parking lot behind her. "Where to?"

"West."

Jenna hit the gas. "Which way is west?"

"Hell if I know." Claire's gaze was glued to the front door of Fast Eddy's. "Just get on the road, we'll figure—"

"Take a right out of the parking lot," Nicole said. "As if we're going back to Theresa's house."

Jenna cranked the steering wheel to turn out of the parking spot, and then cranked it the other way to head toward the exit. She eased up just long enough to notice no cars coming then slammed the accelerator. The tires squealed.

Jenna's heart pounded, but she felt a tickling urge to laugh. That was the first time she'd ever burned rubber.

Claire's whole body twisted in the seat as she kept an eye on Fast Eddy's until she couldn't see the front door anymore. "We have to put some miles between us. A thousand would work. How the *hell* did she find me?"

From the backseat, Nicole blurted, "*Find* you?"

"Washington State plates." Jenna could just see the pale ghost of Theresa's abandoned house as they came up fast upon it. "She probably drove around this road until she found my car. There aren't a lot of those license plates here in Kansas."

"But how did she know I was in *Kansas?*"

"Why wouldn't she know?" Nicole's voice went up in pitch. "You've been talking to Paulina all during this trip. You didn't tell her?"

"I told Paulina what she needed to know and not one iota more—"

"—yet you *knew* Paulina was looking for you!"

"As the firstborn, Paulina believes this bequeaths upon her the royal right to control every detail of her siblings' lives."

"Oh, my God." The teeth of a zipper clinked as Nicole opened her purse. "Has your sister been following us clear across the country?"

"No, no." Claire huffed in frustration. "She's not that crazy. At least, I didn't see her truck in the parking lot. That means she's got a rental car. That means she must have flown in to Wichita or something. Come on, Jenna," she urged. "I know you have a heavier foot than that."

Jenna glanced uneasily at the speedometer as she dared to press it harder. There was a reason why Nicole did most of the driving. This was Jenna's father's old car. Every time Jenna edged over seventy miles an hour she conjured the ghost of her father in the backseat, admonishing her to keep within the speed limit.

Suddenly from the backseat came a blue glow. Startled, Jenna glanced in the rearview mirror to see Nicole's face illuminated by a cell-phone screen.

"Well, for what it's worth, I can guess where Paulina got her information," Nicole said. "Look at this."

Out of the corner of her eye, Jenna saw Nicole's cell phone thrust in the space between the front seats.

Claire leaned over to look only to groan and flop back. "That damn cancer blog."

"Maya must have e-mailed the picture of us to Paulina. Paulina must have posted it on the blog." Nicole withdrew the phone and ran her fingers over the screen. "I didn't mention it yesterday because you've made your feelings about the blog quite clear."

"For the love of Buddha, I hate it."

"I'm glad Maya sent the photo to be posted," Jenna said. "People start to worry if a cancer blog goes silent."

"Well, that's how she found me for sure. Paulina must have contacted Maya to ask where we were going."

From the backseat came a sharp intake of breath. "You were that sure that I'd come to Kansas."

"Nic, not long ago I called you a jet streaking across the sky, but I lied."

"You lied."

"You're a hang glider susceptible to a well-placed gust of wind. After our little talk in the pool hall, at least I finally understand why. Jenna, why don't you take that left at that intersection up ahead? Like Nicole, we need to get off the straight-and-narrow path."

Nicole said, "Explain why Paulina is in Kansas, Claire."

Nicole's voice had dropped down to that soft, dangerous timbre that made Jenna's shoulders tighten, even when she wasn't the focus of Nicole's interest. Still, this time her curiosity was piqued. She waited in the silence, wondering what kind of impulse would send Paulina on an airplane to track her sister down. Jenna made the turn and bumped onto the side road, heading toward a distant glow that was the promise of another small Kansas town.

"Paulina and I don't see eye to eye on a lot of things." Claire twisted to glance out the rear window, scanning the dark road for headlights. "Paulina thinks I should be sitting in my sick chair with a blanket tucked around my knees. She thinks I should be taking medications at the first strike of the hour. She thinks I can't possibly be taking the cancer *seriously* if I'm not eternally grateful and smiling through the tears. Is it too much to ask—for a week or two or three—to just leave Cancer Woman behind?"

Jenna found her breath growing shallow. That speech was perhaps the longest thing Claire had ever said about the disease in the two thousand miles they'd driven together. The high-pitched whirr of the engine seemed all the more noticeable. Lucky's tags rattled as he shifted in his puppy bed.

Jenna knew how this would end. Claire would have to confront Paulina. For all the hijinks in leaving the pool hall, Jenna couldn't imagine Claire would really abandon her sister to wander in search of her among the Kansas cornfields. So Jenna focused on the yellow line dividing the road, seeking a good place to turn off, waiting for Nicole to find the right words. The headlights cast their light only a few dozen yards ahead.

The blue glow came from the backseat again. "Hit the

145

gas, Jenna," Nicole said. "We have to get Cancer Woman out of here."

∽

Jenna woke up knowing what she had to do.

She sat in the breakfast room just off the hotel lobby, digging granola out of a paper cup while she waited for the sluggish communal computer to refresh. Behind her, a family of native Kansans settled in for the free breakfast. A youngish man bit into a donut as he read the paper alone by a window. The TV mounted in the high corner of the room droned the local news, every ten minutes breaking for a weather report, as commodity futures scrolled in a ticker across the bottom of the screen.

She'd been here for the better part of an hour, choking down unbelievably bad coffee while she debated her options. Now she leaned in as the page loaded, then glanced at the clock behind the reception desk and pondered the best path to take, as the Indian clerk briskly tucked a pencil behind his ear. Her finger hovered over the Enter key. With Nicole's pool-hall confession still fresh in her ears and Claire acting all night like a twitchy fugitive, Jenna knew her timing couldn't possibly be worse.

She watched the website timer tick down to less than a minute before she pressed the Enter key.

She didn't have a choice now but to wake up Claire and Nicole. Jenna snagged a bowl, a banana, two tea bags, and some instant oatmeal for Nicole. She'd use the room coffeemaker to make hot water for the oatmeal and tea. For Claire she took a pint of milk and then filled another bowl with two scoops of Cocoa Krispies. Juggling all this, she stepped onto the elevator to the second floor and jiggled her key card in the slot until the light turned green. The room was just as she left it: pitch-dark and filled with snoring.

She allowed them a few more minutes as she turned on the coffeemaker and set the food on the table. Then she crossed the room and flung open the drapes.

Nicole curled up and tried to burrow under the tangled sheets. Claire, her back to the window, shot straight up from the other bed.

In the bright light, Claire's pupils contracted to pinpoints. "Paulina?"

"No, Paulina's not here." Last night, they'd found this run-down hotel about twenty miles from the pool hall. They'd parked the car in the back lot. Claire had insisted that they remove the license plates until morning. "I'm waking you because it's ten o'clock, and checkout time is in an hour."

Nicole groaned as she flung an arm out from beneath the covers. "Oh, my God. What the hell was in that drink last night?"

Claire swung her legs off the bed. "At least you didn't spend last night getting kicked by Jenna."

Nicole said, "I had that pleasure the night before—"

"Hey," Jenna objected. "I don't kick."

The two of them, in unison: "Oh, yes you do."

Jenna gaped at them. "Well, Claire snores, and, Nicole, you steal covers like an anaconda twisting around its prey."

A pillow sailed across the room and hit her in the midriff. Her friends laughed. It reminded her of the laughter that used to come out of the basement in the wee hours of the morning whenever Zoe had a sleepover.

The thought made her feel even more guilty for what she was about to do.

"I can't get up," Nicole muttered. "I'll pay for another night."

Jenna said. "Can't do that."

"Can." Nicole swiveled her wrist and pointed in the general direction of the bureau. "Credit card right there."

"It's not the money, it's the time." Jenna pulled the chair out from beneath the desk and sank into it. "I have to be in Des Moines by five p.m."

In the stillness that greeted this announcement, the coffeemaker gave that long, gurgling breath that indicated it had discharged the last of the water from the filter basket. Nicole raised her head out of the covers like a groundhog out of its burrow. Then she clutched her forehead as if she'd moved too fast.

"Des Moines." Nicole eased herself up. "Isn't that, like, two hundred miles away?"

Jenna said, "Closer to two hundred and twenty."

"And what's waiting at the end of it?"

"An airport."

Nicole came to blinking attention. She squinted at

Claire, who shrugged and then went back to hiding in the shadow of a curtain to scan the parking lot for her sister.

Nicole asked, "Who are we meeting at an airport?"

"I'm taking United Airlines flight 792 to Seattle." Jenna stood up as every muscle in her body went tense. "I'm going to tell Nate that I don't want a divorce."

She walked to the coffeemaker to give the two of them time to absorb that information, to glance at each other the way she had known they would in order to telegraph their mutual shock and dismay. Meanwhile, she ripped the plastic bags off the polystyrene cups. She opened the tea bags and dropped them in. She pulled out the carafe of hot water and filled each cup three-quarters full.

By the time she turned around, Claire sat against the pillows on her bed and Nicole had shuffled to the bottom of hers.

"Frankly, Jenna, my head is still swimming with fumes." Nicole took one of the cups. "A lot happened yesterday, between our talk, coming upon Theresa's house, running away from an angry sister—"

"Six calls," Claire remarked, clanking her phone on the bedside table as she took Jenna's offered tea. "Eleven texts. Determined little bugger."

"The point is," Nicole continued, "I think maybe I piled too much pressure on you about that divorce petition."

"You didn't cause that pressure. Nate did." Jenna retreated to the safe distance of the bureau. "And if I'm going to stop the divorce, I have to do it now."

Nicole kept squeezing the bridge of her nose. "I thought

we'd hashed this out yesterday in the car. Leaving now seems odd, too sudden—"

"I don't want to leave you guys." Jenna splayed her fingers on the bureau, feeling the grit of spilled sugar. "I know it's a terrible time. Paulina is out there somewhere." Jenna watched as Claire once again glanced out the window to the pothole-pocked parking lot. "I know you need to call her today."

Claire clanked her tea on the bedside table. "I'm not calling."

"Let's table that issue for later," Nicole said. "Right now you have to explain what's going on, Jenna."

Jenna's neat, prepared speech flew right out of her head. Her reasons swam in her mind, a strange stew formed from three events, mostly the visit to Theresa's burned-out house. It was while poking around the weeds in front of that house that Jenna couldn't help imagine what Three-Tat Tess would have done had she found herself in Jenna's situation. Theresa wouldn't have filled a suitcase and a box, swept up the dog, and thrown everything in the backseat before taking off across country. No, Theresa probably would have done exactly what Nicole had suggested: doused the porch in gasoline and tossed a lit cigarette upon the stairs.

Unless Theresa had a daughter who was part of that same home and that failing marriage. When there was a child involved, it was selfish to indulge in an act of escape or destructive fury, and a child of Zoe's—or Noah's—age was particularly susceptible. You had to think. You had to be smarter.

You had to be strong.

"Nic," Jenna sputtered. "I spent most of my adolescence watching you with awe from the grandstands. You would step up to the plate when the bases were loaded and there were two outs, and you just grinned like you knew you were hitting a single to left field."

"Wait." Nicole clawed her fingers through her hair. "Are you talking about baseball now?"

"My mom was a Red Sox fan," Jenna explained. "My firm has season tickets to the Mariners."

"How your mind works," Claire commented as she came to the bureau to retrieve milk and Cocoa Krispies, "is one of the universe's great mysteries."

"What I'm trying to say is that I know Nicole is strong and competent and a great mother. And what I saw of Lars makes me think he's the most amazing father. And yet you two still struggle as parents. *Together*."

Nicole said on a breath, "Please tell me your decision to leave has nothing to do with what I told you about Noah."

"Then I'd be lying—"

"We struggle with *Noah*," Nicole said. "Chris's and Julia's issues are garden-variety. But Noah's issues require medication. Zoe won't—"

"Zoe's got a few mood problems herself."

"As does every teenage girl." Nicole leaned forward. "Listen, I know you think I'm some sort of expert. I'm really *not*. But from what you've told me about Zoe, it seems like you've got a daughter who has pinpointed all her rage on *Mama*—not an uncommon thing. All other aspects of Zoe's life function absolutely normally, yes?"

151

"For now." Jenna shoved her fists deeper into her pockets as the small muscles of her neck started to tighten. "Theresa's whole personality changed dramatically between the ages of thirteen and fourteen, to the point of setting things on fire—just," she added, "as her parents *divorced*."

"Zoe isn't going to be like Noah *or* Theresa. You can't think that way. Just because Zoe has some anger issues, just because she has slammed a few doors—"

"More than a few."

"I should have kept my mouth shut." The cup shook as Nicole lowered it to her knee. "I've scared you to death by telling you the details about Noah. And I still don't understand why you're doing this now."

"You will. I told you something in the car yesterday."

Nicole bobbed her head as she pressed her fingers into her eye sockets. "You still love Nate."

"Who do I love more than Nate?"

No one spoke Zoe's name, but Jenna saw it in their eyes, she heard the name like an echo in the room.

She said, "Zoe deserves to be protected from the kind of domestic disruption that can turn a perfectly normal adolescent girl into an angry stoner. Zoe deserves a chance to deal with her garden-variety issues in a stable, supportive, two-parent household. The only way that's going to happen is if Nate and I sit down—now, before these papers have to be dealt with—and work out our differences."

Jenna watched Nicole exchange a look with Claire, a look that made Jenna's heartbeat stutter. She'd never been a good reader of body language and swift, silent communications, but she understood this kind of look. She'd been on the receiving end of it since the age of ten. It was a look of empathy that bordered on pity, a look that suggested that Jenna in her social incompetence didn't fully grasp the consequences of her decision.

She blurted, "I know what you're both thinking."

Nicole braced her hands on her knees and creaked her way into a standing position. "We're worried that this may not work out the way you want."

"The situation is already worse than I ever imagined."

"What you're planning to do will be painful—"

"Is divorce ever a happy process?"

Nicole looked for a nod from Claire. "Considering how fast Nate's pushing this through, it's likely that his feelings for you have long changed."

Her throat constricted. "Of course his feelings have changed."

"You're setting yourself up for failure, Jen."

Jenna looked up at the ceiling, at the blinking light of the smoke detector, seeking a way to explain her new determination in words that would make sense to folks who lived outside her head.

"Nearly two weeks ago, I abandoned my home and my husband to knock on the door of a friend I hadn't seen in years." A watery laugh bubbled up in her throat. "I had this crazy idea that the reason why I'd screwed up every relationship in my life was because I'd never *really* given myself over. I hid. I was too ashamed to share because, if I did, people like you, Nicole, would know that I was on the inside what

I appeared to be on the outside: clueless, awkward, and unworthy of affection."

"Jenna—"

"Something had to change. So I flung myself upon Claire."

Claire sat as still as stone, a Cocoa Krispie stuck to her chin. Jenna wanted to thumb it off her face.

"Now I don't have a choice but to do what I'm afraid of doing. If I fail, I fail for Zoe's sake. And at least I won't spend the rest of my life wondering what could have happened if I'd just had the courage to fling myself at Nate's feet."

Claire stood up. She set her bowl of cereal on the bureau. She walked the length of the bed and took Jenna's hands in hers.

"If we have to break every speed limit on every highway in Iowa, Jenna, we'll get you to Des Moines by five."

❦

"There's security." Nicole fast-walked toward the security area that led to the airport gates. "Thank God the line is short. You know what gate, right?"

Jenna said, "A4."

"You've got your liquids separated?"

She tugged the edge of a plastic ziplock bag out of her purse for what she figured was the third time Nicole had asked.

"Boarding pass?"

"Enough, Nic." Claire slowed down near the line entrance. "Jenna's got twenty minutes at least. She'll make the flight before the doors close."

"With no phone," Nicole said, "how are you going to let us know when you're on the flight?"

Jenna fumbled with the strap digging into her shoulder. "If I don't make this flight, I'll just make the next on standby."

"That could be hours stuck in this place."

"Which is why I'm glad you two are keeping Lucky with you."

Nicole frowned as her phone rang in her purse. "Maybe I should give you my phone—"

"And leave us stuck with only mine?" Claire shifted Lucky into her other arm and stepped out of the way to let someone pass in line. "We can't depend on my toy phone while we're driving Jenna's car and Jenna's dog another thousand miles to Pine Lake." Claire waved at Nic's ringing purse. "Just pick it up—that's the second time in the last ten minutes."

Nic pulled the phone out of her purse, and her expression shifted. "Bad timing. But I have to take this." She flung an arm around Jenna's neck. "Have a great flight, Jenna. And good luck."

Jenna squeezed Nicole, feeling strangely disoriented, and not just by the frantic trip to the Des Moines airport, during which they talked logistics for Lucky, for the car, for meeting up in a week in Pine Lake when Jenna flew out to fetch Zoe from camp. All during the four-hour trip Claire kept twisting in the seat and glancing through the rear window, as if

Paulina were hot on their trail. The irony of the situation wasn't lost on Jenna. She'd been the first one to start this vacation off, running and dodging phone calls. Now that she had determined to stop fleeing, it was Claire's turn to run and dodge calls.

Claire opened her arms for a hug. Jenna closed eyes that were too dry. She felt Lucky's warm body against her, felt Lucky lick her cheek. She didn't want to leave. She wanted to dump this whole crazy idea and return to the Lumina, sprawl in the backseat, listen to Nicole hum some disjointed country song, and watch Claire plow her way through a bag of Cool Ranch chips. She wanted to visit Chicago and go to a Cubs game with Nicole. She wanted to shop for hats with Claire. The longing had a bittersweet edge, something that made her feel sad and warm and full all at the same time.

Maybe she was doing something right. Maybe she'd feel like this even when Nate rejected her.

"United Airlines flight 792 now boarding at gate A4."

"That's me."

She pulled away and gave Lucky a last scratch.

"You'll be fine, Jenna." Claire squeezed her shoulder. "Nate's an idiot, but you'll be just fine."

The stitch in her chest tightened and twisted as she turned to walk away. She was facing forward, but her heart had turned back.

She handed her boarding pass to the TSA agent. She slipped off her sandals, piled her things in a gray plastic bucket, and walked through the metal detector. Once she was past security, she turned around and quick-stepped backward in the hope of one last glimpse of her friends.

Claire smiled and swept one arm in a long, comic wave. Nicole stood stiffly beside her, hugging her elbows.

And behind them came Paulina.

Chapter Twelve

Des Moines, Iowa

C laire didn't have to guess who had tipped off Paulina as to where she was, or who had told her sister to hustle to the security area of the Des Moines airport. It was always the friends with the best intentions who caused the worst damage.

Amid the white noise of the high-ceilinged terminal, she turned away from Nicole's stricken face, determined to deal with her after she'd dealt with Paulina. She focused her sights on her sister. Paulina had the same Petrenko brown eyes and auburn hair, but her face was thinner. Wiry strands of white hair poked out from her braid. Her sister looked tired, her cotton batik top wrinkled, tiny lines etched around her eyes. Yet those bird-bright eyes belied fatigue.

Claire said, "You would have made a fabulous Mormon missionary, Paulina. If you were on the case, by now all of Africa would be evangelized."

"I know you're afraid, Claire."

That whisper-soft, kindergarten voice, like sandpaper to her ears. "Afraid? Please. Ask Nicole. Last night I ordered take-out Kansas Mountain Oysters. I ate every last one of them even after I found out they were fried bull testicles."

Paulina pulled her lips in the kind of smile you'd give a recalcitrant toddler. "You know I'll be there with you through the whole time. Me and Alice and Zuza—"

"Maybe you've noticed I'm on vacation right now. You just missed our driver, Jenna. Though apparently you've met Nicole, at least by phone."

Nicole had the grace to look sheepish.

"A vacation is always a good idea," Paulina said in that voice that never changed pitch, "but it's all about timing."

"Well, we've been talking, talking, talking about timing since I left Roseburg. It's amazing how little you hear when I open my mouth."

Paulina put a hand on her arm. "Why don't I just return my rental car here at the airport and then arrange two flights back to Oregon?"

Claire resisted the urge to pull her arm away. "In Cheyenne, I should have tossed my phone under the same truck that Jenna tossed hers. Life is full of these little regrets."

Paulina said, "There are so many people worried about you."

"I know *exactly* how many people are worried about me." Claire looked longingly down the terminal at a neon sign advertising a bar. "By the way, has Zuza been checking in on my raven? Jon Snow gets cranky if you don't throw out a handful of corn by ten a.m."

"When you come home with me, you can check on him yourself."

She dropped her arm. "You really do think I'm your seven-year-old younger sister who you can just pick up from school."

"Be reasonable, Claire. This is not something you can run away from."

"I'm not running away from *it*, Paulina. I'm running away from *you*."

Paulina's lids fluttered closed. Her nostrils flared ever so slightly. Claire knew that sign, the indication that Paulina was reaching the end of her patience. If only she would reach the end of her determination.

When Paulina opened her eyes, her expression was smooth. "I've set another appointment. The doctor can insert the portacath in three days."

"The nurses will be so disappointed when you cancel it on my behalf."

"You can't put off the chemo any longer."

"I'm not 'putting it off,'" Claire interrupted. "I'm choosing not to do it at all."

ॐ

Claire had always known cancer was coming. The certainty had been born when she sat on a tree bench outside her *guti* in Thailand. She'd fallen into a meditation so deep she'd woken up to find a large blue butterfly warming itself upon her white sarong. She'd remained in place and watched the butterfly on her knee until it flapped its wings and flew away. A few days later, she'd flown away, too.

The six years since she'd returned from Thailand had been a serene pause, pruning squash vines, tending injured goats, blind possums, and broken-winged birds, waiting for the inevitable. When she found the chickpea-size lump under her arm and the oncologist had confirmed the diagnosis, Claire had accepted the news like the arrival of an old friend.

Ah, you're finally here.

"Claire."

Claire pretended she didn't hear Nicole's call as she strode across the terminal. She continued to weave through the crowd in the airport as she strode away from the security area—away from a pale Paulina—tucking a quivering Lucky closer to her side.

Nicole's fingers curled around her arm, tugging. "Talk to me."

Lucky made a whining noise, his neck arched as he sniffed the air. "You're making Lucky nervous," Claire said. "I'll tell you the whole sordid story just as soon as I'm convinced you won't be tipping Paulina off to my location from here on in."

"But we can get you on a flight to—"

"I don't fly, remember? Let's get in the car and head to Pine Lake. Straight-arrow this time, no more detours, just the way you always wanted."

Claire headed toward the glass walkway that led from

the terminal to the parking garage. She heard Nicole reluctantly follow. At the car, she dropped Lucky to his feet where he quivered until the concrete was wet. When he was done and looking up at her with buggy, frightened eyes, she swept him into the front seat with her.

Lucky started a series of little whines as they headed out of the airport north onto Interstate 35. He kept crawling up Claire's shoulder to look out the back window, raising his snout as if searching for Jenna's scent. He didn't begin to settle until they'd cleared the city limits and headed out into the flatland cornfields, the enormous sky a soft-serve swirl of gray clouds. Even then, his toenails dug into her thighs.

"I should have known something was up," Nicole said, her knuckles white on the steering wheel. "I should have known from the moment you showed up at my door in San Mateo."

"I'm surprised my sisters didn't send out an APB. They could have told the police that I'd been kidnapped by you and Jenna. That would have been exciting. If we got pulled over, I could tell the sheriff not to shoot us because we were wanted in two states."

"You're still joking about this."

"Or maybe my sisters would have tried one of those silver alerts, have you heard about these? Like when an Alzheimer's patient wanders off. That's how they treat me most of the time. Like I've lost the capacity to understand what's happening to my body. When I understand it a hundred thousand times better than any one of them."

When Melana had been sick, Claire's older sister would

pop in now and again, bringing food, picking up a prescription, taking stock of things, spewing research, being the controlling busybody that Paulina always had been. Alice had been pregnant and terrified of coming into the house altogether. Zuza had been living like a theater rat in New York City and couldn't afford the fare back. Bill and Henry were, well, Bill and Henry. In a family that once had six women, they did what their older sisters told them, which was mostly to stay out of the way. In the end, Claire had been the one elbow-deep in the caretaking. And even in the late states of her chemo fog, Melana was always piercingly aware of what was going on.

Nicole said, "You intentionally missed your appointment for chemo."

"Nope."

"But Paulina said—"

"I didn't *miss* that appointment because I didn't *make* that appointment. That appointment was made by them."

"You told them you'd be back from this trip by then."

"I lied."

"Claire—"

"Yes, I broke Buddhist precept number four. Even the Dalai Lama believes that you must weigh the price of a lie against the pain of speaking the truth."

Nicole stuttered, "So the truth is painful."

"It appears to be painful to everyone else, because I haven't yet found one single soul who wants to hear it."

Nicole struggled to compose the features of her face. "Paulina told me that your oncologist said—"

"—that when you're suffering from Stage III HER2-positive cancer that includes the involvement of a sentinel lymph node, radiation and adjuvant chemotherapy is strongly recommended."

Nicole's spine didn't quite touch the back of her seat. "You know that Jin's woo-woo pills can't be a replacement—"

"Of course not. What the oncologist really wants to do is give me doxorubicin and cyclophosphamide together for two or three months followed by paclitaxel and trastuzumab for three months, then keep up with the trastuzumab to round out the chemo for an awesome full year." Claire scratched Lucky in that spot under his collar that made the dog sink into an ecstatic swoon. "Jin's woo-woo pills give my immune system a boost, which is something I sure wouldn't get from a year's worth of slow-dripping poison."

"Claire, you had a double mastectomy."

"And I thought I'd hid that so well."

"But you must have known that chemo would be the next rational step."

Claire resisted the urge to close her eyes. The progression of events after she'd found the lump under her arm had been eerily familiar. She'd dreamed her way through them. The sonogram, the MRI, the biopsy, the call into the office for the diagnosis. Her sisters took the news with quivering smiles and determined hope. *It's Stage III, not Stage IV—isn't that encouraging?* The news was a ghoul they draped in blinking Christmas lights.

Claire said, "Do you garden, Nic?"

Nicole blew out a long, frustrated sigh. "Just once, I'd like a straight answer from you."

"I've got a Fuji apple tree in my forest garden that came down with a disease called fire blight. It's a nasty, withering bacterial infection, but if you prune off the infected branches in winter, you can actually save the tree."

"Oh for goodness sake, you're not a tree."

"Bleach, ammonia, copper fungicides, on the other hand, they do very little. And they poison everything around them."

"Those drugs could save your life." Nicole's gaze skittered all over the highway as her jaw worked. "Paulina told me the five-year survival rates."

Sixty-seven percent. The percentage might as well have been branded on her forehead. "Paulina does love her numbers."

"But the statistics are only valid for women who go through treatment," Nicole added. "Not for women who forgo treatment altogether."

Claire dropped her head back on the headrest. She'd had this argument from the beginning. She wasn't thinking clearly, Paulina said. She was still foggy and recovering from the surgery, they insisted. But her mind was fine. She knew that radiation would sap her energy, make her skin dry and itchy until it wept. It would give her aches in her chest and the cough that plagued Melana long after the radiation was done. Chemo would be a thousand times worse. You can't say no, they told her. You have to *fight*. Then they'd babble about how close Melana had come to beating it. They'd chatter about how the medicines were so much better. They'd say wistfully that if Mum had had the drugs that Melana had had, maybe she'd be alive, too. *And if Melana had had the options that you have now...*

Then their voices would waver and the tears would well until Claire, exhausted, couldn't muster any energy to argue anymore.

Back in Salt Lake City, she'd hoped that Jin would be the one who would understand. Jin would grasp the consequences of her decision, and since she used homeopathic remedies in her practice, Claire had hoped she'd keep an open mind. But Claire had hesitated. She and Jin hadn't had enough time together for her to probe her about her philosophies. And in the end, she weighed the promise of Jin's sympathy against the possibility that Jin might contact her sisters if she knew Claire's plan. Salt Lake City wasn't far enough away from Oregon and not close enough to Pine Lake. Claire wanted to be far, far past the midpoint of this journey before her sisters discovered that she'd made her own special plans.

Now Claire opened her eyes to the swirl of slate-bellied clouds, the cornfields of mid-American Iowa, every mile taking her farther away from a confused and disappointed Paulina, finally resigned—she hoped—to returning to Oregon. She just hoped her sister didn't get it into her head to follow her all the way to Pine Lake.

Claire glanced at her friend. Nicole was flexing her fingers over the steering wheel while she chewed a hole in her lower lip. Claire cast about for a way to explain and decided to start from the beginning.

"The problem, Nic, is that everyone thinks they have time."

Nicole didn't answer. She kept staring ahead, tipping the steering wheel with a finger, a line deepening between her brows.

"We rush, rush, rush to get things done, and in the process, our lives rush past us."

"Maybe that's true, but—"

"Life isn't supposed to rush past you like that. You're supposed to *live* it. Moment by moment. Mile by mile. Day by day."

Nicole's throat flexed. "But you would have time in your life—maybe years and years—if you went through chemo."

"There were no years after for my sister. None for my mother, either."

Nicole beat a tattoo on the steering wheel. "That doesn't mean there won't be any for you."

"And who should be the one who makes that call?"

"Paulina told me—"

"For Buddha's sake, it's the voice, isn't it? Everyone listens to Paulina like she's preaching Gospel."

Then a terrible noise came from the engine, a high whine that screamed and then gave a metallic grind before settling into a silence almost as frightening. Nicole startled then glanced at the instrument panel. She flicked the hazard lights on.

Claire said, "What the heck is going on?"

"Not sure." Nicole glanced over her shoulder, then kept her gaze in the rearview window as she switched lanes. She pumped the brake pedal as she steered toward the shoulder. "The engine is stalled. Hold on," she said, as they rumbled over the rumble strips. "This is going to get bumpy."

Claire fumbled for the seat belt she should have been wearing, then strapped in herself and Lucky. Nicole steered the Chevy onto the shoulder, crushing the gravel as they hit it at high speed, spewing up clouds of dust until the car eased to a stop. They waited a moment for the dust to settle.

Nicole pressed a button under the dashboard and popped the hood. "Check the trunk for a tool kit and flares. I'll see what's going on."

Claire settled Lucky in his doggie bed in the backseat and then rounded to the trunk. She pushed aside their luggage and Jenna's crate of mementos while trucks rumbled past. The breeze tossed the hem of her skirt and caused skittering bits of gravel to clink against the car. She pushed aside a first aid kit until she found the yellow tool kit.

Nicole stood cock-hipped in front of the car with the hood up, frowning at the guts of the Chevy. Heat blasted off the metal parts. "Too hot to touch," she said, flicking open the toolbox. "I don't see anything obviously wrong."

"Maybe it doesn't run without Jenna's mojo."

Her attempt at humor sailed right over Nicole's head. Nicole put her face close to the engine to get a better look. She pulled a folded cloth out of the tool kit and shook it out. "Grab the flares," she said, holding the open kit out to

Claire. "Place them right on the rumble strips, a good twenty feet apart. The sun's going down and this isn't the best place to stop."

When she returned, Nicole was getting the cloth good and greasy with all the tugging and checking. She told Claire to try to turn on the car. Claire settled into the seat, put down the window, and turned the key.

Nothing happened.

Nicole's voice, muffled by the hood. "Try again."

Still nothing.

"We've got gas, right? A good half tank?"

"Almost three-quarters," Claire said. "We filled it about twenty miles south of the airport, remember?"

Claire followed Nicole's orders, trying to restart the car a few more times, until Nicole closed the hood and leaned gingerly against it. Then Nicole pulled her phone out of her pocket and dialed.

Claire heard her giving mile-marker directions over the phone as she joined her. When she hung up, Claire said, "We busted Jenna's car, I guess."

"I don't think it's an ignition coil. It hasn't been running rough. And if it were a faulty fuel pump, we should be able to turn it on after a rest, unless it's completely broken."

"I know Thai and a little Pali, but this language is unfamiliar to me."

"Considering the noise we heard before it stalled, I suspect it's the timing belt."

"A little thing like that? And you can't fix it?"

"I could, if I had a car lift and the right parts. For now,

we have to wait on a tow truck to bring us to the nearest garage." She slipped the phone back into her pocket. "Looks like we're becalmed, Claire, right smack in the middle of Iowa. Karmic, wouldn't you say?"

Claire twitched. She didn't want to believe Karma had anything to do with it. So far, the universe had been supporting this crazy road trip, drawing Jenna and Nicole together, putting Maya and Jin in her path. But she couldn't deny that there had been disappointments. Not being able to connect with Sydney. Yesterday, for not finding Theresa. Today, Paulina's arrival. And now she leaned up against a disabled car. She glanced to the skies, which were threatening rain, and wondered why the universe would turn its sunny face away.

"Nicole," she said, "you just don't understand the concept of Karma."

"Maybe I'm confusing it with divine intervention. I just know I didn't break the timing belt only about fifty miles outside an international airport while aiding and abetting a woman evading chemo."

"I wouldn't put it past Paulina—or you—to have engineered this."

"Do you know how long it takes to change a timing belt?"

"Just long enough for you to convince me to go back to Oregon?"

"At least a day. If the dealer has the parts on hand."

"So we'll have plenty of time in some little Iowa town to discuss the true nature of Karma."

"Yup."

Claire said, "While we're at it, we'll discuss free will, too."

"Aren't you afraid of dying?"

Claire didn't answer right away. She kept her eye on the overpass a mile or so down the road. Slowly, she felt Nicole shift against the car, uncomfortable with the stretching silence. Claire suspected she wouldn't be able to explain what happened that day on the tree bench outside her *guti*. She'd begun her sitting meditation as she had so many times before. She'd closed her eyes, and the space behind them became dark. She'd focused on the rise and fall of her abdomen, heard the buzzing of a fly nearby and the gurgle of the stream that wandered through the merit fields down to the eggplant garden. She breathed in the perfume of jasmine in the glade.

And then she'd stepped into a deeper concentration, so deep that she experienced vivid images of friends buying chickens in the market and a flash of a conversation between two monks. She heard the laugh of her younger brother diving into the waters at Coley's Point. It was as if the past and the future had slipped their bonds, and the universe was showing them to her like frames of an old movie flickering.

That was when she'd seen a figure running toward her, her arms wide. Young, plump, vibrant, healthy Melana.

Claire startled as another truck zoomed by, spewing a rain of little stone chips. "We're all dying, Nicole. Right now, little by little, we're dying."

"Thanks for that reminder."

"It's a truth that can be liberating when you believe there's something beyond this life."

"I'm Roman Catholic, remember? But I'm in no hurry to find out what's beyond the clouds." Nicole shifted uncomfortably against the hood. "The fact is, rational people just don't light out across the country when they should be at home getting necessary medical treatments meant to save—"

"—*extend* their lives," Claire corrected. "Chemo extends life for some unknown amount of days, sometimes months, occasionally years. I know I've got a disease that I'm unlikely to beat. I'm giving up treatment not because I want to die." Claire lifted her face to the first drops of rain, closing her eyes so she could feel them, cold and sharp, needling her cheeks. "I'm giving up treatment because I want to *live*."

The tendons in Nicole's throat stood taut. "I'm not going to do this."

"You can go on back to California if you want. I can finish this trip alone."

Nicole pressed the heels of her hands against the cooling hood of the car. "Tell me this isn't some sick death wish."

Claire took in the strain on her friend's lovely face, suddenly understanding that there was another reason why this situation was upsetting her so much. Nicole had left out one important detail in her confession last night in the pool hall. A detail she didn't seem capable of speaking. But Claire had read between the lines. A boy who lights a smoky fire in a closed garage wasn't just "experimenting."

Claire reached for Nicole's hand.

Nicole gripped that hand and whispered, "What kind of friend would I be if I help you escape the medical treatment you need?"

Claire rubbed her thumb against a streak of grease. "Right now, that makes you the very best friend I have."

Chapter Thirteen

Nevada, Iowa

Rule number eleven for organizational efficiency was to take care of the toughest business of the day first. So when a reminder beeped on Nicole's phone—a reminder she'd entered several weeks ago—it jerked her out of the ritual of sorting her dirty laundry, a task she'd retreated to after multiple rounds of verbal sparring with Claire. Now she remembered she had something tougher to do than come up with a way to compel Claire to head back to Oregon for treatment.

Claire sat in a lotus position on the Laundromat bench, her face raised to the gray light siphoning through the plate-glass window. Her friend had been meditating for a good half hour. Nicole assumed this was Claire's way of retreating from their pointed discussions, and she was hesitant to interrupt it. Claire sat so still that Lucky slept in her lap. Claire's T-shirt was printed with the picture of two people in long robes running under the caption, *Pilgrims: The First Illegal Aliens*.

Nicole approached on soft feet. "I've got to make a call," she whispered. "I'll be back in a few minutes."

She pushed through the doors to the little town of Nevada, whose welcome sign advertised it as *The 26th best small town in America!* This had been the nearest town from where the car had broken down, not much more than a nexus of two major roads among cornfields. Fortunately, the town had Bo's Auto Repair, where last night a mechanic with a seed-cap tan promised a twenty-four-hour layover on fixing the Chevy. The tow-truck driver, a cousin of the mechanic, had given her and Claire a lift to the budget hotel ten minutes down the road.

Now she strode down the town's main drag passing Ben Franklin's General Store, Miss Julia's Bakery, and C. J.'s Soda Pop Shoppe. The whole display of flat-front, two-story umber-brick buildings reminded her of the straight-backed toy soldiers on Noah's shelf, lined up and well dusted. Nicole put her head into the gusty winds, smelling of rain, and headed to a small park that they'd rolled their luggage past earlier.

Raising her phone, she checked the strength of the cell-phone signal. If the call dropped in the middle of the conversation, she'd be forced to rerun the gauntlet of administrators for a chance to connect with Noah again. Her heart skittered as if she'd drank one too many cups of the diner coffee.

She scrolled through her contacts until she found the

one for the Hope Recovery Center. Before she could hesitate, she hit Call.

The receptionist answered on the first ring.

"This is Nicole Eriksen calling for the third-floor desk. I'm scheduled to speak to my son Noah today."

As she waited to be transferred, she dragged an image to her mind of young Noah sliding down the hall on his socks. She remembered his high-pitched voice as he thrust a drawing at her, pointing out the boles of the trees and the branches with their ribbed leaves curled like welcoming hands. Then his voice deepened in her mind, and the image on the paper morphed into something inky and sepulchral, the smiles lipless and toothy.

Odd spasms twitched in her back. Maybe she'd overdone it on the hotel treadmill this morning.

The floor nurse came on the line. Nicole spoke briefly to her and waited again. She exchanged words with the station nurse, and then she waited again. Every transfer felt like a click of the treadmill to an increased slope.

Click.

"Mom?"

Mom, I'll be late for school! Mom, I found a bird's nest in the cherry tree! Mom, can I have ice cream?

She tilted her head back to stare at the canopy of leaves. "Noah, you'll never guess what I'm looking at."

"Tell me it's the front door of the Hope Recovery Center."

Pain shot through her, like the tear of a tendon in the space between scapula and spine. "Sorry, Noah. Not this time."

She waited through the pause. She listened to the ambient noises of the room through the connection. She envisioned him shuffling to the farthest stretch of the corded phone and then turning his shoulder to the nurses.

"Hey, a guy can dream." He puffed air into the receiver. "So is it tall or small?"

She let her eyes flutter closed. At least he was trying. "It's tall, but not as tall as most."

"Broad or narrow leaves?"

"Broad and many-lobed."

"Fruit, nut, or seed?"

"I've *neigh*-ver seen such spiny seeds."

"*Neigh*-ver? Really, Mom? What, am I six?"

"You've got an answer, smarty?"

"It's a horse chestnut tree. Obviously."

"You've only seen these in a book." Several books, borrowed from the library when he was in his tree-drawing stage, tomes of classification guides with full-color illustrations. "Right now I'm sitting in the shade of a horse-chestnut tree in Nevada, Iowa."

"Dad told me you cut out of town. Iowa?"

"I was on a road trip until the car died. Now I'm stuck in a small town with an incontinent dog and a Buddhist with a junk-food habit."

"Want to trade places?"

Guilt burbled the stew in her stomach. She clamped her throat to hold it down. Through the connection, she could almost smell the pine antiseptic of the place, see the concrete-block walls behind cheap framed prints. She could hear the silence from the long, deep hallways, the boom of heavy doors opening and closing, the rubber squeak of orderlies' shoes on tiles. She could see the pale blue paint and the dark blue carpet and the rounded corners of the scarred coffee table and the nubby brown-orange upholstery of the sofas, and the TV bolted high in a corner droning endlessly. She could see her son pressed up against the concrete-block wall near the communal phone, his jeans sagging halfway down his hips, his dark hair growing long over his eyes.

Someday, technology would be invented that would allow a mother to reach long arms through the line and draw a son into a hug. "Fifteen days. Then you'll be back home, eating dinner with Dad and me and Julia and Christian."

"Don't make meat loaf. That's all they serve here."

"Don't try to con me, kiddo. I know the food is good."

"Yeah, if you're comparing it to a closed-down psychiatric ward."

Positive. Keep positive. "At least at Hope you can get out in the sun once in a while—"

"To walk in circles with all the other inmates."

"Patients."

"Whatever. I suppose it keeps me from getting bloated again."

Change the subject. "You've got your sketch pad?"

"I can't draw. I'm on clonazepam."

"Clonazepam?" Mentally she riffled through the list of meds they'd sampled over the past eighteen months. "Didn't they give you that in"—*lockdown*—"the last time you were in the hospital?"

"I don't remember. I can barely *think* on this stuff. All I want to do is watch the fucking TV."

The curse was like a slap. She pulled the phone away a fraction as a gust rustled the leaves of the horse chestnut tree. She'd tried to become immune to the language when he first started up. She wasn't sure where he'd picked it up. She and Lars never spoke that way, at least not in front of the kids. TV, she supposed. Video games. His high school friends.

"Sorry," he muttered. "Last week on the meds, I was a zombie. Now they've lowered the dose, and I'm swearing like a rapper. Dr. Kleinberg tells me that this is maladaptive behavior, and I have to work on it."

Nicole took a breath. There was so much to be pleased with in what he'd just said. First, the fact that he'd spoken several full sentences, even if one sounded like a direct quote from his therapist. Second, that the therapist was concentrating on his social skills. Third, that he acknowledged an awareness of the issue. But still, she couldn't pretend that this pained self-awareness didn't also break her heart. "Part of the reason why you're at Hope is to get those darn dosages right."

"They're never going to get the dosages right. Strike that," he said. "The *dosages* aren't the problem. I'm taking too many stupid medicines."

Nicole let her eyes drift closed. This was an old argument, a familiar one, a manic merry-go-round they'd ridden endlessly over the last eighteen months. "Fifteen days, Noah. Two more weeks to follow the program."

"I'm such a *vegetable* on the drugs. My whole brain turns

into mush. I can't think, and what's worse is that I can't draw."

Nicole braced her hand on the lathe of the wooden bench. She squeezed until a chip of old paint bit into her palm. She kept her grip tight, because if she thought of pain and only of this pain then she wouldn't let herself remember the sweet promise of the young boy who once showed such lively potential.

With a huff Noah said, "I'm getting mad."

"Yes, you are, hon."

"I'm supposed to notice when I get angry or upset."

"I'm proud that you're growing more aware of how you're feeling."

"I'm supposed to find something that calms me down. Drawing used to do that, and I don't have that now."

"The drawing will come back." She eased her grip on the bench and then lifted the tone of her voice as if it would lift both their spirits. "How about you tell me something good that happened this week?"

His breathing was muffled as if he'd pressed the phone receiver against the wall. "Dr. Kleinberg says I had a break-through."

She banked the urge to hold her breath. "Can you talk about it?"

"I suppose. He makes me keep diary cards, you know, to write down stuff. He's tough but at least he doesn't bullshit me."

Nicole lifted a bit off the seat. Noah rarely spoke of any of his therapists with anything but contempt.

"So he read one of my cards. He talked about all the people who are trying to help me. You know, you and Dad. How
you basically give a shit—sorry."

"Well," she conceded with a forgiving laugh, "we definitely do give a shit."

"He said that you and Dad just want me to get better."

"Everybody does."

"But that's just it. That's what makes me angry. Everyone wants me to get *better*. As if I'm infected with a
disease."

He's a good kid, the psychotherapist had told her after
Noah's first lockdown. *He's smarter than me, smarter than most
of our staff. He comes up with such creative ways to avoid his
meds.* She heard the rising tension in her son's voice, and Nicole's old suspicions needled her. She wondered if the nurses
had been monitoring him well enough.

He rushed ahead. "So I asked Dr. Kleinberg what these
pills do. He told me that the drugs aren't meant to cure me.
They just take away the highs and the lows."

"Those lows are pretty dark, Noah."

"But they suffocate everything. Feeling strongly is better
than feeling nothing at all, right?"

"Noah, the way you sink into—"

"I know. I *know*. I need to figure out a way to handle that.
Off the meds. But the drugs just mask who I am."

Nicole rubbed the spot between her brows. On the other
side of the street, two men in John Deere caps stepped out
of a pickup truck and headed over to the soda pop shop. Not
far from her, a flock of sparrows swept down to the sidewalk

to pick between the cracks. A car that needed work on its muffler rumbled down the street.

Someday she would call her son and they'd talk about the weather. Someday, she hoped she'd call her teenage son and he'd hurry her off the phone because he had a date with a new girl in school. Someday she hoped she'd call her son and they'd laugh about these days when he tried to convince her he could live without pharmaceuticals.

Noah suddenly said, "I'm *always* going to be like this, Mom. I'm always going to feel things more than other people."

She relived the image of an energized, maniac Noah moving the furniture at 3:30 in the morning so he could paint an oak on the wall of his bedroom; the image of Noah sprawled on his bed, banging his head against the pillow to the beat of Metallica screaming from his headphones; the image of Noah furious over his sketch pad, swinging an elbow that struck her so hard she didn't feel her head bounce until minutes after she landed on the hardwood floor.

A pulse throbbed just over her eye socket. "If I could wave a wand, I'd make you better. But until—"

Crack.

She jumped at the noise. It sounded as if he'd banged the phone hard against the hospital's concrete-block wall. She pulled her cell phone away from her ear as she heard another crack, and then another. He stopped, and she heard him make a strangling noise. She heard a nurse's voice in the background, a level, concerned query.

"I'm fine. I'm fine!" His voice was hoarse as he pressed

his mouth close against the receiver. "This is *exactly* what I told Dr. Kleinberg."

Her whole spine stiffened. "Breathe, Noah."

"Do you know what I hear when you say that?"

"Say what?"

"You want to make me better."

"Of course I want to—"

"What I hear is that you wish I were *someone else*."

Nicole sat stunned. That wasn't true. She didn't wish Noah were someone else. No, she just wanted her active, off-center, curious, and intellectual son back. The little boy she used to read to every night. The young man who looked so much like Lars.

Noah said, "I'm never going to stop being who I am, Mom. So you and Dad need to stop hoping that some stranger is going to move in behind my eyes."

ॐ

Nicole wandered back to the Laundromat to find Claire pulling a T-shirt from a heaping pile.

"Holy Buddha." Claire froze midfold. "Did you at least get the license number of the truck that hit you?"

Nicole dropped down onto the bench where she'd left Claire meditating only a short while earlier. She pulled onto her lap a half-eaten bag of Doritos.

She bit into a chip. "I just got off the phone with Noah."

"Ahh."

"He had a breakthrough." She chewed but tasted nothing. "Apparently, the last year and a half of outpatient therapy with four different therapists, the six different drug regimens, and this four-week stint in a mental health recovery center are just my extreme efforts to change him into a son whom Lars and I can finally love."

Nicole swayed on the seat. When she'd been in labor with Noah, the anesthesiologist had set her up with a spinal epidural after four hours of painful contractions. He'd pumped into her meds so strong that she didn't feel anything from the midriff down. Now, sixteen years after the obstetrician had been forced to use forceps to bring Noah into the world, Nicole felt the same sort of paralyzed numbness.

"Noah complained about his meds again, too." The words pressed against her sternum. "He's got a good reason to complain. The meds ease his dark moods and stop him from isolating himself and skipping school. On the meds, he spends less time closed up in his room. But all this time I've ignored the side effects." She looked anywhere but at Claire. "Imagine a mother giving her son drugs that make him slouch in a chair and drool."

The laugh that came out of her mouth didn't belong to her. Her torso shook with it. It was a misfiring reflex, disconnected from her conscious brain.

Claire's warm hand on her shoulder brought her back to herself. She shut the laugh right down.

"It's a cruel twist," Claire said softly, "that Karma would lay at your feet a problem that can't really be fixed."

Nicole tried to shake away the words. Of course there were problems that couldn't be fixed. Claire's disease, for one. Jenna's marriage, for another, a terrible spectacle she supposed was being played out in Seattle right now. She just refused to believe that Noah's condition was one of them.

Maybe that was the problem.

"I can tell you a story about problems that can't be fixed." Claire flopped onto the bench beside her. "Eight months into my stay at the Thai temple, a Buddhist scholar came to teach. Actually, I think he just came to see the *farang*—me," she said, patting her chest, "the crazy foreigner who'd taken vows. He asked me why I had come, and in my arrogance, I told him I wanted to reach Nirvana."

Nicole could tell by the faint flush that rose on Claire's skin that the memory was still painful.

"He told me that most *farang* believe that pushing forward to reach Nirvana means that the future will stretch before us in unending happiness."

Nicole ran her fingers over her brow, distracted. "Isn't that what Nirvana is?"

"Nirvana is a state of past and present. Yes, the future is joyous. But to reach it, you also have to accept the most painful times in your past." Claire's knees bumped Nicole's as she swiveled to face her. "But more than that, you have to understand that it's in those most troubled times—like you're having right now with Noah—where the seeds of happiness are sown."

Nicole balked. What happiness could possibly come from a son who tried to set things on fire? A son who truly believed that his mother's extreme efforts to help were a sign that she didn't love the person he was? "I'm not getting it, Claire."

"I didn't either, not completely." Claire frowned, two little lines appearing between her brows. "I've spent years waiting for some wisdom to rise out of my memory of those terrible days with Melana. It hasn't come yet. But I guess what I'm trying to say right now is that you just don't know what will come of all of this trouble. So put away the whips and the hair shirt. You've done what's best for Noah."

"Maybe I went too far." She sank her elbows on her knees and then thrust her fingers through her hair. "Maybe, instead of forcing him to do hours of psychotherapy three times a week, I should have encouraged him to join a team sport." Maybe she'd spent the last eighteen months trying to hack her way through a jungle with a steak knife when instead she should have nudged a clear path through the trees. "They haven't been able to pin a label on him, you know; the diagnosis keeps shifting. Maybe, instead of jumping to conclusions, I should have waited, seen how his moods evolved, been patient."

Claire gave her a gentle nudge. "Stop second-guessing yourself. You're becoming your own worst enemy."

Nicole straightened up and clutched her arms, digging her fingernails into her skin. For the last eighteen months, she'd been lashing herself for not recognizing Noah's issues before he set the garage on fire. For the last eighteen months, she'd been nursing the idea that *if only* she'd finished her degree she would have been able to intervene earlier, *if only* she'd made the necessary sacrifices Noah would be all right now. That was all bullshit. Had she, after her unexpected pregnancy, continued to struggle through graduate school and two more years of training to finally become a licensed psychotherapist, she would have cracked and flamed out like a third world missile.

With Noah, she was in way over her head.

"Well, one thing is for sure," she said on an unsteady laugh, "I would have been the world's worst psychotherapist."

"And your situation with your son isn't clouding your judgment about this at all?"

"Oh, no, I would have *sucked*."

Claire's face held a ghost of a smile. "You would have mastered that discipline with your usual attention to detail, my friend. But I suspect, in the end, you would have been very unhappy."

Claire stood up and wandered back to the folding table. Nicole waited for some sort of explanation, but Claire seemed content to pull a T-shirt out of her pile of laundry, carelessly fold it, and drop it straight into the oversize duffel bag yawning open on the floor. Nicole thought about Claire's words. Would she have been unhappy doing what she'd wanted to do since high school? She couldn't wrap her mind around the idea, so she stopped trying. Her head was like a bomb zone; Noah's confession had left her thoughts in shards.

She stood up. The bag of chips crinkled to the floor. Lucky roused from his doze and eyed the bag, so she swept it out of his reach and tossed it in the trash. She strode by

Claire and headed for the dryer, where her clothes lay tangled inside. She yanked the door open and pulled them out into a pile. She returned to the table and put them in a bundle next to Claire's, tugging the jeans from the heap and folding them seam to seam.

"I have a confession, Nicole." Claire plucked at her own laundry. "Remember when Jenna said yesterday that she used to admire you playing softball? Well, I was the one who first took Jenna to the stadium. I used to go to most of your softball games, too."

Nicole smoothed the jeans and tried to reorient herself to the change in subject.

"I didn't suffer through any other sport," Claire continued. "Not the hockey games that obsessed half the school, or football, or track or basketball. But I went to so many softball games that I bought one of those stadium-seat pillows with the Pine Lake Beaver mascot symbol. You know which one I'm talking about?"

"Yeah, the thick vinyl one you could get at Ray's General Store. So you wouldn't freeze your butt off when there was still ice on the metal bleachers in the early spring. I had one for outdoor hockey games." Nicole shook out a pair of capris. "So you were a true softball fan, huh?"

Softball hadn't been a popular sport in high school until Nicole's team started competing in regionals, so there had never been a huge fan base outside of the parents of the players. She remembered Claire's presence only vaguely because she'd been focused on the game, on the team, on the next batter, the choice of the next pitch.

"The first time I went," Claire continued, "I went purely because you talked me into it. It was the regional finals, and if you'd won, the team would play the next county or something. You were bounding up and down the halls, encouraging people to come to give the team moral support, just radiating excitement. I couldn't resist."

Nicole remembered. She'd loved being the captain of the team. She loved every moment of the season. The thrill of standing on the mound staring down to that imaginary strike box, reading Riley's hand signals, feeling the sharp attention of the teammates around her like a multibrained living being.

"At the game, I didn't know what the heck was going on," Claire said. "But when it was toward the end and the Pine Lake Beavers were losing, I was close enough to your bench that I heard you giving the team a pep talk." Claire took great interest in smoothing the wrinkles out of a folded T-shirt. "I don't remember exactly what you said. Something about dragging up the will to do their best. Something about the game not being over until the very last out. Probably a bunch of clichés. For me, it was like you were speaking in tongues. What I really remember is how you said it." Claire tossed the T-shirt with the others. "You were a revival-meeting preacher, Nic. You were a general pinned down by enemy fire. With nothing but words and the tone of your voice and that look in your eye, you worked that team up into such a lather that they shot off the bench and raced across the field like they were soldiers shooting out of the trenches into a hail of lead." She shook her head, remembering. "Heck, I wanted to put on a glove myself after hearing you. You were a sight to behold."

Nicole found herself tugging at a string that had come loose from a seam. An embarrassing prickling started behind her eyes.

"The point I'm trying to make in my backass kind of way," Claire said, "is that I think we are who we are, no matter how much we try to change. Jenna will always be an introvert, no matter how well she adapts. Maybe Noah will always have issues with his own temperament, whether he's on the meds or no. And as for you..." Claire gave her an affectionate bump. "Inside, you're always going to be that girl giving the softball team a pep talk, pushing people to excel to their limits, to take on dreams they'd never thought possible."

Nicole cringed a little, recognizing the language of her own website.

"That's why," Claire continued, "I wonder if you'd really get that same sort of thrill in a clinical situation, with patients whose abilities to improve have more to do with better pharmaceuticals than sheer human will."

A tingling suspicion took hold. "So you've been to a therapist."

Claire gave a brief nod. "Paulina made me go after Melana died. He's the man who encouraged me to go off to Thailand." With one sweep of her arm, Claire shot the last of her laundry off the table and into the open duffel. "So after that confession, maybe now you'll figure out why, ten days ago, I conned Jenna into taking a five-hundred-mile detour just to show up at your door."

Nicole was wondering if Noah's explosive confession had caused some actual concussive damage or if Claire was just toying with her with all these changes in subject. "I thought you came to see me for my wit and good humor. And a free bed."

"Those were bonuses. Like the GPS. But I had an ulterior motive." Claire wandered toward the plate-glass window. "When we set off, I knew Jenna would follow me wherever I led her. Jenna's got a good heart that way. But I knew I needed someone who would make sure I would get to where *I* had to go. Someone who would shore me up when I wavered in my intentions. Like right now."

"Now?"

"You feel it, don't you, Nic?" Claire looked up through the window to the roiling of the gray skies. "Karma has shifted."

Nicole wandered to stand next to Claire, trying to feel what she felt. She smelled the bleach-tinged scent of wet laundry and heard the *thump-thump* of a running dryer. She identified the skitter of leaves against the sidewalk, a sound muffled beyond the glass. She heard the baritone flap of the heavy awning and the whirr of a distant engine. She followed Claire's gaze to the slate-bellied clouds, churning across the sky.

And for a brief, eerily vivid moment, she felt what Claire was referring to. A deepening of the air pressure, a faint ringing in her ears, a resistance more of the spirit than the body.

Claire murmured, "Maybe Jenna chose the right time to bail. Maybe even Noah's breakthrough is a sign from the universe. I just have this terrible feeling that it's time for both of us to go home."

Home.

Nicole hesitated. Yesterday, she had all but begged Claire to return home on a plane with Paulina, to go back with the sisters who were so determined to take care of her health. And last night, she'd plunged the depths of her broken little arsenal of persuasive life coach tricks trying to clear the gears of Claire's muddy thinking. And now, after Noah's painful confession, Nicole felt her heart yearning to return home to Lars. They needed to sit across their kitchen table, where they always discussed family matters, and reevaluate their approach to Noah's treatment. The time had come to reassess every single assumption she'd made. Maybe the time had come to revive the so-called revival-camp preacher she'd apparently left behind in Pine Lake—if only to prove to Noah how much she really loved him.

Yes, she and Claire should go home.

The muscles of her throat wouldn't work. In the light pouring in through the front window, Nicole took a hard look at Claire. She thought about Claire alone on her thirty acres dealing with a sickness that had claimed her mother and her sister. Strangely, she thought of wood smoke, too, not the gasoline-tinged scent of a burned garage but the fresh fragrance of wood smoke on an open prairie. She remembered Claire's confession in the velvet darkness of the grasslands. If Claire turned around before her goal of reaching Pine Lake, she'd be repeating the same self-destructive behavior that had her abandoning her education, her Buddhist vows, and now, perhaps, a chance at a long and fruitful life.

A strange, loosening sensation shuddered through her. Her thoughts began to zip down avenues she hadn't dared to consider. Her mind somersaulting ahead of itself, dreaming up ideas, considering a strategy that now seemed too crazy *not* to consider.

Sometimes, you had to hold up an old goal like a lantern to guide the way—even if it brought you someplace you didn't know you were going.

Chapter Fourteen

Seattle, Washington

In Seattle it was raining, of course.

Jenna stood outside her home garage with rain dripping off the edge of her hood. She stood motionless, feeling the warmth leach out of her body along with the last dregs of her hurling momentum. She stood dangerously close to the garage window, close enough to watch Nate wielding a blowtorch. A metal mask covered his face. Sparks made the faint, fair hairs on his arms glow.

She'd meant to observe for only a minute, just long enough to see if Sissy Leclaire sat on the old upholstered chair in the corner, laughing with both legs thrown over the arm. That chair was empty, but Jenna still hesitated, not sure whether Sissy's absence was good or bad. This confrontation might have been easier if Jenna had walked in on the two of them rutting on the workbench, clawing at each other half dressed, just like in the mental film loop that ran in her head. It would have been a cauterization. Then she'd be freed of the ever-sinking impulse to tell him that she still loved him.

But the hesitation was a mistake. Gazing at Nate through the garage window allowed a different fantasy to unspool, the one where Nate called off the whole situation and set the divorce petition aflame.

She reached for the doorknob. The chill of the metal stole the heat from her hand. She turned it and pushed the door open. The hiss of the blowtorch was much louder than the squeal of the hinges, but Nate must have noticed a flash of light in the glass of a storm door leaning against the wall. The mask turned toward her. He stilled for a moment. Then he switched off the blowtorch.

The urge to run gripped her. Under her raincoat, she grew prickly-heat warm. The doorknob slipped out of her hand, and the door swung shut behind her. She wobbled a little, straddling the crack in the concrete foundation they'd never had repaired.

With greasy knuckles, Nate nudged the mask atop his head. "You're back."

Jenna heard his words and more clearly heard his tone, a combination of surprise and pleasure. It was the way he used to greet her when she'd come home early to find him in a paint-stained apron with an infant Zoe riding his hip.

Her hopes fluttered like a hundred thousand starlings.

"Did you call?" He tilted up his cell phone on the workbench. "I've been working—"

"I threw my phone under a truck in Cheyenne."

"Ah, yes, I'd forgotten. Your friend Nicole told me that."

Nicole?

He gave her a rueful microshrug. "She called and left a message on the home phone. She said I should contact her directly if there was an emergency."

Jenna absorbed that tidbit. The knowledge that Nicole had butted into her private life didn't bother her as much as she supposed it should have. She had a funny feeling—a strange, disconnected, floating, but not entirely uncomfortable feeling that friends sometimes do that for one another.

"I was working on a piece for the Stein Hall installation, but it can wait." He tugged his mask off his head, the straps tugging his shoulder-length hair half out of the rawhide knot that held it away from his face. "Do you need to unload the car?"

"I don't have the car." He was acting as if she'd just driven up with a trunk full of groceries on a random Saturday afternoon. "I flew in last night from Des Moines."

"Tell me the engine didn't seize. The Lumina was due for an oil change before you left."

"The car's fine. Claire and Nicole are driving it to Pine Lake. I'll pick it up when we fly out to get Zoe."

He bobbed his head, but Jenna could see by the way he rubbed his hand across his mouth and chin that his mind was working, working.

"Don't worry," she said. "I've got a rental car and a hotel room by the airport. In case she's here."

No need to define "she," or even raise her hand in the direction of the house.

He showed her a three-quarter profile as he reached for a rag. "She's not here now."

Now. The little word was like the kick of a horse. Likely, Sissy had planned to come later. Maybe even sleep in Jenna's house.

Maybe sleep in their bed.

She wondered when during their marriage he thought it was all right to start fucking another woman. She thought she might know the answer. There was a lot of time to pick over the bones of a relationship when you're driving across the flat prairie in the middle of the country. She'd figured it had been a little more than a year ago when he'd sat at the table tearing a napkin apart over his untouched dinner. Zoe had already left the table. He'd seized Jenna's hand as she'd jumped up to clean the dishes. *We need to talk,* he'd said. Then there'd been a pause, a strange, long pause, before he mumbled the good news about an offer for a new commission.

Nicole had warned her about probing about the details of the affair. Nicole said that it would only force his attention to the past instead of the future.

She bit the inside of her cheek until she tasted blood.

"I'm glad you're here, Jenna." With the rag still gripped in one fist, he leaned back against the workbench. "I've been hoping for a chance for a do-over."

Her breath hovered in the back of her throat along with a laugh that she didn't really want to release. "So you've decided to take a blowtorch to the divorce papers?"

He found new interest in the greasy rag. "I know I've handled this all wrong."

"Oh." A breath of a word. "Was it my disappearance or the dog's that tipped you off?"

"You two are pretty inseparable."

You and I used to be, too. In the early days, anyway. Burrowing into their new house with their new baby, content to spend exhausted Saturday evenings on the couch watching black-and-white crime movies or the Japanese samurai films he preferred, while she lay on his lap and he threaded those work-hardened fingers through her hair.

Did he thread his fingers through Sissy's red hair?

"When I approached you before, I was concerned about the wrong things." He dropped the rag and crossed his arms. "The way I handled it…I should have figured I'd set you off running."

The memory rippled between them. It was the day he'd asked her to marry him. He'd dropped on one knee on the rocky shore of Cape Ann with a backdrop of crashing waves and presented an engagement ring, a ruby sitting in the bud of a platinum rose, a setting he'd designed with the help of a friend. She'd been so taken by surprise that she'd run back to the car, leaving him to walk three miles to the hotel through the rain.

Now the raindrops on the roof of the garage hit like hail. The garage had a damp wood smell. She saw a ghost of a smile pass across his face—saw him remembering, too—and she was launched right back to the bed-and-breakfast that she'd returned to, four hours after he'd asked her to marry him, to throw herself upon him and say *yes*.

The ghost of a smile dissipated. He lowered his head

and spoke to his ankles. "You and I have a lot to talk about."

She said, "We can start with those papers."

"Yeah, that would be reasonable."

"Reasonable? There's nothing reasonable about any of this. I still can't believe that you handed me a petition of divorce."

He pressed his lips together with a rueful tilt of the head. "I started off on the wrong foot, but this doesn't have to be difficult. There are right ways to do this."

"The right way," she said, "is not to do it at all."

He rubbed his jaw with his hand again, feeling up the jawline with his fingers, avoiding her eye altogether. It occurred to her that she'd spent twelve years studying the secret language of the fine muscles of Nate's face. She understood him as she understood no other person in the world. The sudden but calculated stillness of his frame, for example, suggested a surprise he'd already braced himself for. The slow brush of his fingers along the edge of the workbench spoke of a man distracted by the direction of his own thoughts. The flex of that long muscle in his cheek showed his effort to muster patience, to hold back stronger feelings.

She knew what all this meant, and so she rushed ahead, because sometimes you can outrun your fear. "Listen, I know you have feelings for"—her tongue stumbled on the name—"Sissy. I'm not blind, I got that memo."

He stopped rubbing his chin and instead dug the heel of his hand into the ridge of his brow.

"I think I know why, too." Suddenly, she couldn't quite

look at him. "I've been working too much this past year. I thought I was fighting for my job—Scott gave me that impression, anyway. It turns out that he was just trying to raise the sell-out price so he could cash out."

"Yeah, I heard about the layoff."

Jenna paused. She'd forgotten that she'd never told him. So much had happened in so little time.

"I imagine all those times I worked late, you and she were thrown together a lot with the new travel sports schedule. And Zoe spends so much time over at Sissy's house—"

"Jenna." He winked an eye open. "Don't do this."

Words died in her throat. He was right, of course. Her mouth was running away on her. She didn't want the details of the infidelity—they'd just stick in her mind, rise up when she slept, ate, and breathed.

She swallowed, and it was like swallowing a brick. "My point is, I know you have feelings for Sissy. But you once had feelings for me, too."

Metal dust glittered upon his plaid flannel shirt. Debris flecked the curve of his ear. She could see by the way he'd turned his shoulder that he didn't like what she was saying. She could see, too, that he was not unaffected by her words.

He was listening.

She should have let her hair down, the way Nate liked it. She should have stopped in the airport hotel's salon and had it blown out so it would be loose and shiny. She should have parked the rental car at a mall before driving over here. She could have changed out of her travel-weary jeans and puckered T-shirt into something sexy. She could have bought a new lipstick. She'd rarely been the sexual instigator in their relationship, but she also wasn't too proud to start.

Her own voice, husky and raw, surprised her. "You loved me once, Nate."

"Jenna, don't do this."

"Despite everything you've done, pushing those divorce papers across the kitchen table at me," she said, her chest tightening, "I *still* love you."

"You shouldn't."

He pushed away from the workbench. He strode to the back of the room and tossed the dirty rag in a bin. He walked back, his hands low on his hips, dragging the waistband down to show the elastic waist of his black jockey shorts, shuffling in a circle until he finally blew out a breath like he was trying to clear the last bit of air from his lungs.

You shouldn't.

Her mind tripped, tripped, tripped over the meaning of those words. She shouldn't love him, so he said, but did that mean he didn't love her?

He held up his hands. "We should keep this conversation fixed on the issues of the petition—"

"Like we're in a lawyer's office? Like there are no emotional consequences to all this?"

"I never wanted to hurt you—"

"Too late. You're failing." A rush of anger gripped her throat. "And I'm not the only one who'll be hurt if you go through with this. Have you thought about Zoe?"

"Of course. The custody issues—"

"Custody issues." The words sent a drip of cold down her

spine. "Do you hear yourself? How do you think Zoe's going to feel about 'custody issues'?"

"If we remain calm and reasonable, Zoe won't get hurt."

"Then she'll be the first thirteen-year-old in the world who hasn't been affected by her parents' divorce."

"You know what?" He raised a hand in the air again, a flat palm against her. "Let's keep Zoe out of this."

"That's not possible. I know you love Zoe more than me. I know you love Zoe more than *her*—"

"The issue here is not Zoe. It's you and me and the decisions that we have to make to move forward."

There was one person he left out of that equation, maybe the one person orchestrating this whole scene. He was willing to tear apart their family for the sake of some midmorning lust grown out of shared interests and proximity—but Jenna was willing to throw her pride on a pyre if it meant a chance to keep her family together.

"Here's a decision we can make to move forward." Jenna looked around her and nudged a metal pail. "Drop the papers in there and set them on fire."

"Jenna, for God's sake—"

"I know it'll be a sacrifice. For *both* of us. First of all, I'd have to forgive you. I'm not always good at forgiving. Second, you'd have to give *her* up."

"She's not the only one I'd be giving up."

A stillness came over her as Nate dragged his hand down his face. She became aware of something else in the room, another presence, so vivid that she found herself glancing more carefully around the garage as if Sissy were crouched

behind the bikes or hiding under the overturned wheelbar-
row. In the end, she returned to watching the twitch of the
fine muscles of his face, until he tucked his fingers in his
armpits and leaned forward to hide that expression from her
altogether.

"You're going to hear the news soon enough," he said.
"In a month, it'll be obvious to everyone. Sissy is pregnant."

Jenna took the hit like she'd once taken the hit of a
paintball in the chest when she'd been forced to attend a
corporate outing. The blow of that hard nugget had knocked
her off her feet into a patch of mud as blue paint exploded
and splattered across her goggles, blinding her.

"Sit down, Jen, please."

Nate was speaking, or at least, she could see his lips moving. She was staring at him, and then suddenly she wasn't.
In front of her was the door of the garage where steam had
misted the window. She couldn't see outside. Beyond the
door, her subcompact rental car was parked in the driveway.
If she got into it, she could drive to her hotel and lay upon
the bleached sheets of her hotel room.

Nicole and Claire had warned her that this could go
very badly. Jenna wondered if they could have predicted how
badly.

It all made terrible, terrible sense, of course. This was
why he was rushing the divorce. Nate took his responsibilities as a father very seriously. He always had, right from
the beginning. He'd probably demanded full legal custody of
Zoe solely for the purpose of assuring their daughter that she
wasn't being replaced by the new baby.

Jenna stumbled a few steps, and then, realizing she didn't have full control of her own body, she pressed her forehead against the wall and felt the sweat on the raw wood. The head of a nail protruded, digging into her skin, and the sharp feeling brought her back to the garage. Jenna tried to figure out what she was feeling. She found herself imagining Theresa striding out this garage door while tossing a flaming Molotov cocktail over her shoulder. She should be angry like that. She had a right to feel as angry as that.

She didn't. All she felt was shock. The sensation slowly ebbed until she could feel the throbbing hollow in the place where a piece of herself was now lost.

She'd come here in the hopes of changing Nate's mind by telling him how much she loved him. She'd come here to tell him the truth. What she hadn't known was that from the beginning, the situation had been beyond her control.

She pushed away from the wall. The small muscles of her neck and shoulders unclenched. She'd tried her best, for Zoe's sake. And there was something to be said for the value of finality.

She took a deep breath and summoned the plates of mental armor she needed to click over her brain, her ego, her heart. "I've barely looked at the papers since the day you handed them to me. I'll have to read them again."

She turned around to find him sitting on the floor, his back braced against the edge of the workbench. At the sound of her voice, he looked up from under the shade of his hands, his expression unreadable. His eyes were bloodshot.

She said, "I'll need to hire a lawyer."

"Not necessary." He dropped his hands so they hung between his knees. "We can work out a settlement."

"No, I need to hire a lawyer. But I'll have to replace my phone first." She patted her purse only to realize she was patting her hip because she'd left her purse in the car. "I'll call you when I have a phone and a lawyer. In the meantime, you can make another appointment with yours."

Jenna scanned the garage. She took visual inventory of the back shelves, which held soccer equipment, a basketball, a bucket full of children's rain boots, an old pink bike with rainbow streamers.

How do you split a life?

Nate uncurled himself from his seat on the floor. "Will next week work?"

So fast. "Yes. Before we go to Pine Lake."

Nate said, "About Pine Lake..."

Then she realized—*of course*. He wasn't going to fly out to Pine Lake to spend a week with her family this year. They couldn't share her childhood bed for seven days. And if he slept on the couch, that would invite questions. Jenna felt a little flutter thinking about her mother's reaction to this news. Her mother had always adored Nate. No doubt her mother would see the divorce as just another failure by her oddball of a daughter.

He said, "Zoe could spend the extra week after camp vacationing with your family, like she usually does. We'll figure out an excuse for not being there. Then you and I can take that week to work things out here before Zoe comes home."

"So thoughtful of you."

He absorbed that comment on a beat. "Your parents could put Zoe on the plane. We'll pick her up at the Seattle-Tacoma Airport together."

"But I'll be in Pine Lake," she said. "Claire and Nicole have my car. And I'd always planned to spend that week with Zoe and my parents."

Nate's pause was full of the unspoken. Irritation rippled through her. Yes, she and Zoe hadn't had the best of relationships lately. Yes, Zoe would rather starve herself in her room than share a meal with her mother. That didn't mean Jenna was going to avoid spending time with her daughter—quite the opposite. The real problem, she suspected, was that Nate didn't trust that she could keep her mouth shut about the impending divorce until they had a chance to tell her together.

The situation was getting ugly already. "You keep telling me that there's a right way to do this."

"A united front."

"Then trust me that the last thing I want to do is hurt Zoe. While I'm in Pine Lake, I won't say a word about our divorce." The word left a residue in her mouth, a slime she couldn't scrape off. "In the meantime, we have to figure out a way to break this news to Zoe together."

Nate didn't say anything. He sagged against the workbench. His thumbs tatted on the surface. The muscles of his shoulders tightened underneath the stretch of his black T-shirt.

Her suspicions swelled with each passing beat. "Tell me you didn't already tell Zoe about the divorce."

"Zoe doesn't know about the divorce."

The way he spoke the words, Jenna could tell they were true but that he'd left something out. He turned his face away so she could only see his profile. His throat worked. He kept glancing at that old upholstered chair, the overstuffed armchair that they'd bought for five dollars at a garage sale in the early days when they had a house and no money to furnish it. Later, they'd relegated it to the garage when the fabric had torn, exposing the stained foam of the stuffing.

More than once she'd wandered in on a Saturday to deliver lunch while baby Zoe slept, only to end up pressed naked across it—

No.

In her mind, a new film reel flickered: Zoe bounding across the driveway with a school paper fluttering in her hands, calling out over the sound of music in the garage, *Daddy, Daddy, look what I got on my English test*, throwing the door open—

"No." Jenna slammed the back of her hand so hard against her mouth she bit into her skin. "Nate—tell me *no*."

Chapter Fifteen

Chicago, Illinois

"This is why we came to Chicago?" Claire exited the elevated train at Addison station and saw the banks of lights above Wrigley Field. "To go to a baseball game?"

"Not just any baseball game." Nicole marched through the crowd like a pilgrim on the way to Mecca. "We're going to a *Cubs* game."

Claire struggled to keep up with Nicole's city pace as they took the stairs out of the station. Claire had been struggling to keep up with Nicole in a lot of ways since they retrieved Jenna's car from the Iowa mechanic. Nicole spent all her nondriving time on her cell phone, making calls, answering texts, reserving hotel rooms, buying tickets, breaking out in laughter now and again, in a manic way that gave Claire pause. Claire's offer to head straight-arrow to Pine Lake had knocked Nicole back into her über-efficient mode, but the effects were making Claire breathless.

"So," she said, tugging on the hem of Nicole's faded Cubs T-shirt in an effort to slow her down, "you're telling me we drove seven hours to watch a bunch of millionaires throw a ball around?"

"Claire, when we were in Salt Lake City, did we visit Temple Square?"

"No, we saw Jin."

"When we were in Wyoming, did we stop to see the Devils Tower?"

"No, but—"

"When we passed through Iowa, did we pull over to visit the future birthplace of Captain James T. Kirk?"

Claire didn't respond. She'd been particularly scornful of that suggestion, as she had been of most tourist traps.

"Listen," Nicole said, "I've got nothing against roadside pool halls, tacky museums, and friends' pull-out couches. And hauling out to Kansas to chase a ghost pretty much convinced me that you're a back-roads kind of traveler. But it'd be a crime if we continued to blow on past some of the country's high points, especially if they're right on route." Nicole paused at a kiosk to peruse the regalia. "So, today, we're doing something touristy."

"Must we?"

"Baseball is America's quintessential pastime."

"You read that on the back of a Cracker Jack box."

"You're such a heathen." Nicole grinned as she tried to catch the vendor's attention. "You realize that we're here because of you, right?"

"How did I screw up?"

"Back in Iowa, you reminded me that baseball makes me happy." Nicole swept her gaze over the blue-shirted crowd of fans, and the hawkers of hats, bats, and little shirted bears, to the sight of the curved wall of the stadium. "You should think up something that'll make you just as happy. Something that you won't be able to do when you're finally home in your thirty-acre wood."

Claire frowned. She *had* been doing what made her happy—poking about the countryside, meeting up with old friends—right up to the moment Jenna went back to Seattle and Karma completely shifted.

Not going there. "Don't change the subject, Nic. You lured me to Chicago under the pretense that you wanted to do something specific, something you've never done before."

"I did say that."

"But you've been to Wrigley Field before."

"A hundred times, and each time better than the last." Nicole directed the vendor to what she wanted and then she dug out cash. "Claire, just take a good look around you. Look at all the folks here who are excited to watch a bunch of millionaires throw a ball around."

Claire did glance around to view the river of humanity heading toward the gates of Wrigley Field, but her gaze didn't catch on the clusters of bros and the college girls in team T-shirts or the fathers lifting their toddlers so they could better see the red sign that said "Wrigley Field, Home of the Chicago Cubs." What snagged her attention were the same sights and sounds she'd been assaulted with since they'd first driven into the city: an odd, plinking music that reminded her of the hollow wooden ping of a Thai *ranat* but turned out to be an unshaven man making music with rubber bands stretched on a wooden frame. And a rattling of metal that turned out to be a homeless man, thin and stumbling, making the rounds shaking a paper coffee cup.

Sometimes, among her friends, she felt like the little boy in the movie *The Sixth Sense*, seeing the ghosts that others couldn't.

Nicole plopped a Cubs baseball hat on Claire's head and gave her a look, the kind of look you give a kid when offering a lollipop before a vaccination.

Claire tugged on the bill to settle the hat on her head. "So this is it, then? There's nothing else on your agenda for Chicago?"

"Patience, little Buddha." Nicole's grin was that of a sixteen-year-old pitcher confident she could close the game. "That other thing has to wait until dark."

Claire fell into Nicole's wake as she headed for the will-call booth. Nicole retrieved the tickets then waved them under her nose, bouncing on her toes in excitement. Then she turned and led her through the gray bowels of the place.

"Popcorn and peanuts." Nicole savored a deep breath as they approached the entrance to their section. "This is the perfume of my coming-of-age."

Claire thought it smelled like urine and beer, or like a circus just after the elephants had left, but she kept quiet so as not to shatter Nicole's reverie. They climbed up the concrete ramp into the early evening light. The lawn, bottle-green, was scattered with players. An usher checked their stubs, and they followed his directions up the gum-sticky, stained concrete steps into the shade under the upper deck. Peanut shells crackled under their feet as they sidled past a group of skinny young guys with their hair gelled up into blue mohawks.

A shout of dismay rose up around them as something happened on the field. "You're going to have to guide me through this." Claire squinted at the field to watch a player run. "I went to your high school softball games to hear the gospel of Nicole, not to watch the scoreboard."

Nicole perched on the edge of the seat. "And here I thought you wore that T-shirt on purpose."

Claire glanced down. She was wearing a shirt from a hospital walk-a-thon, swag she'd earned in a fund-raiser while Melana was still alive.

"Saint Jude," Nicole explained, gesturing to the emblem on the front. "You know, the patron saint of lost causes?"

Claire gave her T-shirt another rueful look. "If I'd known there was a Catholic saint designated just for me, I might have converted years ago."

But it was true that Claire knew a lot about lost causes. In her opinion, big cities like Chicago concentrated all the lost causes of the world. As she and Nicole had driven through the city earlier, Nicole had shown her the redbricked, copper-roofed public library, the rusting steel supports of the overhead trains, and the slate-blue stretch of Lake Michigan. Claire could barely raise her gaze above the streets. She'd glimpsed a tattered woman lying in the Gothic doorway of a church and felt a piercing guilt for the bag of pretzels that lay open, half-eaten, on her lap. She'd wanted to stop the car and donate one of her growing collection of hats to the man standing in the open sun, his bald head gleaming, while he dug through the garbage for soda cans. She couldn't even appreciate the Egyptian cotton sheets and the Jacuzzi in the pricey room Nicole had insisted on, the one where they'd left Lucky with a doggy sitter. It's hard to enjoy a luxury hotel when she could see, just outside her window, a young man holding up a sign to cars: *Will work for food.*

Nicole leaned forward to hail a peanut vendor. "There's a lot of praying to Saint Jude that goes on here. The Cubs are Saint Jude's most hopeless cause."

"Jenna's mom always said it was the Red Sox who were hopeless."

"The Red Sox killed that curse by winning the World Series after eighty-six years. The Cubs have it worse. It's been more than a century since they won."

Nicole handed her a bag of peanuts. Between cracking and chewing, Nicole told her the whole history, from the Curse of the Goat in 1945 to the time in the 1969 World Series when a black cat came out on the field and stared down some guy in the batter's box. Nicole told her about 1984 when a ground ball went through another player's legs. She told her about 2003 and some guy named Steve Bartman.

"Holy bad Karma," Claire muttered when Nicole had finished. "So they've never won once?"

"Not since nineteen oh eight. No one alive has ever seen these lovable losers win."

"Maybe this is why I don't understand sports." Claire stirred her bag of peanuts and tried not to think about the hungry men panhandling outside. "Wouldn't it be more fun to follow a winning team?"

"Yeah, I suppose it would." Nicole paused with a handful of peanuts halfway to her mouth. "But it's not always about winning. Well, maybe it is for the guys on the field. And the ones in the back office." Nicole rattled the peanuts in the palm of her hand. "But if you're going to condemn yourself to root for a team like the Cubs, you have to do it for reasons other than winning."

Claire waited for an explanation as Nicole ate her peanuts and then pulled unshelled ones out of the oil-stained bag. She watched Nicole dig the edge of her fingernail into another seam, crack out the two peanuts, toss the shells onto the floor, and then eat the nuts, still chewing as she reached for more. Nicole's rhythmic concentration reminded Claire of saffron-covered Buddhist monks clicking their prayer beads as they counted a mantra.

Nicole said, "You know when you work really hard for something? When you spend a lot of time and effort and money in an attempt to be really, really good—only to discover that you're hopelessly bad at it?"

"Story of my life."

"It's like when I'm coaching a pee wee baseball team and *that boy* arrives." Nicole cracked open another peanut. "I can always tell which boy it is by the way he shoves himself in the middle of the huddle. This is the kid who sleeps wearing his batting helmet. He shows up an hour early for every game. He stands on the bench yelling encouragement to his teammates. Yet he can barely run a straight line without tripping over his own sneakers." Nicole gestured to the team spread out on the field. "That boy is the Cubs. Clumsy, overpaid, underperforming strivers. For the whole season, the fans hold their collective breath hoping the team will just this once—*just this once*—make it to the postseason. And if ever they win the World Series"—Nicole's eyelids fluttered closed, her chest rising and falling in a sigh of imagined ecstasy—"it's almost too much to consider. It's the triumph of hope over good sense."

The crack of a bat echoed through the stadium. A tremendous cry rose up around them as the crowd leapt to its feet. Claire winced at the screaming as thousands of eyes followed the trajectory of the ball against the pale sky until that ball—launched by a Cubs player, Claire surmised—cleared the ivy-covered wall. The roar turned to the thunder of approval and stomping and applause.

Nicole settled back in the seat, still clapping. "There's a tradition here I should warn you about. If one of the Phillies hits a home run into the stands, we can't keep the ball as a souvenir. We have to throw it back onto the field."

Claire eyed Nicole's flushed face, brighter than she'd seen it the whole trip. "You really love this."

"These are my people. I love the ball hawks on Sheffield Avenue scrambling after baseballs hit out of the stadium during batting practice. I love the rickshaw cyclists who line up after a game to pedal all these suburban fans back to the far parking lots. And I love these peanuts." Nicole stopped to bury her nose in the bag. "I don't even care that they get stuck between my teeth, or that for the rest of the night my breath is going to smell like sixth grade." Nicole leaned back and pointed to the overhang above them. "Somewhere up there is a peanut-free zone, but I can't imagine coming to Wrigley without grabbing a bag of these and eating them here, one by one, tossing the shells. It's a tradition. It's part of the whole Wrigley Field ritual that keeps all of us masochistic saps coming back."

"I don't remember you following the Cubs in high school," Claire said. "How long have you been a fan?"

"Since freshman year in college." Nicole patted the wooden arm of the chair between them. "This place we're sitting in is like the temple of my youth."

"And here I thought the temple of your youth was Pine Lake."

Nicole's phone suddenly rang. She fumbled for it and glanced at the face. "I have to take this. Watch the field for me and tell me what I missed." She stood up and shuffled past the mohawk twins. "I'll be right back."

As Nicole left, Claire gazed over the emerald field, the ivy-covered walls, the rickety seats, the engaged crowd, in that moment sensing the history of the place in the echoes of the rafters. Wrigley Field must look and sound much the same now as it had a hundred years ago. For Nicole and all the rabid fans, Claire supposed nothing much had changed here since their very first game.

It was funny how the constructs of youth persisted. Sometimes, in the late hours when none of them could sleep, Nicole would rhapsodize about returning to Pine Lake. Nicole's Pine Lake was an Eden of pine-scented backyard parties and cold-lake swims, of endless campfires, of tense softball games played out on dusty mounds as the mountain sun beat on her head. Claire's memories were a little earthier, except for one. Sometimes when Claire thought about returning home, she found herself imagining arriving at her old deep-woods house to find her sisters—*all* her sisters, laughing and lively—helping her mother put dinner on the table.

For a moment that image fluttered in her mind like the enormous luna moths that emerged at night in Thailand, when she would awaken to find flocks batting the air around her like ghosts in the darkness.

She remembered that Jenna would talk about Pine Lake, too, during those restless evenings. Jenna returned every year, so she'd kept tabs on the place. She'd mentioned that the grove by Bay Roberts had been chopped down and the public fire pit removed for insurance reasons. That a Starbucks had popped up on Main Street right down the street from Ricky's Roast. And she'd mentioned that her daughter, Zoe, had once ridden her bike on Nicole's old softball field, which had been relandscaped in favor of a soccer field.

Claire supposed no place stayed the same forever.

She felt a shudder of uneasiness. She'd chosen her Pine Lake goal on a whim—but Karma was never random, was it? Deep down, she had a reason for returning home. Her heart yearned to return to the place where friends once surrounded her, where they remembered her as someone strong and determined, someone worthy, someone who could change the world. Her heart wanted to return to that moment of infinite possibilities. Her heart ached to return to a time when her family was still whole.

She wanted to travel back in time.

"Sorry about that." Nicole slipped back into her seat. "Lars likes to call me in the car on the way home from work. Did I miss anything?"

Her throat was tight as she shook her head. She stared past the banks of lights to the slowly dimming sky, willing Nicole not to see that her eyes were full of tears. She couldn't believe it had taken her thousands of miles to figure this out. All along she'd been running back toward a moment when she felt young and healthy and safe, a time that had long gone. She would *never* find that when she arrived in Pine Lake.

And once again, that wave of sinking dread subsumed her, as it had after Jenna went back to Seattle and their triumvirate crumbled, when Paulina arrived from the past, when the car broke down, when she stood in the Laundromat in Nevada, Iowa, with those cloudy skies pressing down upon her, feeling this same sucking darkness.

Claire ran a hand up her right arm. She probed under her short sleeve for the ridge of the scar that extended to her bicep. Her sister Melana had felt the first tightening of the skin around her upper arm only six weeks after her double mastectomy. Claire had forced her to do everything the nurse had advised, elevating the limb, using compression bandages, concerned when the nurse brushed away Claire's suggestion that the swelling might be an infection so long after the operation. Then one day, Claire had woken up to find Melana moaning. Her swollen arm was streaked mauve and hot to the touch, permanent tissue damage from the lymphedema already done.

Claire squeezed her own arm until it felt sore. She could tell Nicole any medical excuse she wanted. The C card was Claire's ace in the hole, the one card she could play so that even Nicole would agree it was time to turn away from their hometown. Maybe that would be for the best. With just the two of them bouncing around an altered Pine Lake, their arrival couldn't help but be a disappointment.

Nicole suddenly jerked straight in her seat. "Well, well, Claire. Look who the cat dragged in."

Claire glanced up to see a woman sidling down the row toward them. A woman edging closer in a halting, awkward, uneven gait. A woman with a tousled blonde head of upswept hair, hiding behind a huge pair of sunglasses.

"Yup, it's just me, the soon-to-be-merry divorcee." Jenna shoved her sunglasses atop her head. "So, did either one of you road warriors save me a beer?"

Chapter Sixteen

Chicago, Illinois

J enna said, "Can we get arrested for this?"

Nicole rolled her eyes as she dropped onto the sand of Pratt Beach, leaning back as she tried to untie her knotted shoelaces. "I suppose Chicago has laws about public nudity. But that won't matter as long as we don't get caught."

"For the love of Buddha."

Nicole could see Claire's frown by the glow of the distant streetlights. Claire still hadn't risen completely out of the black mood she'd been in since Iowa, although Jenna's arrival had taken the edge off it, thank God. Nicole was just about out of tricks to keep her friend motivated and on track.

"Claire, baby," Nicole said, "you should have had a few more beers at the Cubby Bear."

"Maybe you should have had a few *less*."

"Three beers," Nicole retorted, "over the entire evening. You don't think an ex-jock can handle that?" She stuck her index finger in the back of her sneaker and yanked until she set one foot free. "Besides, I don't have to be drunk to consider taking a swim in the nude."

"Employment applications," Jenna muttered. "They have all those pesky questions about arrests."

"You know I'm always up for fun," Claire said, "but we're in the middle of suburbia." She waved beyond the tips of the park trees toward the glow of a business district. "And until this moment on the road trip, you've always been the sensible one."

Nicole attacked the other set of laces. She wasn't feeling much like the sensible one right now. She didn't know what she was feeling, really, except that it had become vitally important to finish something she wasn't sure any of them should have started, just because instinct told her it was the right thing to do.

"C'mon, ladies." Nicole kicked off the other sneaker. "Are you telling me you've never gone skinny-dipping?"

"Well," Claire confessed, "there was that one time in Sihanoukville on the Gulf of Thailand—"

"Then strip."

"I was a lot younger. There was a hot, young New Zealander involved. And I still had breasts."

Nicole tossed her socks aside. "We've been sharing cheap hotel rooms all the way across country. I've seen your scars." Two wobbly, persimmon-pink crescents tilted across Claire's chest like the stitched edges of closed eyes.

"I'll just stay covered," Claire said. "I wouldn't want to scare the wildlife."

"You should show them off like battle scars." Nicole struggled up from the cool sand, loving the silky feel of it as it shifted between her toes. "Or tattoo them into something dramatic."

Jenna leaned into Claire. "Did someone slip her a roofie when we were in that bar?"

"Damned if I know." Claire shrugged. "There was that weird guy eyeballing us across the room."

"She was only drinking beer," Jenna said, "but who knows what happened between the time the bartender cracked the bottle open and that Frankenstein of a fan handed it over to her?"

"Wait a minute." Claire pointed at her. "This is it, isn't it? This is that thing you've been teasing me about since Iowa. The thing you wanted to do that you've never done before?"

"I married young," Nicole said, grabbing the hem of her T-shirt. "I missed the chance to do all those embarrassing things young adults are supposed to do."

Jenna said, "Clearly I missed something."

Claire explained, "It's not a roofie that tipped Nic over the edge. Nicole told me there was something she really wanted to do in Chicago—"

"—and this is it." Nicole hefted her shirt over her head. "I'm not hanging here all night, ladies. Let's dive in."

Jenna sucked in a gulp of air. "Oh thank God, you're wearing a sports bra."

"Not for long—"

"Stop." Claire held out a palm. "Just stop and think about this for a moment."

Nicole paused with her fingers underneath the elastic band of her sports bra as she caught sight of a jogger heading down the beach. She wasn't shy about nudity in front of her friends, but once she got naked, she wasn't hanging around for the show—she was going *in.*

"What Jenna and I are trying to figure out," Claire said, "is exactly what time during the last few days the pod people invaded your body."

Nicole expelled a breath. In high school, she used to be known as the fun one. "You guys really think I'm a stick in the mud."

"I say it must have happened in Iowa," Jenna said. "If I were a pod person, that's where I'd hide."

"Calling yourself a stick in the mud is a little harsh," Claire added. "But you can definitely be rigid."

"*Rigid* is too strong a word," Jenna countered. "Still, she's not the kind to normally do something impulsive."

Nicole smothered a ripple of irritation. The jocks at Pine Lake High School weren't exactly paragons of virtue. They were usually the ones caught at Coley's Point at three in the morning with two empty bottles of blackberry brandy, scattering like deer at the sight of the police aiming the beams of their flashlights into the woods.

She thought about her truncated first year as a graduate student at the University of Chicago. Like so many other students before her, she spent a lot of time trying to live in the moment and avoid the big decisions. One night she came to Promontory Point with a crowd. Instead of laughing and fooling around, she stared deep into the inky waters of Lake Michigan in the hopes of an answer to a dilemma she—the consummate planner—had never expected to have to make. Then her friends all came and fetched her, shucking clothes in the process, racing one another to the shore as they dared one another to jump into the frigid April waters.

Though she'd wanted to, she hadn't gone skinny-dipping then. She'd had a good reason. Her friends would have seen the evidence if she'd stripped off her clothes. They hadn't yet known she was three months pregnant.

Nicole blurted, "Why do you think we're all here?"

Claire said, "Because after we left that stinking bar, you were the first one to talk to the driver when we stepped in the cab?"

"No, no." Nicole dropped her hands to her hips. "Not why we're on the shores of Lake Michigan. I mean 'why are we here' as in what Maya asked all of us back in South Dakota. Why did we all decide to go on this road trip?"

"Personally, I attribute it to taking advantage of Jenna's good intentions," Claire said. "And maybe a little too much Percocet after the surgery."

"Claire, I can practically see your nose growing."

"Honey, my secrets are all out." Claire rolled her shoulders and turned her face to the silvery whoosh of Lake Michigan, away from what little light fell onto the beach. "I just wanted to get the hell away from my sisters and their grand medical plans."

Nicole glanced at Jenna, who just shrugged and said, "My life is a disaster and I want it to disappear in the rearview mirror."

Nicole waited for Jenna to say something more. During the baseball game, the only news that Claire managed to tease out of a reticent Jenna was the fact that her efforts to save the marriage had failed and that Nate had a pregnant girlfriend. Then Jenna clammed up. Nicole had hoped—wrongly, it turned out—that a postgame noisy bar would be the perfect place to give Jenna a chance to confess whatever other details she seemed to be hiding. But Jenna had kept her secrets to herself.

She decided to cut her friend a little slack. "Okay then," she said, her heart tripping, "I'll confess that I'm here to get away from the reality that in a few more weeks, my son will bring home his behavior and mood issues again, and despite all his sweet promises and honest intentions, his condition will get the better of him just like all the other times before. Once again he'll be suspended from school, and there'll be police at my door, and our whole family will have to watch this boy that we love just *spiral*."

Nicole dropped her gaze to her bare feet. She heard Claire's footfalls in the sand as she tried to close the few feet between them. Nicole shifted away, took a few steps toward the water. It rippled under the light of a sliver of moon. She focused on the glare of the red light at the end of the far pier and tried to parse everything she was feeling, this rush of emotions she'd been suppressing, she supposed, for longer than she would have liked to admit.

Back in Des Moines, Claire talked about finding the seeds of joy in the middle of heartache. Now Nicole stared at the lake and smelled the damp and sand and the vague scent of waterlogged wood from the nearby pier. She listened to the cars rumbling by, muffled by the distance. Water gurgled against the pylons. She used to jog along this area when she was in school, running miles and miles, clearing her mind of worries, opening her thoughts to contemplate her future as the cold Midwestern sun rose over the horizon.

She'd made a life-altering decision back then. She'd taken a turn in an unexpected direction. And every good, difficult, and neutral aspect of her life arose from that terrifying, dangerous choice, in ways she had only begun to understand.

Nicole said, "We're doing this road trip all wrong. We can't keep dragging all these problems along behind us."

In the pause, Jenna murmured, "Like Marley's clanking chains."

"We're worrying too much about the past," Nicole continued, "when we should be living in the present."

Claire's voice, low and sly: "I'll make a Buddhist of you yet."

"We need to crack open our thinking. So let's start right now." Nicole turned to Jenna. "We've got days before we reach Pine Lake. If you could do anything at all, Jenna, what would it be?"

"I asked myself the same question just yesterday." Jenna hugged her elbows as a breeze swept off the lake. "I spent that day talking to a three-hundred-dollar-an-hour lawyer going over the divorce papers and plans for our response. When that was done, I found myself tooling around in a hotel room with nothing to do but watch *Law and Order* reruns."

Nicole said, "That gave you lots of time to think."

"Exactly. I have ten days or so before I have to face Nate in a divorce lawyer's conference room." Jenna traced patterns in the sand with the toe of her sneaker. "I decided that more than anything, I'd rather be hanging around with friends."

A flash of headlights set Jenna's blonde hair momentarily alight. Nicole felt the tingling awareness that told her there was something more Jenna wanted, something bigger, but now didn't seem the right time to probe.

"All right then." Nicole turned to Claire. "If you could do anything, Claire, what would it be?"

"Change the world."

Claire chased those words with a sarcastic smile. Her teeth gleamed in a flash of light that swept quickly over them, the headlights of some distant car turning. Nicole sensed her friend meant them, bone deep, meant them so much that it hurt too much to take them seriously.

"That's a tall order," Nicole said, "but tomorrow morning, we'll all sit down and brainstorm. For now, what I want to do," she said, as she flicked the button of her jeans, "is take a nice, long swim in Lake Michigan."

Jenna looked away in sudden embarrassment as Nicole shimmied out of her jeans.

"Are you guys in?" She stood on the dark beach in her underwear and a sports bra. "Or are you just going to stand here and watch me from the shore?"

Claire groaned and reached for the hem of her T-shirt. "Promise me absolutely no pictures."

Nicole grinned. "Not even shoulders up?"

Jenna muffled a laugh as she kicked off a sandal then wriggled like a kid trying to tug her shirt over her head.

Claire tossed her shirt on the sand. "I just know I'm going to regret this."

Nicole yanked her sports bra over her head and shot toward the surf. "No more regrets."

"*Stop.*"

At the sound of the masculine voice, Nicole froze and slapped her hands over her chest as a beam of light rolled past her, casting her shadow on the sand.

"Ladies," the voice said, "I'm going to need you to come away from the water. This is the Chicago PD."

Chapter Seventeen

To: Paulina, Alice, Zuza Petrenko
From: Jenna Hogan
Subject: Claire and Officer Gomez
Attached: NotaNudeBeach.jpg; BreakingTheLaw.jpg;
RideInaCruiser.jpg

Hey, Petrenko sisters, it's Jenna here. Don't be alarmed by
the picture of a wet Claire with her arm around Officer
Gomez of the Chicago PD. Although last night Officer
Gomez surprised us on Pratt Beach as we were about to
take a swim in Lake Michigan, he was very accommodating
once he caught sight of Claire's mastectomy scars. It turns
out his mother is a ten-year breast cancer survivor. So
under the cordon of two of Chicago's finest, we all had a
good, long, naked splash before getting a free ride to the
hotel in the back of a cruiser.

I noticed that the "Claire and the Big C" blog has gone real quiet over the past few weeks. It occurred to both Nicole and me that all of Claire's friends might start to worry if they aren't kept up-to-date with how she's doing. We'd be happy to share some photos from the road trip along with a few PG-13 stories. We hope you post them on the blog. As you can see, Claire is taking full advantage of this pause in her treatment.

We're making our leisurely way east, planning a few more stops. Barring further interaction with the local police, we should make it to Pine Lake before long.

Chicago, Illinois

Jenna shifted Lucky's weight on her lap, trying to avoid his tongue as the pup snuggled close to her. She scratched him behind the ears as she scrolled down the little screen, nervously rereading the e-mail on her phone amid the white-noise burble of coffee shop conversation.

"Just send it, Jenna." Nicole rolled a large paper cup of coffee between her palms as she slouched behind dark glasses. "Enough fiddling, it's perfect as written."

"The last time Paulina got an e-mail from one of Claire's friends she hopped on a plane to Kansas and hunted us down in a pool hall." Jenna raised her screen. "This might make her call out the National Guard."

"It's a risk I'm willing to take. As it is, I've been answering Paulina's texts practically every day. I know more than I ever wanted to know about the signs of lymphedema." Nicole shook her head. "Maybe if her sisters see Claire relaxed and enjoying herself, then they may relax a little, too."

Jenna winced as she tapped the Send button, eyeing the bar until the phone beeped that the e-mail and its attached photos had gone through.

Just then Claire appeared from around the coffee line to slip a corrugated flat of four hot coffees next to its twin on their table. Claire's T-shirt bore a picture of a round, jolly Buddha with the words *I Have the Body of a God.*

"Second batch." Claire sucked a sticky drip of coffee off her thumb. "One more batch of coffees and we're off."

Jenna watched Claire head back to the counter to wait for the rest of her order, still feeling a bit off-kilter. She'd only been gone for a few days, but she sensed she'd missed some change in the air, a shift in the relationship between her two friends that left her feeling one step behind. This morning, Nicole had sat them all down in the luxury room's seating area with a pen and a paper, intent on making plans for the rest of the trip—but Claire had blown those plans to pieces. Claire had something she wanted to do. Nicole, with a secret smile, had pushed the pad of paper aside and reached for her purse. That's how the three of them ended up in this fair-trade organic coffee shop purchasing twelve hot coffees to go.

Now Claire called out to them from the front of the shop where she waited, balancing the third tray of coffees. Slipping her phone in her purse and Lucky to the floor, Jenna picked up a tray and strode away from the dark-roast aroma into the heart of Chicago.

They passed a bakery and a bodega and a check-cashing store while Claire strode fiercely ahead. Straining against the leash, Lucky froze and nearly had a seizure as they passed underneath an elevated track and a train clattered overhead. A breeze ruffled off the Chicago River, pushing papers and leaves across the sidewalk like skittering insects. Jenna finally swept him up into the hollow of her waist. The poor little pup quivered against her, unnerved by the traffic and the milling crowds.

The first victim of Claire's generosity lay dozing on the stairs of an old stone church. Claire climbed up the steps and leaned over to say something to the man who barely moved in the cocoon of his blankets. Jenna wrinkled her nose. She could smell the ripeness of him even from a good distance. Claire didn't make any sign of noticing. She talked to him as she tugged a coffee out of her carrier. She put the coffee down close enough for him to reach but in a place unlikely for him to tip over.

Jenna watched her old friend turn and descend the stone stairs, and she was reminded of a time Claire had bounced down the stairs of the Baptist church in the cannery section of Pine Lake after delivering three boxes of shoes out of the trunk of Jenna's car. Jenna hadn't always paid attention to exactly *what* Claire was involving her in—which of the many coat and clothing and toy drives her friend took it upon herself to coordinate—because she had just been so gratified to be invited to the planning meetings, put in

charge of the logistics, and given responsibility in a committee of smarter and more enthusiastic students. It never struck
her until now, with a flat of hot coffee in her hand, that all
along she'd been following the trail of a comet.

Nicole must have remembered something, too, for she
suddenly leaned into Jenna. "Claire would have made a fabulous nun."

Jenna paused, confused. "She *was* a nun."

"I mean a Catholic nun. Working with the homeless.
Just like this. Honestly, if she were willing to shave her head
and eyebrows and put on a white sari, then I can't imagine
she'd object to the black habit."

"There's that little issue that she's not Roman Catholic."
Jenna tried to remember what church the Petrenkos attended. Not the Episcopal church, like her own family.
"Also, she already rejected the contemplative life in Thailand. I think she's too much of a rebel for a convent."

"My aunt is an Ursuline nun in Quebec. She's been arrested three times for civil disobedience."

Thinking about Nicole's puckish sense of humor last
night, Jenna was no longer surprised Nicole had a rebel aunt.
It was funny what you learned about people after fighting
with them for blankets.

Then the small muscles of Jenna's neck tightened. Last
night at the Cubs game, she'd been very grateful of Nicole's
hesitation to prod her for more details of her visit with Nate
in Seattle. She hadn't been ready to spill the whole tale
while drunken Cubs fans jolted up around her and cursed the
blindness of the third-base umpire. The subsequent excite-

ment with the police had absorbed them, and this morning Nicole had been adamant about sending photos and an e-mail to Claire's sisters.

Now they walked in companionable silence under the bright light of a Chicago August. Lucky raised his snout and licked her face once again. Jenna took the look in his bulging brown eyes for encouragement.

"While Claire is playing coffee fairy," Jenna said, "I thought maybe I could ask you for some professional advice about—"

Her question was interrupted by the sound of Nicole's sandals scuffing against the pavement. Jenna glanced at Nic only to find her friend staring at Claire offering another homeless man a cup of coffee. One glance and Jenna knew this man wasn't quite right. He shuffled in nervous circles in front of a bus stop avoiding Claire's eye. He wore a stained T-shirt and a pair of pants that slid low enough on his hips to show the ragged gray band of his underwear. He'd intentionally cut the front of his sneakers open. The toes of his shoes curled up like smiling mouths. His dirty socks flopped out like thick tongues.

"I read a statistic once," Nicole said, "that sixty-six percent of the homeless suffered from some sort of mental illness."

Jenna looked at the man more closely as Claire stood, calm, proffering the coffee with a steady hand. A patchy beard softened the line of his chin. One of last summer's interns at the hedge fund had sported that kind of beard. That young man had been a college student trying so hard in his ill-fitting suits to look like a future Master of the Universe. *This* young man was thin also, but in a different way. His ribs pressed against the worn weave of his T-shirt as he shifted his weight and eyeballed the cup of coffee. The man raised an arm and waved it through the air as if he were erasing something from a chalkboard with his forearm.

Nicole visibly relaxed after Claire placed the coffee at the man's feet and moved on. She said, "About that professional advice, Jenna."

"It's about Zoe."

"I figured as much." Nicole dropped her gaze to stare into the four coffees, as if they held the secrets of life. "If you're looking for professional advice about how to deal with a troubled teenager, you might want to go to someone with an actual degree. But if you want advice from a friend, I'm all ears."

Jenna bobbed her head as Claire returned for a moment and relieved her of her coffee burden. Nicole's distinction seemed a thin one. Jenna figured that beyond Nicole's work as a life coach, her eighteen months of personal experience dealing with Noah had to earn her the equivalent of a PhD.

"Last night," Jenna began, shifting Lucky to her better arm as Claire led them down a side street, "I didn't tell you everything about what happened in Seattle."

"I figured there was a lot more to the story."

"All along, I had assumed that Zoe didn't know about anything," she said. "But it turns out Zoe already knows about Nate and Sissy's relationship."

Coffee gurgled through the plastic tops as Nicole momentarily fumbled her grip. "Really? How?"

"Zoe came home from school one day to find her father bending a naked Sissy over the couch."

That wasn't really the truth. She didn't know the truth. Nate had gone tight-lipped about the nitty-gritty details of what he and Sissy had been doing when Zoe burst through the front door to find them together. Since then, Jenna's mind had filled in the blanks about a hundred different disturbing ways. Still, the words left a bitter taste in the back of her throat. Jenna tried to swallow it away as she followed the bounce of Claire's braid.

Then Jenna realized that she was walking alone. Nicole had stopped paces behind her, dead in her tracks.

"When," Nicole breathed when she caught up, "did this happen?"

"I'm not sure." She had tried to put herself in Zoe's shoes. She'd wondered how she would have reacted, at the age of thirteen, if she'd come home to find her own quiet, book-loving father making the beast with two backs with, say, old Mrs. Handley down the road. The image always turned absurd. Maybe it just wasn't within her mental or emotional capacity to imagine that kind of mind-blowing betrayal. Then she remembered how she felt when Nate pushed that petition across the kitchen table. She had packed her bags and run far, far away.

Zoe had had no place to run.

A familiar shudder vibrated through Lucky. Jenna slipped him down near a spindly tree just as he let loose.

Nicole stood in front of her, all wide brown eyes. "You're telling me that Zoe has known about this for a while."

"I think it happened nine months ago."

Nicole covered her mouth with a shaky hand.

"I'm guessing because my bastard of a husband went mute when I asked. I suspect it was in early December. I remember that Zoe wouldn't come downstairs to decorate the Christmas tree. All her young life, she'd marked that first Saturday in December in red ink on the family calendar; it was one of her favorite days of the year. But she wouldn't come down, and Nate was wound up tight. He told me some boy had broken up with Zoe. I hadn't even known she had a boyfriend. Nate said it had only been a few weeks, a lifetime for a twelve-year-old. He wouldn't let me go up and see her. He kept saying she needed privacy. Fool that I was, I just accepted it." Guilt like a sucking sinkhole. "I accepted too many things."

She'd always ceded to Nate's judgment in issues of parenting. He was home with the baby all day. So if he insisted on letting a fourteen-month-old cry herself to sleep, it wasn't Jenna's place to countermand him at one in the morning while Zoe wailed. Nate was the one who'd have to deal with a cranky toddler the next day. Yes, she'd thought it harsh when he refused to let Zoe wear the sparkly red shoes to school every day, or gave her a time-out for not making her bed. But it was Nate at home who'd have to deal with the fallout of those disciplinary choices, so Jenna had deferred to his judgment, time and again.

She'd been determined not to be one of *those* working

moms. The ones who come home to doubt and criticize and, out of guilt for not baking cookies, micromanage every move her husband made. So over the years, she'd watched Zoe grow up to be a lovely, confident, loving creature, even-tempered until about nine months ago. She could only assume that it was Nate's discipline that helped shape Zoe this way.

Jen buried her face in the back of Lucky's neck as she heard Claire's jogging steps. Claire arrived on a wave of cucumber-mango scent, the aroma of the hotel shampoo she'd used that morning.

"Hey, Nic, I'll take that flat. After we give these away, let's go find another coffee shop."

Then Claire was gone, her footsteps echoing as she headed farther down the side street.

Her hands free, Nicole slapped them both on Jenna's shoulders. "You're not the fool here, Jenna."

"Oh, I definitely am."

"Think about this. Zoe knew about Nate and that woman a long time ago, and yet Zoe never said a word."

Jenna squeezed her eyes shut. She'd spent days trying not to think about the consequences of that truth.

Nicole said, "That means Nate forced Zoe to keep it secret."

She shook her head. She couldn't believe Nate would do that. Not the man she'd once come home to find stirring a pot at the stove while his hair stood up sporting twenty-three crooked plastic barrettes.

"Nate probably told her that he'd made a mistake with that woman." Nicole let go and paced a little between the tree and the shaded edge of the building, her mind working. "I'd bet, when she witnessed it, he told Zoe that it was one incident, one moment of idiocy, something that would never happen again."

"Oh, God."

"How else would he justify it? If this fling were just a mistake, then there would be no reason to tell you. In fact, it'd be *dangerous* to tell you. Who knows how you'd react? It could end in divorce."

"I can't believe he would do that." No, not from the man who'd played airplane with Zoe in the backyard, risking elbow dislocations because he couldn't resist the happy pleading of the girl who loved to fly.

"Zoe complied," Nicole continued, "because Nate promised it wouldn't happen again. What else could he do? What girl wouldn't want to believe her father?"

Jenna closed her eyes and saw a gap-toothed, seven-year-old Zoe sprinkling her bedroom sheets with black pepper because Daddy said it would make the tooth fairy sneeze and lose extra change from her fairy pockets.

"Imagine," Nicole said, "if it happened again, how betrayed she'd feel, how angry at you for not noticing."

The thought sent a seismic tremor through her. Lucky, sensing it, pressed against her ankle and whined.

Nicole pressed her fingers against her head as if holding in the pulsing of her brain. "You do realize that this explains all of Zoe's angry behavior for the past nine months."

You're so stupid! You're so blind!

She cringed. She didn't want this to be true. She wanted

Zoe's fury to stem from some normal reason that she'd read about or heard about in her desperate search for understanding. She'd rather Zoe grew angry because her mother interrogated her about school over dinner. She'd rather Zoe felt besieged by the suffocating pressure of being an only child, the sweet beating heart of the family. She'd rather that Zoe's hair-trigger temper be due to something biological and passing, like the usual early-teen fluctuation in hormones, or even to some Freudian idea that Zoe was competing with her mother for affection from Nate.

Jenna thought about all the times Nate waved away her concerns, insisting Zoe's behavior was just a phase, as he changed the topic of the conversation.

Nicole lifted her fingers and started counting. "Zoe was afraid she wouldn't be able to keep the secret. So she avoided you."

All those days rushing home through Seattle traffic in time for seven p.m. dinner in the hopes of a few minutes with her daughter. Only to come home to see Zoe's face close up tight before asking permission to be excused from the table.

Nicole bent back her second finger. "Then when you tried to get close to her, she lashed out at you in order to push you away."

"She didn't want to slip up," Jenna said. "She didn't want to be the one held responsible for destroying our family."

The tendons in the back of her knees softened. She felt a scorching heat on her palm as she braced herself against the hood of a parked car. She ignored the burn as she leaned her weight against it so she wouldn't sink into a puddle on the dirty street. Her bad leg slipped out from under her. She twisted and banged her hip against the car.

Nicole seized her shoulders and held on until Jenna felt the ground beneath her feet again.

"I want you to think about this, Jenna." Nicole's fingers dug into her skin. "Your husband manipulated Zoe. Rather than coming clean, he made his twelve-year-old keep a terrible secret."

Jenna's humorless laughter certainly came from someone else's mouth. "And all these years, I believed I was the bad parent."

"Oh, Jenna, we all believe we're bad parents."

Her mind rolled back to when she came home from work to have Nate show her the video of Zoe rolling over for the first time, of Zoe scooting across the floor on her belly, of Zoe rising to stand, all the precious moments she missed. She remembered an evening when Nate said something to Zoe about her preschool teacher and Zoe laughed. She'd laughed, too, not understanding the joke but so aching to be part of it. She also remembered skipping out of an office meeting to make a six p.m. grammar school basketball game in order to catch Zoe sitting on the bench for all but one minute and sixteen glorious seconds. She remembered the rhythm of early shopping trips to the mall, pennies tossed in the fountain, a quarter to crank out a plastic egg holding a gummy lizard.

Had the situation been reversed—had Zoe come upon her in flagrante delicto with one of her coworkers, say—Jenna would have confessed the infidelity to Nate that same night. Then she would have set her sights on doing whatever it took to see forgiveness in Zoe's eyes.

"I'm not the bad parent," Jenna heard herself say. "Maybe I never was."

Then she dropped her head back to stare at the blue sky between the Chicago skyscrapers, feeling the first shimmering sliver of comfort, an unexpected gift out of the fissure of a broken heart.

Chapter Eighteen

To: Paulina, Alice, Zuza Petrenko
From: Nicole Eriksen
Subject: Dancing with Rastafarians in Cleveland
Attached: NicoleAirGuitar.jpg; JennaMovesLikeJagger.mov;
BuddhistsCantDance.mov

Paulina, so glad you loved the photo we sent yesterday of
Claire mugging by a Grateful Dead poster in Cleveland.
That was taken at the Rock and Roll Hall of Fame, and we
were thrown out of the museum for it. Go ahead and
share it on the blog like the others. After our adventures
there, we spent the evening at the House of Blues listening
to Zydeco and enjoying gumbo and some amazing baby
back ribs. Then we walked the East Fourth Street
neighborhood and listened to a street band. Here are a
few short clips of Claire and Jenna dancing with a busker.

We're heading for Niagara Falls today. I want to scare the wits out of Claire by showing her real waterfalls before she tackles the rapids of the Hudson Valley Gorge.

As Jenna mentioned in an earlier e-mail, we haven't been arrested yet, so we should make it to Pine Lake before long.

Niagara Falls, New York

C laire," Nicole whispered. "We're attracting the kind of attention usually reserved for cults."

Claire shifted on the wooden boards of one of the viewing platforms on the United States side of Niagara Falls. The three of them were sitting cross-legged in a close triumvirate, so close that their knees touched. "Just ignore them," she said. "Tune out every sensation around you. Close your eyes and concentrate only on your breathing."

Nicole sighed. "We couldn't do this in the privacy of our hotel room?"

"Open air," Claire said. "Open mind."

Jenna ventured, "Can I concentrate on Lucky's breathing? The walk from the hotel killed the poor guy. He's slobbering all over my lap."

"Just concentrate on the movement of your diaphragm and then acknowledge in your mind any other distractions."

Claire admitted there were a lot of distractions. The air swirled with a palpable mist. The waterfall roared just past the edge of the wooden platform. Though this cataract was a noisy, angry beast, the vitality of it reminded her of a much smaller one back at the *wat*, the little trickle of a waterfall whose gurgle she used to concentrate on during her first desperate attempts to still her mind.

Breathe in, breathe out. Breathe in, breathe out.

She acknowledged the sound of footsteps coming toward the railing. The boards vibrated under her bottom. A family standing somewhere to her right kept up a muted conversation. *Mom, what are those people doing? Resting, dear. Come and look at the rainbow.* Claire felt another vibration, a tinny one she couldn't identify that came in through her knees.

She peeped an eye open to find Nicole sneaking her cell phone out of the pocket of her capris.

Nicole grimaced. "I know, I know. Just one more text, I promise."

Claire shifted her weight to give Nic's knee a nudge. "Is there some kind of crisis going on? Your phone has been pinging and ringing nonstop."

"Today it's a cleat crisis. Julia can't find hers." Her fingers flew over the screen keyboard. "Lars needs to know where to buy them. I'm telling him that Julia probably left them under the sofa in the TV room downstairs."

Claire said, "He can't wait half an hour?"

Nicole's shrug was sheepish.

"Let me guess," Jenna said, scratching a grateful Lucky under the collar. "The game's in twenty minutes."

"It's in ten. Okay, done." Nicole shoved the phone back in her pocket and straightened to schoolgirl attention.

"Sorry about that. Before that text, I was sort of falling into a zone."

"Yeah," Jenna teased, "the *hangover* zone."

Jenna leaned away from Nicole as Nicole gave her a harmless slap. Lucky startled as his lap chair tipped, and Jenna released him to protect her head with her hands. All innocence, Nicole brought her hand right back down on her knee like she hadn't done a thing, then settled into perfect meditation position.

The peace lasted no more than a minute.

Claire chided, "Jenna, you're squirming."

"Lucky's heavy on my leg."

Nicole laughed. "He weighs, like, ten pounds."

"Just note the sensation," Claire insisted. "Think, *Warm dog on my leg*. Keep noting the sensation over and over. Eventually, the sensation will slip to your subconscious, and your mind will drift to more important things."

"My aunt is twitching in Quebec." Nicole raised her chin as the mist started to thin under the heat of sunshine. "I'm not sure she'd approve of me doing this without a rosary in my hands."

"I promise," Claire said, "your soul is in no danger."

Jenna picked Lucky up and rearranged him on her lap. "Okay, I'm trying to do what you say. So I'm breathing in, and I'm breathing out. I'm thinking, *Warm dog on my leg*. Then I'm thinking, *Dog lifts head*, followed by, *Dog sniffs the scent of a waffle cone*. Then, *I sniff the scent of a waffle cone*. And then my stomach rumbles."

Claire said, "Great observations."

"I just don't get it," Jenna said. "Exactly what are we trying to accomplish here?"

"Mindfulness."

Jenna repeated, "Mindfulness."

"It's the ability to be intensely present." Claire noted the dampness of the boards soaking the seat of her jeans. "It's a way of being aware of everything you sense and feel. It's a way to shut off the constant roll and tumble of your thoughts so you can finally identify what you're really thinking. You'll recognize how you feel. You'll acknowledge those feelings. Then you can respond to them better."

Splinters plucked at the fibers of Claire's jeans. The mist churned up by the falls bathed her skin and gave her a chill. The August sun broke through long enough to burn a swath across her forehead and lighten the space beyond her eyelids. Soon all sound became subsumed by the roar of the falls. Behind them, she heard the muffled shouts of children and the thud of feet upon the deck, as if her own consciousness had slipped amid the foam.

She willed herself to remember all this. The air had an iron-tang taste to it. She heard the rumble of wheels as a vendor passed, trailing with him a roasted-honey scent. She became conscious of the slight pressure of their knees touching. She made herself feel the strength in her own still-supple spine, the force of life as her heart pumped blood through her body, the ease at which she could suck in a breath.

There would come a time when the cancer would migrate to her vertebrae, stealing the strength and flexibility from her spine. There would come a time when the effort of consciousness would drain the life force from her body. There would come a time when it would be a chore to suck in air, and Paulina and Alice and Zuza would sit vigil waiting, like Claire had for Melana, for the rhythm of her breathing to slow to a stop like the unwinding of an old clock.

Until then, she would vacuum-pack these memories in imaginary snow globes to put up on high shelves until the time she needed to take them down and shake them back into vivid life again.

I mustn't think of that yet.

Yet that singular thought had kept rising into her mind ever since they drove along the southern shore of Lake Erie out of Cleveland, through Pennsylvania, to the wooden placard that announced *Welcome to New York*. Only about three hundred miles now separated them from Pine Lake.

Not yet.

The air had grown thin, as if she stood again at the top of Thailand's highest mountain. Doi Inthanon was only a bus ride away from Chiang Mai. She'd gone there before her Buddhist vows. On arrival she and her friends had roamed around a Hmong roadside market before discovering that there were no hiking trails to the summit, so they paid their two hundred baht to hire a private car and drove their way up. They stopped at Sirithan Waterfall and oohed and aahed over the ornate twin temples built in honor of the king and queen of Thailand. Finally, at the peak of the mountain, they waited in line for a good hour to get their picture taken in front of a teak sign, only to be hustled away to make room for the next tourists. Then they'd milled about, admiring through the haze the blue outlines of the mountains. The return trip to Chiang Mai was an uneventful slide back to the youth hostel.

This was the problem with goals, Claire thought. Once accomplished, they were chased by disappointment. The moment the three of them turned their faces back west, Jenna would summon her energies to the upcoming fight for custody, and Nicole's worries would shift to Noah's return from the residential facility. There would be no more moments contemplating mountains or waterfalls in blissful peace.

Claire tried once again to clear her mind. Perhaps she could talk them into a side trip to the wineries of the Finger Lakes region. Maybe she could convince them of the fun they could have swinging through the Catskills. Maybe she could pass out coffee in New York City before heading to Pine Lake. For as long as possible, she wanted to delay her return to her thirty-acre wood with Jon Snow, her raven, and the three-legged goat and the blind possum under the porch, and her forest garden, where she would stay until the end of all things.

Breathe in, breathe out. I hear the rush of the water. I feel the chill upwind seeping from under the railing. Goose bumps spread along my arms. I smell a pink smell—cotton candy, carnival-sweet. I hear Lucky whining.

"Jenna?"

Nicole's voice was full of concern. Claire blinked her eyes open to find Lucky with his notched ears perked. The dog stretched up to his full height licking Jenna's jaw. Jenna sat with her wrists limp on her knees, trembling.

"I'm okay," Jenna said, but her voice was shaky. "I feel sort of strange. Like I'm riding a swing."

Claire raised her brows. She hadn't expected this out of Jenna—out of anyone—and certainly not on the first try. Only after three months of intensive meditation did she herself experience this kind of physical reaction. Her teacher called it "the rapture," one step closer to the tranquility and sharpness of mind that all good Buddhists sought, and it came with shivering gooseflesh.

Jenna said, "I know what I want."

Nicole said wryly, "A jacket, I assume."

"No, not that. Back in Chicago," Jenna said, gripping Lucky, "Nicole asked us both what we really wanted to do on this trip. Now I know what I want."

Claire felt a pinch of envy at Jenna's good fortune. In the silence of meditation, wisdom sometimes snuck up on you, like a bubble working its way through a viscous consciousness until finally it exploded to the surface, only to leave you wondering why it took so long.

"I should have known from the beginning," Jenna said. "After what Nate has done, he has no right to keep me away from Zoe. That's what I want more than anything else: to speak to Zoe."

"Seeing Zoe isn't going to be easy." Nicole wrestled out of her sweater and then draped it over Jenna's shoulders. "Camp Paskagamak is like Fort Knox for teenagers. We'll have to figure a way past Master Ranger Garfunkle."

No, please. Claire's spine tightened as she realized what they were planning. *Let's stay here. Just a little longer.*

"I don't care if we have to lock Ranger Garfunkle in the janitor's closet," Jenna said. "I am going to see my daughter."

Chapter Nineteen

To: Paulina, Alice, Zuza Petrenko
From: Nicole Eriksen
Subject: What's a little criminal mischief among friends?
Attached: StockingUpOnCourage.jpg

While heading in the general direction of Pine Lake, we stumbled on a trail of wineries in the Finger Lakes area. It was Claire who insisted we stop. What kind of West Coasters would we be, she said, if we just passed right by wineries? We're only a couple of hours from the homeland, but Claire insisted we spend the night. In this picture, you'll see that Claire has taken a liking to the mead, Jenna is wrinkling her nose at a white, and that's me, fortifying myself well with some sweet ice wine. (Don't worry, Jenna's driving.)

The good news is that we've finally passed over the blue boundary into Adirondack Park, which we all would have known by instinct even if a sign hadn't marked the border. Now, every time the car climbs, we get a glimpse of those hazy peaks, and with every descent, the thick spruces drown us in shadow. Jenna cracked her window, and we can all smell the pine air.

This part of our road trip is soon coming to an end, but we have one secret adventure to accomplish before riding the rapids. Fair warning: this next lark of ours may force the Great Sachem of Camp Paskagamak to defrock both Jenna and me of our Master Ranger Badges...if not lead us to actual legal detention.

Which is why, first, we're swinging by Pine Lake.

Pine Lake, New York

I n the sweet, long-grass days of Nicole's youth, whenever she perceived a blue luminescence rising from the far hills or a thrumming electric whine just at the edge of her hearing, she knew it was time to leave the shore at Bay Roberts. Lightning storms in the mountains came swiftly. So she'd jump on her bike and race the rumbling clouds, hoping to make it home before the air crackled, before the first heavy drops sizzled on the asphalt, before the first branched lightning bolt pushed a charge through the humidity and raised the little hairs on the back of her arms.

Charged, electric, breathless—that was exactly how Nicole felt now, sitting in the driver's seat, when she finally glimpsed the exit ramp to Pine Lake. After more than four thousand miles of anticipation, she turned the car onto the off-ramp. At the bottom, she took a left onto the rural road. The steering wheel dug into her sternum as she pressed close to read the old wooden sign:

Welcome to Pine Lake.

In the passenger seat, Claire released a long, slow sigh. In the back, Jenna shifted into life. A church-morning silence descended as they made their way down the half mile toward the center of the town.

Nicole recognized a patch of birch trees that marked the turnoff that led to the Historic Sayward Sawmill, a field trip destination for every Pine Lake middle schooler. She could still hear the drone of the docent's voice telling the story of the first Vermont settler, a soldier who'd fought in the French and Indian War. He returned to his native mountains after the war long enough to convince his family of the riches waiting for them if they built a sawmill in these deep woods. Behind that sawmill's waterwheel she'd shared her first sloppy kiss with Joey Colfax while moss squished beneath her sneakers.

The hairs on the back of her arms rose as she glimpsed the buildings on the north edge of Pine Lake. She saw the gas station, the machine tool and die shop, and, most important, the auto body shop that her uncle had once owned. She eased her foot off the gas, wishing she could pop in for just a few minutes to breathe in the smell of the grease and hear the whirr of power tools and the banging of pneumatic hammers. For two years, she'd pestered her uncle to allow her to work in that shop until he'd indulged her during senior year. He spent the next year trying to convince her to forgo college and take it over so he could spend his time fly-fishing. Now the new owners advertised a thirty-minute oil-and-lube with one of those tall, floppy-armed undulating balloon men.

At thirty-five miles an hour, she raced past it with her heart feeling like a rubber band pulled backward. It sprung back as she glimpsed a converted railroad car belching blue smoke. How many platters of greasy burgers and French-Canadian steak fries with gravy had she eaten in the laminate booths of that diner? Back in his train-obsessed days, Emile's had been Noah's favorite eatery.

She drew in a breath to say, *Let's stop in Emile's for an early lunch*—but she halted before the words formed. Nicole had promised Jenna she would get them to Camp Paskagamak by one in the afternoon, the only free time in the campers' tight schedule. In the rearview mirror, she saw Jenna clutching Lucky close, scratching the pup into an upright doze while her gaze fixed on some middle distance.

Nicole forcibly calmed herself down. She felt like a six-year-old waking up in the dark of an early Christmas morning, her hopes flaring to life with the intensity of a Roman candle, forced by a solemn promise to stay fixed in bed until gray slats of light filtered through the blinds. Only then could she leap upon her parents' bed to announce the arrival of Christmas morning.

She told herself they'd be back in Pine Lake tomorrow

afternoon. She would have *days* to play tourist, even to un-familiar neighborhoods like the one they were now entering. Nicole slowed down in the residential area of Cannery Row. She used to be afraid of passing through this area in her youth, partly from her mother's warnings and partly because of its shady, seemingly shiftless collection of men loitering on corners. The small two-family houses stood only a few feet back from the sidewalk. Their porches sagged and their shutters peeled and they were bleached gray, like Monopoly houses that had baked out in the sun too long. Between the buildings, she glimpsed cluttered backyards that sloped to the water's edge. One house bore a sign that said *Antiques*. The little patch of front lawn was cluttered with an exuber-ant collection of birdbaths and whirligigs and resin replicas of the Virgin Mary.

The cannery itself loomed into view, a four-floor struc-ture by the banks of the river, stained with streaks of rust and pocked with broken windows. In the early twentieth cen-tury, it processed a motley mix of Hudson River fish but later turned to pickled cabbage and red beets and sauerkraut until American tastes changed and the costs of improving mech-anization proved too much for the owners. She knew, from several forbidden youthful trips into the building, that it was dark and excitingly creepy and still smelled vaguely of vine-gar. She wondered if her initials were still spray-painted in black next to Drake's on the second floor wall.

Claire shifted forward to get a good look at the place. "I'm astonished that old thing hasn't become a galleria or a mall by now."

"Bite your tongue," Nicole said. "If they developed it, where would the next generation of Pine Lake get into mischief?"

Jenna shuffled forward between the front seats. "My mother told me that it took the city council two years to commission a new sign for the town. Just imagine how long it's going to take for them to sell that property."

Claire stopped braiding her hair to squint down the road. "Hey, is that really Ray's General Store up ahead?"

Jenna said, "It's run by Ray's son now—Bob."

"My dad used to say there wasn't a piece of fishing or camping equipment known to man that you couldn't find in those aisles."

"I used to buy pine tar there," Nicole said. "And softball bats."

Jenna made a muffled snorting sound. "Like you didn't wander up here just to watch Drake Weldon unloading stock."

Nicole's face went warm at the memory of the tall, lanky hockey player with the charming broken canine.

"Yeah, Barbie and Ken." Claire eyeballed the beach balls and folding chairs and plastic kayaks piled up outside the old store. "I was sure you two would give birth to two-point-five children destined for major league sports."

"Pul-eese." Nicole paused at one of the three stoplights in town. Then, from old habit, she turned right toward the old square. "That boy spent more time on his hair than I did on mine. I don't think we exchanged more than six words all year. He kept trying to get me to the cannery to—"

Her words stopped on a breath. The beating heart of the town spread before her in full end-of-summer vacation mode. The streets teamed with tourists in khaki capris and flip-flops, wearing straw hats and carrying oversize canvas beach bags. The porch of the Adirondack Inn was full of folks eating brook trout seared in a butter sauce. Even Josey's, the tiny restaurant that served five-dollar pancake breakfasts with real Adirondack maple syrup, had set a couple of plastic tables on the sidewalk in front of their establishment. Among the little boutiques strolled the better-dressed tourists, the ones who'd probably taken rooms in one of the Victorian B&Bs that graced the slope of the old town.

Claire reached back to tap Jenna on the knee. "Jenna, look—the Book Bag. It's still here."

"Yes it is." Jenna glanced balefully at the tiny storefront. "I single-handedly kept that bookstore afloat during my high school years."

Claire said, "Maybe now it's kept afloat by that chain store café that opened up beside it."

Nicole said, "That didn't kill Ricky's Roast, did it? I'll be so mad if it shut down because of some chain."

Jenna asked, "What's the fascination with Ricky's Roast? Did you really drink coffee in high school?"

"How else do you think I managed two sports, three clubs, and a college-bound course load?"

"You're perfect."

Nicole snorted. "You were woefully misinformed. Caffeine, the magic elixir." She did a little leap in her seat when she caught sight of her old haunt. "There it is—Ricky's Roast. Oh, my gosh, it hasn't changed."

Claire murmured, "It's still full of men with scruffy beards."

"God, yes," Nicole breathed.

Jenna shook her head. "Wow. Two coffeehouses in town now. The Saint Regis brats are really taking over the place."

Nicole reached back to slap at air as Jenna cringed away, laughing. Then, suddenly, they were driving out of the square and onto the winding residential roads past all the neat little cape houses that were rented out during the summer. The swiftness took Nicole by surprise. The square had seemed endless to the high school girl she once had been, and also to the summer tourist that she had become. Then again, most places seemed endless when you're tugging three children alongside you.

Nicole tried to keep her eyes on the road and her mind on the route to Camp Paskagamak, but the pattern of the dappled light—so lovely, so familiar—brought on memories both old and new. Late August was the season of fund-raising car washes, of watching the returning college boys sprawl on the lake beaches. Late August was the season of menthol-scented sunburn cream, of shopping in Ray's for packages of clean white paper and fresh spiral notebooks. Late August was Noah and Christian and Julia toasted golden and coated with coarse-grained lake sand that she'd still be scrubbing out of their hair in September. Late August was when time felt elastic, stretched to its limit as she swam in warm waters under cool skies.

Her heart leapt as she caught sight of another sign on the west edge of town.

Claire drawled, "Well, look at that. Bay Roberts, just beyond those trees."

A grove of quivering aspens revealed teasing glimpses of the lake. Nicole tried to keep her eyes on the road but somehow she saw it all anyway, the winding shaded path, the picnic tables, the bright water, the long gray dock.

The urge was almost unbearable. She imagined herself pulling the car off the asphalt onto the soft dirt shoulder. She imagined racing down the pine-needle path, over sand that sizzled and gave under her toes. She imagined the soles of her feet hitting the weathered boards of the old pier as she made a beeline to the far edge. She imagined raising her arms above her head and pushing off the end of the pier, sailing through the air before plunging into the cool green underwater world.

"Hey, Jenna," Claire asked, "how's Lucky doing?"

"He's just fine." Jenna set his tags jingling with a scratch. "I'd say he's good for an hour or so—"

"Are you sure about that?" Claire interrupted. "There's pretty much nothing between here and the camp, nothing but trees and hills."

"What else does a dog need?"

"Maybe he needs a little time romping in the water. Maybe he needs, say, ten minutes to bask in the sun." Claire lifted her arms. "I know I'm ready for a stretch."

Nicole figured she must be glowing with a sort of blue luminescence, or her yearning was emitting a high whine just on the edge of hearing, because why else in the sudden silence of the car would Claire be looking at her with a sly smile on her face?

"Hey, Nic," Jenna said. "Promise me you'll wear a bathing suit, okay?"

Chapter Twenty

Camp Paskagamak, Pine Lake

J enna last laid eyes on the entrance to Camp Paskagamak nearly twenty years ago, when she'd finished her final summer as a Master Ranger. Now the Chevy rocked over the same dirt road, plunging into the same ditch of tire tracks, only to clamber over a ridge into a second puddle-pocked set of tracks. She leaned forward to get a better look at the bent-wood lattice that arched over the entranceway, trying not to whack her head against the back of the driver's seat as the car lurched. The sign still spelled out the name of the camp in woody letters. Beyond, the road opened up to a clearing faced by a familiar log cabin. The word *Office* had been charcoal-burned into the gable.

The nausea that rose up her throat wasn't from car sickness. It was an echo of anxiety and excitement that used to grip her whenever her parents dropped her off here in early July. In the sweaty humidity—or in the pouring rain—there had always been a confusion of cars and luggage and green-shirted Master Rangers with clipboards doing their smiling best to herd her away from her parents and through the office door. She'd be worrying that her campmates from Canada hadn't signed up again; she'd be wondering if any of the new girls in her bunkhouse would be mean; she'd be anxious at being forced to play the first-evening ice-breaking games that required tying her wrists up to strangers or accepting random hugs.

With all its forced communal activities, all signs indicated that as a child, she would hate this camp. But at the mess hall, she never ate alone. At the lake, she never lacked a swimming partner. And the cabins proved to be potent incubators hatching the kind of instant friendships that could be stretched for a month and then linger for years of pen-pal closeness.

Jenna rolled down the window and filled her lungs with the scent of green growing things and sticky sap. It was a singular source of joy that Zoe loved this place, too. Over the years, Zoe had zoomed her way through Fox Circle to Wolf Pack Den to Brown Bear Lair to Moose Marsh to Hawk Heights. Maybe, if Zoe set her mind to it, she'd make it to Apprentice Forest Ranger this year, as every Hogan had done for the past three generations. The blood-sister secrets of this camp had been one of the few things Jenna could share with Zoe alone, impishly holding them back from Nate, who would just shake his head and smile.

As Nicole pulled to a stop, Jenna clicked a leash on Lucky and shoved the door open so he could tumble outside to do his business. Cicadas screamed in the trees. The sun baked the russet needle carpet of the clearing. The trunks of the white pines, arrow straight, formed a formidable fence beyond the camp office.

She tightened her grip on the leash as her mind raced. Even if she could finagle her way past that front desk—an unlikely process—there was a good chance that Zoe wouldn't even want to talk to her. Zoe probably treated this place as the perfect one-month retreat from the trouble at home.

And here Jenna was, dragging that trouble right to Zoe's cabin door.

"So," Claire mused, "this is the famous Camp Paskagamak."

Claire stood arms akimbo, eyeballing the main office cabin and beyond to the emerald shadows of the woods. Jenna forgot that Claire hadn't attended the summer camp. Most of the kids who grew up in Pine Lake attended, but Claire was considered a come-away because she'd only moved to town in middle school when her father got a job as a park ranger.

"I expected sniper's towers and barbed wire." Claire pulled her braid through the back of her Iowa seed-cap hat. "I'm terribly disappointed."

"They're hidden in the trees." Nicole rounded the car to join them. Her hair was still damp from her swim at Bay Roberts. "Jenna, are you sure you want to play this straight?"

Jenna nodded as a sudden pressure squeezed her chest.

"As far as I know," Nicole continued, "no excuse less

than a death in the family will allow a camper to see her parents before End-of-Days."

Jenna raised a two-finger salute. "Camp Rangers don't lie."

"For the love of Buddha," Claire said, "I knew this place was a cult."

Nicole glanced warily toward the office. "Okay, here's my advice. Don't let Mrs. Garfunkle frazzle you. You know the rules, you respect the rules, you understand the rules. But you've driven clear across this great big country to see your daughter. Look Godzilla in the eye. Be assertive. Be reasonable. Be unafraid."

Jenna nodded her head so hard that the clip in her hair wobbled.

"And if that doesn't work"—Nicole slapped the hood of the Lumina—"we've got flashlights, water bottles, good walking shoes, and a map of the camp. My phone has a compass if we get lost. We'll head around to the main electric shed on the northwest side and hike a mile to the wigwams."

Claire said, "Wow. Next time I plan to rob a convenience store, Nic, I'm calling you."

Jenna tugged Lucky into action and headed toward the porch. The screen door squealed open to the chemical smell of mosquito repellent and coconut sunscreen. It slammed shut behind them as Jenna's eyes adjusted to the dim interior. On the wall hung a large map of the camp complex, pinhole-studded and curling at the corners. Around it were scattered framed photos of campers past, from the grainy black-and-white shots of solemn children in woolen bathing suits from the 1920s to the mud-smeared and chalk-tattooed urchins of the more recent crop. Behind the battered counter, an older woman sat in front of a computer monitor, her head tilted up so she could see through the narrow reading glasses perched on the tip of her nose.

"Welcome to Camp Paskagamak," she sang, raising a hand. "I'll be right with you."

Mrs. Garfunkle had been at least sixty when Jenna had been a camper. At least that was what she and the girls had estimated back when Jenna was thirteen and sixty years old seemed just one bout of poison ivy short of the grave. Now the camp director stretched up to her full four feet seven inches, all dentured smiles and snow-angel white hair.

Claire leaned in and whispered, "Godzilla?"

"Another group of lost sheep, I see." Mrs. Garfunkle planted her hands on her square-bodied hips. "You ladies must really be lost if you found your way all the way out here."

"We're not lost," Jenna said. "We've come to see you."

"Ah, well, we don't do tours during the season." She reached for a map and a booklet entitled *Historic Camp Paskagamak*. She pulled a pencil from behind her ear. "Touring interferes with the disciplined schedule we set up for the young men and women, so today I'm afraid you'll be confined to what you can see of the place from the back of this cabin. You are welcome to come back in a week when we've—wait." Mrs. Garfunkle squinted at her. "I know you."

Jenna swore she could smell it: that strange mix of onion and lavender that billowed off the camp director, as if the woman bathed in bath salts in the morning then ate a burrito for breakfast.

Mrs. Garfunkle seemed to be laboring, so Jenna decided to help her along. "Master Forest Ranger Jen Hogan, here," she said, cutting herself off before adding *reporting for duty*.

"My faith, it is you, Jenna." Mrs. Garfunkle's blue eyes were swallowed by a bed of happy folds. "Between the dog and the fancy hair you fooled me for a minute. But there's no hiding the straight posture of a girl who in her sixth year made Ranger of the Year."

Claire exploded in a coughing fit.

Jenna tried very hard not to flush. "I'm sure there have been many since."

"Oh, no, only a few sixth-years ever made that distinction, and all in better days. Still, I try to remember every last brave, every last squaw, even if it is politically incorrect to call the girls that these days." She glanced behind Jenna, to Claire swallowing her humor and Nicole standing by the door. Her gaze hesitated on Nicole's face before giving her a nod and returning her attention to Jenna. "It's a pleasure to see you, Ranger Hogan, but certainly you didn't come all the way up here to see the camp?"

"That would be against regulations," Jenna said. "Ordinance number three section D, expressly prohibiting any individual or individuals not previously sanctioned by the Council of Elders to stray into Paskagamak hunting lands during the season of the Long Days."

Mrs. Garfunkle pulled off her reading glasses to look at Jenna more closely, ignoring Claire's next coughing fit. It occurred to Jenna that her first introduction to a foreign culture was here at camp, with all its protocol and particular rules and muddled Indian culture references and language. She'd thrived under the strictures. Unlike the fluid social soup of high school, here she understood the rules. Here, she felt like she was home.

"Well." Mrs. Garfunkle took great care cleaning her glasses with the hem of her camp polo shirt. "I must say, most campers forget the rules from one year to another."

"I wouldn't dare. I have a daughter in her fifth year."

"Do you?" She tugged at the whistle hanging from her neck, puzzling. "I would think I would have remembered you had I seen you at the Opening or at the End-of-Days."

"My husband or my parents usually take care of the drop-off and pickup."

"Oh?"

The camp director's response was distracted. Jenna could tell she was mentally flipping through her memory of current campers in an effort to identify her daughter. Then the director waved a hand in the air. "Well, End-of-Days is this coming Sunday, so I suppose I'll be seeing you then—"

"Actually, I'd like to see my daughter now."

Jenna watched as Mrs. Garfunkle's smile hardened and cracked like clay left too long in the sun. Those blue eyes narrowed. The director's shoulders slid back and her spine straightened and her lungs expanded so she seemed to grow and lengthen like some cartoon superhero. Here was the sachem with the jaw of iron. This was the woman with a set of lungs that could blow a whistle until Canadian wolves howled over the border. Here was the Godzilla stare that could make a teenager blurt all the camp-bed secrets she'd drawn blood and pinkie-sworn never to tell.

"Ranger Hogan, you know perfectly well there's a strict prohibition on family visits except on the two prescheduled End-of-Days."

"I realize that my request violates protocol."

"Rules, not protocol. Rules are the very pillar—"

"—of civilization. I'm willing to abide by the rules, Master Ranger Garfunkle. I came today to ask for sanction by the Council of Elders."

"A situation covered by regulation seventeen part B." Mrs. Garfunkle's eyes narrowed to slits. "Has there been a sudden major illness or a death in the family?"

Only a death of the family.

Jenna bit back the words. She couldn't mention the divorce. A divorce meant a conflict between parents. Mrs. Garfunkle would defy taking a side in any domestic dispute, and Jenna didn't want to give the camp director any reason to have her escorted off the campgrounds.

She said, "No, not a death."

"Well, that settles it then." The director slipped on her glasses. "You know that we here at Camp Paskagamak take special pride in nurturing in our young rangers the importance of personal responsibility and growing independence, and these rules serve to foster those qualities that are ever more important in today's society." Mrs. Garfunkle strode to her desk and splayed her fingertips over the surface. "Ranger, I must admit I'm disappointed."

Jenna felt the little muscles at the base of her neck contract. She wasn't a thirteen-year-old girl anymore. For all the camp's rules, she knew very well that there was no legal way Mrs. Garfunkle or anyone else could keep her away from her daughter. So, as Claire had taught her while meditating at Niagara Falls, she mindfully noticed her body's physical reaction to the stress. She noted it, sensed it, admitted it, and dismissed it. Then she pressed her sneakered feet flat on the pine-knotted wood of the floors.

"The Council must reconsider." Jenna heard Claire and Nicole shuffle close behind her. "There are extenuating circumstances of a personal nature that will have a direct effect on Zoe's sense of self-worth—"

"Zoe?" Mrs. Garfunkle froze as she tugged her glasses off her face. "Do you mean Zoe *Elliott?*"

Jenna realized she'd neglected to mention her married last name, a lapse that caused so much confusion among teachers, doctors, and coaches at home that she just let them all call her Mrs. Elliott.

Mrs. Garfunkle's liver-spotted hand fluttered to her chest, where it lay, patting, patting, patting. The older woman opened her mouth and then just as quickly shut it. She pressed her mouth so tight that her lips went white. Then Mrs. Garfunkle dropped into the desk chair and attacked the keyboard.

Jenna pressed against the counter, trying to see what the camp director was typing. A terrible foreboding gripped her. Zoe was okay, she told herself. Zoe couldn't be hurt. The camp would have contacted her parents. Her parents would have contacted her. She had a new phone but the same cell phone number. If they contacted Nate, then he would have called her from Seattle if something was wrong.

Another thought arose, an ugly thought, like a troll waddling from under a dank bridge. Nate knew she was coming to Pine Lake. Maybe Nate flew in and took Zoe away before she could have a chance to talk to Zoe alone.

Mrs. Garfunkle said, "You're in luck. Zoe is just about to start archery."

Jenna collapsed against the counter so hard that the edge dug into her solar plexus.

Mrs. Garfunkle reached for the corded phone. "I'll have your daughter report to Wawobi Point. I assume you remember the way?"

༕

Zoe had dyed her hair purple.

Sitting on a fallen weathered log at Wawobi Point, Jenna watched that bobbing purple head as Zoe wound her way through the pine woods. Jenna wondered where on earth Zoe had bought the dyeing kit. They certainly didn't sell things like *that* at the camp Trading Post. The closest general store to the camp was a tiny grocery in a one-crossroads town six miles away, an escape-and-return that no girl had ever accomplished without being caught. Zoe must have bought the kit in Seattle and smuggled it in. Jenna imagined she'd done the dye job in the communal bathroom sometime in the middle of the night.

Jenna understood the act of defiance. Zoe had a reason to be suspicious of authority figures she'd once trusted. She watched Zoe approach while her heart stumbled through a three-step shuffle in her chest. Her daughter dug her high-top sneakers deep in pine litter and dragged the rubberized toe through. Her shocking magenta hair lay over her brow in choppy pieces. As she came closer, Jenna realized it wasn't just the bangs that had been cut short. All that lovely, light blonde hair that once fell to the middle of her back…Zoe had taken scissors to that, too.

Look what you've done to our strong young fledgling, Nate.

Zoe shuffled to a stop on the other side of the log. "I guess this means the bitch is finally expelling me."

The expletive exploded between them. Jenna lost the power to speak while she waited for the shock wave to pass. She'd never before heard such a word in her daughter's little-girl voice. She tangled with the competing urges to reprimand her or ignore her.

When unsure, Nicole had advised, speak the facts in a nonjudgmental voice. "Master Ranger Garfunkle is not expelling you, Zoe."

"Man, what do I have to do to break out of this place?" Zoe kicked over some reedy wild mustard. "She's been riding my ass all summer about my hair, about my eyeliner, about my piercing, about my 'attitude.'"

Zoe turned her head just far enough so Jenna could see a flash of silver hanging from her ear. Right next to the little silver stud from Zoe's first piercing, Jenna caught sight of a paper clip holding up a long chain of other paper clips.

Neutral voice. "I hope you iced that ear good before you put the needle in."

"I didn't even feel it."

"I'm glad it's not your eyebrow." She glanced at the hem of Zoe's T-shirt. "Or your navel."

"I'll be getting a navel piercing on my fourteenth birthday." She crossed her arms. "Dad promised."

Jenna absorbed that little tidbit thinking it sounded like a pie-crust promise, thinking it sounded like a bribe.

"Look," Zoe said, "if I'm not being expelled, then who died?"

"Nobody died."

"It has to be something real bad for Godzilla to break, like, a thousand regulations."

Jenna forced her voice calm. "I'm here because I need to talk to you about what's going on between your father and me."

Zoe's face went still. It was a cold, swift tensing of muscle that looked so strange on a face still round with baby fat.

Jenna knotted her fingers together and then braced them against her knees. "It's about nine months too late, but your father finally told me about Siss—Mrs. Leclaire."

"Well, it's about fucking time."

"That wouldn't be Algonquin for 'finally,' would it?"

Zoe twisted and sat down with a huff on the log. "How did you figure it out? Did you catch him sneaking out her back door at night when he was supposedly working in the garage? Or did you catch them doing it on the living room couch? Or did you find her tent-size cotton underwear under that chair in Dad's workshop?"

Jenna felt like she'd been struck in the back of the head. She unlocked her fingers and flattened them on the gnarly bark of the log. "That was a multiple-choice question, and you didn't offer me a 'none of the above.'"

"Gawd, Mom."

"It's actually a virtue to have absolute faith in someone's loyalty."

Zoe's whole body heaved as she made a huff of such cynicism that Jenna winced.

"I only found out after we put you on the plane," she explained. "That's when your father handed me the petition for divorce."

Zoe's head swiveled. One incredulous blue eye peeped out from a rim of black eyeliner. "Divorce?"

"Alas."

"Wow," Zoe said, blinking. "He's really doing it."

"I'm afraid so—"

"After all that," Zoe barked, her voice rising. "After all that, he just went ahead and did it anyway."

The words rang in Jenna's head. *He did it anyway.* As if Nate had discussed the possibility of divorce with his thirteen-year-old daughter before he'd talked about it with his own wife. *He did it anyway.* Her mind tumbled, struggling to think up a different scenario—any scenario—that would prompt Zoe to say such a thing.

Zoe's blue gaze skittered away to find interest in something on the other side of the lake. "So, did Daddy also tell you that he knocked the bitch up?"

Jenna raised a hand as if to catch her brain before it exploded out of her skull. To think she'd worried about how unethical it was to visit Zoe without Nate's knowledge. To think she'd almost texted Nate ten minutes ago to let him know she and Zoe were going to have a one-on-one. To think she'd been ready to reassure him that she'd only wanted to let Zoe know that she didn't have to keep secrets anymore.

"He knocks up a neighbor, and you've got nothing to say?" Zoe said. "Aren't you furious at him?"

Jenna thought about the tangle of emotions she'd carried with her when she'd flung a box of mementos in the trunk of her car and set off for a new life...the shame and the shock and the crushing sense of worthlessness and failure. Later there had been anger, too, but it had been like a comet, a flare and then a flameout.

"Anger is like a hot coal, Zoe. If you hang on to it for too long, then you're the one who'll get burned."

"What, did you read that on a Hallmark card somewhere?"

"Wisdom from a Buddhist nun."

Zoe cast her that blue eye again. "Well, if you're not angry, that means you can't ground me."

"Ground you for what? A bad purple dye job and a piercing?"

"For keeping those secrets for Dad."

Jenna managed to just brush her fingertips against the frizzing purple ends of Zoe's hair before Zoe shifted away, scuffing down the log out of arm's reach. Jenna sat there with her arm outstretched and her ribs squeezing her breath out of her body.

"I was never mad at you, Zoe, never, ever, not once."
What could she say to make everything better? "Your father
shouldn't have burdened you with such a secret. It was
wrong. He wasn't thinking clearly."

"Yeah, I saw that much." Zoe took intense interest in the
chipped purple nail polish on her fingers. "So I guess that
it's going to be me sharing a room with my new stepsister
Natalie while Dad shares a room with his second wife Sissy
and we all wait with joy for the arrival of our new little half
brother or half sister like one big weirdly fractured dysfunc-
tional family."

Jenna's mind was starting to hurt. "That's something
we'll have to work out."

"Whose house, ours or...*hers?*"

"Your father wants to keep the house."

"After all he's done?"

"Oregon is a no-fault state." She shrugged as if she could
dismiss fourteen years of joyous nesting. "I'll probably get an
apartment nearby."

"Where would I stay, in the house or your apartment?"

"The house. It'll always be your home." Jenna braced
herself to hit Zoe with the next wave of truth. "You should
know that your father is asking for full legal and physical custody."

"What does that even *mean?*"

"He wants to be the main parent. I'll get visitation
rights."

"What, like I'm in prison?"

"It's going to be complicated."

"No shit, Sherlock."

"It's going to be complicated," she repeated, "because I'm going to counter and ask for *shared* legal and physical custody."

Zoe turned her face away, but Jenna knew her baby. She knew the curve of that cheek. She knew when it quivered a certain way that Zoe was biting the inside of her lip, that her chin was starting to pucker. This was a lot for a thirteen-year-old to absorb, too much, all at once. Jenna had vowed she wouldn't make the same mistake Nate had by putting too much of a burden on those slim shoulders.

"So," Jenna said, changing the subject, "did you get any of my postcards?"

"Yeah."

"Nice vacation, huh?"

"It's *weird*. Did you really camp out at an archaeological dig?"

"In South Dakota. I also went skinny-dipping in Lake Michigan."

"Gawd, Mom, TMI."

They sat in silence for a little while. A woodpecker clattered away in the trees. A chipmunk darted out from a root, crossed in front of them, and burrowed in the litter. Jenna recognized the birdsong of a cardinal whistling through the woods, and after a long pause, she heard another cardinal respond in the distance.

Zoe finally said, "You still haven't told me how you convinced Godzilla to break, like, four epic rules to let you in here."

"I'll explain that as soon as you tell me why the Great Sachem tossed those rules to the wind upon hearing your name."

"You go first."

"Would you believe I threatened to break in from the northwest with a SWAT team?"

A spark of a smile, extinguished far too quickly.

"Actually, I was ready to have my Master Ranger badge ripped off my chest for the chance to talk to you. I had a backup plan that involved trekking to the wigwams after dark, but first I tried a frontal assault. I figured it would fail. Then Godzilla heard your name and she practically drove me here in the camp golf cart."

Zoe's mouth curved. "We hijacked that golf cart just last week."

"Well, that does raise some interesting questions. Your turn."

Zoe's smile fell. "You should know right now that I won't be making Apprentice Ranger."

Jenna heard a ribbon of regret amid the defiance. "Five years to Apprentice Ranger is almost unheard of, you know. There's always next year to earn that badge."

"That badge doesn't mean *anything*. This whole place is a joke. I won't be coming back next year."

Zoe launched up from the log. Jenna saw little bits of bark peppering the backs of her thighs as Zoe strode down the path. Nicole had warned her that a lot of teenage mood swings stemmed less from hormones than from the stew of confusion, self-doubt, ambivalence, guilt, and anger that young adults were just learning to handle. Jenna's instinct was to run after her daughter, pull her into an embrace, and hold her little girl until Zoe stopped fighting. But Zoe wasn't a little girl anymore, and Jenna sensed that holding her like that would only make her feel smothered.

Jenna caught up with Zoe just as the archery range came into view. "Listen—"

"You didn't come to get me out of here, Mom. So why don't you just go back to your *friends?*"

"I intend to."

She let Zoe absorb that as she walked in the flat-footed way she'd once been taught in these very woods.

"I am going back," Jenna repeated, "because you need a few days here to make a certain decision."

"What?" She flung her arms up. "Am I supposed to decide *now*? Between you and Dad?"

"You'll never have to make that decision. It's been a horror show lately, Zoe, but your father and I both love you, and in the end, we'll do what's best for you."

"Blah blah blah."

"I realize that over the past months you've had to grow up much faster than you should have—"

"Am I old enough to get a navel piercing now?"

"Those secrets your father made you keep put a big distance between you and me."

Zoe made a noise as if she'd wanted to say something but then, at the last moment, swallowed it down.

"So, respecting the fact that you've had to grapple with big issues, I'm going to make you an offer."

"Can I refuse it?"

"I wouldn't blame you if you did. It's a radical change of plans. You'd be giving up a week at Nana's. You'd be giving up all those home-cooked meals and daily trips to Six Flags."

"It better be good."

"I drove all the way here from Seattle in Grandpa's old Lumina. I have to get it back home. If you can stand being in that car with your less-than-perfect mother for five or six days," Jenna breathed, "I would love for you to join me for the road trip home."

Chapter Twenty-one

To: Paulina, Alice, Zuza Petrenko
From: Nicole Eriksen
Subject: Camp Rule #34: Never Come Between a Mama Bear and Her Cub
Attached: GodzillaLives.jpg; BreachingThePerimeter.jpg; MissionAccomplished.jpg

We can neither confirm nor deny that these photos were taken yesterday at thirteen hundred hours (during the "Long Days") near Paskagamak Lake at an undisclosed location deep in the Adirondack Mountains. What I can tell you is that it took Herculean restraint not to toss my smelly old sneakers over the bentwood entrance sign like we all used to do at End-of-Days.

According to Jenna, we've added 4,470 miles onto the odometer in order to get us right here. Our reservation is set for eleven thirty this morning at the old Birchbark

Rafting Company. Claire will finally get to check the box—come hell or, more likely, high water.

It's been a long, wonderful trip. It's doubly strange to find ourselves home at this time of year, when the sun still sizzles during the day but the air goes cool in the evenings, when, in the old days, we'd be growing nostalgic about summer even as our minds turned to the new school year. It feels the same way for us as we count down the last days of our adventure here in our old stomping grounds.

The only thing that's missing is all of you.

As they drove closer to the Hudson River Gorge, Nicole pulled the plug on the GPS and let the screen go dark. She didn't really need directions. These roads followed the familiar meanderings of shallow, rock-strewn streams that now and again revealed a fly fisherman or a pair of helmeted kayakers. While navigating them, she heard in her mind the shout-singing of her softball team as if she were riding not in Jenna's Lumina but instead in a hired bus to an away game in high school. She and her teammates used to stand in the aisle or braced their arms against the backs of the chairs, howling as they sang the Pine Lake Beavers song. Not just the official one, but the one with all the dirty jokes, too, as the bus careened far too fast around the hairpin turns or rattled over potholes not yet fixed after the long winter.

She sidled a glance at Claire, who wasn't meditating but had nonetheless grown unnervingly still since they'd left the inn this morning. That stillness made Nicole anxious. She wished Claire was as lost in youthful memories as she was and not worrying herself into knots about the prospect of whitewater rafting.

A phone beeped, breaking the silence.

Claire spoke without glancing from her window reverie. "Nic, darling, you must get a thousand texts a day."

"That's not my phone."

Claire nudged her tote bag with her foot. "I know it's not mine."

Jenna jerked up in the backseat and dug for her cell. She sucked in a breath as she glanced at the face. "It's a text from Mrs. Garfunkle."

"That's impossible." Nicole flicked a look in the rearview mirror. "The phone in that office was tethered and had a rotary dial."

Claire said drily, "Apparently Godzilla owns a cell phone, too."

Nicole shook her head. "First Mrs. Garfunkle lets Jenna onto the sacred grounds during the Season of the Long Days, and now she's allowing electronic communications. All the sacred institutions are falling. What's next, a satellite dish on the Trading Post?"

Nicole watched in the rearview mirror as Jenna's face, awash in the light of the cell-phone screen, became suffused with nothing less than a heavenly glow. Nicole's heart did a little leap of relief. After everything Jenna had told her yesterday, Nicole hadn't been so sure that her discussion with Zoe would end well.

"Let me guess." Claire rolled her head against the headrest in order to glance into the backseat. "Zoe said yes to the road trip."

"Yes." Jenna's laugh was shaky with relief. "Yes! Mrs. Garfunkle also says she only allowed this communication because Zoe promised not to toilet-paper any more buildings in the last few days of camp."

Claire said, "A girl after my own heart."

Jenna pressed her phone against her throat. "I hope you two don't mind. It's going to get crowded in this car on the way back home."

Nicole said, "No, it won't."

"But with Zoe's duffel in the trunk and Lucky's bed taking up half the—"

"No, no," Nicole interrupted, "Zoe doesn't want to do this trip with two middle-aged women sitting in the backseat breathing all over her. And just imagine how much you two could talk if you were alone in that car for thousnads of miles."

"But what about you and Claire?"

"If you're okay doing the drive, then Claire and I will fly home."

"But Claire doesn't fly."

Claire made a snorting sound. "I lied about that."

"What?"

"Back in Oregon, I told you I didn't fly because I wanted to convince you to drive across country. It's a much more mindful way of travel, don't you agree?"

"Why, you lying Buddhist."

"Even Buddhists allow for an occasional evasion," Claire said, "as long as it does some good and no harm."

Nicole eased up on the gas as they approached a hairpin turn.

"Jenna, are you worried about driving all that distance by yourself?"

"No, I'm fine driving. It's talking to my teenager that has me in a cold sweat."

"I hear you. I'll make all the flight arrangements when we get to Pine Lake."

In truth, Nicole was relieved to be flying home. Not just because she was developing a swollen rock of a calf on her gas-pedal leg, but because they were running out of time. Noah would be coming back from the residential facility in ten days. Even a direct route home meant driving three thousand miles, and she'd hoped to stay for at least a long weekend in Pine Lake.

Nicole snuck a glance at her other lost sheep, who was staring out the window as if to map every curve of every stream. With one arm pressed against her midriff, bracing her other elbow, Claire chewed on the end of her thumb. On her lap sat a package of chocolate pretzels, unopened.

Nicole understood how Claire felt. At least, she thought she understood. For Claire, this final goal was the equivalent of, say, the last, tense, all-or-nothing playoff game of a long high school career—with all the fierce expectations, pressure to perform, and the stomach-churning conviction that failure and disappointment were inevitable.

Nicole understood the feelings even though she *hadn't* experienced them on her last, tense, all-or-nothing playoff game of her high school career. That special morning she'd woken up intensely aware that once that playoff game was over—and win or lose, it would be epic, every bright crack of the bat seared in her mind—then never again would she arrive on the softball field on a bright April morning with the chill of snow in the air. Never again as captain would she grasp the icy iron of the lock as she opened the shed to the musty blast of wood and mold. Never again would she set out the bases and the bats and balls while the other players sleepwalked onto the field. For all intents, the high school career she loved was over and the halcyon days done. All that remained was to enjoy the moment.

"Hey, Claire," Nicole said, her heart rising in her throat, "do you remember that Cubs game in Chicago?"

Claire stopped chewing on her thumb long enough to give her an odd look. "Is this a pop quiz?"

"I've been thinking about that rookie closing pitcher who came out on the field in the ninth inning."

"I remember the pitcher we drank in the Cubby Bear after."

"The game was tied. There was a man on first." Nicole kept her eyes on the road, but she could feel Claire's reluctant curiosity. "You have to remember it. We stood up because everyone in the whole stadium was standing up, and roaring, and watching the pitcher's every wind-up. The whole ball game hung on how well that one guy pitched."

"Do I get extra-credit points for remembering I had to pee?"

"Forty-one thousand nineteen people were watching that poor sap. That guy should have been a wreck. He should have been sweating bullets."

Claire paused, as if remembering the focused, unwavering, cold-as-ice look on the rookie's face at the same moment she realized what Nicole was trying to say. "At least he wasn't facing mortal peril."

"Wasn't he?" Nicole said. "A ninety-six-mile-per-hour fastball can do a lot of damage if someone hits it straight toward his head. That boy," she said, knowing the Cub's rookie was only twenty-two, "knew that he had to focus on getting into position, on the signals the catcher was sending him, on settling his fingers just the right way along the seam, on the feel of the wind on his face, on winding up and letting athletic instinct take over as he threw a pitch the same way he's been throwing a pitch since his high school coach chose him from the crowd of hopefuls and put him on the mound. Claire, you have to do the same thing today."

"Pitch in a major league baseball game?"

"Approach this situation in the exact same way I've watched you handle everything that's been thrown at you."

"Give up?"

The words hung in the air. Nicole forced herself not to be angry, even though what she wanted to do was pull the car over and give her friend a good, long shake. Instead, she took one deep breath and then took another so she would feel the blood rush to her brain. Yes, Claire had given up on many things. But Claire didn't see herself the way the rest of the world did. She didn't see a strong, determined woman who was her own worst enemy.

Nicole said, "You've driven forty-five hundred miles in a creaking car that smells like ranch-flavored potato chips and wet dog. You've put up with me listening to a hundred hours of country music, without a word of complaint—"

"No risk of drowning there."

"You've publicly line-danced in Cheyenne. You escaped out of the back door of a pool hall in Kansas. You swam naked in Lake Michigan—"

"Still, no mortal peril."

"Is it mortal peril that's got you chewing on your fingernails?" Nicole asked. "You've faced that, too. And you have been facing it since the moment you were diagnosed."

Claire opened her mouth and then shut it. She shifted in her seat. The word *cancer* seemed to whisper through the car. Nicole paused to give Claire a chance to spit out another sassy reply, but Claire had gone mute, finding intense interest in the seam of the bag of chocolate pretzels in her lap.

Nicole said, "The Claire I've come to know is a woman who accepts what the world has thrown at her, as bad as it is. The Claire I'll never forget is the one I saw in that airport terminal in Des Moines, when you planted your feet and stood up to your formidable sister to assert—for better or for worse—your own free will about treatment." The words came fast, her tongue tripping over them. "Your giving-up problem, my old friend, lies in an utter lack of confidence in yourself. You have always, always, *always* underestimated what you are capable of accomplishing."

The car rumbled over a pothole. Lucky's dog tags jingled in the backseat, as if the pup had just woken up to the charged atmosphere in the car. The hum of the tires over the road went up in pitch as they traveled over one of the many little bridges that crossed the streams.

Nicole fixed her gaze on the winding road as the air stretched tense and her confidence began to waver. She once thought she knew how to ferret out people's weaknesses and the unconscious habits that sabotaged their better intentions. She once thought she knew how to nudge folks over the fence to better pastures. Even Claire once claimed that Nicole knew how to inspire people. Still, it took a long time for her to muster the courage to look over and gauge the expression on Claire's face.

Claire looked straight at her, blinking, her brown eyes full of gratitude…and tears.

Nicole let out a breath she felt as if she'd been holding for about eighteen months. She let out a breath that seemed to expel so much air that her belly button touched her spine. She felt adrenaline shaky, nicotine shaky, caffeine shaky, public speaking shaky, both jittering and relieved and strangely, oddly thankful. She wanted to stick her head out the car window and feel the wind rush past her ears. She wanted to pull the car over and run circles around it until she stopped trembling.

Then Claire started to laugh, and Jenna laughed with her, and they all scrambled for the last of the tissues and whatever scratchy fast-food napkins they could rustle up, as the road opened, as buildings appeared through the trees. She caught sight of a sign ahead, a rustic placard of elaborate lettering swinging on a pole, and her heart did another Olympic leap knowing that the real test of their friendship was coming.

Gravel popped under her wheels as she pulled the car into the parking lot of the Birchbark Rafting Company. She turned to Claire as she shut the car off. She waited until her friend lifted her face from the T-shirt she was using to dab her eyes.

Nicole sensed the high wattage of her own expression. "Are you ready?"

Claire nodded once. "Bring it on."

Nicole swung open the door, stepped out, and bounced to the front of the car. She shaded her eyes with her hand as she squinted down the slope to the water's edge. Her heart gave a little leap as she caught sight of a group of folks getting ready to go rafting, then stilled in disappointment when she realized the group was not who she expected—only a bunch of guys.

Claire hefted her hands onto her hips as she joined her. "I see we're not the only fools to be doing this today."

One of those "guys" suddenly turned and shouted in their direction. What he shouted sounded very much like *Claire*.

Nicole froze as the rest of the group swung around and looked their way. She stuttered in disbelief as she watched the whole group rush up the slope with a collective squeal that didn't sound in the *least* bit like it came from the throats of men.

Nicole counted them. Then she pressed her hand against her mouth as she counted them again.

Yes, they were all here, exactly as she'd planned.

But every last woman was bald.

Chapter Twenty-two

Claire first felt the cold edge of a razor against her scalp in a Bangkok barber shop on the night before her ordination. Her sponsor, Narupong, had made a party of it, inviting a motley assortment of her Thai and traveling friends. As curls of her auburn hair whispered to the floor, Claire began to realize how radical a decision she'd really made. The French eco-traveler who hadn't been back to Lille in seven months hung back in horror. The two Aussies who'd narrowly missed being shot during a forest trek in the Golden Triangle covered their mouths as the buzzing continued. She'd seen the same expressions on their faces when they witnessed the bloody cheek-piercing rituals at the vegetarian festival in Phuket.

At first, all she'd felt was cold. The metal edge of the clipper mowed a path across her scalp. It left a chill in its wake. The buzzing continued, unrelenting, tufts of hair brushing her neck before slipping to the floor. As the barber worked his way to the top of her scalp, the spaces between her neck vertebrae were no longer compressed by the weight of her hair. Her throat lengthened; her head felt helium-light.

When it was all over and she finally glanced in the mirror, she looked Bambi-eyed. She saw the true shape of her head, the funny curve of her ears, and the length of her neck. It was odd to see oneself shorn of a universal indicator of femininity and yet feel more intensely feminine than ever.

She felt naked, vulnerable, exposed.

She felt like herself.

Now Claire watched five shorn women hurry up the slope from the water's edge. Her mind balked at what her eyes were seeing. What were a clutch of Buddhist nuns doing at a river-rafting company on the Hudson Valley Gorge? But they weren't swathed in white robes. And they weren't walking the serene pace of venerable *maechis*. They were struggling up the hill and laughing and slipping in the mud and trying to outrace one another.

Leading the charge was a tiny pip in a bikini top with her arms outstretched. Claire had a sharp, sudden flashback to a photo of a bald doctor leaning over the hospital bed of a thin, young patient.

Jin.

Not. Possible. Jin was in Salt Lake City with her husband and her twins, holding vigil for a pediatric cancer patient.

The woman-who-couldn't-be-Jin stopped short in front of her, vibrating like a hummingbird. She ran her hand over her bald head while dropping into a pose.

"Like my new do?"

293

Claire saw Jin's almond-shaped eyes and the winged brows and the impish chin and the little brown mole just above her left eyebrow. Claire willed her mind to accept the evidence of her eyes, while the midday sun beat on her hair, while she felt a sliver of gravel biting into the sole of her foot, while she heard the faint pop and crackle of the car engine as it cooled behind her.

Then Jin couldn't wait any longer. With a laugh, she launched herself into Claire, sending her stumbling back. Over Jin's shoulder, Claire saw a dark-haired woman with a hairline of sharp stubble.

Maya.

Maya, who hadn't told Claire in South Dakota that she was planning to join them. Maya, who had insisted that soon she'd be returning to her wooden drawers of old bones and the musty lecture hall to terrorize the next crop of archaeology students.

Claire looked beyond Maya, to the other women rubbing their hands over their heads with bashful awareness. That couldn't be Sydney, because Sydney hadn't returned her calls when Claire was only a hundred miles away from her hometown of Denver. That couldn't be Riley, because Riley no longer had her fire-red hair, though she still had freckles that stretched over her pale, pale scalp. Another woman stood separate from them all with a smirk on her face and a cigarette dangling from her fingers. Claire didn't recognize her as Lu until she got a glimpse of the dragon tattoo on Lu's forearm.

Sometimes in meditation, especially in those last few

weeks before she left the *wat*, Claire had gone so deep into the dusky silence that she'd caught flashes of imagery—of her sister Melana as a girl climbing a tree to return a fallen starling's nest, of Pine Lake just as the first drops of a summer storm pattered the lake, of two strangers in yellow scarves riding a motorbike through Bangkok. She'd become a conduit for both past and present, where distance made no difference. The images rolling through her consciousness like the flipping of television channels in which she had tuned in, watching.

Like now.

But with each hug, she felt her senses come back to this place. With each greeting, memories flooded her senses. Unable to speak, she ran her hands over one bald head, and then another, and then another, two heads at the same time, gazing into those laughing faces as her mind worked the features into familiarity.

Jin leaned in. "We thought about dying our hair pink again, just like in high school. But then we remembered, heck, you lopped off your boobs. We can lose a little hair."

Claire couldn't gather enough air in her lungs to speak. It was all too much. Five of them here, and all of them bald. She imagined them each feeling the cold bite of the clippers against the napes of their necks as they, too, committed to exposure, vulnerability.

"Solidarity." Jin held her by the shoulders and gave her a little shake. "Remember?"

One guilty part of her wanted to confess the truth—*I'm not going to go through chemo; I won't be going bald*—but she couldn't. She wouldn't disrespect their sacrifice, or the fact that Nicole and Jenna had honored her secret when they arranged this.

Because it had to be Jenna and Nicole who'd arranged all this. Claire glanced over her shoulder and saw Jenna standing with Nicole a little apart from all the others. Claire remembered all the calls to "Lars" this past week, the text messages that couldn't be ignored at Niagara Falls, the midnight arrival of e-mails marked by the dinging of phones, and Jenna's insistence on sending travelogues and pictures to Paulina so that the cancer blog would not go silent. Now the two of them leaned in the shade against the office, flicking worried glances in Claire's direction.

Maya said, "Nicole was a jackhammer. She texted and e-mailed and badgered until she got a yes from every one of us."

Lu added, her voice whiskey-rough, "It was Jenna's posts on the blog that hooked me. It reminded me of the old days. I wouldn't have missed this for the world."

Jin bounced into the conversation, cocking her head toward the bank where the guides waited by several blow-up rafts. "I knew how important it was for you to do this white-water rafting thing. We weren't going to let you and Nic and Jen have all this fun on your own."

Claire crossed the small distance between her and her road-trip buddies as they both pushed away from the wall.

Jenna smelled like the menthol-sunburn cream they'd both used this morning.

Nicole did, too.

"It's a gathering of the tribe," Nicole said as she pulled away from Claire's hug. "Isn't this what you wanted all along?"

～

The last time Claire had dipped an oar in these waters, rain had tapped frigid needles into the back of her neck. The last time she'd braced her feet against the bottom of a blow-up raft, her toes had gone numb with cold in spite of the wool socks and rubber boots. The last time she'd dared this route, she'd been with many of the same women, and to the last one, they'd been grim with purpose.

Now in sun-dappled waters, they razzed one another across the river, amusing the guides by shooting spray at one another with their oars. Sydney bleated like a herded sheep when they all piled up at a narrow channel. Jin's high-pitched, never-ending chatter was interrupted by Maya teasingly asking her if she ever took a breath. Lu piped in to ask if anyone remembered to bring a flask of blackberry brandy.

Claire allowed herself to enter into the same lightheartedness. It was easier to act unafraid at the beginning of a run, anyway, when the river still gurgled gently around them. In places, the water became so shallow that the guide wove them single file through the deeper channels so they wouldn't be beached. As they edged closer to the banks, she distracted herself by gazing through the tea-colored water speckled with skimming bugs and alive with frogs. Here she could hide her face for a while. Here she could try to get a grip on how grateful she was for the lengths to which Nicole and Jenna had gone to bring her friends together.

Amid this momentary calm, the memories flooded in like the white water she knew they would ride soon. The sound of Sydney's rolling laugh reminded her of a night when a bunch of them had gathered in her attic under the boards of the eaves—the only place she could get privacy from her sprawling family. While the printer spewed out posters that they'd tape throughout the high school the next day, they chatted over a freshly delivered pizza about the unfairness of some assignment or relative hotness of the high school boys. The attic had smelled of sauce and cheese and drying ink long after it had gone silent.

Most of all, she remembered coming home afterward to the scent of a roast wafting out of the kitchen, blessing the house with sage and thyme. She remembered coming home to her brothers racing up and down the stairs and all her sisters arguing over shoes and her mother wearing that silly green apron with the frills.

Her mother, before cancer took her.

Claire plunged her oar into the water, forcing her attention back to the task at hand. She heard a rumble in the distance, a thrumming vibration in the atmosphere. She flexed her fingers around the oar. She was ready for this. Maya and Jin led the way in the front raft. Lu and Riley and Sydney were in the raft behind her. No matter how swift the raft flew across the current, no matter how close they skimmed the collection of water-worn rocks, no matter how the thin floor of this vessel buckled and bucked against the churn of the waters, she would stay in this boat. Her friends all knew she'd come here to complete something she'd abandoned years ago. They were watching.

This time she would not let them down.

At the first gentle dip of the riverbed, the water gripped the bottom of the raft. A breeze lifted the hair around her helmet as the raft skimmed the surface. She raised her oar when the guide directed and dipped it back in when he commanded. She eyed the foaming eddies around the rocks for whirlpools, the ones she'd been so terrified of getting caught in. Jenna occasionally shouted "Rock" before twisting her oar to guide them away from it. No sooner had they crested the first run when they sluiced all the way through it.

Her feet were still dry.

She sat nonplussed. She remembered the shock of that first run much differently. It had been a snarling roller coaster of spray and foam. Now she twisted in the raft to look upriver. She must have conflated it in her mind with a later, longer, more perilous run. She faced forward in search of that run but found herself in a part of the river that bulged wide into a pond. Maya and Jin paddled in circles around Riley's raft to make it twist backward. Riley and Lu collapsed in laughter at their uncoordinated efforts to face forward again.

Nicole cast a glance over her shoulder. "Are you guys getting hungry?"

"I'm thirsty," Claire said, though she wasn't sure she could keep anything down until they were done.

Nicole thrust a water bottle at her.

Claire said, "Tell me there's whiskey in there."

"Whiskey's against the rules," Nicole said, rolling her eyes at the guide. "And we're not eating until Elephant Rock." Nicole poked the guide with the end of her oar. "About how far away is that?"

"A good half hour," he said. "Longer if your friends keep horsing around."

Nicole said, "Well, I'm starved. We should take the lead and show those clowns how whitewater rafting is *really* done."

Goose bumps rose on Claire's skin. She blanched at the idea of being in the front raft, the boat that blazes the trail that all the other rafts follow, but with a word to their guide and a little whoop of excitement, Nicole plunged her oar into the water before Claire could object. The guide with his young-man's shoulders braced himself in the front as Jenna pulled hard. Claire joined them with a shivering lack of enthusiasm. When they ripped past the two rafts twisting idly in the shallows, five bald women lifted their heads. With shouts and exclamations the race was on.

She strained her ears, listening for the roar of the white water downstream and looking for a curl of mist rising between the trees. Then she saw it loom right ahead, like the rim of the world.

The oar nearly slipped through her hands. She tightened her grip as the guide shouted to veer to the right, and then to the left. Then the boat dropped out beneath her. Her stomach slammed into her throat. The floor of the raft bowed as they hit water again and skimmed down the current, following the sluice to one bank and then steering to avoid an outcropping of rocks. She didn't have time to think as they took a channel around a sand bank before escaping through an easy drift into another run so shallow it was like sliding over a pit of balls.

In the midst of all this, Jenna nudged her, shouting, "Look!"

Jenna gestured to the opposite bank. A young man sporting the T-shirt of the rafting company waved an arm where he stood atop a boulder. He lifted a camera into view. The guide in the front shouted something that sounded like "Smile!" Nicole twisted her oar to bring them closer for a better shot.

Claire squinted as she looked up at the blue sky and thought about the poster board her sisters would eventually display in the McCreery Funeral Home. It would be like the boards they'd scrapbooked for Mom and Melana after they'd died. Claire had already made a file for her sisters that now lay on her desk in Roseburg. It held a copy of her baby photo, a few shots of her as a gap-toothed child, the one with her father in the canoe holding up a brook trout, a group shot on a rope swing with her sisters, the high school graduation photo of her and her pink-haired friends, and one picture of her bald-headed in the white robes of a Buddhist nun.

She'd always known that the board lacked one last photo, the vivacious, triumphant one that her sisters would need to pin in the middle.

Claire pulled her oar out of the foaming water and smiled at the camera as she lifted the oar above her head.

Moments later the run was done. Claire paddled down

a calm, deep section of the river and wondered why her clothes were still dry. Her feet were barely wet, and only from a thimbleful of water that had sloshed into the boat. She bent over the edge of the blow-up raft and slipped her fingers through the water to scatter a school of silver fish.

She glanced behind as the other rafts came into view. "I guess the real white water comes closer to Elephant Rock, right?"

Nicole twisted to meet Claire's gaze, and there was a gleam in her eyes that Claire didn't quite understand.

Nicole said, "Do you remember when you last did this?"

"High school, of course."

"No, what *month*."

"April. A frigid, sleety, nasty, mountain April."

"And what month is it now?"

"August."

"Uh-huh."

Nicole held her gaze for another moment, eyebrows raised so high as to nearly disappear under her helmet, until what she was saying began to dawn on Claire. Then Nicole, with a triumphant smile, turned away to dig her oar back into the water.

"It's summer," Claire muttered, "and this river is at its lowest ebb."

Nicole wielded the oar in a way that proved she'd earned some special canoeing patch at Camp Paskagamak. "This little excursion is going to be nothing but a little raft ride down a lazy stream."

Claire sagged against the rear of the boat. She pulled the

dripping oar onto her lap, not caring that it was soaking her jeans. Had she paused long enough to think about this, she would have realized this was true.

She lifted a wet foot and nudged Nicole's butt. "You knew this all along."

"Yes, Claire, I did."

"More than four thousand miles in the car and you never once said a thing to me."

"I made sure you got a good look at *real* rapids at Niagara Falls."

"You're a sick, twisted bastard, Nicole Eriksen."

"What we fear, Claire, is mostly in our minds."

Claire shoved her oar back in the water and yanked it so hard that a wave of river water rained down upon Nicole. While Nicole squealed, cringing, Claire did it again to soak Jenna, too. Not long after that, in a hail of squeals, there wasn't a piece of clothing on any one of them that remained dry.

Riley's boat sailed by, and Lu cupped her hands over her mouth. She shouted, "Last boat to Elephant Rock has to buy the first round tonight."

Claire, Jenna, and Nicole weren't the first to reach the outcropping of rock where everyone beached the boats for lunch. But Claire was the first at something.

She outraced everyone to leap off Elephant Rock.

Chapter Twenty-three

Camp Kwenback, Pine Lake

Maya said, "I brought a little game."

Nicole groaned good-naturedly along with the rest of the crowd as Maya flourished a silk drawstring bag. They'd all just come in from the great lawn of Camp Kwenback, Riley's family compound on the wooded edge of Pine Lake, after watching the sun set. The lodge had originally been built by Riley's great-grandfather for the Teddy Roosevelt–era titans of New York to enjoy lavish, weeklong hunting parties. Riley had recently inherited the main lodge and all the outlying buildings. Over the past year, she'd been doing her best to make the camp habitable, with the hope, eventually, to restore the place to its former glory.

Now they all gathered in the pine-forest cathedral of the main hall, their bellies full after dinner and their moods mellow from the local white wine. Under the perusal of the enormous moose above the stone fireplace, Nicole dropped into one of the overstuffed chairs only to sink into the hole of a broken spring.

"Aren't we a little long in the tooth," Nicole said, slipping a foot on the glass-top coffee table, "for Truth or Dare?"

Lu barked, "Speak for yourself!"

"There are no dares in this." Maya pulled the drawstrings loose. "Just truth, however you want to tell it. It's an icebreaker." Maya winked. "Just like in South Dakota."

Nicole smiled more widely to hide how her stomach did a sudden flip.

"Claire, you're the guest of honor." Maya held out the bag. "You go first."

Claire sat in the middle of the most exuberant plaid couch that Nicole had ever seen. It was a relic from the nineteen seventies, Riley had explained, which was the last time the camp had turned a profit. In the midst of this vintage décor, Claire raised her glass for a toast before putting it down, her cheeks flushed with happy color.

Claire pulled a slip of paper out of the bag and read, "What is the strangest decision that you've made, postgraduation?" Claire swept an incredulous gaze across the room. "You mean other than taking a road trip to find all of you bald?"

Nicole laughed along with the crowd. She saw Sydney adjust the bill of the baseball cap she'd taken to wearing. She witnessed Riley running a distracted hand across her head as if she'd forgotten amid the details of hosting that she was actually bald. And Nicole caught Jenna's look from across the room, a steady, questioning look as Jenna adjusted the clip that held her hair. Tugging the short ends of her own hair, Nicole let her gaze skim away, pretending she didn't understand what Jenna was mutely asking her.

"Well, the strangest decision I made postgraduation," Claire said, "had something to do with shaving my head, too."

"Yes, yes!" Jin bounced in place on the couch beside her. "What in the world made you take Buddhist vows?"

"Now there's a story…"

Claire launched into a description of her decision to take vows, beginning with the agonizing months when she took care of her sister Melana. To Nicole's surprise, Claire shared details that Nicole had never heard during the road trip. Claire described her sense of dislocation after Melana's burial, about the irresistible urge to leave the familiar behind, and then about the thrill of traveling in Thailand. The women leaned forward in their seats, rapt, nodding, injecting their own observations, and just when Claire started to get a little weepy, she shifted the mood by relating an anecdote about the pit toilet in her *guti*.

Nicole had already heard this tale while traveling somewhere through Wyoming. Three weeks into her stint as a nun, Claire woke up to go to the bathroom only to catch sight of something popping out of the pit toilet.

It was the hooded head of a cobra.

The group collectively gasped and lifted their feet off the ground and then squealed in horror.

"I couldn't pee in that hole for *weeks*." Claire described how the cobra slithered out and flopped against the wall until it found a chewed-out hole in the corner where it slid out to disappear into the forest. "I kept wondering if the thing had laid eggs."

When the chatter finally died down, Maya stood up and shook the bag at Jin.

"Me? How am I ever going to top *that?*" Shaking her head, Jin reached in the bag and pulled out a sliver of paper. She read, "Fill in this blank: None of you know this, but in my twenties I…"

A chorus of eager *ooooooooooohs* rose up. Jin flushed as she raised her eyebrows and covered her mouth.

From across the room, Sydney said, "I want to know about that Ukrainian guy you were dating when we were living in the city."

"Wait, wait." Maya leaned forward in interest. "Was that the guy in that band we saw at the dive bar on the Lower East Side?"

"Let Jin answer." Riley slipped a tray of cookies on the table. "I had no idea the good doctor had a wicked past."

"All right, I'll confess." Jin dropped her hands to her lap and let out a theatrical sigh. "For about nine glorious months on a break from medical school, I was an indie-band groupie."

Nicole couldn't help laughing as Jin told her story, a tale of backstage antics that occurred during a year of what Jin called "existentialist confusion about my career as a pediatric oncologist." Jin dished frankly about the mistakes she'd made during her first year of medical school, as well as the grief and the miracles she'd witnessed, both of which had sent her in a tailspin.

As the tale unwound, Nicole found herself admiring Jin's honesty even as her own throat closed up. Soon it would be her turn. She'd already mentally flipped through her own life's stories to find one with an appropriate mixture of humor and pathos that would satisfy any question. She would talk about the day Lars proposed to her. She'd tell these friends about the unplanned pregnancy that had thrown her for a loop. She'd tell them how he dropped to his knees when she told him about the baby. She'd tell them about the engagement ring that he'd plucked from a candy bowl in his dorm room, a bright purple, grape-flavored Ring Pop left over from Halloween.

She drew her knees up to her chest and held them tight, just as she did under the South Dakota sky when Nicole had turned from the light of the campfire to find Maya's wise eyes upon her. Nicole had chosen the proposal story because she knew it had a happy ending.

She was too much of a coward to share the truth about Noah.

Nicole hauled herself out of the chair and murmured an excuse. She slipped between the couch and a taxidermic black bear to wind her way in the general direction of the bathroom. Halfway there, she changed direction and slipped out the back sliding doors.

She wandered to the edge of the porch and leaned against a pillar. Riley had given them a brief history of the camp when they arrived this afternoon, entertaining them with tales of bootleggers during Prohibition slipping Canadian whiskey over the border in canoes they paddled across the lake that now spread before her. The cabins, a row of dark shadows beyond the trees, had once been used for storage, and the boathouse on the shore had been built as an unloading dock.

Now, moonlight cast a strip of silver upon the water. She closed her eyes and soaked in the ambiance of Pine Lake. Katydids sang in the trees. She smelled the tang of lake water, the earthiness of damp moss, and the scent of smoke.

Cigarette smoke.

Her eyes flew open. A creak of a floorboard drew her attention to the porch shadows where the end of a cigarette glowed bright red.

"Another escapee, I see." Lu spoke through a blue cloud. "Welcome to the club."

Nicole hadn't seen Lu leave the room. Lu must have slipped out just as silently as she herself had. Now she lifted the wineglass that until now she hadn't realized she still held in her hand. "I needed to clear my head."

"That's a good excuse, too."

Nicole gave Lu a long look. Some of the women who'd shaved their heads could pull off the cue-ball look. Jin, for example, was petite and confident enough to get away with it. Maya looked exotic, her Mohawk cheekbones far more prominent without her hair hiding her features. Sydney took to wearing a baseball hat and long, dangling earrings that showed off her Cleopatra neck. But Lu was not so fortunate. Gristle-thin and angular, Emma Lu of Cannery Row looked like she hadn't lived the easiest of lives.

Lu said, "You know, I've checked out your website."

Nicole tensed. "It's a work in progress."

"Well, some of those women back there called it their bible, you know, like they couldn't raise their kids without it."

"They're just being kind."

"They're proud to see another Pine Lake girl done good. Of course, everybody always knew you'd do great things, Nic." She slapped the arm of the Adirondack chair beside her. "Come sit. For a woman who's been on vacation for almost three weeks, you look like you could use some rest."

Nicole hesitated, gazing past the eaves to the smear of stars, so many that she couldn't pick out the usual constellations. "I'll sit if you promise you won't talk about my job."

Lu's laugh was like gravel. "I'll welcome you as long as you don't lecture me on the evil of cigarettes."

"We have a deal."

Nicole crossed the porch and settled in the chair, stretching her legs out as she leaned back.

"It's strange," Lu said, "how a bunch of women who haven't seen one another in ages can just get together, and suddenly it's like we're all in high school spilling our deepest, darkest secrets."

"Well, not everyone spills so easily, right?" Nicole gave Lu a pointed look. She remembered the tough teen that Lu had tried to be in high school, the enforcer on the hockey team, the small, combative woman with the snarky attitude and the bruised eyes. "It's a beautiful thing, though. The way things are going, we'll have a crying couch by Sunday."

"But you and I won't be on it, will we?"

Nicole hesitated. She thought about the hours and hours

she and Claire and Jenna spent in the Chevy Lumina. She thought about the long nights they spent exhausted in sketchy roadside hotel rooms, eating fried chicken on the beds for the lack of a table. Could this three-day gathering of the tribe—no matter how miraculous—possibly encapsulate the same intensity of a three-week road trip?

Claire's words floated back to her.

Your mistake is thinking you always have time.

"Nic, Nic, Nic." Lu made a tsking sound. "I never thought I'd see the day when you and I would have so much in common."

"Well, we were both pretty good athletes."

"You know what I'm talking about. I'll tell you what. I'll show you my troubles if you show me yours."

The truth Nicole could barely admit rose to her throat like a hard capsule of poison. Her first reflex was to swallow it down, deep down, and resist the urge to bring it into the light. That was what she'd been doing every day for eighteen long months. This time she made herself resist the urge to push. This time she let the words she couldn't bear to say rest there, a hard lump lodged in her neck.

In the end, she didn't know exactly what alchemy gave her the courage to finally speak the truth about Noah. Maybe it was the quiet, patient woman sitting next to her, a wise and solemn old friend who was still part stranger, a woman who'd seen hard times and yet seemed willing to listen with empathy and without judgment.

But more likely it was the lake breeze that chose that moment to sift through her hair like a mother's comforting hands. It was the soothing haze of darkness, the rhythmic music of the katydids, and the air that smelled of river reeds and damp leaves and white spruce. As a girl, she'd sprouted amid these woods like a sapling aiming straight for the sun. Now, with her life in shadows, she'd shot clear across the country just to experience the old magic, to find, in the familiar natural rhythms of her hometown, some measure of bravery.

She took a long, deep breath and finally admitted what had always been too painful to confess.

"Eighteen months, three weeks, and six days ago," she heard herself saying, "my oldest son attempted suicide."

Chapter Twenty-four

Pine Lake revealed itself to Claire in pieces both old and new.

On the porch of the Adirondack Inn—where Claire had never eaten before—the eight of them sat in the shade with a view of the lake. They clinked glasses of iced tea and watched the sporty sailboats pass by as they ceded all choice of lunch foods to Sydney, who revealed herself as quite the foodie. Sydney eyeballed the menu, stroking the silk ends of the scarf she'd wound gypsylike about her bald head, and then crooked a manicured finger at the waiter. That waiter soon delivered loaves of warm artisan bread and small bowls of sweet whipped butter followed by an endive salad studded with Roquefort cheese. Plates of rainbow trout in citrus vinaigrette, smoked venison with cranberry chutney, and slivers of roasted duck ensued.

Claire feasted, swooning at every bite. She couldn't remember when she last ate such a meal. Sydney sampled each plate, leaning toward Claire to share lively anecdotes about a dish of trunkfish she'd tried in the Caribbean, the best gumbo she'd ever had in New Orleans, and the time she ate wild boar in Montreal.

They all worked off desserts of apple crumble and mountain berry pie by taking a walk down Main Street, breaking up into small groups. They all agreed to meet at the city hall flagpole in an hour.

Claire took advantage of the opportunity to set off on her own, wandering amid the flow of visitors and natives, just listening to the broad vowels of the accents that at times sounded Canadian, at other times veered closer to New England, but blended together formed the verbal soundtrack of her summer youth. She passed the bike store where she'd once bought a wicker basket and inner tubes to replace the ones busted on her hand-me-down bicycle. The ancient, overstuffed Smoke Shop that used to stand beside it had been replaced by a tiny cupcake bakery, all powder-pink paint. Though the confections were artful, Claire remembered with a pang of nostalgia how much time she'd spent in the musty, old place perusing magazines and buying bubble gum and flavored lip balm.

She slowed to a full stop as she reached the town library. She stood in front of the bulletin board to read the announcements tacked up under glass. It felt as if she were reading an activity list from her childhood. They announced Monday Movie Night, the Tuesday Tales for children, the Swinging Wednesday concert on the lawn (weather permitting), the next town council meeting, the summer book club, and a gathering of the hikers club.

She also noted the *Save the Adirondacks* sticker slapped on the glass, an image of a straight pine topped with a fist on a red-white-and-blue background. It was the kind of in-your-face icon that Claire knew represented yet another rogue, local political action committee. The Adirondack Park was an odd mix of public and private land. Tension between developers and environmentalists ebbed and flowed as predictably as the phases of the moon. It gave her a pleasant little buzz to see that her hometown was still a hotbed of activism.

Claire caught up with Jin just as she bounded out of the sports shop where Claire had bought her first pair of ice skates—well, the first pair she hadn't inherited from her older sisters, anyway. The shop had flourished and expanded into the adjacent space. Jin seized her hand and dragged her inside to point at the photos of the local sports teams, old and new, hanging on the walls above the racks of bathing suits. Together they found Lu's hockey team, with Lu in full goalie gear, as well as a yellowed newspaper clipping of Nicole's team deliriously celebrating their regional softball championship win.

Claire stood beside Jin and gazed at the photo of those happy young women, and she found her thoughts drifting to her own sleepy, rural town in Oregon, eight miles away from the nearest library, the high school a mixed regional one, the only restaurant on the crossroad strip a restaurant that closed at two p.m. that was simply called The Diner.

She shook herself. It wasn't fair to compare. And surely,

she said to Jin, it must be time for them to gather at the flagpole.

The others were already there except for Nicole and Jenna. Maya and Sydney dug into their bags to show off jars of elderberry jelly, bottles of maple syrup, and hunks of local cheeses they'd bought at the farmer's market. Claire settled in the grass and listened as they worked out the logistics for a dinner picnic at Coley's Point, watching the ease at which her old friends arrived at a consensus.

Claire squinted, recognizing the cadence of Jenna's walk as she and Nicole made their way across the green. Watching them, her throat closed up. Their heads were lowered, close to each other. Jenna stopped now and again to twist and point to different places on her wonky hip.

Claire didn't have to hear what Jenna was saying to know she was describing the developmental hip dysplasia that Jenna had been born with, the Pavlik harness she'd worn as a baby, the pelvic osteotomy surgery she'd suffered in her childhood, the hip abduction braces she'd later hated. Jenna had told Claire the whole difficult story in high school, then confessed that Claire was the only friend who'd dared to ask. It was a litmus test, of sorts, Jenna admitted. She always felt great warmth for anyone who ventured a question rather than pretending her rolling little limp didn't exist.

But Nicole and Jenna's deepening rapport wasn't the sole reason why Claire pushed herself up from her seat by the flagpole, her eyes prickling, waiting with a pounding heart to greet the two women who knew everything.

"Sorry we're late." Nicole swung an arm around Jenna's shoulders as she joined the group. "Jenna's hip was acting up, so we took it slow. Anything exciting happen while we were gone?"

Claire pressed her hands against her cheeks as everyone laughed and gathered around and ran their hands over Jenna's and Nicole's newly shorn heads as if this were some strange female bonding ritual. With her short hair sheared off, Nicole looked strong and fierce, like G.I. Jane. Jenna was a creature transformed, a young Sinead O'Connor, fey and otherworldly. Her lashes swept her cheeks like long, dark wings.

Claire hugged them both while one word rang in her head: *solidarity*.

Later that evening, when they gathered blankets and baskets of food to take up to Coley's Point, she made sure she gave Nicole and Jenna one of her many hats so they wouldn't get cold as the picnic inevitably morphed into a late-night bonfire, and then, just as she expected, into a sleepover under the star-blasted skies.

Somewhere around five in the morning, as the embers of the fire smoked and most of the women still huddled under blankets, Claire stood up to watch the first rays of the morning light peep between the distant trees. One by one, her friends joined her at the edge of the clearing. The sky brightened. For a single transcendent moment, their faces smoothed and the few extra pounds dropped off and their muted voices rose in pitch, as if they were standing barefoot in sateen during the morning after their senior prom, as they had all those many years ago.

Perhaps it *was* possible—for one winking moment—to go back in time.

Even the sensation she was feeling was familiar, a thrumming connection to her true community, the quivering of the strands of memory that tied her irrevocably to these friends. As a girl, she'd reveled in this tangle of human connection, but then she'd shucked it—person by person, year by year—as too painful to maintain. Now, on this hilltop overlooking the place where she'd come of age, she realized that the world she'd created for herself after Pine Lake had become a small, meager place, bereft of joy but never of suffering. *This* feeling was what she'd craved, this was the source of that yearning she'd experienced the day Jenna had arrived at her door and offered up a fairy-godmother wish.

For four thousand miles she'd been following her heart, but she hadn't truly understood what it had been whispering to her until now.

She needed to stay close to the people she loved, no matter how much it hurt.

🙟

Claire stole away from the main lodge. She'd been hoping for a moment alone at the boathouse from the moment she'd set eyes upon it. The building sat over the banks of the lake within a stand of yellow birch. The coiling twig work gave the pillars the look of sun-bleached trees. It had an elfish look, a Thai-temple look. Now she slipped off her sandals and pressed her palms together. With the boards hot under her feet she walked with attention, keeping her gaze on the ground just in front of her. Mindful of each step, she wandered up the four sun-drenched bays before plunging back into the cool shade, seeking calm in Buddhist walking meditation.

Sometime later, she settled cross-legged at the end of one of the docks to listen to the gurgle of water. Beneath her, the wood vibrated with every knock of the tethered rowboats in the bays. Her head filled with the aroma of reedy lake shallows, warm wood, and the iron tang of rust.

She heard their footfalls on the grass. She recognized Jenna by the hitch in her cadence and, once they reached the boathouse, the distinctive click of Lucky's claws. She recognized Nicole by the athletic grace of her tread and the soundless breeze as Nicole dipped down to settle cross-legged right beside her. Nicole had been spending a lot of time with Lu; a vague scent of cigarette smoke clung to her clothes.

They sat together in comfortable, effortless silence. Claire breathed in this feeling. In the weeks and months to come, she would meditate in the shade of her forest garden or in the spot in her den where the sun poured through the window. She wanted to be able to remember the pulse of their presence, every physical tic, every subtle rustle of their clothing. She wanted to be able to summon the spirits of her friends like ghosts.

A warm pressure clambered against her thigh. She opened her eyes to see Lucky climbing into her lap.

Jenna slackened the leash. "Boy, he's going to miss you."

The pup stretched under Claire's fingers, closing his big,

brown eyes as she gave him a good rub. "He's got a long way to ride home, poor little pup, but at least he'll have Zoe to scratch his ears. Have you come here to fetch me back to the lodge for dinner?"

"Not just yet." Nicole shifted her seat, the boards creaking beneath her. "Riley promised to ring the bell when dinner is ready."

"Sorry I bugged out of cooking."

"Everyone did, once Sydney took over." Nicole raised her face to the sun. "It's sad to think we're all leaving tomorrow."

Claire felt a pang so sharp she winced. "The flights are all arranged then."

Nicole said, "Jenna's leaving at nine a.m. to fetch her mother and pick up Zoe at camp. Lu offered us a ride to the Albany airport at noon."

Jenna piped up, "It's not too late to change your minds, you know. I could use some help with a certain cranky teenager."

"Sorry." Nicole nudged off one sandal and then reached for the other. "I wouldn't inflict upon Zoe the sight of Claire cross-legged in the back humming '*Ommmmmmm.*' And besides, as a group, we're a little scary." Nicole put her sandals aside and brushed her hand over her shorn head. "No reason to give Zoe an excuse to escape the car screaming she's been captured by a cult."

Claire still wasn't quite used to seeing Nicole and Jenna bald. Of all the women, Jenna might just benefit the most from the change. Already there was a brave tilt to her jaw. On the other hand, by the frequency at which Nicole ran her hand over her head, the buzz cut had apparently left Nicole feeling unnerved.

Claire hoped Nicole would look in the mirror soon and see what Claire saw: someone fresh, peeled, newborn.

Three days and four nights with these old friends—not just Jenna and Nicole, but all of them—and she felt as if they'd hardly cracked the surfaces of one another's lives. Last night they'd designated the wicker love seat at the far end of the back porch as the "crying couch." This morning they'd take a group picture in the same positions as their high school graduation photo—the one where everyone sported hot-pink hair. Even if they'd all stayed a month, Claire wasn't sure that would be enough time to get as close to each one of them as she'd become to Jenna and Nicole after so many miles together.

Already her eyes began to prickle. She couldn't fully absorb what her friends had done for her sake. And yet, as with any act of love, it came with the weight of hesitant and yet so very hopeful expectations. It was the weight of those expectations that had propelled her to this boathouse, to this lakeside, to the hour of walking meditation in search of clarity.

Claire said, "Do you guys remember when we gave out coffee in Chicago?"

Nicole unfolded her legs to swing her bare feet into the water. "Is this a pop quiz?"

Claire smiled. "Do you remember that one guy by the street sign, right in midtown? He was scruffy and thin, hungry looking, alone. Wild blue eyes."

Jenna nodded. "He was jittery and not in a good way."

"He wouldn't take the coffee." Claire combed her fingernails down Lucky's back. "I stood there holding it out, waiting. I just wanted to give him something warm. A simple gift. So I left it on the ground in front of him. When I looked back a few minutes later, I noticed he'd shoved his hands in his pockets and crossed the street. He'd left the coffee just sitting there, abandoned."

Nicole said, "You give out three dozen coffees and the guy you remember is the one who refused you."

"All my life, I've been the one giving charity. I've been the one delivering the winter coats, handing over the tip jar, offering my time after hours for tutoring. I've seen stone faces like his before." She thought of Theresa, glaring at her from a Cannery Row stoop as Claire unloaded charity coats from the trunk of her car. "But only now, today, do I really understand."

Nicole asked, "Understand what?"

"Accepting help is a very hard thing to do."

She became aware that Nicole had gone very still. Her friend leaned over to peer deep into the water.

"But it wasn't difficult for my sister Melana." Claire summoned her ghost to this place, Melana as she wanted to remember her—full-cheeked and rosy, joking about her generous hips and laughing at her own bad puns. "Every time my sisters and I talked with her about her treatment, Melana always chose the route we wanted, the route that offered hope. She always said, 'We're going to fight this,' or 'We're going to beat this.' She chose those words because they always made us feel better." Claire pressed her face against Lucky's warm back. "Later, when I remembered those conversations, I got so furious at myself and my sisters. I felt that we'd pushed Melana into treatments that stole what little life she had left in her. For a long time, all I could remember was her suffering."

Jenna and Nicole sat so still beside her that Claire couldn't even hear them breathing. A fish leaped out of the water and splashed back down. A birch leaf descended, twirling and sweeping, skidding to rest with its edges curled up.

"Now I realize that when Melana said, 'We're going to fight this,' or 'We're going to beat this,' she wasn't just talking about surviving her own disease." Claire remembered Melana covered in a hand-sewn quilt sitting in that big chair, her eyes too large for her face. "She knew she was second in line—but there might easily be a third. Melana meant 'we' as in *all* her sisters. We *all* had to find a way to survive this disease. She just happened to be the one suffering from it at the time."

Claire sensed their silent understanding as she watched three loons descend from the sky. They cut close to the water and then skidded across the surface of the lake. Tucking in their feathers, they glided in perfect collusion to the far bank.

"Anyway, I thought you two might want to know that you didn't shave your heads in vain." Claire handed Lucky over to Jenna as the first tones of the dinner bell rang. "I'm not giving up this time. What the Petrenko sisters need is a survivor."

Chapter Twenty-five

L eaving Pine Lake was harder than Jenna expected.

Just yesterday, she'd glanced in the rearview mirror as she pulled out of Camp Kwenback and watched her friends waving good-bye on the porch. Her trunk had rattled as her single suitcase jostled against the plastic crate of mementos. The car had felt silent, hollow, as she tried to focus on the road ahead. Lucky had felt the loss, too, lifting his head from his puppy bed in the passenger seat, rattling his license tags as he pleaded with her with bulging brown eyes.

Now, a day later, she took the highway west through New York State. Claire's and Nicole's absence in the car was like a pulled tooth, an ache in a space she kept probing. Her daughter had made no effort to fill the void. Zoe sat slumped in the passenger seat, tapping her feet against the glove compartment to the tinny beat buzzing from the buds buried in her ears.

Jenna had been getting this silent treatment since she'd showed up at Camp Paskagamak as bald as any of the fathers.

Zoe had convulsed with embarrassment and hurried them both away as if her mother's shorn head was a personal affront. During the afternoon and evening at her mother's house, no amount of calm explanation could shift Zoe's sense that Jenna's choice had been a selfish bid for attention. And Jenna's mother, aghast, didn't help matters by suggesing that Jenna start therapy again. Their combined reactions had irritated Jenna to the point of dismissal.

She figured that was a step better than feeling guilty.

Now she ran her fingers over the peach fuzz on her head, still flashing hot and cold with the boldness of what she'd done. It was unfortunate that this act had put yet another wall between her and her daughter. With Zoe silent and Nicole and Claire ever farther away, Jenna felt very much alone.

The next day as they pulled out of Chicago, Jenna remembered something Nicole had suggested to her during long discussions on the Kwenback porch. Figuring she had nothing to lose, Jenna rifled in the papers between them and then tossed a ragged, coffee-stained map of the United States into her daughter's lap. Zoe startled and caught it. Seeing what it was, she gave her mother one of those world-weary looks.

Reluctantly, Zoe tugged the buds out of her ears. "You know I failed map-reading, right?"

"I'm driving. It's your job to navigate."

"I managed to get six Fox Cubs lost in a wood full of marked paths, and now you're putting this on me?"

"It's not rocket science. Besides, we've got two hundred miles before we have to make a decision."

Zoe huffed out all the annoyances of the world, but at least she opened the map. For a brief, glorious few months in third grade, Zoe had been obsessed with a project that involved collecting postcards from as many states as possible. She and Nate had elicited the help of family all over the country. They'd bought a map so Zoe could see where the postcards came from. The little girl who gleefully put pins in the map hadn't completely suffocated under the thickness of eyeliner, apparently. As the miles flew by, her daughter became increasingly absorbed.

"Both northern routes bring us close to Yellowstone and Little Bighorn," Zoe finally announced, furiously thumb-typing on Jenna's smartphone. "What route did you take to get here? I remember a postcard from Sioux Falls."

"We were on Interstate 90 through just about the whole of South Dakota, but then we went south to Kansas."

"Kansas?" Zoe traced a finger over the map. "Are you kidding me?"

"We were searching for an old friend. All we found was her burned-out house." Jenna dropped that little breadcrumb then moved right on. "In any case, I flew back to Seattle out of Des Moines. I didn't meet up with Nic and Claire again until I flew into Chicago for a Cubs game."

"I thought you hated baseball."

"I just say that to piss off your grandmother."

Jenna didn't know what caught Zoe's attention more, the mild profanity or the statement itself. In any case, Jenna made a point of ignoring Zoe's surprise. "So just pick whatever route you prefer, Zoe. It'll be new to me, too."

Zoe returned her attention to the map, but Jenna noticed that now and again she glanced out the passenger-side window to watch the traffic passing by on the interstate before returning to her task.

Later, sucking on a straw as they sat at a laminate table at yet another fast-food rest stop, Zoe said, "I think we should take Interstate 94. It's the northernmost route, and it takes us past Teddy Roosevelt National Park. There's also Powwow in North Dakota in a couple of days, and that would rock."

"Sounds like a plan."

"I suppose it's not every day you get a chance to see Bismarck, North Dakota." Zoe took the burger in her hands and examined it, her voice casual. "So, what ever happened to that woman you and your friends were looking for in Kansas?"

Jenna took her time unwrapping her grilled chicken sandwich. She felt an unfurling in her chest like the damp wings of a newly hatched bird.

"You mean Theresa." Jenna took a healthy bite and waited until she'd chewed it down good. "Now there's a girl who had a lot of reasons to piss off her mother..."

꙳

The long stretch of the northern prairie, with its unrelenting fields of alfalfa, prodded Zoe to ask the first hard question. Just as Nicole had predicted, there was no more warning than the sight of Zoe pulling a bud out of her ear.

"I suppose," Zoe said, "that there's no chance that you and Dad will get back together?"

The question yanked Jenna out of the zone she'd been drifting in. She turned the volume down on the radio, set on a country station that reminded her of Nicole. Her heart heard the ribbon of hope in Zoe's voice despite the effort her daughter made to sound nonchalant. Zoe wasn't going to like her answer, but somehow it was a small comfort to know that Zoe could still dream of miracles.

"I'm afraid not, Zoe." What had Nate been thinking when he got Sissy pregnant? Had he been thinking at all? "There's a baby in the picture now. Your father takes his responsibilities seriously."

"Some of them, anyway."

That was the end of the conversation. Zoe popped her earbuds back in as the alfalfa gave way to a field of heavy-headed sunflowers.

Later that evening, as they settled down in a nondescript motel in Bismarck, Zoe spoke into the dark. "I hope the baby is a boy."

Jenna rolled over and peered at the lump in the other bed. "You don't want a little sister?"

"Dad already has a daughter."

A sharp little burn in the center of her chest. It had never occurred to her that Zoe would fear being replaced. Jenna supposed it should have. Zoe was the only child, the princess of the house. How could she convince Zoe that she wasn't going to be loved any less for the new sibling that came into her life?

"There is going to be a lot of excitement when the baby is born." Jenna hoped Zoe wouldn't be there to witness it. "But your father is never going to love you less."

"If there wasn't a baby, would you have forgiven Dad for cheating on you?"

Jenna lay back against the pillow to better absorb the next blow to her solar plexus. Would she have forgiven Nate if he'd come clean before the pregnancy? Would she have forgiven Nate for having slept with a neighbor? Would she have forgiven Nate for putting her daughter in a position of hiding a secret from her own mother?

Yes.

God help her, she would have tried.

Jenna heard a rustle as Zoe turned her head on the pillow. She debated the wisdom of telling Zoe everything, and then knew, instinctively, that it wouldn't be fair to drag Zoe into the muck. She also suspected that if she told Zoe the whole unvarnished truth, she'd be handing her daughter a scapegoat.

"That's all hypothetical, Zoe. What matters now is that your father kept a terrible secret from me. Secrets tend to build walls between people. Like the wall this secret built between us."

"Mom, just answer."

"Don't blame the pregnancy," Jenna said. "That baby is an innocent in this mess. Just like you."

A day later, hiking through the wind-sculpted sandstone of Theodore Roosevelt National Park, Jenna was sucking on her water bottle as Zoe hit her with another tough one.

"You're going to move out of the house now, aren't you?"

No.

She screwed the cap back onto her bottle. "I don't know yet."

"What do you mean you don't know? We can't all live in that house. Sissy and you and Daddy and me and Natalie and the new brat."

"New *sibling*."

She debated how much to say. Nate had asked for the house in the divorce petition. He'd argued that the garage was his place of self-employment. He argued that it would be a great hardship for him to move it or refit a new workshop. Jenna suspected that argument—along with Nate's position as the main domestic partner—would go a long way in convincing the family judge to grant him full legal custody as well as the house.

She wouldn't mind Nate living in the house with Zoe, but she couldn't bear the thought of Sissy Leclaire in her marital bed.

Jenna reached out to touch Zoe's hair, slowly fading to its natural caramel color. "I won't move far, I promise," she said, drawing her hand back as Zoe ducked out of reach. "Like it or not, you're stuck with me."

The hardest question came a day and a half later, standing amid a crowd of tourists in Yellowstone Park. They'd spent the morning hiking to the observation point for a view of the Grand Basin. Zoe's ponytail bounced as she took the trail by leaps and bounds. They'd passed by evidence of a large quadruped. That had Zoe chatting about the disgusting job of having to identify animal scat as part of the Master Rangers badge. That led to a debate on Mrs. Garfunkle's tutorial about how to be safe from bears. Soon they were whistling and stomping about until they laughed so hard they couldn't whistle anymore.

But now, waiting for Old Faithful to erupt, Zoe went silent where they stood on the edge of the crowd.

Zoe said, "Why did he ruin everything?" She kept her gaze fixed on the hole in the ground, granting her mother no more than a three-quarter profile.

Jenna thought how ironic it was that Zoe had been spending this whole cross-country trip staring out the car window asking the exact same question that Jenna had spent the whole journey trying to answer herself.

She knew she hadn't been the perfect wife. She didn't bake cookies, or cook dinner, or go to all the soccer games. After twelve-hour days she rarely mustered the energy to cuddle up to him when they were finally together in bed. It was likely she'd rarely told him how much she admired his sculptural artistry, how much she appreciated coming home to a house that smelled of bay leaves and thyme, to a dinner warm on the table, to Zoe done with her homework and bathed and ready for a story.

But she'd come to believe that these were the slicing knife points of her own insecurities. These were the faults she'd magnified in her own mind. When she stepped out of herself and looked at them objectively, they bore little relevance to reality. She made omelets most Sunday mornings. She went to every weekend soccer game. She even bought lingerie once in a while, swinging it merrily home in little pink store bags.

She'd spent a lifetime caught in the thrall of insecurities. She couldn't allow them to rule her anymore.

Her daughter's smooth brow grew furrowed as if she were confused at her mother's stretching silence.

Jenna could tell Zoe that this was the oldest, saddest story in the book. The bored housewife takes up with the milkman. The boss sleeps with his secretary. Somehow, Nate had put himself into a situation where he spent too much time with a free spirit who decorated her house with the branches of pussy willows because she knew they'd burst into fluff on Easter. Jenna could tell Zoe that her father had been thinking with his limbic brain. He'd acted like a thirsty man who reached for the nearest beer.

What was it that Claire once said? It was okay for a Buddhist to tell a little white lie, as long as it was done for the greater good. Well, Zoe was thirteen years old. She was just starting to feel the tidal pools of emotional attraction. The last thing Jenna wanted was to see her daughter poisoned with cynicism. Love came only with trust and faith and hope. This situation mustn't destroy Zoe's sense of goodness in the world.

So Jenna drew her hoodie closed and fixed her gaze on the stretch of pines beyond the geyser. "Honestly, I've been asking myself that same question, Zoe, over and over and over, for close on to five thousand miles. Maybe someday I'll realize I played a part in what happened."

"He's ruined *everything*."

"Not everything."

Zoe peered into her mother's face as if she were trying to gauge the weather. "You're forgiving him."

Jenna's jaw muscles tightened. She certainly hadn't reached a state of forgiveness, but she was willing to take a step on the road to trying.

Then Jenna did what she'd wanted to do since she followed Zoe to the observation point for the Grand Basin. She reached out and threaded her fingers through the hank of choppy hair that obscured her daughter's face, surprised when Zoe didn't jerk away. Jenna didn't want Zoe to hide behind all this hair anymore. So she pushed it back, back, so she could better see those beautiful, hurt eyes.

"No matter what happens," Jenna said, "I'll forever be grateful to your father that he gave me *you*."

༈

Zoe's nervous chattering about the first day of the school year sputtered to a stop just outside Spokane. The kid who'd sprawled in the passenger seat cradling Lucky in her lap, crunching on SunChips, and pointing out the rainbows in the fog-shrouded foothills of the northern Rockies popped her buds back in her ears once she realized they'd be in Seattle before nightfall.

Caffeine was the only thing keeping Jenna alert at the wheel. The last stretch since Yellowstone had passed in a two-day blur of quick rest stops and the scent of exhaust and burning rubber. She'd promised Zoe she'd get her back home before the first day of school, which was tomorrow. The next two hundred and thirty miles loomed before her, miles and miles to go.

Yet, despite her fatigue and the ache in her lower back, she felt an almost uncontrollable urge to ease up on the gas. These miles with Zoe—now dozing, her head rocking on the seat, her eyes finally clear of the eyeliner that had rimmed them since Pine Lake, her face creased with the press of piping against her cheek—had been some of the best times she'd ever spent with her daughter. Yet every mile closer to the house that was once her home brought her closer to the troubles she'd run so far away from.

She would have closed her eyes against those troubles if she wasn't going seventy-six miles an hour. She would have blocked them out of her mind if, every time she tried, Nicole's face didn't rise up in her mind to insist she stop avoiding conflict, if Claire's voice didn't remind her to live mindfully, to acknowledge her thoughts and feelings rather than push them aside. Her friends hadn't been in the car for the last three thousand miles, but they were traveling with her nonetheless.

It was 6:30 in the evening by the time Jenna turned the balding tires of the bug-splattered, mud-stained Lumina onto their street. She pulled the car into the driveway next to Nate's Prius, but not before noticing the *For Sale* sign on the front lawn of Sissy's house.

She turned the key, and the car shuddered off. Zoe straightened up, shoved her iPod in her backpack, and bounded out of the car. Jenna pulled the key out of the ignition. Through the curtained window, she saw Nate's familiar shadow moving in the kitchen.

"Mom, pop the trunk."

Jenna realized she was still gripping the steering wheel, immobile. She hit the yellow button and the trunk opened. She pushed open the driver's-side door and unfolded herself from the seat, slapping a hand on the gritty car roof as her cramped legs nearly gave out beneath her. She shook them out and noticed that the small front lawn had been neatly mowed. Nate had edged the flower beds and added a fresh heap of mulch.

She heard the front door squeal open. Nate walked out to the edge of the porch. A dish towel lay over his shoulder. He rested his hands on his hips, his gaze and his smile fixed on Zoe.

Zoe didn't acknowledge him at first. With Lucky tucked under one arm, Zoe tugged her enormous camp duffel out of the trunk to hit the driveway with a thud. She strode down the sidewalk toward the walkway, her chin puckered in that stubborn, I'll-do-it-myself way as she rolled the heavy duffel on its back wheels. When Zoe turned into the walk and finally looked up at her father, her face was stone.

Nate padded down the steps to intercept. "Hey, pumpkin," he said, reaching for the handle. "How was your trip?"

Zoe turned a shoulder so her father couldn't reach the duffel. "It was fine."

"C'mon, hand it over." He reached for the strap again. "Something tells me it's full of laundry—"

"Dad, you don't make it out of Wolf Cubs without knowing how to do your own laundry. Right, Mom?"

Not waiting for an answer, Zoe shot by her father and yanked the duffel one-handed, bump-bump-bumping it up the stairs before disappearing into the house.

The small muscles of Jenna's neck tightened as the plates of her mental armor clattered into place. Now that the Zoe buffer was gone, she braced herself for the angry accusations she'd known would fly from the moment she decided to short-circuit Nate's end-of-camp plans and instead drive cross-country alone with Zoe.

He stood empty-handed in the driveway looking through the open door. "Now I know what it feels like."

"What?" She threw the word like a gauntlet.

"To have Zoe angry at me instead of you."

Jenna swayed from bracing for a hit that never came. She took a hard look at Nate as he jerked his hand through his hair. His T-shirt formed loose folds across his abdomen. Mauve hollows set off the color of his eyes. He looked like he needed a shave, a haircut, a good meal, and about twenty hours of sleep. He certainly didn't look like a man upended by love.

His mouth moved in what may have been an attempt at a smile. "I know Zoe hasn't been acting like that the whole trip."

"She's been wonderful."

"She's grown about four inches."

"She also dyed her hair purple."

He raised his brows.

"You'll see when she takes off her baseball cap. Plus the new piercing."

She didn't add anything more. She had a feeling Zoe would be displaying a lot of war paint and attitude in the days to come.

He said, "Anything left in the car?"

"Nothing but chip bags and half-filled water bottles."

And Jenna's own luggage, of course. Plus the box of mementos—Zoe's old lovey, Pinky Bear, and the photos she'd taken off the mantelpiece. The French press. And trinkets she'd gathered from Salt Lake City, Cheyenne, Chicago, Niagara Falls, nothing but pinpoints on a coffee-stained map that now held a hundred thousand memories.

She heard a happy yelp from inside the house and, with a twinge, she realized that Zoe had taken Lucky inside with her. It was a seven-year-old Zoe who'd insisted on rescuing the ragged little creature from the pound all those years ago. Lucky was Zoe's dog. Suddenly Jenna understood the impulse three weeks ago to sweep Lucky into her arms and make Zoe's pet her buddy on the road trip.

Nate still hesitated where he stood on the walkway. He shifted his stance and rubbed his jaw, as if he were searching for something to say. She didn't know what to say, either. Maybe it would be better if they didn't say anything outside the presence of lawyers.

She swung back to the car, resting her hand on the open door. "The mediation meeting is still set for next Friday, I assume?"

"Yes."

"Tell Zoe I'll see her after school tomorrow."

"Wait. Where are you spending the night?"

"A hotel," she said. "As usual."

"I've seen some of those hotels you've been staying in." He thumbed the scruff on his chin. "The Silver Dollar in Reno. The Hotel No-tell in Iowa? That sleazy honeymoon place in Niagara Falls? Hell, I know you're out of a job, Jen, but we've got enough savings. You could have kicked it up a notch."

Jenna froze with her hand flat on the roof of the car. Her mind stumbled, raced. She knew that Zoe had been posting photos of their road trip online. She knew that Nate would be able to see those updates. In fact, she'd taken a measure of guilty vengeance in knowing he would see her having a great time on vacation with the daughter he'd all but single-handedly turned against her. She ran her hand over her head and felt again the soft peach fuzz. He hadn't made a single comment about her baldness.

Then she realized that she hadn't been in Reno, or Iowa, or Niagara Falls with Zoe. But she'd been all those places with her friends.

If Jenna had to guess, she'd say Nicole must have invited Nate to subscribe to Claire's cancer blog.

Nate said, "Stay here, Jenna."

He spread a hand toward the open door. She looked at him, at the house, not understanding.

"Stay here," he repeated. "Sleep tonight in your own bed."

Out of the house drifted a mouthwatering smell. A sirloin roast, she was sure of it, that lovely blend of juices and rosemary and thyme, dissonant now, because this was once the smell of homecoming. Jenna looked at him more closely. She saw the shame sweep over his expression like a shadow. Once again he couldn't meet her eyes. His shoulders bowed as he found great interest in something lost in the grass by his feet.

He said, "I fucked it all up, didn't I?"

The admission should have filled her with self-righteous triumph. It just made her feel sad.

"This past week I've been doing a lot of thinking." He swayed back on his heels as he shoved his hands into his pockets. "Someone has to leave this house. That someone has to be me."

Chapter Twenty-six

Bertha the goat *baa*ed an enthusiastic greeting as Claire pulled her luggage out of the trunk of Paulina's car. As the goat, teetering on three spindly legs, strained against the leash, Claire approached and dropped her bags on the grass in order to grant the little beast a vigorous scratch. Behind her, the tires of Paulina's car bit into the gravel as her sister pulled away, Paulina's promise to return early tomorrow still ringing in Claire's ears.

Now she lifted her face to the sunshine and looked at her thirty-acre wood. This cabin had always reminded her of the forest hut where she'd lived in Thailand, a natural Nirvana, a sanctuary of serenity that she could retreat into should the secular life once again wear her down.

Now she looked at the sagging porch, the tingling wind chimes, and the morning glory vines choking the posts. She realized if left unattended, in a year or two this whole place would be swallowed by the forest vines so thoroughly that no one would ever remember it had existed.

Claire huffed out a humorless little laugh for finally seeing what had always been right in front of her eyes. Long before she'd been diagnosed with cancer, she'd set out to bury herself.

She shook the thought out of her head and headed to the cabin. She had a bag full of laundry and a forest garden that needed tending. The floorboards creaked as she stepped up the stairs, waking the crow. He cocked a black eye in her direction. She pulled out a handful of corn from the bin by the door and tossed the grains on the porch. Jon Snow did his awkward glide-drop to the boards to fill his belly.

Inside, the house smelled mediciney and musty. Dust whirled in the shafts of light pouring through the front window. Her tattered slippers lay discarded on the braided rug, as if she'd just stepped out of them. Through the hall, she saw a stack of mail teetering on the butcher-block counter of the kitchen along with a note from the teenager who'd been looking after the animals. Claire dropped her bags and pulled open the cabinet in search of cat food. Then she wandered to the porch, where she sang in Pali until she saw the blind possum poke his nose from underneath. She left him to his dinner and then got to work.

She stripped every linen in the house, pulled down the towels, and piled them up. While the washing machine vibrated in its alcove, she pulled a stool by the counter and used a butter knife to open the bills and the credit card offers, the belated get-well cards, tossing the outdated grocery circulars and the mail-order catalogs into the recycling bin. She cleared a shelf of books she would never read and placed in their stead her new collection of hats. When that had all been taken care of, she booted up her computer and took a rag to the smudged front window while she waited for updates to load.

The square of light coming through that window had passed from one side of the room to the other by the time she finished her e-mail. She ate a dinner of grilled zucchini from her own garden while she clicked through the photos of the reunion in Pine Lake that the ladies continued to post to the blog. Her favorite shot showed all of them posed in the same formation as the high-school graduation picture. She set that picture as the background on her computer.

She gazed at her friends as her throat started to tighten. She'd set out on this trip convinced she'd been a fool to believe that one person could ever change the world. And yet seven people had managed to make a profound change in hers.

Maybe, after you've thrown enough good Karma into the universe, it gathers and boomerangs back.

And maybe it wasn't the world that needed changing.

Claire reached into her pocket and pulled out the business card that Jin had slipped her last night. Scrawled on the back in Jin's messy script were a name and a phone number for an oncologist in Portland. He was a colleague, Jin had told her, working on a stage IV double-blind clinical drug trial for a targeted form of chemo for a certain type of breast cancer. Jin warned that she might not qualify. Jin warned that it might be too early in her treatment to even think about something like this. Still, Jin encouraged her to call and get more details. Every promising new drug ever developed, she said, began with a trial just like this one.

Claire glanced out at the afternoon light. Her sisters would visit tomorrow morning. They would sit on the couch while sunlight set fire to the frizz of their hair. They'd perch on the edge, the three mages, trembling with hope and fear, to deliver the speech they'd no doubt been planning from the moment Paulina returned from Kansas with the news that Claire was bypassing radiation and chemo altogether.

We're going to beat this.

Claire glanced at her computer screen to check the lateness of the day. Office hours were not yet over. She still had time.

She picked up the phone.

Chapter Twenty-seven

R ise and shine, Noah."

Noah's face was buried in his pillow, but Nicole could sense the rolling of his eyes. She understood his annoyance. Anyone would be pissed off at being woken up at six fifteen in the morning to the sight of their mother shaking a bottle of pills.

"Come on." She cracked the bottle open and tipped a pill into her palm. "You've got fifteen minutes before your father leaves without you."

Noah took his time rolling over, grunting all the while. The neck of his T-shirt stretched to one side. His black hair stuck up at odd angles, not much longer than her own hair, now coming in thick. After Noah's release from the residential facility, they'd determined through trial and error that morning was the best time for him to take his meds. In these few moments in the semidark, Nicole could still see a glimmer of the amenable young boy lurking behind the stubble.

He opened his mouth like a bird. She laid the pill on

the back of his tongue. His throat flexed as he swallowed. He rose up on an elbow to take the glass of water she held out for him. After much discussion, Noah's main therapist had agreed to whittle Noah's meds down to a single mood-stabilizing drug. Nicole had promised her son that if he took this one drug, she would forgo the usual tongue inspection. They could reboot their relationship on a basis of mutual trust.

So far, so good.

"Turkey or ham for lunch?" She slipped the bottle of pills in the pocket of her bathrobe as she stood up. "I bought some soft rolls yesterday."

He swung his legs out from beneath the covers and answered with another grunt.

"Turkey then," she said, swiveling on a heel.

"No chips."

She paused. "Are you sure?"

"I have to cut back or I'll never make the team."

Since Noah had begun jogging with Lars, he'd lost some of the puffiness from the long merry-go-round of potent meds. She held on to the hope that Noah's surprising urge to try out for the track team would serve the dual purpose of getting him to a healthy weight as well as start a lifelong habit for the sake of the all-natural, mood-smoothing endorphins.

"An apple then. Get dressed fast. Your father's already stretching."

She closed the door and padded down the stairs toward the kitchen, where she'd set coffee to brewing. Christian and

Julia didn't have to wake up for another half hour, which gave her enough time to slice strawberries and cook up some real oatmeal.

Lars wandered in, shaking his legs as he paced in a little circle in the kitchen. "Is he coming down?"

"Five minutes."

"He take his meds yet?"

"Half-asleep. Just like the doctor ordered. Do you think his crankiness at dinner last night was a blood-sugar thing?"

Lars grimaced. "He'll tell me if there's anything going on in school."

She nodded, grateful, as she poured herself a cup of coffee and added some half-and-half. Within a matter of weeks, it had become clear that Lars had a way of coaxing Noah to open up emotionally that was far more successful than anything she'd ever tried. A simple precept, but one she'd nearly forgotten: a teenage boy needs the advice of his father.

She took a quick sip of her hot coffee and let herself enjoy a moment of hope that even though she still spent every moment with Noah trying to gauge his emotional temperature, there might be long, blissful stretches bereft of mood swings and school suspensions and dismayed calls from teachers.

Her son now bounded down the stairs with all the grace of a water buffalo. He popped his head into the kitchen. "Dad?"

Lars straightened. "Ready."

Nicole heard Noah say, "Beat you to the park."

"Like hell you will."

Lars bolted out of the kitchen, and then they were off, pounding out the door and slamming it in their wake, their voices fading as they tore down the street.

Then Nicole's day began as it usually did, as Julia stumbled down the stairs complaining about how noisy Noah had been, followed by Christian rubbing his eyes. Nicole served them hot oatmeal and juice, then emptied the dishwasher and put away the pots drying on the rack. She officiated the bathroom fights as she picked up towels and dirty clothes. By the time Lars and Noah returned from their run, Julia was fixing her bangs in her room and Nicole was sorting laundry while testing Christian in Spanish. Noah showered quickly and then charged down the stairs, hair wet, for the mad dash for backpacks, purses, lunches, car.

Lars, wrapped in a towel, grabbed her arm before she ran out the door. "Good luck today."

Her breath faltered, remembering the day's plans. "It'll be fine." She nodded. "I know I'll be fine."

"Good luck anyway."

He smelled of hot water and soap. He tasted like bubblegum toothpaste.

She dropped the kids off at two schools and then swung by a bagel store to buy her second cup of coffee. She lingered in her car before setting the cup in the holder and heading toward the local hospital. In the parking lot, she ran her hand nervously over her head, feeling the crisp growth feather through her fingers. She became mindful of the return of that old balking reflex. The idea that she didn't need to do this, that she had everything under control at home, that her life was clipping away at its usual frantic but controlled pace.

For now.

Nicole signed in at the front desk and took the elevator to the second floor. Her heels clicked on the linoleum floor and echoed down the corridor as she searched for the right room. She zeroed in on a schedule taped up on the wall beside one door. *9 a.m. Support Group for Parents of Troubled Teens.*

As she walked in, Dr. Jayson, her therapist, waved to her from the donut table. Four other women and two men were already present.

Nicole joined them amid the circle of chairs.

Chapter Twenty-eight

M om, *please* come pick me up. This is so *awkward*."

Jenna grimaced as she heard Zoe's discomfort beamed through the cell phone. She struggled to unlock the front door to her house while squeezing the cell phone between shoulder and ear.

"Honey, I don't know what to say."

"Sissy's making cookies in the kitchen," Zoe wailed. "Like Natalie and I are *ten years old* again and we've come over to ice the gingerbread men."

Jenna flicked on the lights. She slipped her dripping umbrella into the umbrella stand and clanked her purse on the hall table. "I suppose Sissy is just trying to make you feel welcome—"

"Welcome," Zoe snarked. "She's got a bowl full of stale popcorn she expects us to string. And she's playing this ridiculous Christmas music. You know, the old Charlie Brown music?"

Jenna pictured a much younger Zoe racing into this

house with her red reindeer sweater, hopping from one foot to another humming the Snoopy song while she flung her ponytails like floppy ears.

Poor Nate. Jenna could practically smell his desperation. "That was once your favorite Christmas music."

"When I was a kid! Meanwhile, Dad is in the other room cursing and making all this noise trying to mount the new TV on the wall."

Jenna bit her tongue so she wouldn't release the ungracious laugh that rose to her lips. "Zoe, he's been looking forward to having you over for a good long stay, now that they have a house."

"It's just too weird. I feel like I'm stuck in one of those black-and-white Christmas movies where everyone smiles too much and pretends everything is all right when it's all twisted and stuff."

Jenna kicked off her heels and nudged them toward the pile by the door. She padded to the kitchen. Nicole had warned her that this was going to be part of the new paradigm. Though Jenna and Nate were a few weeks from being officially divorced, the dysfunction in that other household would always seep into hers, simply because it would always involve Zoe.

Her gut instinct was to get back into the car, drive across town, fetch Zoe, and shelter her from the inevitable difficulties that came with a new stepfamily. Jenna would have loved to spend the evening pulling out the old ornaments and decorating their own Christmas tree. She'd have loved to watch *Elf* while sipping eggnog with Zoe. That was what they'd usually do in this house that now held fewer of Nate's sculptures—and no more Nate. But Zoe hadn't yet spent a full weekend with her father, never mind a whole week. Now that Nate and Sissy had settled into a new house, he was determined to settle into the shared-custody arrangement.

"Okay, tell me this," Jenna said, opening the fridge to see what's for dinner. "How awkward is it?"

"Like what?"

"Is it missing-the-goal-when-you're-wide-open awkward?"

"Not even close."

"Is it burping-while-you're-giving-a-class-presentation awkward?"

"No!"

"Is it getting-your-period-in-gym awkward?"

"Mom!"

"So then it must be I'm-going-to-need-time-to-get-used-to-this awkward."

Zoe sighed, and it was a sigh that Jenna could *see*, as if the girl were standing right in front of her with her gaze rolling toward the ceiling.

Jenna said, "Do you remember after I got this new job at the bank, when I told you how uncomfortable I felt every time I walked into the office?"

"I know, I know," Zoe muttered. "You told me you felt like you were exploring the dark side of the moon."

"It took me weeks to figure out that I shouldn't talk to my boss before her second cup of coffee. But now it's hardly awkward at all." Jenna felt a little frisson of excitement. "Today I even hung around for the Christmas party."

A Christmas party where she'd summoned the courage to walk across the room to strike up a conversation with that stock analyst she'd just met, the one who was fluent in Chinese. She'd been curious about a phrase she'd heard during yesterday's talk with the factory manager of a company they were researching in Guangzhou. The analyst had shuffled his feet. He'd bent his shoulders down in a shy way that she recognized all too well.

Seeing it through Nicole's eyes, she thought, *Interesting.*

Zoe sighed into the phone again. "So you're not going to pick me up."

"Not until next week. Eat one of Sissy's gingerbread men for me, okay?"

"You want me to disembowel it?"

"Absolutely. Tear it apart, limb by limb. Pick out its eyes. Anything that makes you feel better."

"Okay."

"Love you, pumpkin."

"Love you, too."

Jenna ended the call and stared at the screen. She would be alone for a week, the longest stretch she would be without Zoe since she had returned from Pine Lake. Though she would miss her daughter, Jenna suddenly found herself in possession of a freedom that shimmered with possibilities.

She flicked her thumb over her smartphone and opened her contacts list. She scrolled down the names. Sydney and Lu. Riley, still fixing up the main lodge in Pine Lake. Jin back at her clinic in Salt Lake City. Maya off on a dig in South America. Nicole, weeks into therapy, working hard on the New Year's launch of her updated life coach website.

And Claire in Oregon, newly bald as she finished her scaled-back chemo, as she geared up for the clinical trial.

Jenna paused. Her thumb hovered over Claire's name. On the last video blog entry, Claire claimed she was running low on material, so instead she introduced Bertha the goat to all her friends. Although the video had made Jenna laugh until she spit coffee on her keyboard, she also sensed that her friend might be going a bit stir-crazy in the woods.

Jenna pressed the Call button and lifted the phone to her ear. She glanced out the kitchen window to the car parked in her driveway. Before the first ring, she'd mentally packed, called in a few vacation days, and made the time-distance calculation to Roseburg, Oregon.

"Hey, it's your fairy godmother," she said with rising excitement, as Claire picked up the phone. "Make a wish."

A LETTER FROM THE AUTHOR

Dear Reader,

I guess it's no secret that I adore traveling. Those of you who've read my previous books have already journeyed with me to India and Burundi in *The Proper Care and Maintenance of Friendship* and all over Europe in *Friendship Makes the Heart Grow Fonder*. So I'll confess that the cross-country expedition in *Random Acts of Kindness* mirrors a road trip I once took with an interesting young man. That adventure made me realize that any guy who can abide retro music, fast food, and driving ten hours through cow country is definitely worth marrying. He's now the father of my three girls.

Like most young couples, my husband and I imagined that we would continue our bohemian way of life after we had children. Yes, I can hear you all laughing. We might have attempted that lifestyle if our kids weren't so sensitive to car and air sickness. Instead, we sought adventure only a few hours from home in old Catskill resorts, kitschy Adirondack towns, and rustic cabins in the Poconos. We ate meals in community halls, played board games in the main lodges, danced the Chicken Dance and the Hokey-Pokey, and were entertained by ventriloquists and Elvis impersonators. We toured caverns and old farms, took hayrides, and visited petting zoos. Veterans of gritty European back-packing trips and one voyage around the world, we teased each other that we no longer vacationed abroad—instead, we vacationed in 1956.

And yet we loved every minute of it. Those very different journeys are what inspired me to create Pine Lake. This college resort town in the historic Adiron-dacks is the home of our perpetual youth. In Pine Lake, folks escape from trouble, heal in body and mind, and often stay for good.

With a great, heartfelt sigh, this happy traveler is going to nestle in for a while. I'll be keeping tabs on Claire, Jenna, Nicole, and all the other Pine Lake women, even far-flung Maya and Dr. Jin. I hope you'll join me for the next book to discover what Riley makes of Camp Kwenback and learn exactly what happens when Three-Tat Tess comes back to town.

It's a natural evolution: all roads lead to home.

DISCUSSION QUESTIONS

Lisa Verge Higgins loves to meet new readers. If your book club has chosen a book by Lisa and you're interested in arranging a phone or Skype chat, feel free to contact her at **http://www.lisavergehiggins.com/contact.htm**.

1. *Random Acts of Kindness* is written around the theme that even small acts of generosity can cause great changes in people's lives. Jenna's initial kindness to Claire kicked it all off. Is it possible that Jenna's first act of generosity ultimately led to Nate's final change of heart?

2. Road trips are the quintessential American vacation. We travel for pleasure, for curiosity, for education, or just for a change of scenery. Have you ever driven cross-country or taken an extended driving trip with friends and family? Was the trip a disaster or a success? During those long hours driving, what did you learn about your traveling companions that you hadn't known before? What did Claire, Nicole, and Jenna learn about one another that they hadn't known before?

3. Claire gives her friends a number of reasons for wanting to spend three weeks on the road. First, she wants to escape from the label "cancer victim" and just be Claire in the big,

wide world. Second, she wants to finish running the rapids of the Hudson Valley Gorge. And third, she wants to avoid her sisters' medical interventions. Which reason do you think is the primary one? Do you think Claire, the disillusioned idealist, has other, underlying reasons that she doesn't admit, maybe not even to herself?

4. Nicole is undergoing a crisis of confidence because of her failure to identify and effectively manage her son's mood and behavioral problems. She sets off for Pine Lake in the hopes of rediscovering the confident, capable woman she needs to be in order to help Noah upon his return from the Hope Recovery Center. When does she first start to find her mojo? Does Pine Lake prove to be the magic elixir?

5. Jenna, like many introverts, has learned to adapt her temperament to function in a world that favors extroverts. Can you relate to Jenna's social difficulties? Do you know people like Jenna? What about you? Are you an introvert or an extrovert?

6. Claire, Jenna, and Nicole are all facing crises that will result in profound change in their lives. Jenna is fighting against the destruction of her family, Nicole grapples with her son's behavioral issues, and Claire is facing her own mortality. Their issues cannot really be solved, only managed. Who, in your opinion, handles these life-altering issues with the most grace?

7. Before Claire has a change of heart about her medical treatment, she is certain about the decision she has made, even though her friends and family disagree. How do you feel about Claire's choices? By initially refusing treatment, is she showing wisdom at the inevitability of mortality? Or is she being irrational? Even selfish?

8. Jenna remarks that her daughter, Zoe, has "a touch of the changeling" because of how temperamentally different they are. Nicole could say the same about Noah after her once-amenable son morphs into a moody, unpredictable teenager. Perhaps most children, in the eyes of their baffled parents, have this "touch of the changeling." How about your children? And what about you? Did you grow up to baffle your own parents?

9. The fate of one of the ladies of the Pine Lake Sisterhood, Theresa, remains a mystery, a thematic reminder that not everyone will find a happy ending. If you had to speculate, what do you think happened to Three-Tat Tess?

10. Who is your favorite character, and what is it about her and/or her situation that you most relate to? Who among the secondary characters—Jin, Maya, Sydney, Riley, and Lu—are you most drawn to?

11. Each woman remembers her hometown of Pine Lake differently. To Nicole, it's the land of her heavenly youth. To Claire, it's a town that had more than its share of socioeconomic problems. To Jenna, it's a place she visits regularly and the site of many a middle-school gaffe. Would you approach a visit to your own hometown more like Nicole, Jenna, or Claire? Are your remembrances also colored by the experiences of your youth?

12. Jenna makes a decision in the middle of the road trip to return to Seattle to confess her love for Nate. Was Jenna being courageous for putting her heart on the chopping block? Or was she just being foolish for giving Nate another chance to hurt her?

13. While in Thailand, Claire had difficulty accepting one particular Buddhist concept. In order to reach Nirvana, one
must acknowledge the sufferings of one's past and understand
that it was in these most troubled times where the seeds of
happiness were sown. Jenna gets a hint of this when she finally realizes that maybe she *isn't* the bad parent she secretly
believed she was. Thinking back on your own difficult life
experiences, do you believe there is truth in this Buddhist
concept?

14. Sometime during the journey, Nicole finally realizes that
even a therapist can benefit from a support group. Accepting
help can be a very difficult and humbling thing to do—
especially if you are the one who usually does the giving.
Have you ever been in a position of physical, financial, or
emotional need to the point where you required outside
help? Was it difficult to ask for that help? What was the trig-
ger that pushed you to find the help you needed?

15. Nate's request for a divorce is such a shock that Jenna fills
a crate and leaves their home. Based on how Nate behaves
whenever Jenna confronts him, what do you think Nate's
real feelings are about the adultery, the divorce, Sissy, Jenna,
and the new pregnancy?

16. In one of the most surprising random acts of kindness in the
story, the Pine Lake women shave their heads to show solidarity with Claire. It's a bold sacrifice in a society that puts
so much weight on a woman's physical appearance. Yet several of the women find the act liberating. If you had a good
friend undergoing chemotherapy, could you make that same
choice?

ABOUT THE AUTHOR

While studying for her PhD in chemistry, Lisa Verge Higgins wrote and sold her first novel. Now an author of sixteen books, this opera-loving mother of three has twice had a novel listed among the top twenty novels of the year by Barnes & Noble's General Fiction Forum. Her stories about women's lives and women's friendships have been described by reviewers as "joyous, uplifting life lessons" that "inspire us to focus on what's really important in our lives." When not writing stories, Lisa works as a reviewer for the *New York Journal of Books*. She currently lives in New Jersey with her husband and their three teenage daughters, who never fail to make life interesting.